continued . . .

D1009256

Also in the Dog Walker Mystery Series

Begging for Trouble

A DOG WALKER MYSTERY

JUDI McCOY

AN OBSIDIAN MYSTERY

OBSIDIAN
Published by New American Library, a division of
Penguin Group (USA) Inc., 375 Hudson Street,
New York, New York 10014, USA
Penguin Group (Canada), 90 Eglinton Avenue East, Suite 700, Toronto,
Ontario M4P 2Y3, Canada (a division of Pearson Penguin Canada Inc.)
Penguin Books Ltd., 80 Strand, London WC2R 0RL, England
Penguin Ireland, 25 St. Stephen's Green, Dublin 2,
Ireland (a division of Penguin Books Ltd.)
Penguin Group (Australia), 250 Camberwell Road, Camberwell, Victoria 3124,
Australia (a division of Pearson Australia Group Pty. Ltd.)
Penguin Books India Pvt. Ltd., 11 Community Centre, Panchsheel Park,
New Delhi - 110 017, India
Penguin Group (NZ), 67 Apollo Drive, Rosedale, North Shore 0632,
New Zealand (a division of Pearson New Zealand Ltd.)
Penguin Books (South Africa) (Pty.) Ltd., 24 Sturdee Avenue,
Rosebank, Johannesburg 2196, South Africa

Penguin Books Ltd., Registered Offices:
80 Strand, London WC2R 0RL, England

First published by Obsidian, an imprint of New American Library,
a division of Penguin Group (USA) Inc.

First Printing, March 2011
10 9 8 7 6 5 4 3 2 1

Copyright © Judi McCoy, 2011
All rights reserved

Acknowledgments

To my partner in crime: Jessie Esposito, retired Port Authority of New York and New Jersey police detective, and one of the most decorated in their history. Jessie tries to keep me on the straight and narrow when it comes to police details, but sometimes Rudy and Ellie get distracted by a new scent or sound and take off on their own. Thank you, Jessie, for leading them back to the correct road.

To Piper Rome, author, attorney, pilot, singer, chicken farmer, cat lover, and animal-rescue expert. Piper gave Rudy his lawyer jokes, and she gave me all the info I needed on appointments to the appellate court.

To Bobo, (aka Gary Wallace) for his help and encouragement with this story.

To Gino Canzanetta, for his help and encouragement, as well.

Chapter 1

"Swear to God. Ellie, next year you're getting flowers, candy, perfume. Hell, I'd even go to one of those prissy operas before I'd let you drag me to one of these so-called extravaganzas again," groused Sam Ryder, as he hunched forward in his seat.

Ellie ignored his complaint and people-watched instead. She'd never been to a show like this before and was looking forward to the antics predicted. Sam had been behaving like a spoiled brat for the past week over this one night, and she'd simply pooh-poohed his griping. In fact, she found the idea that a crack homicide detective on the NYPD force was uncomfortable in these surroundings to be pretty entertaining in itself.

Vivian smirked. "Excuse me, Detective. Did you say 'drag'? Because I thought I heard you announce that this wasn't your idea of fun entertainment."

"Ha-ha." Sam loosened the knot in his necktie, as if the very air in Club Guess Who was choking him. "If Vince or any of the guys find out I was here, I'll be the laughing-stock of the department for the rest of the year."

"Poor baby," said Ellie, patting his fisted hand. She grinned at Viv and Dr. David Crane, the couple sharing their table. "Tell me, Dave, how do you feel about being here?"

The placid veterinarian smiled adoringly at Vivian. "It's not my first choice for an evening out, but my lady wanted to attend, so why not? I'm secure in my masculinity."

Vivian winked at Ellie, then focused on Sam. "A little bird told me that you've done nothing but complain about tonight since you heard about the tickets, which, by the way, didn't cost you a dime. It's a free show at the most trendy playground in Manhattan. Why not sit back and enjoy it?"

Sam slouched in his seat, his expression that of a five-year-old waiting to see the dentist. "I'd rather pay a couple hundred bucks for two tickets to a Broadway flop than suffer through this—this fiasco," he answered. "A production like this belongs in Miami or Vegas, not anywhere near where I live."

Ellie suppressed a sigh. Rob Chesney, one of her clients, had given her passes for the opening night of his new drag show, and the event was a sellout. It looked like everyone in Manhattan wanted to see a host of female impersonators strut their stuff in a fun show filled with one-liners, songs, and plenty of dancing.

"You live in the Big Apple, and Manhattan has hosted a lot of things more outrageous than this. Remember the revival that got rave reviews on Broadway this past December? Everybody in the production was naked, even Scrooge, or so the newspaper said."

Ellie had read the show's description with her mouth open. She'd even thought about going, but figured if her mother found out she'd attended, she would never let Ellie forget it. It was going to be difficult enough having to explain to Georgette why she was here tonight. "Just be glad I didn't push for those tickets as a Christmas gift."

Sam growled ... actually growled. Jeez, what a grouch.

Resting a forearm on the table, Ellie sipped her glass of white wine and continued scoping out the cavernous venue. The deep tiers seemed to go on and on. With four-seater tables clustered side by side, the place reminded her of a nightclub on steroids. And the customers seated around her were a show all by themselves.

She'd never been to this kind of performance, but Rob had given her the tickets as a peace offering after he realized that he'd offended her when he didn't inform her of his unique profession. By the time she'd convinced him it wasn't *what* he did for a living that ticked her off, but the fact that he hadn't clued her in, he'd already committed to the freebies and passes to the backstage party when the show finished.

Considering that her ex had never done more than send her a dozen roses or a gift certificate to her favorite spa for Valentine's Day, Sam's dinner at one of Bobby Flay's restaurants, Bar Americain on West Fifty-second Street, and a carriage ride around Central Park made this the best sweethearts' holiday she'd ever celebrated.

"When the hell are they going to get this business moving?" said sweetheart ground out, drumming his fingers on the table.

Ellie checked her watch. "Any second now. Don't tell me you've changed your mind and you actually want to see it."

"The sooner it starts, the sooner we can leave."

As if on cue, a drumroll sounded from the band situated at the rear of the stage, and the audience's raucous laughter turned to an expectant murmur. Then the bright red curtain closed, a trio of colored spotlights arced across the forefront, and a man wearing formal dress, complete with a top hat and tails, glided from the wings to the center of the stage.

Bowing to rousing applause, the snazzy dresser grinned and began a stand-up routine that started out tame and built to a bawdy climax. His parting words, "And now, ladies and gentlemen, and everyone in between, please give a warm welcome to the drag stars of tomorrow," revved the crowd, and the orchestra struck up introductory music. Then the lights dimmed and the curtain parted.

Ellie gazed openmouthed as a sea of men dressed in feathery boas, five-inch stilettos, and sequined costumes in every color in a paint chip display stomped, strutted, and high-kicked across the stage. The music, more exhilarating than what she remembered from *A Chorus Line*, brought the performance to life. Minutes later, the band changed tempo and seamlessly segued into the second number, a slinky rendition of an old vamp song accompanied by a second group of dancers.

"Wow," Vivian said as she watched. "Who knew men could do women better than women?"

"Certainly not me," said Ellie. She gave Sam a sideways glance and breathed a sigh of relief. His body posture was less rigid and his scowl had morphed to a thin-lipped grin. "Don't tell me you're starting to enjoy this," she whispered, leaning into his shoulder.

"If you imagine the performers are real women, then yeah, it's an eye-popper."

To Ellie, half the fun was knowing that the stage was filled with men dressed like women, but she didn't want to ruin Sam's fun. She wondered about Rob's role in the show, and recalled their first meeting, when Randall, the doorman in one of the buildings housing her dog-walker clients, had sent her to Rob's apartment to interview for the job of walking Bitsy, his Poodle-Chihuahua mix.

She'd guessed then that he was some sort of entertainer, but had believed he'd been born a female. It was a complete surprise when he showed up last November at a neighbor's party in an Armani suit that declared him to be undeniably male.

After patiently sitting through several dances, Ellie was sure that her client had been stretching the truth. Each of the four numbers had been big, brash, and beautiful, but none of them included Rob. Then, when the troupe bowed to applause and left the stage, rolling platforms split the orchestra in two, and a spotlight shone on a set of stairs. The comedian dressed in the top hat and tails entered from the right and the audience grew quiet.

"Ladies and gentlemen, please welcome our first feature player of the evening. I give you Miss Bobbi Doll."

Rob stood in the spotlight's glow wearing a formfitting red sequined gown, a feathered headpiece that had to weigh ten pounds, and a pair of slingback pumps with stiletto heels. As he glided down the steps, Ellie smiled and poked Sam's shoulder. "It's Rob," she whispered. "The guy who gave us the tickets."

"Yippee."

"Pay attention. I've been waiting to hear him sing for three months now."

"Yeah, me, too."

"Sam, be nice," she warned. "I plan to introduce you at the backstage party later."

"I can't wait," he said in a smart-ass tone. "It'll be a perfect end to the night."

Bobbi Doll stopped at the foot of the stairs and gave a sweeping gesture of welcome. After a clever intro, she—or was it he? Ellie still had no idea which pronoun to use when talking about a cross-dresser—began a stirring rendition of "Diamonds Are a Girl's Best Friend."

She sat back, amazed at the sound coming from Rob's mouth. The tone was pure Marilyn Monroe, his body movements identical. The crowd roared encouragement when Bobbi finished and strutted off the stage as dancers returned dressed in fresh costumes for the next number.

"That was your guy?" Vivian asked her.

"Uh-huh."

"I'm impressed. He was even better than Kylie Minogue doing Marilyn. What do you think?"

Ellie had never heard Kylie Minogue's impression of the iconic blonde, but she had seen Marilyn in the classic movie and Rob—er, Bobbi Doll—was better at doing Marilyn than Marilyn had ever been. Unfortunately, if she confessed the bit about not knowing Kylie to Viv, it would give her friend another reason to lecture her on getting in tune with the entertainment of the twenty-first century.

"I still wish he'd told me he was a female impersonator as soon as we'd met," Ellie said, showing her naïveté.

"The way you explained the meeting, I can't believe you didn't know," answered Viv. "I wonder if he'll do Christina Aguilera."

Ellie frowned at the name of another singer who was unfamiliar to her. "Trust me, if you'd seen him the way I did that first day you wouldn't have guessed either. But tonight, well, it's not just the clothes, hair, and makeup. He has the voice and mannerisms of Marilyn down perfectly. I wonder if he does anyone else." She turned to her date. "Sam, care to comment?"

Sam raised both brows. "It was an okay job."

"He did a great job," she countered. "It's hard to believe he's straight."

Vivian sighed. "You can't possibly still believe that."

"But Rob told me so. Why would he lie?"

Sam snorted so loudly that a woman sitting at the next table, who could have passed for a cross-dresser herself, gave him a dirty look.

"You are so narrow-minded," Ellie said, glaring at him. "If a woman wore a tux would you automatically assume she was a lesbian?"

"And please bear in mind that I wore one on New Year's Eve," Viv, one of the girliest girls Ellie knew, reminded him.

"You looked adorable," Dave said, his eyes shining. "It was an honor to be your escort for the evening."

"Aw, you're so sweet," Viv said, blowing him a kiss.

"Get a room," Sam grumped, instead of answering Ellie.

"I'm waiting," she prompted, brushing imaginary lint from the front of her red-and-gray-checked sweater. Viv, of course, was in Donna Karan. "Do you really believe that what a person wears defines who they are?"

"Okay, okay," he conceded. "But remember the old adage—if it looks like a duck and it quacks like a duck . . ."

The latest dance number wound down and the top-hat-and-tails guy returned to the stage. "And now, for your listening enjoyment, I give you Frieda deManeata."

"Holy crap," muttered Sam, "now what?"

"Shh," Ellie told him when the person at the other table again glared in their direction. "For now, this discussion is over," she told him. "But just wait until we're alone."

Sixty minutes later, the show was near completion. After the third headliner, Sheleata Burrito, performed, there'd been a short intermission, which allowed the patrons to order another round of drinks and stretch their legs. Then a second comic appeared, this one in a black bustier, mesh thigh-highs, and the necessary stilettos, and did a risqué skit on the joys of being a girl.

When the applause tapered off, the red curtain

opened, the orchestra began another number, and the scantily clad comic introduced Miss Bobbi Doll for the second time. Rob entered from stage left on a gilded pallet carried on the shoulders of four muscle-bound men dressed in little more than loincloths.

Wearing a formfitting gown of ice blue satin, he slipped to his feet, stood in a circle of light, and waved to the admiring crowd. Then he broke into a number Viv said belonged to Christina Aguilera. When finished, he blew kisses and scampered offstage, but the audience continued to applaud. A minute later he came out for an encore and sang a Barbra Streisand tune that sounded very close to the real deal.

"Wow," said Ellie, when Rob left the stage, "who knew?"

"I can't believe you didn't introduce me to him the night we were at Flora's party," said Viv. "Some friend you are."

"If I remember correctly, you were doing more important things that night," Ellie told her. "And I was still shell-shocked from seeing Rob in normal guy clothing." The night had gone to hell in a handbasket, ending with the authorities driving her and their host downtown for questioning in a murder investigation. "Stop complaining. You'll meet him soon enough."

Another troupe of dancers, these performers wearing hot pink and black with twelve-inch-wide headpieces fitted with fuchsia and black feathers, took the stage, and the orchestra played the opening bars of "I'm Every Woman."

Midway through the number, shrieks rang out from a distance and several audience members sat bolt upright in their seats. Seconds later, the music stuttered to a stop and the dancers clustered on the stage, staring into the wings on the right side.

Ellie grabbed Sam's hand when he shot upright in his chair. The scream built to a crescendo, and he stood and scanned the audience. "Stay here, and don't move," he ordered, and took off at a jog.

Jumping to her feet, she watched him thread his way to the bottom of the tiers, where he disappeared through a door she assumed led to the dressing rooms.

"Where are you going?" called Vivian as Ellie raced down the steps.

"Someone's in trouble," she shouted over her shoulder. *And Sam might get hurt.* She headed in the direction he'd taken, hit the bottom of the seating area, and stumbled into a dim hallway.

When her vision grew accustomed to the pale light, she noted that the backstage area was teeming with stagehands, costumed performers, and catering staff, who'd been there, she imagined, to set up for the party. Pushing past them, Ellie made for the crowd hovering around an open door on the right. After working her way through the mob, she stopped short in the doorway.

Rob knelt next to a body lying facedown on the dressing room floor, his beautiful gown soaked in blood, the scissors in his hand covered in the same sticky liquid. In a far corner stood one of the dancers, still in costume from an earlier number, staring openmouthed and wide-eyed.

Before Ellie could speak, Sam took a swatch of cloth from his jacket pocket, used it to remove the scissors from Rob's hand, and wrapped the cloth around the weapon. After setting it on a counter, he grasped Rob's elbow and pulled him to his feet. Then he flipped open his phone and made a call.

Rob shivered and glanced at the doorway. When their gazes locked, Ellie sent him a smile of encouragement, then stepped back into the hall and rested her backside against the wall. Tears sprang to her eyes while she struggled to process the terrible scene. Rob couldn't have done whatever it was she'd just seen. He was a sweet guy she'd grown close to over the past few months. Now he was a friend.

A siren wailed in the distance, its piercing sound growing louder, and she knew it was Sam's backup. She ordered herself to take slow, deep breaths, hoping it would calm her pounding heart. The lights overhead flickered to life. A man wielding a clipboard walked into the room and quickly returned to the hall, his face a pasty white.

Officers marched in from what she assumed was the rear entrance of the building and began clearing people out and into another dressing area. Ellie closed her eyes and pressed herself against the wall, hoping to remain invisible, but when she raised her lids, she saw Vince Fugazzo, Sam's partner, eyeing her intently.

"Ellie?" He wore an expression of both confusion and surprise. "What are you doing here?"

"I'm—I was watching the show."

"And Sam was with you?"

She jerked her head to the left. "He's in there—with the victim."

An officer she thought looked vaguely familiar grasped her elbow and Vince gave the guy a look. "She can stay, Murphy. Just secure the area." Heaving a breath, he stared at her in full police mode. "Stay here, and do not move until either Sam or I come out to get you. Understand?"

Nodding, she slumped forward, still taking deep breaths. Who was on the floor lying in that pool of blood? Why was Rob holding what could only be the murder weapon? What the heck had happened?

EMTs and a cadre of crime scene investigators

charged in from the rear entrance, probably because everyone in the audience was being cleared out through the front. Moments later, more men entered and she recognized them as the forensic team. Finally, after what seemed like an eternity, Dr. Emily Bridges quick-stepped past her along with a slim young woman with almond-shaped eyes and short dark hair.

As the medical examiner charged by, she did a double take and stepped backward. "Ellie?"

Ellie heaved a sigh. This was the fifth time she'd met Emily Bridges. Four of the meetings, if she counted this one, were at crime scenes where Dr. Bridges had been the medical examiner of record. The fifth was at a Christmas party Sam had taken her to given by Captain Carmody. The woman probably thought she was some kind of jinx. At the very least, she would agree that Ellie was living up to her reputation as Sam Ryder's bad penny.

"Dr. Bridges. I—uh—hello."

"Is Sam with you?"

Sure. She followed him around like a gore-hungry groupie, always hoping to be involved in his latest murder investigation. She nodded toward the dressing room doorway. "He's inside with the victim. We were here watching the show when it happened."

The ME gave a faint smile. "I'd like to say it's nice to see you again, but it seems that every time we meet there's a dead body lying around."

"I didn't have a thing to do with this," she said, feeling the heat rise from her collarbone. "Honest."

"Oh, I believe you." Dr. Bridges nodded at the young woman on her left. "This is Dr. Jordan Kingsgate. She'll be training beside me for a while. Jordan, this is Ellie Engleman. You might run into her from time to time in the course of learning the ropes. It seems that being in the wrong place at the wrong time is a hobby of hers."

Great, thought Ellie. Thanks to the episodes she'd been involved in over the past year, she now had a reputation as a permanent fixture with the crime scene teams working Manhattan. "I don't look for trouble. It just seems to find me," she said, shaking Dr. Kingsgate's hand.

"Nice to meet you, and call me Jordan."

"You ready?" Dr. Bridges asked her. "It's time to go in."

The two women disappeared through the door, and Ellie drew in a breath. Then she pulled out her cell and called Vivian. "It's me."

"Ellie? Where are you? And what's going on?"

"There's been an accident. Someone was stabbed."

"Stabbed. Like in murdered?"

"I'm not sure," she whispered. "I'm backstage, waiting to talk to Sam. According to Vince, I'm supposed to stand here and not move."

"Sam's partner is there, too?"

"Yep. I can only assume they'll be working together on this little . . . er . . . problem. Where are you and Dr. Dave?"

"On the sidewalk out front. Dave's trying to catch a cab, but with this crowd it might take a while. When the cops announced everyone had to leave, I was hoping you'd come home with us."

"I'm fairly certain I'll be staying for a bit."

"So give me the scoop. Who got stabbed? And why?"

"I think it was Rob."

"Your friend got stabbed?"

"No. But Sam found him with the body." She swallowed. "It doesn't look good."

"He thinks your client is the killer? Are you sure?"

Ellie ran a hand across her forehead, shoving her

damp curls into further disarray. "No, I'm not sure, but when I peeked into the dressing room I saw Rob kneeling over the body and—"

"The dead body?" Vivian asked, as if Ellie had just told her there was a live cow backstage.

"I think so." Was the person really dead? Maybe not, though there was an awful lot of blood. "Probably."

"And you're going to wait for Sam?"

Not just Sam, but Rob, too. He was her friend and could probably use some support right now. At least, this time she wouldn't have to be taken in for questioning. "Those are my orders, and when the officers in charge are in official detective mode, there's no point in arguing."

"Then you won't be upset if Dave and I go to my place?"

"Of course not. Just do me a favor and walk Rudy. He'll worry if I'm not home soon, and he needs to go out before bed."

"Okay, sure. Dave and I will take him when we do Mr. T. We can talk tomorrow."

Ellie closed her phone, stuck it in her bag, and slouched against the wall. She still heard low voices muttering and saw flashes of light shooting from the crime scene doorway, which told her the investigators hadn't finished their job. She spotted a metal folding chair a little way down the hall, retrieved it, and took a seat. If this was going to take a while, at least she could be comfortable.

She closed her eyes and time seemed to stop. Next thing she knew, she was glancing at her watch and realized that close to two hours had passed. The EMTs took that moment to exit the room pushing a gurney with a zipped body bag resting on top, which gave Ellie the answer to Vivian's question. Dr. Bridges and Dr. Kingsgate filed out, and finally Vince, Sam, and Rob entered the hall along with two patrol officers.

Rob appeared nothing like the confident performer he'd been just a few hours ago. His dress was covered in blood, his wig was gone, his makeup was a runny mess, and his hands were cuffed behind his back. When their gazes collided, he tried to approach her, but Sam held him back.

"Ellie, thank God you're here. You have to help me. It's Bitsy. She's—"

"Take it easy, Mr. Chesney. Ms. Engleman can't help you. We're taking a trip downtown."

Ellie stood, remembering to act professional and calm so she didn't agitate Sam. "Detective Ryder. If you could give us a minute?"

Sam traded frowns with Vince, who said, "I don't see the harm. We've done all we need to for tonight." He glanced at the floor. "Hell, we couldn't even get a decent footprint what with all the idiots tramping up and down the hall."

Ellie gave Sam a pleading look.

"All right, but just one minute. Mr. Chesney still has to be booked," he told her.

She smiled at Rob. "You don't need to worry about Bitsy. I have keys. I'll pick her up from your apartment on the way home and keep her at my place."

"But she isn't at the apartment. She's—she's here," he said, his voice breaking.

"Hang on. Your dog is in the dressing room?" asked Sam.

Rob kept his eyes on Ellie as he spoke. "She's supposed to be under my makeup table, unless whoever did this stole her—or something worse."

"I'll take a look," said Vince, raising his still-latex-gloved hands in front of him. He went back into the room and returned toting a small pink dog carrier. "Is this what you're talking about?"

"Where did you find that?" asked Sam.

"Right where he said, but pushed all the way to the wall. The room was so damn tight. My guess is no one noticed it." Vince narrowed his gaze and inspected the carrier. "It looks clean, but you never know. What do you want to do with it?"

"It's part of the crime scene," Sam answered. "It has to be dusted for prints, photographed, treated as evi—"

"But Bitsy can't stay in that room overnight. She needs to go out, to be taken care of, f-fed—" Rob stuttered.

Sam gazed at the ceiling, as if he hadn't a clue.

"How about we give Ellie the dog, like he asks, and I put the carrier back exactly where I found it?" Vince suggested. "The dog's not going to tell us what happened, so we don't need it for evidence, but there could be something on the case."

Ellie peered into the mesh opening on the side of the carrier and saw Bitsy, her eyes closed, shuddering. "What would you normally do with a dog found at a crime scene?"

Sam shrugged. "It rarely happens, but we're supposed to bring them to the city shelter. I don't know if—"

"The city shelter? God, no!" Rob cried. "She's my baby, the only thing I have in the world I can count on. Please, Detective, let Ellie take her for tonight, and ask someone for permission tomorrow."

Sam and Vince exchanged looks of impatience.

"I'll sign papers—do whatever I have to do so she can stay in Ellie's custody," Rob continued.

Vince opened the top of the carrier and held it out to Ellie. "Don't touch anything. Just remove the dog."

She slipped her hands inside, cupped the tiny pooch,

and lifted Bitsy to her chest. The adorable dog weighed all of four pounds and was trembling like a scoop of Jell-O on a plate. "You okay, little girl?"

Bitsy snuggled into her arms.

"We're taking Mr. Chesney to Green Street," said Sam. "Where he'll be processed for arraignment. I'll phone you about the dog tomorrow."

Chapter 2

Ellie arrived home from the club, paid the cabdriver, and pulled the extra leash she carried for emergencies from her bag. After snapping it to Bitsy's rhinestone collar, she walked the pup to the corner. Bitsy squatted, did her business, and huddled at Ellie's ankles until she was picked up and carried to the apartment building.

She'd made a few tries at getting the poohuahua to talk on the taxi ride, but so far Bitsy hadn't said a word. Ellie imagined the pup was probably still in shock from all the terrible things that had gone down in Rob's dressing room. Between the screaming, the police, the EMTs, the swarming investigators, and seeing her owner covered in blood, she'd had a night filled with chaos and upheaval.

At the top of the porch steps, she held the still-shaking pooch in one hand, dug for her keys with the other, and unlocked the door. She juggled the tiny dog until she got inside, then held Bitsy close to her chest and climbed the two flights to her condo.

Ellie thought about knocking on Vivian's door on the way up, but it was after one, too late to disturb her friend when there was next to nothing she could say. Hoping to calm Bitsy and get her settled, she continued the climb while she whispered soothing words. "It's okay. You're safe now. Nothing's going to happen while you're in my care."

No comment from Bitsy.

"I know you're upset. I would be, too, if I saw what you saw. But Rob will be fine, and you'll be back together soon."

She sighed. The poohuahua didn't make a sound, just continued to tremble, ratcheting Ellie's worry quotient to the breaking point. On their twice-daily walks, Bitsy had no problem speaking her mind, but when Rudy was with them she was a regular chatterbox. The dog's absolute silence now was a concern. Maybe if she got Bitsy together with her yorkiepoo, she'd be more willing to speak.

After doing another juggling act to open her apartment, she went into the kitchen, set her tote and Bitsy on the table, and removed her coat. "Do you want to walk or should I carry you to the bedroom?"

Not a sound, not even a plaintive whimper, escaped Bitsy's doggie lips.

Ellie scooped her up and held her near. "I feel your pain, sweetie, but you'll sleep next to Rudy tonight. I'm sure that will make you feel better."

They entered the bedroom and she smiled at her boy, curled on the pillow next to her own. "Now that's what I call being a good watchdog," she teased, setting Bitsy on the foot of the bed. "Did you help the robbers clean out the apartment?"

"I knew it was you the second the door opened," Rudy answered after yawning. Then he stretched and gave a sneeze. *"Why'd you bring Bitsy to our house? Was Bobbi-Rob's act so bad she decided to leave home?"*

*Tsk*ing, Ellie started to undress. Rudy had known

about Rob Chesney's cross-dressing from the moment they met. The stinker thought it amusing that she was in the dark right up until Rob came to that party in regular male clothing. Calling him Bobbi-Rob was her dog's way of continuing the joke.

"Don't be silly. Rob was great, very talented. The whole show was amazing . . . until the murder."

Rudy gave a full-body shake. *"Not funny, Triple E. You promised there'd be none of that talk ever again, remember?"*

"Oh, I remember," she said, pulling her sweater off over her head. Walking to the closet, she folded the garment and put it on a shelf, then slipped out of her gray wool slacks and hung them up. "But it couldn't be helped. There was a"—she glanced at Bitsy, who was huddled into a tight ball, and held a finger to her lips—"problem at the club tonight. Someone got killed and they arrested Rob."

"What? Bobbi-Rob? Our Bobbi-Rob?"

"Yep." Ellie donned a sleep shirt, gave Bitsy a pat, and headed for the bathroom. After performing her nightly ritual, she returned to the bedroom and found Rudy lying next to their houseguest, his pose protective.

"Has she said anything?"

"Nope. But she stopped shiverin' when I got close to her, so I'm stayin' down here for a while. Is that okay with you?"

"I was hoping you'd do that. Bitsy is always talkative when you're around, but she hasn't said word one to me." She doused the light and snuggled under the covers. A few minutes later Rudy gave her cheek a sloppy lick. "I thought you were sleeping next to Bitsy."

"I will, but she's out like a light, so I have to ask, was there really a murder?"

Ellie ruffled his ears. "Yes. One minute the performers were headed into the finale; the next someone off-stage was screaming like a freight train. Sam left to—"

"Detective Doofus? It figures he'd stick his nose in it."

"He was simply doing his job as an officer of the law."

"So how did you get involved?"

"I followed him, of course. I didn't want him to get hurt."

"As if you could stop a bullet."

"I didn't hear any shots, so I thought it might be a fight. When I got to the backstage area, I took a look in the room with a crowd at the door and . . ."

"And . . ."

"There was blood. Lots and lots of blood," she said in a hushed tone. "And Rob was kneeling over the body with a pair of scissors in his hand."

"Somethin' must have happened, because the Bobbi-Rob I know would never kill anyone."

"Exactly what I thought, but nobody asked for my opinion."

"Then the cops arrived?"

"Not just the cops. Vince, the medical examiner, her new assistant, the EMTs, the whole investigative team. Before I could find out more, the place was crawling with officials."

"Where was Bitsy when it happened?"

"Under Rob's makeup table. She would have been left there overnight or, worse, taken to the city pound if he hadn't asked me to look after her."

"Typical cop reaction," the yorkiepoo pronounced. *"Forget the canines. They're not worth a second thought."*

"You're being too harsh. Vince and Sam could have insisted they take Bitsy to canine prison, but they agreed to let her stay with us. They did the best they could." She rolled to her side and gave him a shove. "Now get down there and stay close in case she has a nightmare or something. If she wakes up, try and get her to talk. I'll find out what else we can do in the morning."

"Bitsy is totally traumatized," Ellie said as she and Rudy accompanied Vivian to her subway stop. "On this morning's walk, she did her business, then sat in a trance until I picked her up and carted her the rest of the way home. If she doesn't act normal by the end of the day, I'm taking her to Dr. Dave for a checkup."

"Where is she now?" Vivian asked as they headed up Lexington.

"Asleep on my bed, I hope. She didn't spend a very restful night." Rudy had complained that Bitsy had awakened him several times with pathetic-sounding whimpers. Ellie hadn't heard the noise because she'd been too enmeshed in her own nightmare involving bloody scissors and blue-dressed harbingers of death. "I can only imagine the horrific scenes playing over in her mind."

Viv hoisted her Valentino rosette bag onto her shoulder and smoothed the lapels of her full-length black leather trench coat. "She's a dog. Do you really think something like that would bother her?"

"I can't believe you just asked me that," Ellie said, frowning. Viv knew how in tune she was with her charges and she usually put up with Ellie's views, especially when they were relaxed and having fun. But today was a workday, and Vivian was more professional . . . in every way.

"Sorry. I'm aware you're wrapped up in your dogs and their lives, but I'm not. I didn't mean to sound snotty."

"No snot taken," Ellie said with a smile.

She could only imagine the contrast they made standing side by side. Vivian was almost six feet tall and model slim. Though also considered tall, Ellie stood about four inches shorter, and even when she had been married and starving herself to stay in a single-digit dress size, she hadn't been model thin since she was a ten-year-old.

Today's temperature was warm, the sky sunny, the morning breeze balmy, and Viv looked as if she was on her way to a *Vogue* photo shoot. Ellie, of course, wore her usual yellow rain slicker over a nubby yellow and navy sweater, worn jeans, and her most practical hiking boots. If the temperature climbed, she could fold up the slicker and hide it in her Fendi peek-a-boo tote, a Christmas gift from her mother and one of the few designer pieces she owned.

Standing at the subway entrance, Viv said, "So what's your plan for the day?"

"First thing I'll do after morning walks is find out where Rob is and try to get a visitor's pass to see him. Then I'll go home for lunch and take Bitsy out." *And let her know how Rob is doing.* "After that, it's second rounds. If Rob is still in custody, I'll stop at his apartment and pick up whatever will make her comfortable at our place."

"And you're going to call Dave?"

"If she's still acting weird, yes. Why? Were you planning on seeing him tonight?"

"Not really, but phone me if he agrees to come over and I'll call in a dinner order for the three of us." Viv headed down the stairs to her subway. "You can bring the dogs to my place, and Bitsy can have her exam there."

"Sounds like a plan," Ellie said, giving her a wave. "I'll let you know."

Ellie and Rudy started their morning rounds at the Cranston Arms, and were on the way to collecting their first customer: a rather plump Pug named Sampson, who belonged to Mariette Lowenstein. Ellie had given several potential helpers a tryout at walking the six dogs in this building, but unfortunately, none of them had worked out. She was disappointed that her last assistant, Joy, had quit with no warning, even though she'd been paid a good salary, with bonuses for any extra time she spent lending a hand.

"Why don't you call her?" Rudy asked, as he often did when he was in mind-reading mode.

She and the yorkiepoo were fast approaching their one-year anniversary, so she was getting used to his uncanny ability to sneak into her brain. It happened most often when she was preoccupied or worried.

"I've tried Joy a few times, but she never answers, and she doesn't call back when I leave a message. I wish I knew what kind of problem she had that forced her to stop working for us."

"Keep tryin'. Maybe now that the weather's gettin' nicer, she'd be willing to come back."

"I guess I'd better hang another round of flyers in the local college bookstores. Those sites brought me the most applicants, even if Joy was the only one who worked out."

They arrived at Mariette's apartment and knocked, though neither of the Lowensteins was usually home at this hour. Ellie used her key to enter, but before she could open the door it swung inward. She gaped at a puffy-faced Mariette, her eyes swollen, her expression sour.

"Mrs. Lowenstein, is everything all right?"

The usually attractive and personable middle-aged woman nodded and stepped back to let them in. "I had a bad night. Couldn't fall asleep, even after I took a pill."

"Can I do anything for you? Call the doctor, maybe? Or your husband?"

Mariette jumped at the suggestion. "Heavens, no. Norm has a full calendar today, as usual. He never has time for—I mean, he doesn't have time for my problems."

Ellie had met Mariette Lowenstein and her husband through Ellie's stepfather, Judge Stanley Frye. Norman Lowenstein was a judge for the U.S. district court, where, according to Stanley, the cases he tried involved everything from organized crime to people suing the government.

"Judge Frye told me how hard he works. Isn't he up for some big-time federal appointment?"

Mariette heaved a sigh. "Second Circuit Court of Appeals. It's something I thought we both wanted, but I'm beginning to think—" She put a hand over her mouth. "Lord, just listen to me, going off on a tangent when you have work to do."

"I'm always willing to lend an ear to my clients, both human and canine," Ellie assured Mariette, following her into the kitchen. "So, how have things been going with Sampson and his diet?"

Shrugging, Mariette ran a shaky hand through her straight brown hair. "You tell me. You're the one who cleans up after him."

Rudy snorted. *"Yeah, and it's always a treat."*

Ellie jerked his leash. "There hasn't been another incident like the one I had in November—"

"That blue poo was gross."

She tapped her boy in the rear with the toe of her boot. "But Sampson still processes a large amount of waste, and it doesn't look like he's lost any weight, which is my main concern."

"I've managed to keep him out of the wastebaskets, even the one in Norm's office, which is where he got hold of that transfer paper. But he still begs food at the dinner table, and if I don't keep the trash up"—she nodded at a metal container on top of the counter—"he's in it all the time, even though I've warned the housekeeper to stow it out of reach. It's just that ... well ... I hate saying no to him."

Ellie hated saying no to Rudy, too, as did most owners who cared about their dogs. But pet lovers had to stand firm, exercise their pooches, give treats in moderation, and serve their animals healthy food with no chemicals or additives if they wanted their four-footed friends to enjoy a long and healthy life.

"Sounds like she's a pushover, Triple E. You could take a lesson from her every once in a while."

Ellie made a note to list the treats she gave her boy, including the number of times each day she fed him a bite from her own fork or spoon, and read it to him the next time he complained. She knew darn well she shouldn't be giving him anything extra, but a forkful every once in a while wasn't that bad. It was the owners who made a habit of indulging their dogs' every whim who weren't being fair to their pets.

She gave Mariette a smile of encouragement. "I know what you mean, but you still have to stick to the rules."

Sampson ambled in from the hall and plopped his extra-wide bottom on the tile floor. After emitting a large burp, he yawned. *"Morning, all. Here for a breakfast nibble?"*

Ellie reached down and gave his wrinkled face a scratch. "Has he had breakfast yet?"

"He hasn't even been out," Mariette answered. "I got in late and— Well, I got in late and took him out to calm myself down. He lost sleep and so did I."

"Then you can feed him after we return from his morning walk. We'll be back in about thirty minutes."

"But I'm hungry now," the Pug said with a moan.

Ellie raised an eyebrow in his direction. "And make sure it's a half portion. Not one kibble more."

"Aw, Ellie," Sampson said as they ambled into the outer hall. *"You take all the fun out of my life."*

They stepped into the elevator, rode to a different floor, and set out for their next stop while Ellie lectured the overweight Pug. "Fun is one thing. Eating food that's bad for you is something else entirely."

"How'm I supposed to know what's not good? Everything is tasty when my tummy is empty," he groused. *"Besides, I got a supercharged metabolism. I need more food than other dogs."*

"Hah!" Rudy said, his voice snarky. *"What you got is too much nap time."*

Ignoring their chatter, Ellie knocked on Freud's door, then used her key. Most mornings, Esther Gordon left early for her sculpting studio and her psychologist husband had appointments. "Hey, Freud," she told the cocky French Bulldog. "How are things going today?"

"Great." He gave Rudy and Sampson the usual buttsniff welcome. *"Whoa, smells like the big guy's gonna need some extra outside time today."*

"Oh, goody," commented Rudy.

"I'll take care of it, but we still have to get Roscoe, Arlo, Lily, and Rocco."

She led them to the elevator for another climb. Twenty minutes later she and the canines were outside and across the street in front of the park. The sun felt warm, even at this early hour, so after the pack's normal route she took a seat on a bench. When Sampson sat at her feet, she thought he wanted to continue the discussion on his dietary needs.

"I'm not going to tell your mom to ease up on the food restrictions, so there's no point in asking."

"Big Momma will do whatever you say, Ellie. She

thinks you're the man—er—woman," the Pug pronounced. *"After she got in last night, she kept tellin' me over and over how much she loved me, and how we'd never be apart."*

Generously proportioned, Mariette stood about five-ten, which made her a very formidable woman. So formidable that the Pug's pet name for his mistress made perfect sense. But to Ellie, the conversation sounded much too dramatic for Mariette. "That's surprising. I always thought your Big—er—Mariette was a bit more practical."

"She was sad, even a little upset, kinda like she is when she and the judge argue."

"Have they argued a lot lately?"

"Yeah." Sampson rested a paw on her knee. *"But Norm wasn't there when she got home. He walked out when the news finished and stayed away most of the night. Then, a little while ago, her and the judge were in the back room, arguing about more stuff."* Sampson sneezed, blowing dog spit over her legs. *"He left right before you got here."*

Ellie took the spittle as part of the job. She listened to her dogs when they confided in her about their home lives, even if in jest, but this sounded more serious than usual. The Pug had complained a couple of times about the way his mom and dad did verbal battle, but she assumed it had to do with the pressure Judge Lowenstein was under regarding the position he hoped to be appointed to on the Second Circuit Court of Appeals.

"Parents argue. It's the way humans work out their differences. I'm sure Judge Lowenstein is worried about his future on the bench."

"I don't think his job was the problem. Big Momma's always sayin' he does bad things."

"Well, she's home now, and the judge is gone, so I'm

sure she'll calm down. Her and Norm will work things out." Standing, Ellie headed the pack across Fifth Avenue. "Time to go inside. Rudy and I have three more buildings to take care of."

They dropped off their charges, finished the walks for building two, and were at the Davenport in record time. Randall, the daytime doorman and Ellie's good friend, shot to attention when they entered the foyer. "Did you make Mr. Chesney's opening-night gala? Did you see him afterward, when the trouble began?" he asked, rounding the counter with a newspaper in hand.

"We were there for the whole magilla. Had a great time, or rather Viv, Dr. Dave, and I did. Sam, on the other hand—"

Randall cleared his throat. "I can well imagine what Detective Ryder thought about attending a drag show. He appears to be a very—I believe the term is 'macho'— type of man."

"He's macho, all right, sometimes a little too mucho macho for me, but I've learned to take the good with the not-so-good."

"So he enjoyed the show?"

"I think so, at least until the moment the screaming started."

"Ah, yes. The entire evening was reported in this morning's paper. I assumed that Detective Ryder would be in the thick of it if he was there."

"It made the papers?" Since the murder had occurred around eleven p.m., she thought it would be on the local news, but not in print.

The doorman held the newspaper in front of her face and Ellie read the headline: MURDER AT GUESS WHO. DRAG QUEEN'S DEATH STEALS THE SHOW. "The entire story is covered here."

"I sometimes wonder where the heck newspaper reporters get their info. I mean, I was there and I don't know the whole story. Sam finished the night as the detective in charge, and it was a zoo backstage—worse than when Arnie Harris died."

He cocked an eyebrow in disapproval. "And how did you get backstage?"

"No biggie. When the racket started, I followed Sam. I was worried he might get hurt."

"I'm sure the good detective loved that move."

"Not so much, but he'll get over it. So what else does the paper say? Anything about Rob?"

"It just says there was a stabbing, and the police—that would be Detective Ryder—caught Mr. Chesney with the supposed weapon in hand. The paper is calling it a crime of passion."

"Really? That, I hadn't heard. Of course, it sounds lurid enough to be information dreamed up by some reporter hoping to make a name for himself."

"That's possible, but—" Randall's eyes lit up as if a lightbulb in his brain had suddenly switched on. "Are you telling me you once again stuck your nose in a crime scene?"

"I didn't 'stick my nose in,' as you so nicely put it," she said on a sigh. "When I went after Sam, I had no idea there'd been a murder."

"Ellie," he warned.

She rolled her eyes. "I know, I know. Stay out of trouble, mind my own business, blah, blah, blah. I was, I tell you. If I'd known what was going on, I'd have kept my bottom in my chair."

"I understand. Still—" The doorman tipped his cap to a tenant leaving the building. "Please don't get involved."

"I didn't do it on purpose. I had no idea that whatever was happening had to do with murder and would have to do with Rob."

Randall glanced at the paper again. "The scenario certainly seems to incriminate Mr. Chesney."

"Sam did find Rob with the weapon in his hand, but I think the rest is speculation on the reporter's part. I simply can't imagine Rob is capable of doing anything that horrible. And the 'crime of passion' thing doesn't ring true."

It hit her that except for Rob holding the scissors and Bitsy being under the dressing table during the murder, she knew virtually nothing about the crime scene. "Does the paper give the name of the victim?"

"I'm sure it does," the doorman said, scanning the columns. "Yes, here it is. The dead man was Arthur Pearson, also known as Carmella Sunday. It says he—er—she had been arrested on several occasions for lurid acts and prostitution, but in the last several years she'd done a turnaround and gone into the entertainment business."

"She had a part in the show. If I remember correctly, she was wearing a big dance-number costume when they found her, but she wasn't one of the three headliners."

"Mr. Chesney planned to take Bitsy to every performance. Do you know what happened to her?"

Ellie realized all this chitchat was making her late and headed toward the elevator. "Bitsy spent the night at our place. Rob asked me to keep her and I couldn't say no." She pressed the call button. "If he doesn't get out on bail, I'll stop in his apartment this afternoon and gather her things. Someone has to look after her. She's too tiny to go to a shelter." She waggled her fingers when the elevator door opened. "I'll be down in a minute."

On the ride up, she gazed at Rudy. "You're too quiet. What are you thinking?"

"I got a lot on my brain. Who killed that Carmella person? Why was Bobbi-Rob holdin' the weapon? What will

happen to Bitsy if he gets convicted?" He sneezed. *"We have to help them."*

"My thoughts exactly," she said as they stepped onto Buckley's floor.

"But you shouldn't get involved in the actual find-the-murderer scenario. This one sounds like a bigger mess than any of the others."

She knocked, then used her key to get Buckley, a small black maltipoo with a cranky disposition. "Hey, Buck. How are things?" she asked when he trotted to the door from somewhere in the rear of the apartment.

"Hazel's on a tear about my health again, just because I been chewin' my paws."

Ellie stooped to hook his leash to his collar. "So why are you chewing?"

"Itchy is all. No big deal. But she took me to that dopey pet psychic for another reading."

The trio aimed for the elevator. Ellie had four more dogs to retrieve. "What was her name again?"

"Madam Orzo. According to Hazel, the woman's a wonder, but she has yet to get me right."

No surprise there, thought Ellie. Buckley had a bad opinion of everyone and a complaint about everything. "Hmm, I can't imagine why," she said jokingly. "I haven't seen your mistress in a while. Still off the cigarettes?"

"She's been good, but I bet that once the nice weather's here she'll start again. She always sits on the patio and takes a hit. Bet she thinks I'm too stupid to figure it out."

"She knows you're a smart little guy," Ellie said. They arrived on Sweetie Pie's floor, walked down the corridor, and opened the Westie's door. "Hey, Sweetie. You ready for us?"

The adorable West Highland White Terrier greeted Rudy and Buckley in typical doggie fashion, prompting her yorkiepoo to say, *"You smell like you've been through the wash cycle. Mom using a new shampoo?"*

"Not Babs, but the groomer thought it was a nice change of pace. Personally, I hate it."

The details on the Westie's shampoo sent the dogs off on a tear about groomers that continued until the pack was outside and crossing Fifth Avenue. When they got nitpicky about telling one scent from another, Ellie's mind went into overdrive. Was it possible Bitsy had smelled something during the murder that would identify the killer?

She'd never find out until she got the poohuahua to talk, and that might take time. Meanwhile, she still needed to know if Rob had been released. Until then, there wasn't a thing she could do to help him or his dog.

Chapter 3

Sam read the caller ID on his cell phone and leaned back in his chair. Paying attention to Ellie now would go a long way toward keeping the peace and deflecting invasive questions later. He had, in fact, expected her to call him before this, but then he remembered that she'd taken home a suspected killer's dog, which might have caused a problem.

"Ryder," he said, though Ellie had to know he'd be the only one on the other end of the line.

"Do you have time for a few questions?"

He smiled at the greeting, happy to know they'd grown so close over the past couple of months that Ellie didn't feel it necessary to announce herself. Positive he knew the topic she wanted to discuss, he heaved a sigh. There was no use trying to pretend he didn't have the answers, and after only four hours' sleep last night, he didn't have the energy to play the avoidance game or give her a lecture, something that never worked with his "bad penny" anyway.

"Can you keep it to five minutes? Because that's about all the time I have right now."

"I'm outside the station. Can I come in?"

Sam ran a hand through his hair. "Don't take this the wrong way, but no. Just ask what you have to and I'll do my best to tell you"—*get off my case*—"what you need to know."

"It's about Rob Chesney."

Well, duh. No surprise there. "I figured. Go ahead."

"Where is he right now?"

"Probably in a holding cell."

"Has he had a bail hearing?"

"And you need to know that because . . ."

Ellie blew out a breath. "Because I have his dog. I want to know if I should keep her with me or drop her at his apartment."

"I believe Mr. Chesney's attorney is in the process of amassing the funds needed to set him free."

"How much did the DA ask for?"

He drummed his fingers on the desk. "I fail to see what the amount of Mr. Chesney's bail has to do with his dog."

"Come on, Sam. Bend a little. Rob's a friend and I want to help him if I can."

"Why? Did he ask you for the money?" He'd heard Chesney was a trust fund baby and didn't need a cent from anyone.

She waited a beat before saying, "You're being difficult."

He shrugged. "Unless you're an attorney or an eyewitness to the murder, you don't need to know anything about his finances or the state of his stay here." Of course, he knew darn well that wouldn't stop her from prying. After a long silence, he said, "Bail was set at half a million. I believe he's made arrangements with a bondsman, but there's paperwork to finish. With luck, he could be home by the end of the afternoon."

"Okay, fine." She exhaled another breath. "Would it be possible for me to see him?"

Sam gazed at the ceiling. "You're kidding, right?"

"I would never kid about such a serious matter. I'd like to see him, and I know you can get me in."

Okay, he could, but that would be a bad move for a couple of reasons. First off, just about everyone in the station knew he and Ellie were dating, and they'd consider it extending special privileges if he did what she asked. Second, they also knew she continually horned in on police business, which didn't endear her to the cops. Third, she wasn't a relative of the perp and therefore had no credible reason for a visit, which would steer them back to reason two. Fourth—well, hell—the list went on and on.

"Can't it wait until he's home?"

"I guess." Another pause, then, "The papers are calling it a crime of passion. Any idea where they'd get that idea?"

That was his girl. If one direction took her nowhere, she'd head off in another. "Not from here. Must have been someone in the DA's office."

"And those scissors were the murder weapon?"

"We're waiting for confirmation from forensics and the ME, but I'm guessing so."

"Is there any other evidence?"

"Not much. The crowd that tromped in and out of the room obliterated any footprints, but forensics might come up with something."

"What about—"

"Sorry, Nancy Drew, but that's all I can say for now."

Ellie's *tsk* shot across the phone line. "But you have an opinion. I know you do."

"All I have right now are the facts. Until the entire

story comes to light, and that's up to the evidence Vince and I gather, I don't know anything for sure."

"Okay. Be that way."

The huge sigh she dropped onto the end of the sentence made him want to bang his head against a wall. "Are you really going to make me recite the list of reasons why I can't discuss this with you?"

"You could discuss it if he was innocent."

"You know better than to say that, and as far as I'm concerned, he isn't." Neither he nor Vince had bought Chesney's story of walking into the dressing room, seeing the victim, and falling to his knees to offer assistance. Only an idiot would pull a weapon out of a body. "I have to go."

"Can you stop by my place tonight? I want to talk to you about Bitsy."

Sam closed his eyes. He recalled the fuss about the dog, but what the heck did it have to do with him? "Did something happen to the little mutt that I need to know about?"

"I think Dr. Dave has to make a house call."

When the word "mutt" didn't get a rise out of her, he said, "Why? Is it sick?"

"Not in the physical sense."

Was she saying the dog had a mental problem? Did he really want to know? "And you need me there . . . Why?"

"Just to talk over a few things. Come on, I promise I won't go overboard with the questions."

Impossible. "I'll drop by if I can, but I'm not making any promises. What time?"

"Anytime. In fact, if you're free around seven you can stop by Viv's place. She's ordering dinner for me and Dr. Dave, and there's always more food than we can eat."

"It all depends on how the investigation goes. Vince

and I are still questioning people who were allowed backstage last night, even if they were performing at the time of the murder. Vince is lead on this one, so he's calling the shots."

"Why Vince? You were the first officer on the scene."

The answer to her question was the same as the list of reasons he had for not allowing her to visit Chesney in jail. They were personally involved; she'd been with him at the site; she knew the supposed killer. But if he told Ellie she was the reason he had to play second fiddle, she'd have a full-blown fit.

"It was Vince's turn," he stated simply. "He had no problem taking whatever I told him as fact and assuming command."

"Is that the truth?" she asked, her tone rife with suspicion.

He crossed mental fingers. "Yes. Now hang up. I'll call you later and let you know about dinner."

The connection dropped and he tossed his phone on the blotter. He'd been waiting for Ellie's call, knew what she would ask, was even prepared for her bossy attitude. So why did their dialogue bother him so much?

Get real, Ryder, a voice in his brain growled. *You care about the woman. You don't want to create hostility, especially since things have gone so well for the past four months.*

Ellie had let him back into her bed. They enjoyed being together, verbal sparring included. She always knew what to say to ease his anger and make him laugh. She was a good person, a saint really, when compared to most of the people he had to deal with, including those in his own family.

More important, she knew the rules. She usually backed away when he asked her to, and made him smile when she did it. She was the bright spot in his day, the reason he now saw the good in people he used to write off as crackpots or fools. She complemented his contrary and disbelieving nature, made sense of the things he sometimes found it impossible to understand. To put it plainly, Ellie was the very best of his better half.

Except when a friend or a client was in trouble. Then all bets were off, and she fought as dirty as any street fighter.

And Chesney was both.

Leaning back in his chair, Sam heaved another sigh. He could give orders, make demands, and set as many boundaries as he wanted, but it wouldn't do him a damn bit of good. Vince had already told him he was a goner when it came to Ellie Engleman and he didn't doubt it for a second.

Instead of saying good-bye to Sam, Ellie simply ended the call and headed for home. The man was so frustrating she wanted to scream. Then she remembered the hellacious wail that had erupted from backstage at Guess Who and thought better of it. She'd only hurt her voice if she raised it that many decibels, and the last thing she needed was laryngitis—not a good thing in her line of work.

"Didn't sound like the deceptive dick was any help," Rudy offered, trotting beside her.

"He told me as much as he could, I guess. I'll just have to get the rest of the details from Rob."

They made it home in twenty minutes. After Ellie gave Bitsy a cuddle and a walk, they came back inside, and she was now studying Bitsy in silence. She planned to eat lunch and leave Rudy here babysitting while she completed her afternoon rounds. Right now, the poohuahua was huddled on a floor mat and trembling, exactly where she'd been when Ellie first came in the door. Best she could tell, the pup was still traumatized from the events of last night, but without verbal contact, she had no clue as to why.

"You gonna give me orders or what?"

She cocked an elbow and rested her cheek in her palm, still gazing at her houseguest. "Just take care of her. Stay close and give her a shoulder to cry on if she needs it. If she starts to talk, try to remember what she says so you can repeat it when I get home. Think you can follow instructions?"

"That's as easy as polishing off a Dingo bone, Triple E. I can handle it."

"Then I'm out of here. I probably won't be back until it's time to go to Viv's for dinner. I guess I'd better call Dr. Dave and ask him to meet us there so he can give Bitsy a once-over."

Rudy settled on the mat, curling his body around the tiny pooch. *"Got it. And don't worry about us. We'll be fine. Won't we, Bits?"*

Bitsy snuggled closer to him and closed her eyes, which again tore at Ellie's heart. As soon as she finished the afternoon runs, she'd visit Rob, get his version of what had happened in his dressing room, and see if there was anything she could do to help. She hated lying, but she had to tell Rob his dog needed a checkup, which meant she had to come up with a story that would convince him to leave Bitsy in her care for another night.

She left her apartment with Bitsy's predicament in the forefront of her mind. The idea of the tiny dog so in tune with her owner that she could do nothing but shake and whimper at his misfortune brought tears to Ellie's eyes. Anyone who believed that canines didn't experience emotion was an idiot. The dogs she walked felt sorrow, joy, pity, love, and every emotion in between, and they were proud of it.

Heading west on Sixty-eighth, she crossed Lexington and passed Hunter College. Great. She'd been so enmeshed in Rob's dilemma she'd forgotten all about dropping off Help Wanted flyers at the local colleges. *I'll do it first thing tomorrow,* she told herself, striding across Park Avenue. She figured she might as well talk as she walked, so she pulled out her cell and rang Dr. Dave.

"Hi, David. It's Ellie," she said when he answered.

"Hey, what's up?"

"This is a twofold call. First, you're invited to join me for dinner at Viv's place around seven tonight. Think you can make it?"

"Barring a four-legged emergency, sure. What else?"

"Bitsy needs a checkup."

"Bitsy? What's wrong with the little girl?"

"I assume Viv told you I brought her home with me last night."

"She did. But what happened that made you think she needs an exam?"

"The poor thing hasn't stopped trembling since they pulled her carrier out from underneath Rob's dressing table. And she hasn't so much as touched a single bite of kibble either. She's all of four pounds, and I'm pretty sure a dog that small can't go too long without eating, right?"

"You're absolutely correct. So, you'll bring her to Vivian's and I'll look at her there?"

"Yep, and thanks. I appreciate it."

Crossing Fifth, she dialed Viv's office line and left a message about dinner. Then she dropped the phone in her bag and aimed for the Beaumont, after which she planned to skip the Davenport, take care of her two northernmost buildings, and swing back around. Keeping things tight, she took care of her charges and was at the Davenport in under two hours. Now that she was here, she would walk the dogs, bring them home, then go to Rob's for a quick talk.

She entered the building to the sound of angry chatter and the booming voice of the evening doorman, Boris Kronkovitz.

"You must wait," he told the crowd gathered around the front desk. "I need identification before you go up."

Huh? Ellie glanced at her watch as she skulked past the unruly tenants, praying she wouldn't get caught. She didn't have time to wait for the people who were complaining to get through.

She'd made it to the elevator and pushed the call button when Kronk's voice, sounding much too close, chimed, "*Ell-ee,* my dar-*link* girl. Where are you go-*ink*?"

She turned to give the doorman a wave and bumped smack into him. Rubbing her nose, she took a step of retreat. "Stop sneaking up on me, Kronk. I have dogs to walk."

He shook his leonine head. "Sorry, but no. *Ees* impossible."

"What do you mean '*ees* impossible'? I have keys and you're holding permission slips from each of my clients." She peeked around the doorman's beefy chest and found a dozen people glowering at her. "Uh, hi. I don't suppose any of you need a dog walker?"

"If she's allowed up, we're all allowed up, Mr. Kronkovitz," said a woman wearing Prada and pearls. "This business of having to be cleared before we go to our apartments is ridiculous. The police can't keep us from our homes."

Shouts of "Yeah," "She's right," and "You tell him, Sharon," rang out when she finished.

"What the heck is going on, Kronk?" Ellie asked, hoping the tenants would view her as a friend if she was able to get the crazy Russian to change his tune.

The doorman stretched his six-foot-four frame to an even more imposing height and scanned the crowd. "*Ees* not my idea." Stepping into the elevator, he removed an enormous key ring from his pocket, chose a key, and fiddled with the control panel. Then he marched back to the desk, calling over his shoulder, "*Ell-ee-vay-tor* not work until I check you in."

The tenants continued to grumble. A gentleman rushed to the stairway entrance, grabbed the door handle leading to the steps, and gave a tug. When the door failed to open, he swung around. "How dare you disable the elevator and lock the door to the stairs. I'm reporting you for a fire code violation."

"*Ees* not me," Kronk explained. "*Ees* management."

"But we're not criminals," the woman named Sharon said.

"Management say police advise them to keep build-*ink* free of trespassers and news *pipple*. I only do-*ink* my job." With that, Kronk raised a clipboard and waited.

The residents continued to argue, but it appeared they'd gotten the message. Ellie watched while the burly doorman did his thing, matching each person's identification to a list of names on his clipboard. Finally, he walked to the elevator, again took out his key ring and fiddled with the control panel, and stepped into the foyer.

One by one, the tenants entered the waiting car, leaving her to get to the bottom of the story. "Okay, spill," Ellie ordered, following Kronk to the front counter. "What's this all about?"

"I am only obey-*ink* orders," he said, his expression soulful. "Authorities say no one goes up unless they prove they *leeve* in build-*ink* or someone already here gives okay."

"So the cops are trying to keep reporters and thrill

seekers away from Rob Chesney? Is that what you're saying?"

"Yes, is what I'm say-*ink.*" He gave her a grin. "But *ees* not for you. I am sure you are approved."

Ellie opened and closed her mouth. While she and Kronk had a decent relationship, she'd never found the man to be totally trustworthy, but every now and then he surprised her. "That's nice of you, Kronk."

"But I *haf* favor."

She rolled her eyes. She should have known it was too good to be true. "And that would be . . ."

"You are great crime solver, yes?"

Fairly sure she knew where this was leading, she raised an eyebrow. "I have had some success at scoping out murderers."

"And *eef* you find *geel-tee par-tee,* you go to police?"

"I definitely go to police—er—the police."

"So, before you do, you tell Kronk who *ees keel-air.* I call reporter and get paid for news. You get credit for solv-*ink* crime. *Ees* what you call a win-win deal, yes?"

"Ah, no," Ellie stated, heaving a sigh. She'd learned from past experience that the Russian was all about the cash, but this was too bold to be real. "And you should be ashamed for asking me."

Kronk's expression grew wounded. "*Ell-ee,* why you say such a *theenk*? I merely share in your wonderful luck."

Luck? Now that was a real insult. She'd been tied to a chair and left for dead, had her dog stolen, and just four months ago had been held at gunpoint and threatened with poison. Getting out of those situations had taken a heck of a lot more than luck.

"We split *mon-ee*? I give you ten—no—*twen*-tee percent," he continued.

She pivoted on her toes, walked to the elevator, and

pushed the call button. The suggestion wasn't even worth a second "no." When the door opened, she stepped inside and punched the number for her first client's floor.

Finished walking the Davenport pack, she managed to slip past Kronk, who was busy checking in more grumbling tenants, and back into the elevator. She probably should have phoned Rob and asked if he wanted visitors, but she assumed he would expect her to bring Bitsy home without a call. Which she would have done, except for the fact that the poohuahua was too traumatized to leave her condo.

But how to explain this to Rob?

After returning the dogs to their homes, she knocked on his door and waited, positive that someone was watching her through the peephole. When no one answered, she knocked again and heard the dead bolts slide open. Then the door swung inward.

"Ellie. Thank God it's you." Rob stepped back and allowed her inside. Then he slumped against the hallway wall and ran shaking fingers through his hair. Throwing her a mournful smile, he said, "I guess I don't have to tell you about last night, do I? I mean, you were there and all, and—"

He headed down the hall, as if expecting her to follow, and she obliged.

"The first detective on the scene was your date, right? I figured that out when I met you outside the dressing room." Now in the living room, he dropped onto a butter yellow leather sofa and crossed his legs. Wearing faded Levi's and a claret red cashmere sweater, he looked sad yet determined. His disheveled hair only added to his pitiable expression. "So did Detective Ryder tell you anything? Is there any word on the real killer?"

She dropped into a matching wing chair across from

him. "Yes, Sam was my date. We've gone out for a while now, but he won't—I mean, he rarely discusses his cases with me. In fact, I probably know less about what happened than was reported in the papers."

"But you've solved crimes, caught killers and all that. Doesn't he ask for your help?"

My help? She wanted to laugh, but knew it wouldn't be appreciated by a guy who'd just been charged with murder. "He hasn't approved of anything I've done to solve the murd—er—the cases I've been involved in. He thinks I'm inept and a danger to myself, so, no, he does not ask for my assistance."

"I'm sorry to hear that, because the way Randall talks you're a regular Sherlock Holmes." He leaned back on the couch. "I was hoping I could hire you to lend a hand in the investigation."

Hire me? "Rob, I'm not a PI or anything like one. To tell you the truth, I'm a nudge." Great. She'd just slotted herself in the same category as Sam put his mother. "I really don't know what I'm doing, but I push and push until I manage to stumble onto the facts."

"But you've caught the guilty party."

"Yes, but . . . How about I ask you some questions? Maybe if we talk it out, something will come to you that you haven't thought of before. Then you can tell the cops and they'll look into it."

"Sure, fine." He narrowed his eyes. "Hey, where's my baby? Why didn't you bring Bitsy home?"

Ellie swallowed hard, determined to tell a convincing story. "Bitsy is still at my place. I wasn't sure you'd be here, so I thought it best she stay with me until I knew for certain."

"I'm out on bail. It took the entire day to get that straightened out." He started jiggling his leg in a twitchy, nervous kind of manner. "Little did I know there are some restrictions on my trust fund that don't allow for a withdrawal of a large amount of cash unless I can prove to the attorney in charge that it's necessary."

"I heard bail was set at half a million. Isn't putting up ten percent the norm?"

"Yes, but everything I have is invested. I didn't trust myself to have that kind of money at my fingertips, so I put myself on a budget. My attorney pays the mortgage on this place, the tenant's fees, all of it, and deposits a monthly allowance in my checking account. He had to liquidate some bonds to—" He rubbed his hands over his eyes. "Listen to me, going on about money when I'm facing a murder charge. If my mother and father hadn't already disowned me, this would have sealed the deal."

Right around Christmas, Rob had told Ellie a sad tale about his dreadful family life, and since Sam was on duty and her mother and the judge were in Barbados, she'd invited him to spend the holiday with her and Flora Steinman. But it hadn't been necessary. Rob was still on good terms with his sister in Phoenix, and he and Bitsy had flown there for the week.

"Do you think they know you were arrested?" Ellie asked, uncomfortable with the personal questions.

"I haven't a clue, but I've talked to my sister. Kayla's agreed to stay with me until I'm cleared of the charges. And if I'm not, well . . ." He shook his head. "She'll take Bitsy home to live with her and Bradley."

Hoping to drop the dismal family business, Ellie decided it was time to get down to the nitty-gritty. "I don't mean to be intrusive, but can you explain what happened last night? I'll understand if you don't want to tell me anything, of course, but I ran into Kronk and a group of angry tenants downstairs, so I know about the restriction management has put on allowing reporters and thrill seekers into the building."

"Amazing, isn't it? No one gives a damn about me. All the tenants care about is their precious right to privacy, and the newspapers can't seem to talk about anything except the fact that I'm a drag queen and so was the victim. I have to be the killer. It's nothing less than what any pervert would do."

"So you've seen the papers?"

"I read them, and afterward I was ordered to clam up by Keller Williams, my attorney. He'd probably have a fit if he knew I was talking to you, but I really could use a friend right now, and the guys in the revue . . . Well, let's just say I wasn't close to any of them."

"Okay, fine. I'll be your sounding board until your sister shows up." Ellie rested her elbows on her knees. "Why don't you tell me what happened?"

"Why not? It's all going to come out anyway. The victim was Art Pearson, stage name Carmella Sunday. We weren't lovers, as the papers suggest, and we certainly weren't friends. In fact, Carmella could barely tolerate me."

"So he—er—she was just someone working in your show?"

"She danced in the revue, but she wasn't just any performer. Carmella was my understudy. If I got ill or couldn't go on for any reason, she had my numbers down pat." Rob stood. "Hang on a second. Let me show you something."

He left the room and Ellie bit back a sigh. It sounded as if this Keller Williams guy had a pretty good idea of how to handle the press. She only hoped he was a decent trial attorney.

Rob returned and passed her an eight-by-ten glossy. "Take a look at this."

Ellie gazed at the photo, a picture of Rob in full drag, complete with the ice blue satin gown he wore during his second number. "Um, I don't understand. This is you the way you looked in your final song last night."

"But that isn't me," he said, his expression bleak.

She held the photo at arm's length and studied it. The person in the picture wore the same blond wig and elbow-length gloves, the identical headpiece. . . . If this guy wasn't Rob, it was someone who had him down cold. "It's not?"

"Nope. That's a picture of Carmella Sunday, vamping as my understudy."

Chapter 4

Ellie blinked back her surprise. "But he—er—she looks exactly like you."

"Spooky, isn't it?" Rob shrugged. "It's the makeup, of course, and the wig. Cosmetics work wonders, but Art and I do have the same basic features, eye color, face shape, that sort of thing. Trouble is . . ."

She moved to the edge of her chair. "Go on."

"The trouble is he auditioned for the part I have in the show as well, only we were called up in last-name order so I performed ahead of him. Apparently Carmella's act was similar to mine, our wigs are almost identical, and we sing a few of the same songs. When she heard me onstage, she raised a huge stink, claimed I'd stolen her shtick, said she'd take me to court, the works."

"But you didn't copy her act?"

"Lord, no. I'd been playing in small clubs around the country for a couple of years, even before my parents disowned me. Carmella was strictly a Big Apple celebrity. She claimed I must have seen her act after I moved here, then worked up something just like it and come to the tryouts ready to go."

"How did you find out about the show's casting call?"

"I subscribe to a couple of Web sites that announce openings for movie and television roles, plus live shows as they become available. I assume Carmella did, too, but we never discussed it. Apparently she canceled her last gig at a small club in the Village because she was positive she'd get one of the leads at Guess Who." He ran a hand through his already messy hair. "I still can't believe this has happened."

"How are the police tying you to the murder?" Ellie bit the inside of her cheek before she could add "other than finding you next to the body with the murder weapon in your hand." "They need a motive to make a good case, and since Carmella wanted your job, I'd be more willing to believe she was planning to kill you, or at least find a way to take over your role."

"Funny you should say that, because I often thought she was looking for a way to get me kicked off the show. Things calmed down over the last month and she seemed to accept the job of understudy, and that's what I told the cops, but they didn't believe me. Said they had me at the site with the weapon in hand, and I had a motive—getting rid of my competition."

Ellie cringed internally. She'd been involved in the murder investigation business for a while now, and she knew what the cops would believe. Unless someone could convince Sam and Vince there was a more logical motive, they would never listen to a word Rob said. "Then you'll just have to find a way to prove them wrong."

He shook his head. "My attorney said they'd come around once he had a chance to run a background check on Carmella. He claims she could have been killed by anyone: a past lover, a current lover, a random murder by someone who hated gays—"

"So Carmella was definitely gay?"

"That was the talk around the dressing room. The gay drag queens outnumber the straight ones by ten to one, and the straight guys don't talk about it for fear of being snubbed by the others. I just kept my mouth shut, but I'm sure people in the cast figured it out."

"Are you aware of anyone who might have it in for you enough that they would frame you for the crime?"

He shrugged again. "I doubt it, but who knows. It was just such a shock returning to the dressing room and finding her like that. I saw her lying in that pool of blood and thought I could help." He stared at the floor, as if trying to recall the details. "When I bent down, my feet slipped out from under me and I sort of fell against her body. My hand touched the scissors and it was automatic." He rested his head on the sofa back and closed his eyes. "My fingers curled around them and I pulled."

"Was it you that screamed?" Ellie asked.

"I was too terrified to say a word. The screamer was Regina Devine. She was standing in the corner of the room when you looked in. The three headliners shared that dressing room with their understudies: Carmella, Regina, and Frieda. It's convenient for rehearsals, so I imagine she was coming in to take a break. When she saw me with the body, I guess she just lost it."

"And you think Carmella was in there to freshen her makeup or redo her hair?"

He raised his hands in a who-knows? gesture. "Those are the obvious choices, but she had a couple of minutes before performing in the finale. Maybe she just wanted to sit and put her feet up."

Sliding back in her chair, Ellie decided it might be less than smart to press Rob any further. He needed time to go over things, maybe consult with his attorney again, or merely get a good night's sleep. She only wanted to clarify two more points. "Are you sure you didn't see anyone run from the room as you made your way there?"

"It was opening night and I was a hit. Instead of leaving the wings immediately after the encore, I hung out for a minute or two, basking in the applause and congratulations from the stage people." He ran a shaky hand over his face. "Hell, I don't know. I vaguely remember someone walking toward the back of the building as I approached the room, but I have no idea who he was or where he'd come from. I'm not even sure it was a man. It could have been a crew member, one of the other girls going to a different dressing room . . . anyone."

"It's just my opinion, but I think you should take some downtime, relax and try to recall everything that happened. Let it play over in your mind, maybe write it down in an outline—whatever works."

His shoulders dropped as he looked at her. "You're probably right. I'm so damn tired I can barely think straight. My brain should be clearer in the morning."

"That's the spirit. Now, last thing—do you have any idea why someone would want Carmella dead?"

"You'd have to ask the other girls. There were a few I thought she might be close to. I only know most of them by their first name, but I did give the cops a list. I'm sure Detective Ryder would let you—"

"Ah, no. He wouldn't." After glancing at her watch, Ellie stood. "I'm sorry to leave you, but I have dinner plans, and I'll be late even if I go now."

"But you'll bring Bitsy home tomorrow, right?"

That depended on the outcome of Dr. Dave's exam, but she'd worry about it after he checked the poohuahua out. "Um, sure. When is your sister scheduled to arrive?"

Rob stood and followed her to the door. "Her flight gets in at three, but she may have a bit of trouble getting here."

"Trouble? Just have her catch a cab. They'll be lined up and ready to go outside the terminal."

He leaned against the hallway wall. "That will all depend on Bradley, I'm afraid."

Ellie had assumed that was the name of Kayla's husband or son. Now she wasn't so sure. "Does Bradley have a problem?"

"Not according to Bradley he doesn't, but the choice of a ride won't be up to him. It's going to depend on the cabbie."

"Okay, now you've lost me." She grabbed the doorknob. "Speak English, please."

"Sorry. I guess I'm too wrapped up in my own problems to discuss my sister's. Bradley is a dog."

Ellie grinned. "A dog? Well, that should be a piece of cake. Almost every driver in this city will transport a canine. They might charge her an extra fee, but if it's the cost of the ride you're worried about, they all take credit cards. They'd probably even give her a hand juggling things if she had too much luggage. If that didn't work, I'm sure Randall would ring you when they arrived so you could come down and pay the tab."

"It's not the money. Kayla has a trust fund, too, and she's been careful with her investments."

Tired of playing the guessing game, Ellie said, "Well, then, don't keep me in suspense. What the heck is Bradley's problem?"

Rob gave his first real smile of the visit. "How about if I let you see for yourself? Consider it a surprise."

She raised an eyebrow. "I don't like surprises."

"Oh, I think you'll like this one. Bring Bitsy home after you finish second rounds tomorrow. Kayla and Bradley should be settled in by then, and you'll see what I mean."

"Okay, now I'm really curious—but I can wait." Before stepping into the hall, she reached out and touched Rob's hand. In an instant, he was clinging to her the way a drowning man clutches a life preserver.

"I don't know how to thank you."

She hugged him and moved away. "Thank me? But I didn't do anything."

"You took Bitsy into your home without asking a single question, and you've treated me as if you know I'm innocent. That's huge in my book."

She smiled encouragement. "That's because you *are* innocent. And Bitsy's like family. If I needed help, I'd expect you to do the same for Rudy and me."

"Then you have my promise. If I get out of this situation with my life intact, I'll owe you one."

Ellie took the direct route home. After entering the building, she retrieved her mail, still pondering what Rob had told her. The idea of him being a murderer was preposterous. She couldn't envision him killing anyone for any reason. He was a nice guy, intelligent and reserved, who seemed to let go only when performing onstage.

Climbing the stairs, she told herself there had to be more to the story, something Rob wasn't telling her. Something he'd forgotten. It was important for Sam to question the girls Rob said were Carmella's friends, but if she told him how to do his job, she'd be so deep in trouble that she would need a ladder to climb back to ground level. She would have to drop a hint or make an innocent statement that would put the idea in his head.

Then again, her darling but wily detective had probably taken care of it already, or was going to. And if he had, she'd love to find out what those other girls had said. If they could shed some light on Carmella's life, or know a reason why someone might want her dead, the case would practically solve itself.

Ellie was hardly an expert on drag queens, but she had become fairly good at figuring out what made people tick. Those hoping to succeed in show business were well aware of the competitive world they wanted to enter. Carmella had disliked Rob and considered him a rival—that much was clear, but it still wasn't motive enough for Rob to kill him—er—her.

Still thinking, she unlocked the apartment door. According to Rob, Carmella had jumped to conclusions and assumed things that weren't true. Was it possible she had been so insulting and rude to another performer that he or she had been out to get her, or had there been an outsider with a jaded sense of morality who had simply committed a random act of violence? Had Carmella been the real target or had it been someone else who'd shared the dressing room?

After storing her coat in the hall closet, she looked for the dogs. When she found them, her throat closed and tears blurred her vision. Her boy and the tiny pooch were in the bedroom, cuddled up on Rudy's favorite pillow, with Bitsy asleep between his forelegs.

She tiptoed in and sidled over to the bed. Sitting carefully, she reached out and cupped a palm over Rudy's head in a caress. He was all bluster and talk on the outside, but inside her boy was pure mush.

"I know you're there," he muttered under his breath.

"I know you know," Ellie answered, a smile in her voice.

"How'd things go with Bobbi-Rob?"

"We had a talk, but I didn't learn much. I'll catch him again tomorrow afternoon, when we take Bitsy home."

She walked to the closet, where she removed her heavy sweater and pulled a clean baby blue T-shirt over her head. Dr. Dave only had eyes for Viv, and Ellie's best friend wouldn't care what she wore. Sam had seen her dressed in worse plenty of times, so it wasn't necessary that she fuss for a casual in-home dinner.

She returned to Rudy's side of the bed and sat again, noting that Bitsy was still asleep. "Has she said anything?"

"A couple of whimpers is all." He unwrapped himself from around the tiny dog and walked to the middle of the bed, where he performed a full-body shake. *"I think she might have somethin' like what Gary had. That post-trauma thing."*

"Post-traumatic stress disorder." Ellie recalled the homeless man they'd befriended. She ran her fingers over Bitsy's spine. When the pup relaxed and rolled onto her back, Ellie was happy to give her a tummy rub. "Are you feeling better, little girl?"

Bitsy didn't answer, but she did seem calmer than she had earlier. "That's it—take it easy. No one is going to make you talk before you're ready."

"Go over that post-whatever-it-is thing again for me," Rudy said, nudging her free hand with his nose.

"It's better known as PTSD. And it is possible that's what's wrong with Bitsy, though I've never heard of a canine being diagnosed with the condition."

"Of course not," Rudy grumped, plopping his bottom on the green-and-burgundy-striped duvet. *"Humans don't give dogs any credit for having regular emotions. What have we got to be depressed about?"*

"Not all humans feel that way," she corrected. "That's why I want Dave to conduct an examination. He's one of the few professionals I know who give canines credit for having human reactions. He and I have already talked about a couple of the dogs in our pack. Mr. T, for one."

"Oh, boy. Don't let T hear that. He's already too much of a complainer. If he knew you were talkin' about him behind his back . . . Well, there's no tellin' what he'd do."

He stretched out his front paws and dropped to a down position. *"Who else have you discussed with the vet? Lulu? Arlo?"*

"None of your business," Ellie answered.

"I know. You told him about that dopey Poodle Ranger and his nutty opera-star owner. They're both nothin' but hypochondriacs, and Ranger can be a real pain."

"I would never discuss a human client with the vet, and I'm not telling you which of the pack I've asked him about either, so stop badgering me." She glanced at her watch. "It's time we got downstairs. Dr. Dave is probably already waiting for us at Viv's." She bent forward and nuzzled Bitsy's head. "Think you feel good enough to spend some time with Dr. Crane?"

The dog laid her muzzle on her paws and sighed.

"It's okay. He just wants to be sure you're physically fit. Isn't that right, Rudy?"

"Huh?" He took a look at Ellie, who nodded encouragement. *"Oh, uh, yeah, yeah. That's right. Dr. C is a good guy. I'll even hang with the two of you to watch the exam, if you want."*

His offer lightened Ellie's heart. Just as she'd suspected, her boy was all bluster, but happy to lend a hand when needed. In fact, Rudy's presence would probably go a long way toward keeping Bitsy at ease.

"Do you two want to eat up here, or shall I bring your supper to Viv's place?"

Rudy inched over to Bitsy and nuzzled her ear. Then he jumped off the bed. "Bitsy says she's not hungry, but she says I should eat if I want."

"Great. That's the first positive thing I've heard in hours." Then she frowned at her boy's guilty expression. "Hold on. I didn't hear her speak. Are you making it up just so you can get your dinner right away?"

"Uh, not exactly. But she was thinkin' it."

Ellie shook her head. "Not fair, big guy. Don't get my hopes up and let me believe she was talking if she wasn't. It won't help her recovery."

"No, honest. Bein' with her this afternoon, I learned how to read her body language. She's all right with seein' Dr. Dave, and she won't mind if I eat now."

"Hmm." She gave Bitsy another measuring glance and realized the little dog was still sitting calmly. "Maybe she'll nibble a little if she sees and smells the food. Come on, baby girl, let's go to the kitchen. I'll make an extra portion of Rudy's dinner and it might spark your appetite." Ellie carried Bitsy down the hall, talking while Rudy stayed at her heels. "He has special kibble, not exactly like yours, but just as good. And I'll mix in a little of Grammy's Pot Pie to make it extra tasty."

That was her boy's favorite flavor of canned food. It was expensive, but it was one of the best brands around and if her yorkiepoo enjoyed it, that was all she needed to know.

She set Bitsy next to Rudy's water dish, then filled it from a pitcher she kept on the counter. "How about a drink? We don't want you to get dehydrated. It's not summer, but that's still something I need to worry about."

The poohuahua obliged by taking a few licks. Seeing that Bitsy was more eager to cooperate, she brought the dry food from the cupboard and the can of Grammy's Pot Pie from the fridge. After mixing Rudy's helping with a small addition, she removed a tablespoon of the food, mounded it on a saucer, and put both servings on his place mat. Then she held her breath.

"Come on, Bits. This stuff is great," Rudy said before digging in.

Bitsy sniffed the plate and gazed over her shoulder at Ellie. When the poohuahua picked up a kibble covered in Grammy's Pot Pie and began to chew, Ellie dropped into a chair and heaved a sigh. Even if Bitsy ate just half, it was one less thing to worry about.

She nodded when the pup gave her another questioning look. "That'a girl. Finish it up and we'll go for a quick walk. Then we'll see Dr. Dave and Mr. T."

She had high hopes that once Bitsy moved past her fear she would overcome her trauma and willingly talk about what she'd seen from her spot beneath the dressing table. As the only witness to the murder, she was the one who could clear her master, but Ellie refused to tell her so. Pressuring someone with PTSD was not a good idea. Bitsy needed to recall what had happened when she was ready and not before.

And when she did, Ellie would find a way to let Sam know, so he could catch the real criminal and set Rob free.

"How's Bitsy?" Viv asked when she opened the door.

"See for yourself." Ellie stepped aside so the poohua-hua and Rudy could enter together.

"She seems good," Viv pronounced. "At least she's not acting like a coma patient."

Ellie followed her friend into the kitchen and took a seat at the table. "She's definitely better. I left her with Rudy while I made afternoon rounds, and when I got home she seemed more relaxed and less traumatized."

"But you still want Dave to give her an exam."

"You bet. I have to cover all the bases before I send her back to Rob." She gazed around the kitchen. "Where's T?"

"Watching Animal Planet, like all good dogs should." Viv opened a couple of cartons of Chinese food and set them in her microwave. "Maybe Bitsy and Rudy want to join him."

"Give me a minute to get them settled and I'll be back." Ellie waved a hand at her boy and he took off for the living room with Bitsy trailing behind. When they arrived, Mr. T was too busy viewing *Groomer Has It* to turn his head.

"Get comfy, fools, but don't expect no cocktails from me. This show is too dopey for words."

"Be nice, T. Bitsy's had a rough twenty-four hours. She needs lots of TLC." Ellie bent and rubbed his ears. "I know you can be polite if you put your mind to it."

The Jack Russell sniffed, then gave a doggie shrug. *"I am bein' polite."*

Rudy nosed Bitsy into Mr. T's bed and waited for her to settle down. Then he trotted to T's side and sat on the room's Oriental rug. *"So, what else is on tonight's schedule?"*

The dogs began a spirited conversation and Ellie smiled. Bitsy was falling asleep and the boys were chatting. Things would be all right for a while. She returned to the kitchen and found her friend setting the table.

"I thought we'd eat in here. Is Sam coming?" Viv asked, taking plates out of an upper cupboard.

Ellie opened the utensil drawer, grabbed forks and serving spoons, and brought them over. "I invited him, but I can't say for certain he'll show. When do you expect Dave?"

"He left a message saying he'd be here by seven thirty. You want wine?" Viv automatically withdrew four glasses and set them on the counter. Then she pulled a bottle of Sauvignon Blanc from the fridge and took a bottle of Merlot from her wine rack. "I guess Sam's busy with that drag queen murder, huh?"

"Very," said Ellie, nodding at the white wine. "And he wasn't thrilled when I called him this afternoon either. We talked, but the conversation was short and not so sweet. Rob's out of jail. They set his bail at half a million."

Viv let out a low whistle, poured Ellie a glass of wine, and placed it on the table. "I know Rob has a trust fund, but can he get his hands on that much money?"

"Bail bondsmen only require ten percent in cash, so it wasn't too difficult. His sister's flying in from Phoenix to stay with him." She sipped her Sauvignon Blanc, pleased that it was crisp and dry. "I've never met her, but Rob says she's nice and, unlike his parents, she's fine with his line of work."

"Lucky for him." Viv opened the Merlot, poured herself a glass, and took a seat across from Ellie. "It's a bummer if you don't get along with your family."

Ellie had always wanted a little sister, but that had never occurred, and it might have been for the best. She spent so much time trying to stay on her mother's good side, she probably wouldn't have had a spare minute to interact with a sibling.

"Speaking of family, how's that crazy sister of yours?"

"Arlene or Adrianne? They're both nuts if you ask me."

Ellie had never met either sister, just heard of their oddball shenanigans from Viv, who was the youngest. "I don't remember which one, but she wanted a dog."

"Ah. That was Arlene."

"That's her. You said her boyfriend was buying her a dog as a Christmas present. Did he get her what she wanted?"

Viv rested her elbows on the table. "Dr. Kent bought her three Boston Terriers. Apparently when they went to the breeder, she couldn't make up her mind, so they took all the dogs that were left in the litter. She e-mailed me a picture. There's Isabella, Darby, and Corey."

According to Viv, Arlene's boyfriend was a general

practitioner named Martin Kent, and he took care of the rich and famous on the far end of Long Island. Viv said he sounded like a pompous ass, but Ellie knew she was exaggerating. Still, she wouldn't mind meeting the man for herself.

"Wow, three puppies. Boston Terriers are intelligent and gentle, and they're a great dog for an apartment, too," said Ellie, remembering what she knew of the breed. "But they must be driving her nuts."

"The way Arlene tells it, she's puppy-proofed the summer cottage she inherited from Myron, who was her first husband, and Dr. Kent turned the bottom floor of her guesthouse into offices. T and I are supposed to visit her for a week over the summer, probably for the wedding." Viv threaded her fingers through her thick brown hair. "Of course, Ms. Mensa will insist that her dogs are smarter than T, which will really tick me off because no canine can beat my Jack Russell in that category." She rolled her eyes. "I'm sure we'll have a lot to discuss."

Ellie knew Viv had an IQ high enough to allow her entrance into Mensa, too, but she'd never tried to join. Being the youngest of three overachieving but flaky girls, she'd made a point of dancing to a different drummer while growing up. "So she's moved to the Hamptons permanently?"

"Yep. Says it's a fabulous house right on the beach. I can't imagine being that far out, but she loves it there, and her fiancé makes a fortune treating every star and celebrity in the area. I'm starting to think he's some kind of Dr. Feelgood."

The doorbell rang and Viv stood. "That's probably Dave. I'll be right back."

Ellie stayed in her seat and waited patiently for her best friend. Viv and Dave were sure to share a kissy-face greeting and she didn't want to intrude. Though she and

Sam were affectionate in private, they did little more than hold hands in public. She didn't mind, though, because Sam more than made up for it when they were alone.

Standing, she started the microwave to heat their food. It was possible Sam wouldn't show, which was fine. There was plenty of time to quiz him about Rob's supposed crime, and she still had a lot to go over with Rob in order to lend him a hand. Then she would come up with a plan.

Sam would understand her need to help a friend. Once she convinced him.

Chapter 5

Ellie and Vivian sat in the living room drinking wine while Dr. Dave gave Bitsy an exam. In the course of their chat, Ellie discreetly checked out, as she usually did, the regal decor of her best friend's apartment. Viv had been born into wealth—not a huge amount, but certainly more than the median income level of most Americans. Ellie had been here a thousand times and Vivian's sense of style always impressed her. Though this apartment wasn't the moneyed display that Ellie's ex had insisted upon, it was more elegance than she wanted in her own home.

Their condo layouts were identical, but Ellie had done everything imaginable to avoid her ex's opulent taste. Since being granted her unit in the divorce settlement, she had completely erased the dickhead's presence. After receiving a loan from her mother, she'd painted the entire place, added hand-painted borders, hung her favorite artwork, purchased new area rugs, and changed out every stick of furniture. Instead of screaming upscale, expensive, and snooty, it now shouted "come in, kick your shoes off, and stay a while," something she thought all homes should profess.

Sitting in "wait" mode, she'd watched Rudy accompany the poohuahua and vet to the spare bedroom in order to keep Bitsy calm. Ellie was more than ready to hear Dave's take on Bitsy's odd actions since the stabbing, but what she really needed was Rudy's observations. Her yorkiepoo was a sharp little guy, very in tune with the dogs they walked. He would notice things the vet missed, and he'd be sure to inform her if Bitsy said anything important.

"Why are you fidgeting?" asked Vivian, who was perched on the sofa. "It's just a normal checkup, and Bitsy seemed okay to me."

"You call sitting like a statue and refusing a treat *okay* for a dog who's usually upbeat and playful?" She snorted. "That only proves you know squat about man's best friend."

"I never proclaimed to be a canine expert, but I do care. Bitsy isn't puking or whining, and she still wants to be held and scratched. For me, those are all positive signs in a dog."

Ellie twined her fingers in her lap. "Sorry. I didn't mean to jump down your throat. It's just that . . ." She shrugged. "I can only imagine what Bitsy saw from underneath that makeup table, and I'm positive it wasn't a pretty sight. Remember what happened to Gary when he witnessed his parents' murders? It ruined his life."

"But Gary was a teenage human, not a puppy," Viv said, her tone that of a kindergarten teacher explaining the meaning of life to one of her pupils. "Death hits all of us in one way or another, and we have to accept it."

"People, yes, but dogs—" Ellie stopped her tirade before she was in too deep. "The deaths most of us experience aren't violent or shocking. Bitsy's a puppy who loves her owner, which means she feels with Rob. And she shares a bond with him that's stronger than the one many humans share."

Viv grinned. "You mean like you and the exterminator?"

"Don't be a smart-ass. Georgette and I have a bond, when she chooses to be motherly." Ellie sipped her second glass of wine, then set it on the side table. "If I wanted to be snide, I could compare it to the bond you and your sisters have."

"One of these days I'm going to take you to the Island to meet Arlene. Then you'll understand what I've been talking about." Viv drained her glass of Merlot, then glanced at her watch. "I wonder what's taking so long."

The comment shook Ellie to her core. Was it possible Dave had found something serious? A skin condition or a tumor that flagged a more frightening problem? Maybe Bitsy wasn't suffering from PTSD, but was physically ill and it simply hadn't come to light until now.

"Should we send Mr. T in to take a look?" She gave a weak smile. "He might report back to us."

"Say what?" T gruffed from his spot on the floor. Still engrossed in Animal Planet, he hadn't said a word since Rudy left with the vet and poohuahua.

"I doubt T has any idea what's going on," Viv offered.

"Oh, yes, I do, fool," the Jack Russell insisted. *"You just don't know it."*

"I was only joking," said Ellie, hoping to defuse T's temper. Unless absolutely necessary, he was not the kind of canine to show a soft spot for any dog or human. If something bad happened to his mistress, she was certain he'd be upset, and it might bother him if she or Rudy was in trouble, but that was about it. "Besides, he's too fascinated with *Dogs 101* to pay attention to whatever's going on in Bitsy's life."

"He does seem self-absorbed," Viv agreed. "Maybe if I—"

Rudy took that moment to trot into the room with Bitsy at his side. When he reached Ellie, he jumped onto the chair and nuzzled her ear. *"Talk about a nail-biter. You were right. Bitsy's body is fine, but her mind is confused and hurting."*

"Is it serious?" Ellie murmured.

"Nah, not really. Dr. Dave just—"

"What the heck are you whispering about?" Viv interrupted.

Ellie settled Rudy on her lap, then picked Bitsy up and let her get comfy next to him. "I just praised him for staying with his bitty buddy."

Dave walked in carrying his black bag and took a seat alongside Viv, who then stood and went into the kitchen. "I've done all I can without running blood tests and X-rays." His expression remained firm. "But you were right to be worried."

"What's wrong? What happened to her?" Ellie ran a trembling hand across Bitsy's spine. "Is it serious?"

The vet continued to frown. "On a scale of one to ten, I'd rate her condition a six. She's definitely not the Bitsy I'm used to treating, but she isn't totally lost or out of normal range."

Ellie gazed at the petite pooch, who was now sleeping on her thigh. "What the heck is that supposed to mean?"

He accepted the beer Vivian handed him and moved over to give her room. "I've seen it before in patients, but not very often. Normally, dogs live for the moment. Once the danger or traumatic event passes they perk up and, with a bit of kindness and the return to a regular routine, go back to being their usual happy and trusting selves."

"I know dogs are resilient. I also believe they have a very forgiving nature and react to the vibes given off by their owners," Ellie added.

"Where canines are concerned, you and I see things the same way, but not everyone agrees." He gave Viv a look and smiled. "Vivian and I had this very discussion just a couple of months ago, if I remember correctly."

"We talked over T's inability to understand why I didn't want him wearing that stupid sweater he got at Flora's." Viv sat closer to the vet and snuggled into his side. "Dave said Mr. T wanted—no, he *needed*—to wear that outrageous garment, and I said T didn't know the first thing about style. He liked the coat because it was loaded with feathers, and since it's natural for dogs to chase birds, that's what drew him to it."

Ellie had heard a few of their talks, and most had fallen just short of an argument, so she'd tuned them out. When she took T for a walk, she let him wear the silly sweater. It was no skin off her nose if he looked outrageous, and it made the Jack Russell feel good. Who cared if people pointed and giggled when they saw him?

"All I know is Mr. T enjoys that outfit," said Ellie. "His step is quick, he holds his head high, and his attitude is that of a Best in Show winner when he has it on. It you ask me, that's reason enough to give in to his demand."

"Okay, okay. I let him wear it, don't I? But that doesn't mean I can't wait for spring to arrive so I can toss it onto the top shelf of my closet. It's not my fault I can't talk to dogs the way you two can."

"Now, babe—" Dave held her free hand. "I never said I could *talk* to dogs."

Ellie suppressed a grin. One day she was going to tell her best friend that *she* could. Viv's reaction was sure to be priceless.

Dave went on. "It's more an inborn understanding, and I don't expect everyone to have it. Just because you don't doesn't mean we're poking fun or thinking any less of you."

Viv stuck out her lower lip. "Yeah, right."

"So, Dave," Ellie continued, "what did you find when you examined our little girl?"

"She's definitely in a funk. I don't know if it has something to do with Rob and the murder, or if it's simply because she's away from him. All I'm sure of is that Bitsy is not the carefree dog I'm used to treating." Dave upended his beer bottle and took a long swallow. "When do you think you'll be taking her home?"

"Tomorrow. Rob's sister is supposed to arrive sometime in the afternoon and I'm fairly certain he has an appointment with his attorney, so it's better if Bitsy's with us for the day." Ellie rested her head on the chair back. "I was planning to drop her off after my last round of walks."

"I think that's best. In the meantime, do what you've been doing. Keep her calm, see that she eats, and let her rest. If she really was a witness to what went on in that dressing room, it might have caused a shock to her system. Let's wait a while before I start her on a drug."

"A drug?" Viv exclaimed. "You're kidding, right?"

"Nope. There are mood enhancers for dogs just as there are for people, but they're usually given in only the most serious cases," explained the vet. "Or we can go the holistic route, maybe try some valerian or another calming herb, but I think that with time and care Bitsy will come around."

Ellie said good-bye to Viv and Dave and left them making nice on the love seat while Mr. T kept his eyes on Animal Planet. Her best friend and the vet could walk the Jack Russell on their own, but her charges needed to go out before they settled in for the night.

Thoughts of Sam's no-show for dinner filled her head as she led Rudy and Bitsy down the front steps and onto the sidewalk. When Sam was on a case, everything else in his life took a backseat, and she figured that was the reason he hadn't stopped by or called. Though dedication to his profession was one of the things she admired about him, it was also a concern. Did she want to spend the rest of her life with another man who put his career first and her second?

No need to worry about it now, she decided. They were just starting to get comfortable with each other. Sam had yet to say he loved her, and she hadn't said it to him. The only future plans he'd mentioned were in reference to next year's Valentine's Day, which had been more a joke than an invitation. But she was head-over-heels crazy about him, and she suspected he knew it. They'd both been through the wringer in their first serious relationships, so it made sense for them to wait a while before committing fully to another person.

As they neared the corner, Ellie's cell rang and she retrieved it from her tote. Though it was nearly ten, she answered when she read the display. "Hey, Joy. I was wondering if I'd ever hear from you again."

"Ellie, hi—uh—it's me."

"I hope you're calling to tell me you're ready to come back to work."

"Um—no. I mean, I'd like to come back, but I . . . can't."

"Is something wrong, Joy? Something you need to discuss? Because you know I'm more than happy to help." Ellie waited while Rudy and Bitsy did their business. "I don't mind."

When Joy didn't answer, she headed back to the apartment. Finally, as she approached the steps, her ex-assistant said, "Ellie, this is nothing personal, but you have to stop calling me."

The statement took her by surprise. Had she been that much of a pest? "Okay, if you don't want to hear from me, you won't, and I apologize if I've overstepped my bounds."

"It's not me that—I mean—" The girl heaved a sigh. "I can't explain. Just don't phone me anymore. I'll get hold of you if I need you, but until then . . ."

"Okay, sure, but—" She stopped talking when Joy disconnected the call. After dropping the phone in her tote, she opened the inside door to the condo and headed up the steps.

"So what did Joy want?" Rudy asked as they climbed the two flights to their floor.

"She asked me to stop phoning her."

"But why?"

"Do you think I've been that much of a bother?"

"You do know how to gnaw on a bone when your hackles are up, but with Joy, no. You only called her what? Every couple of weeks?"

"Maybe twice a month is all. I thought I was simply keeping in touch, but I guess not." She unlocked her apartment and the trio continued down the hall. "Let me change and we can talk about you-know-who."

In the bedroom, she set Bitsy on the bed while Rudy jumped up and plunked onto his pillow. Then Ellie changed into a sleep shirt, took care of business in the bathroom, and returned. After pulling down the covers, she settled in while Bitsy curled up in the center of the bed. Snuggling nearer to her boy, she asked, "Okay, let's hear what went down in Viv's spare room."

Rudy gave an exaggerated stretch, walked in a circle, and lay back down. *"Dr. Dave did the usual: thermometer up the butt, heart check, ear check, eye check—you know, all the stuff he does when he looks me over every year."*

"I do know. So what else?"

"After that, he stared into Bitsy's eyes and started talk-

ing to her. I always knew he was a good guy, but I never realized how good until I saw him with our little girl."

Was it possible she and Dave shared the same psychic link with canines? "Please don't tell me Bitsy answered him and he understood her."

"Not the way you and I do, but he does send out a vibe that tells us dogs he cares. Makes us want to trust him when we know other humans are only pretending."

"And he made Bitsy feel that way, too?"

"I'm not a hundred percent sure, but I'd say yes."

"Can you ask Bitsy if she's willing to talk to me now?"

Before Rudy answered, Bitsy tottered to Ellie's side and jumped onto her chest so they could gaze eyeball to eyeball. *"I'm ready to talk, Ellie, and I'm sorry if I've been worrying you."*

She laid a hand on the poohuahua's back. "Oh, sweetie, I'm so happy to hear you. Are you feeling better?"

"Dr. Dave said I was supposed to relax and trust you. He said you'd take care of me."

"He's right. I'm here for you and Rob."

Bitsy shivered. *"There was so much blood, and angry men took him away. It's all I can think about."*

"Rob is home. I saw him this afternoon and he's concerned, but he's all right." Hoping to put the little dog at ease, she added, "His sister and Bradley are coming to visit."

"Bradley's coming? Really, truly he is?" Bitsy panted in excitement. *"I can hardly wait to see him again."*

"I take it you like Bradley?"

"I love Bradley, and he loves me."

"Rob wouldn't tell me, but I know you will. What kind of dog is Bradley?"

"Ahh . . . a big one?"

Ellie grinned. Because of Bitsy's size, almost every canine she met would be big. "How about his breed?"

"I'm not sure. But he's ginormous."

"Let's try to whittle that down. How large is he when you compare him to Rudy?"

The poohuahua gazed at the yorkiepoo as if she were sizing up a biscuit. *"Bradley is way, way bigger."*

Since her boy was only twelve pounds, that figured. "Can you be more specific?"

"Maybe as big as Rob?"

"That doesn't make sense. Rob's almost six feet tall."

Bitsy gave a doggie shrug. *"All I know is I have to look way up to see his muzzle, just like I hafta do with Rob."* She heaved a sigh. *"I miss him. When can I go home?"*

"How does tomorrow afternoon sound?"

Bitsy moved closer and licked Ellie's chin. *"It sounds great."*

She gathered the dog in her arms. "I don't want to upset you, but you have to help me get to the truth about last night. Can you tell me what happened in the dressing room before Rob walked in?"

Bitsy started to shiver. *"I don't remember all that much."*

"Were you awake? Did you actually see Carmella come in, and . . . whoever killed her?"

"I'm not sure. I was sort of dreaming, cuz I remember thinking about a squirrel I saw in the park. You know, the one that's bigger than me?"

"The one we saw the other morning?"

"The sucker with the black bushy tail?" Rudy asked.

"That's the one. I dreamed he was chasing me and—"

"Whoa-hoa. You weren't havin' a dream. That was a nightmare."

"Let her finish." Ellie gave the poohuahua another pat. "Go on, tell us more."

"I remember running from that squirrel, and then I heard voices. Human voices. I guess that's when I woke up. I saw high heels. Then I saw pant legs. The shouting

got louder, and I closed my eyes. Next thing I knew, Rob was on the floor holding that sharp, pointy thing."

Ellie bit her lip. Bitsy's memory did not bode well for her master. "Was Rob the other person arguing with Carmella or was it someone else?"

"Someone else. But I'm not sure who."

"You don't know or you don't remember?"

Bitsy's whimper tore at Ellie's heart. "Both, I guess. Is that important?"

"I'm afraid so, because right now you're the only witness to the crime. We need you to recall exactly what happened."

"But I heard Rob tell the big men he didn't do it."

"I heard him say that, too, but without someone to corroborate his story—"

"Co-rob-er-what?"

"Corroborate. It means to agree with what Rob said. No other human was a witness, just you, and since you can't tell them . . ."

"But I told you. Why can't you pass along what I say?"

"It's not that simple. First of all, no one would believe me if I said I heard the story from you. It's bad enough some folks think I'm nutty for talking to the dogs I walk. If I said you gave me the details of the crime—"

"I thought that detective, the one Rudy knows, was your boyfriend."

"Detective Demento?" Rudy broke in. "He's a putz."

Ellie wrapped her fingers around her boy's muzzle. "What Rudy means is Detective Ryder is all cop when he's on a case. He doesn't understand that some people can communicate with their pets. He'll only believe what can be proved, and that's not talking dogs."

"Oh."

"Yeah, 'oh,'" Rudy repeated. "So unless you can give

us a name or a description of whoever was in there before Bobbi-Rob arrived, his ass is grass."

"Enough," Ellie muttered, grabbing his muzzle again. "There has to be a way to make this work."

Bitsy nuzzled into Ellie's chest. *"I'll try to remember, really I will. I don't want Rob to go to the big house."*

"The big house?" Raising an eyebrow, she stared at her boy. "Where did you hear that?"

"Rudy told me—"

"I just told her that humans put other humans in jail—"

"You said the big house—"

"Jail, big house—same difference," the yorkiepoo gruffed.

"The term 'big house' is frightening," Ellie scolded. "Bitsy's worried enough without you upsetting her."

"Okay, okay. I didn't mean to scare her, but she has to know the truth."

"Not to worry, sweetie. Once we iron this out, nothing will happen to Rob and life will go on just like before." She rubbed Bitsy's ears. "How about you sleep on it, think about remembering, and see where that leads you? Maybe you'll have some answers in the morning."

The poohuahua yawned. *"I am kinda tired."*

"I imagine so." Ellie rolled to her side. "If you want, you can snuggle with Rudy and close your eyes. I'm here if you need me."

Bitsy yawned again and scratched at the duvet. After walking in a circle, she lay down and did as Ellie suggested. A moment passed; then Rudy sniffed the top of the poohuahua's head and snurffled her ears. *"She's almost asleep,"* he whispered. *"Wish I could zone out like that."*

"Since you've never had the problem Bitsy has right now, I know you always zone out like that."

"Hey, there were times when I was scared. When that water delivery guy pulled a knife on you, and when Gary's brother tossed that sack over my head. Then there was the gig with that stone-faced woman and her—"

"Okay, okay. I get the picture." She stroked the spot between Rudy's ears. "It's just that Bitsy's a baby. She hasn't been around the block, so to speak, and—"

"That ain't so. She goes 'around the block' whenever you give her a walk."

"Ha-ha. You know what I mean."

The yorkiepoo snorted. *"So maybe I do. That doesn't mean I don't worry about you."*

"Like I worry about you." She turned off the light and pulled up the covers. "What do you think I should do next?"

"Don't you mean what do I think we should do next?"

"Fine. Me. You. We want to help Rob and Bitsy. What do you think we should do next?" Ellie stifled a yawn. "And make it fast because I'm beat."

"Talk to Detective Demento. Question Bobbi-Rob again. Snoop around the club holdin' that revue to see if any of the other performers can give you a clue. Take your pick."

"I'll sleep on it. Maybe something will come to me overnight, just like I hope things will straighten themselves out in Bitsy's head."

"Give her a while. She'll remember."

"Why are you so sure of that?"

"Because Bitsy loves Bobbi-Rob, just like I love you. She's not gonna rest until she helps prove him innocent." He licked Ellie's cheek. *"And neither will we."*

Chapter 6

Bitsy woke the next day more alert and talkative than she'd been since the night of the murder, so Ellie decided to take her along on her round of morning walks. She figured the exercise would keep the poohuahua's mind occupied for a few hours and help calm her nerves. Over breakfast, Bitsy confessed that she hadn't remembered anything new about the night of Rob's arrest, but she felt certain she'd recall what had gone down at the club if she were given a little more time.

On the way to the Beaumont, their first building of the day, the trio stopped at the nearest Joe to Go to pick up Randall's twice-weekly tea and Natter's regular coffee. Ever since Rudy had been kidnapped from in front of the store, Joe Cantiglia, her old college buddy, had allowed Ellie to bring her boy into the coffee shop disguised as a "service dog." Since no one had ever asked to inspect his completion certificate, and not a single person had complained about having a canine in the shop, she hoped she would be safe this morning with two dogs in tow. She had immense respect for service dogs and what they did for humankind. Eventually, she thought she'd take Rudy through their training steps and actually have him awarded the designation, but not today.

"Hey, Nancy Drew. You're early today," said Joe when she walked to the counter.

"Not funny, pal." She knew Joe was trying for humor, but it wasn't always welcome.

"Sorry. Is something up your—" He narrowed his eyes. "Uh-oh. Don't tell me you're involved in another murder thing."

"Not involved, exactly. But I do have a new companion."

Striding from around the register, Joe squatted. "Hello, fella." He gazed at Ellie. "He's a bitty thing, isn't he?"

Seeming to not care that Joe had guessed her gender incorrectly, Bitsy nuzzled his palm while Rudy gave a doggie snort. *"Guess again, paisan. That's a female you're strokin'."*

Ellie jerked the yorkiepoo's leash, her unspoken warning to be polite. "Bitsy is a girl. If you were a canine expert, I'd have called her a bitch."

Joe rose to his feet but continued to stare at the dog. "She may be a girl, but she certainly doesn't look like a bitch to me. Is she your new pup?"

"She belongs to one of my clients, but I've been watching her the past two days. She's a sweetie, but she's under a bit of stress right now."

"Stress?" Joe asked. "I can't believe there's an iota of stress in her life if you're on guard. When I die, I want to come back as one of your dogs. Nothing better than being treated like royalty, right, Rudster?"

Rudy stood on his hind legs and rested his paws on Joe's calf. *"I'm worth every bit of special treatment, Bozo,"* he wisecracked. *"Dogs as good as me deserve the best."*

"What kind of stress?" Joe said, unaware of Rudy's comment.

Ellie spotted a newspaper stand in front of the register and nodded toward the top publication, which carried a smaller headline and sidebar on the death of Carmella Sunday. "Have you been reading the papers?"

"Yeah, sure, but the only thing making the front page these days is a story about some drag queen and her dead lover."

Ellie shrugged and his eyes opened wide. "Holy cannoli. Don't tell me you're involved in another—"

Her ragged sigh stopped Joe in his tracks.

"Jeez, I don't believe this."

"How about giving me a shortbread cookie?"

When she glanced at the dogs, he went behind the counter, retrieved a cookie, and brought it over. After handing it to her, he grabbed her elbow and hauled her out of the foot traffic. Ellie pulled napkins from a holder, broke the cookie into pieces, and set everything on the floor.

Rudy and Bitsy dived into the treat and she faced Joe. "The accused killer is my client, and Bitsy is his dog." She raised her hand in a hold-your-horses gesture. "And before you give me a lecture—"

"What the heck is wrong with you, sticking your nose into another crime?"

Ellie grimaced. "I was there when it happened."

"There? What there?"

"At Guess Who on opening night. Remember, I told you I had tickets. My client, the alleged murderer, is a headliner at the club, and he shared a dressing room with the victim."

Joe rolled his eyes. "I don't get it. You look like such a nice normal pers—"

"I am normal," Ellie interjected. "I didn't have a thing

to do with it. Sam, Viv, and Dr. Dave were with me in the audience when the ruckus broke out. Sam took off and I followed him."

"I bet Ryder loved that."

"I haven't really talked to Sam since he commandeered the case, but Rob begged me to take care of his dog before they carted him away, so I brought her home. She's been with me ever since."

Joe gazed at Bitsy, now sitting at his feet. "That little doll was there when the murder occurred?"

"I like him, Ellie," the poohuahua said. *"Think maybe he'll give us another cookie?"*

She smothered a smile, lifted Bitsy in her arms, and held her close. "Rob sometimes took her to rehearsal, and she loved the attention the performers gave her, so it was only natural he wanted her to share his big night. She was in one of those pet carriers, hidden beneath the dressing table, when the cops found her."

Joe scratched Bitsy under the chin. "Poor baby. Now I get why she's stressed."

"I don't have time to explain more. I'm early because I need my weekly thank-you drinks for the doormen." The line of customers had dwindled, so she headed for the counter.

"I guess you didn't notice the sign," he said, walking to the register.

She focused on a blackboard tacked on the wall behind the counter. "Deli-style sandwiches available from eleven to three every day. Aw, how sweet. You decided to take another of my suggestions to heart."

"You were right about those punch cards, so I thought I'd try this one, too. Yesterday was the first day, and I sold over fifty sandwiches. By the first of next week, I'll be doing the same in the other stores."

Ellie paid for the filled drink carrier. "If we can, we'll stop by at lunchtime."

"Hang on," said Joe, again stepping to the side of the counter. "Have you taken a look at the store next door? I can't believe I'm gonna have more competition."

"Next door?"

"It's a bakery, and I hear they'll be serving a free cup of java with every purchase. That's sure to cut into my trade."

Her college buddy had done well for himself, running a successful business amid direct competition from the city's booming Starbucks trade, as well as the delis, diners, and drink joints scattered around town. She was proud of the fact that he used one of her sales ideas and now offered the free-coffee punch card. With the addition of sandwiches, his foot traffic was sure to grow.

"What do you mean, 'you hear'? Don't you think you should check it out before getting annoyed? That's the sensible thing to do."

"Since nothing goes better with fresh baked goods than a cup of coffee, I get where they're going, and it's bound to put a dent in my croissant, cookie, and muffin trade. Next thing I know, they'll be offering sandwiches."

"Have you met the owner? Maybe you should talk to them, get the skinny yourself."

Joe scowled. Her friend was a very attractive guy, maybe more so with the lines bracketing his tanned face and dark brown eyes. Why was it okay for men to show their age, but not women?

"I've thought about it, but if I go over there I'm afraid I'll say something I'll regret."

"You need to stay friendly with the locals. We can talk about it later, but I have to leave."

On the sidewalk, Ellie hoisted her tote bag onto her

shoulder, juggled the drink carrier until it was safely in hand, and took a quick look at the store next door. It was empty, but she could tell by the glass counters that some type of work was being done. Joe was probably right about getting competition. She'd look into it when she had the time. Right now, all she could think of was Rob.

Since he'd given her the story of his life, both private and professional, and explained his parents' blatant disapproval while growing up, she'd made it a point to become his friend. Now she wondered whether Rob had made up his sorry tale just to garner sympathy. Had he lied about his stiff and unbending parents? Had he lied about being straight? More important, had he lied about committing a murder?

Though she hated to admit it, some of Sam's ideas made sense. Greed was the cause of as many crimes as jealousy and hatred were. Carmella was jealous of Rob's chance at fame and the opportunity for a successful career. Was it possible Carmella had something Rob wanted?

Turning into the Beaumont, she grinned at Natter and passed him his coffee.

"Thanks, and have a good day," the doorman said with a smile.

Hearing that Rob was innocent was the only thing that would make her day good. "Looks like I'll have to take a trip to Guess Who today," she muttered as she led the dogs to the elevator.

"Since when?" Rudy asked from the floor.

She gave Natter a wave when they entered the elevator. "Since now," she told her boy. "There are a couple of things I need to look into."

Ellie walked to her next stop, breathing deeply of the cool air. She couldn't remember the last time there'd been a snowfall, and there was rain in the forecast, which

she hoped would bring the April showers six weeks
ahead of time to herald an early spring. The weather had
been so nice, in fact, that she couldn't recall the last time
she'd wrestled one of her charges into a coat, sweater,
or booties.

Now at the Davenport, she made a point of handing
Randall his tea. Fearful that the poohuahua might cry or
throw a fit at not being able to see Rob, she also passed
the doorman the dogs' leads and raised an eyebrow that
asked if he would keep them.

Randall, being a good friend, acknowledged her with
a nod and led the pups behind the front counter, in ef-
fect blocking them from the view of anyone walking by.
After collecting the last dog in the Davenport pack, she
herded Sweetie Pie, Buckley, Jett, and Stinker to the elevator and gave them a lecture as they waited for their
ride down.

"Okay, everybody, listen up," she began. "Bitsy's
downstairs with Rudy, and I expect you to be on your
best behavior. No arguing, grumbling, or commentary."

"Tell that to the boys," Sweetie Pie advised. *"I'm always on my best behavior."*

"Ha!" shouted Stinker. *"That's not what we hear."*

"Uh-huh, sure," said Ellie. "What about when Babs
brings home an overnight guest?"

"You're talking about a man, right?" The Westie
snorted. *"That's so different."*

The rest of the pack, all male, yapped at once.

"You're such a girl."

"Little Miss Fussypants."

"Someone grab me a cryin' towel."

"Enough," Ellie ordered. "Bitsy is your pal. I don't
want to hear a word about Rob's arrest. You got it?"

Mumbles of *"yeah"* and *"if you say so"* filled her
head and she smiled. These dogs had been her first cli-

ents, so each of them held a special place in her heart. Even Buckley, the grump, made her grin.

She led them into the elevator. Time to change the subject. "So, Buck, tell me a little more about your last visit to Madame Orzo. Did she read your mind? Do you have another appointment?"

"I say she guesses, because she can't really see into my head, but Hazel made another date with her," the maltipoo yipped. *"That woman gives me the creeps."*

"Everything gives you the creeps," said Jett, her Scottie with an attitude. *"I never heard any dog complain like you do."* He gave his muzzle a toss. *"'Cept for Stinker."*

The comment started another round of insults that continued until the elevator hit the ground floor. She collected Rudy and Bitsy, and aimed for the park, where she gave everyone an extra amount of time to do their business. When the canines treated Bitsy the same as usual, she was so relieved that she pulled a bag of biscuits from her tote and gave each dog a reward.

Back in the Davenport, she again passed Rudy's and Bitsy's leads to Randall and made quick work of returning her charges to their homes. "Thanks," she told the doorman when she returned to claim the pups. "I figured you'd understand."

"Of course," he said, his expression Yoda-like. "You didn't want Miss Bitsy to be reminded of her master. Mr. Chesney is still up there, you know."

"Did he tell you his sister was flying in today to oversee damage control?"

Randall tipped his hat to a tenant and reached under the counter. "Here you are, Ms. Shelton," he said, handing her a package with a Bergdorf logo.

Ellie remembered the pencil-thin woman from yesterday. She seemed to be the leader of the group of troublemakers who'd argued with Kronk when he asked for IDs before allowing people into the building.

Ms. Shelton nodded her thanks, then gazed at the pups with a sneer etched on her snooty face. "Isn't that the dog owned by that—that pervert?"

"If you mean Rob Chesney, then yes," answered Randall.

She gazed at Ellie. "And you're his dog walker."

The tone in her voice made Ellie sound like a criminal. "I am. Do you need someone to take care of your pet?" She grinned when the woman's expression segued to one of horror. "My rates are reasonable. Just ask Rob."

"Me? Own a dog?" Ms. Shelton shook her head and her fall of straight blond hair swung rigidly across her pashmina-clad shoulders. "I should say not. Filthy creatures." She tapped the counter with a manicured nail and returned her focus to Randall. "I take it you gave management our demand?"

"It's taken care of," he assured her.

"Then we should hear something soon." Ms. Shelton stomped to the elevator on her four-inch Manolos and stepped inside.

"Demand? What demand?" Ellie asked when the door closed.

Randall heaved a sigh. "It's something I was hoping you wouldn't hear about. A group of tenants signed a petition and asked me to hand-deliver it to the consortium that manages this complex. It's about Mr. Chesney."

She lowered her voice. "What do they want to do with Rob?"

"They want him evicted, of course. Claim a person of his ilk isn't welcome in their building. They're also annoyed over the way Kronk handled the security check after the murder. They claim he treated them badly, and they tried to blame that on Mr. Chesney, too."

Ellie's mouth dropped open in shock. "That's ridiculous. I was here, and Kronk only did what management ordered him to do. You know Kronk. He's not the most tactful guy in a difficult situation, but I thought he did an okay job."

"Boris Kronkovitz has no tact in any situation," Randall said, frowning. "But I was very careful to go over the handling of the tenants with him when I left for the night. I think they're merely using him as an excuse to see Mr. Chesney out."

"Great. Just what Rob needs."

"I agree." He rested an elbow on the counter. "But I'm sure it will take some time for management to make a decision. If you come up with something that might delay his removal, let me know and I'll pass it along."

Ellie, Bitsy, and Rudy left and walked north to their next stop, a building that was smaller and less ostentatious than most on the Upper East Side. Because there were only five dogs on her list, the run was usually quick and uneventful.

It was only after she arrived to pick up Pooh and Tigger that she began to worry. Sara Studebaker, a woman near Ellie's age, lived here with two adorable West Highland White Terriers, the same breed as Sweetie Pie. She and Sara sometimes held conversations about their dogs or whatever was going on in their lives. She knocked, let herself in, and found it odd that Sara wasn't there to say hello. Stranger still was the fact that Pooh and Tigger were missing.

She called the dogs' names, then Sara's, and got no answer. Concerned, she walked down the center hall of the comfortably appointed unit checking the rooms. "What do you think? Should we be worried about the situation?"

Rudy sniffed the doorway of each room. *"I'm not get-*

tin' a whiff of trouble, so my guess is the car girl forgot."
He loved referring to Sara as Sara Sedan, Sara Ferrari,
sometimes even Sara Convertible, depending on his
mood, even though her family had no connection to the
automobile industry.

Ellie stopped in the kitchen and went to the spot
where she left her daily progress reports. "Maybe you're
right, but I'm still worried. There's no note, and she usually leaves one if she has to go out."

Without a clue on how to proceed, she left Sara's
place and moved down through the floors, picking up
Scooter, Fred, and Spike. With two fewer dogs to walk,
she finished in twenty minutes, returned them all home,
and headed for the Cranston.

"You sure got a lot of us to walk," chimed Bitsy, who
had never accompanied them on their entire route before.

"I had an assistant until last November," she told the
poohuahua as they entered the Cranston Arms lobby
and headed for the elevator. "I'm advertising for another right now."

*"Was that the pretty girl who walked us a time or two
the day you were at that show?"*

Ellie unlocked Freud's door, introduced him to Bitsy,
and let the dogs get acquainted in the usual manner.
After a round of sniffing and bowing, she answered the
question. "Her name was Joy. Did you like her?"

*"She was okay, but she talked on the phone a lot. And
sometimes she forgot to give us our biscuit."*

Joy spending time on the phone didn't bother Ellie.
It was easy to walk and talk at the same time. But not
giving the dogs their treats was a different matter. "No
biscuits? Why didn't one of you tell me?"

*"We knew you were extra-busy so we talked it over
and agreed not to,"* Bitsy explained. *"It sorta just slipped
out."*

"Did you know about that?" she asked her boy as they arrived at the next apartment.

"Who, me? Nope. Didn't know a thing."

"You are such a liar," she scolded. "Someone should have told me, so I could deal with the situation."

"I thought about it," said Rudy. *"Then Joy quit, so I figured 'no biggie' and filed it away."*

They collected Freud, a French Bulldog; Arlo, a miniature Dachshund; Rocco, a black toy Poodle; Dilbert, the long-haired Chihuahua; Lily, a tiny Bichon with a sweet disposition; and finally Sampson, the extra-large Pug.

On the sidewalk, Ellie noted the weather was even more agreeable than she'd first thought, and so she let the pack take their time. Then she sat on a bench and inhaled the fresh air. When her phone rang, she checked the number. Though it didn't register on caller ID, she picked it up anyway. "Paws in Motion. How may I help you?"

"Are you the person lookin' for a dog walker?" asked a male voice awash in a Brooklyn accent. "Ellie Engleman?"

"That's me. Are you interested in the job?"

"Uh, yeah. I mean, maybe." The man cleared his throat. "How much does the gig pay?"

Ellie recited the amount she'd been giving Joy, which was 50 percent of what she charged for the walks.

"So, uh, what would I have to do?"

"Before I answer, maybe you could give me a name, Mr. . . . ?"

"Rizzoli. Tony—er—Anthony Rizzoli."

"Thanks, Mr. Rizzoli. I'll explain what the job entails and you feel free to ask questions." She went over the times of day he would need to work, as well as the bonding and insurance papers he would need to fill out. "How does that sound to you?"

"Easy enough. So what do we do next?"

"How about a meeting? Say, this afternoon around five thirty at the building I need you for?" She gave him the name and address of the Cranston Arms.

"Sure, fine. Whatever you say. Meet you in the lobby at five thirty."

"We gonna get another new walker?" asked Arlo when Ellie ended the call.

"Maybe. He'll have to try out first."

"That means we'll be missin' you again," complained Lily.

"I'll choose someone dependable and pleasant. I promise."

"Big Momma ain't gonna like it," Sampson warned. *"Seems like everything makes her miserable these days."*

Standing, Ellie led them across Fifth Avenue and entered the Cranston while assuring each dog she'd find the perfect walker. She kept it up while dropping off each of her charges. Finally, at Sampson's door, she knocked, then used her key, but like the other morning Mariette swung open the door.

"You're home," Ellie said, surprised to see Mariette, who was usually at a spa or a fitness appointment. "Since you didn't answer when I picked Sampson up, I thought you were out."

Mariette blew her nose into a wad of tissues, shocking Ellie with her red face, swollen eyes, and rumpled hair. Then she grabbed the Pug's leash and unclipped it from his collar. "I've been under the weather, so I haven't been out lately."

"Is there anything I can do for you? Maybe pick up a prescription or warm some chicken soup?"

"It's nice of you to offer, but I'll be fine." She glanced at Sampson. "How was my boy today?"

"Fine."

"I've been extra careful with his treats and his diet."

"And it shows," said Ellie. "Are you planning on going to the doctor?"

"Don't worry about me, Ellie." The door closed and the locks clicked into place.

Ellie raised her hand to knock again, then thought better of it. If Mariette had wanted help, she would have accepted it when first offered. According to Judge Frye, the woman loved her socialite lifestyle and enjoyed the prestige garnered by her husband's successful judicial career. Whatever was bothering her would probably take care of itself soon enough.

The trio headed toward the elevator. Ellie planned to take Rudy and Bitsy home, grab lunch at Joe's, and go to Guess Who. She wanted to talk to a few of the "girls" and find out if they knew anything that might help Rob.

On the street, she hailed a cab and herded the dogs inside. After giving the driver her address, she leaned against the backseat. When she laid a hand on Bitsy's head, she sucked in a breath. "Hey, baby girl. What's wrong? Why are you shivering?"

"She's been like that for a while, Triple E."

"Shaking like one of those battery-powered monkeys?"

"Pretty much," said Rudy, putting his paw on her thigh.

Ellie gathered Bitsy in her arms. "What's wrong, sweetie? Did something frighten you?"

When the poohuahua continued to stare straight ahead, Ellie groaned internally. The little dog was acting the same way she had the night of the murder. What had happened to put Bitsy in such a state? And what could she do to bring her out of it?

"Bitsy, talk to me. Please tell me what's wrong."

The poohuahua sniffed out a breath, but she didn't speak.

"Want me to give it a try?" asked Rudy.

"Sure, go ahead. Just don't frighten her."

He nosed Bitsy's ear. Ellie didn't hear anything, but she knew the dogs were communicating in their own language. After a few seconds, Rudy sat back on the seat.

"What? What is it?"

"You ain't gonna believe this one."

"What did she tell you?"

"Bitsy says she heard something . . . a bad voice."

"Voice? Whose voice?"

Rudy again nudged the poohuahua. After a moment, he sighed. *"I ain't gettin' nothin'. She says she can't talk about it. She wants to go home and sleep."*

"She's probably confused because she's tired. A canine her size isn't used to trudging the number of miles we do each day. Rob always said the only long walks she got were with us, and that's not really much."

Rudy gave a doggie shrug. *"That's all she's willing to say, and from the looks of it, I think you should give her a break."*

Ellie gazed at Bitsy, curled in a ball on her lap. Her eyes were closed and her panting had slowed, but she was still trembling. Cradling the poohuahua in her arms, Ellie nuzzled Bitsy's neck. "It's okay, little girl. I'm here and so is Rudy. We'll figure this out and we'll help Rob, too."

Chapter 7

Ellie dropped the dogs off and returned to Joe's flagship store on Lexington off Seventy-fifth for a quick lunch. As the week progressed, her college buddy rotated to each of his three stores, but he lived above this one, so he spent the majority of his time here. Walking through the front door, she found him scowling behind the counter.

"Why are you grumpy? Has the new menu hit a glitch?"

"The new menu's working out just fine. Thanks. What can I get you?"

"A turkey on whole wheat, lettuce, tomato, and mayo sounds perfect. And my usual Caramel Bliss. Now, about the store next door—"

After handing register duty to a coworker, he motioned Ellie to the side of the counter. "Did you get the chance to look inside that bakery?"

"Just for a second this morning, but I didn't see anyone."

"Well, check it out before you tell me I'm wrong." Joe grabbed her tray from the clerk and carried it to an empty table, still scowling. "I thought about what you said, but I doubt I can go over there without starting a fight."

Ellie rolled her eyes. Men! After taking a swig of coffee, she stood. "Watch my sandwich. I'll be back in a second."

She was out of her seat and on the sidewalk so fast he didn't have time to respond. Before entering the building next door, she did a full inspection, noting its sparkling windows, freshly painted exterior, and shiny brass doorknob. Peering inside, she saw several men hanging shelves, a large bakery case, and a woman arranging round tables and matching chairs in the area in front of the case.

The workmen looked like the typical construction workers hired for a renovation job, so she concentrated on the woman, who was of medium height with straight blond hair and a healthy build. Ellie guessed she was the owner and headed inside. When the woman glanced up, Ellie stepped forward in surprise. "Sara?"

"Ellie?" Sara Studebaker dusted her hands on her snug jeans and smiled. "Oh, gosh. I guess I forgot to tell you. I'm opening a bakery."

It was then Ellie spotted Pooh and Tigger, peeking out from behind a rear door she guessed led to the kitchen. "Hi, girls," she said, waggling fingers at the Westies. Then she focused on her client. "I'm glad to see you're okay. I got worried when I arrived at the apartment this morning and you and the dogs weren't home."

Groaning, Sara rolled her big green eyes. "I am so sorry. I knew there was something I forgot to do when I left. I meant to call and tell you I had the babies, but with all the excitement I forgot."

"So," said Ellie. "You've decided to follow in your family's footsteps." She gazed at the antique bookshelves, which she imagined would soon be filled with goodies. "Have you developed any new items?"

Sara pulled out a chair and gave a nod, encouraging Ellie to sit. "Sort of, but not exactly."

Sara's grandparents had secured a fortune back in the sixties, when they won a lawsuit against a company that stole their first-on-the-market, all-natural baked-goods recipes. A few years later, they compounded their wealth by selling the company, Mother Millie's Home-made Treasures, to a high-end food conglomerate.

"You did say it was a bakery, right?"

Pooh and Tigger trotted over, stood on their hind legs, and rested their front paws on Sara's thigh. She gave each of her girls an ear rub before saying, "The Spoiled Hound will carry goodies for canines only. A sign company's scheduled to dress up the door and windows sometime next week."

"A dog bakery? Like Bread and Bones?" B&B was Ellie's favorite spot for fresh dog treats, but they made goodies for humans and canines alike. Because it was several blocks from home, she stopped there only if she had extra time.

"The canine cookies will be one hundred percent natural, with no chemicals or preservatives. They're so pure that babies can use them for teething biscuits," Sara assured her.

"Is it one of Grandma Millie's recipes, or did you come up with it yourself?"

"A bit of both," said Sara. "I took one of the Treasures' cookie recipes and played around with it until I knew Pooh and Tigger loved it. Then I decided to get off my butt and work for a living instead of existing on my overblown trust fund."

"What do your mom and dad have to say about the venture?"

Sara shrugged, her expression forlorn. "I think they're okay with it. Then again, it's hard telling how they really feel. A once-a-month phone call from Jamaica isn't exactly the best way to gauge a person's true reaction to things."

Ellie and Sara had talked about their parents before, comparing Paul and Bunny Studebaker's lack of involvement in their daughter's life to Ellie's buttinsky mother. Sara wished she had a mom and dad more like Georgette, and Ellie wanted a mother who interfered in her life only when asked.

"I'm sure they're proud of you," Ellie told her. "Send them an invitation to the grand opening. I bet they'll come."

"Maybe, but who knows?"

"Still, you should send them an invitation."

Sara heaved a sigh. "I guess."

"Great. What's the date of the grand opening?"

"I'm not sure. Four weeks or so. I'm still waiting to set up an inspection by the city, and I can't do that until the kitchen is fully operational and I can post the permits. Right now, I'm making trial batches of the cookies in my apartment and passing them out to whoever I see walking a dog. Why?"

"Because I plan to mark the date on my calendar. Rudy and I will be here with bells on, and I'll be happy to hand-deliver invitations to all my clients." She remembered the reason she was in the shop and smiled. "I don't mean to be a mooch, but do you have any samples with you?"

"Sure do. Give me a second." Sara disappeared through the rear door and returned with a bag. "These are apple-carrot, Pooh's and Tigger's favorite."

"And you'll be making other flavors beside these?"

"The plan right now is for cranberry-orange and carob

chip. I'm also working on a recipe for liver treats and dry kibble, but that one might take some doing. I'm almost ready with an all-natural wet dog food you keep in your freezer, too. It'll be packaged in quarter-cup servings. Just take out however many you need, nuke them for a minute per, and dole them out alone, with my kibble, or with your own. Whichever your dog likes best."

"Wow! I'm impressed," said Ellie, studying the cookies. She knew the perfect way to show Joe how wrong it was to jump to conclusions. "I have to get moving. If you're bringing the girls in every day, I guess you won't need me for a while."

"No, but I'll call you if I leave them home and they need a walk. And if you come by this way again, feel free to stop in and take them out if you can." Sara rested a knee on the chair and leaned into the table. "I didn't know you walked dogs on this street."

"I don't, but I have a friend near here. I stop in to say hello a couple of times a week."

"Then I'll still see a lot of you. That's great. And don't worry about my account. I'll get my money's worth if you promise to use my biscuits as your special treats and keep reminding your clients to do the same."

"Will do," Ellie said, standing. "Oh, and don't be surprised if you have a visitor."

"A visitor?"

"Be patient. You'll meet him soon enough. Catch you later."

She stepped outside, thinking. She'd used up her free time scouting for Joe, so she would need to wrap her sandwich and eat it on the way to the club. But first, she had just the thing to teach her pal a lesson.

"Look what I've got," she said when she returned to the coffee shop. Joe was still sitting at the table, his expression grim. "Free samples."

"Some friend you are, going to the dark side and accepting contraband."

She opened the bag and held out a cookie. "Stop being such a grouch and try one. Tell me what you think."

He grabbed the treat and gave it a quick study. "Shaped like a carrot? These must be for kids."

Ellie recalled Sara's teething biscuit comment. "Yep." She waited while he took a bite. "Well?"

Still frowning, he swallowed. "They're good, but they're hard as roofing tiles." He took another bite. "I have to admit, the taste does grow on you."

She choked back a grin. "Great, considering they're dog biscuits."

Joe's eyes opened wide. He swallowed what was left of his cookie. "What?"

"I said they're dog biscuits, you dope. And you would have known the 'bakery' was for dogs if you'd bothered to do a little investigating."

Still wearing a stern expression, Joe crossed his arms. "You did that on purpose."

"Of course I did. Now go next door and introduce yourself to Ms. Sara Studebaker. Tell her you have an idea that will benefit both of you."

"I do?"

"Yes, you do." Ellie wrapped what was left of her sandwich in a napkin and tucked it in her bag. "Tell her when she rings up a sale, she should hand the customer a coupon for a free cup of coffee next door. That way she won't have the hassle of making pots of coffee and supplying sugar and cream, and people will stop in your store to buy something from your case for themselves to go with the coffee. It's a win-win deal."

Smiling for the first time since she'd arrived, Joe said, "Maybe you should open a promotions firm instead of a dog-walking service."

"You like the idea?"

"I'm going over there right now to discuss it. Want to come along?"

"Sorry. Don't have time. But I'll be by soon to hear how you made out. Maybe tomorrow. See ya."

Ellie caught a cab on Lexington and finished her lunch while she rode to the Village. Turning down the alley behind Guess Who, she walked into the building through the back entrance. Inside, she gazed at the line of doors running up the left side of the hallway. When she peered to the right and saw another corridor with more doors snaking around the rear of the stage, she slumped against the wall. She'd always thought her powers of observation were decent, but she didn't remember seeing this many doorways the other night.

Of course, she should have figured as much. Rob had told her the cast of the revue numbered close to sixty, and each performer had three to four costume changes including wigs and headpieces. With six to a dressing room, there had to be ten-plus rooms to inspect, and more than a few participants to interview. Unfortunately, due to her appointment with Anthony Rizzoli, she would probably have only enough time to talk with a couple of cast members before she had to leave, pick up Bitsy and Rudy, and head for the meeting.

Glancing to her right again, she heard voices from somewhere behind the stage, so she moved in that direction. On the way, she pulled a notebook much like Sam's, only bigger, from her tote bag, intent on holding a logical conversation with one or more of the showgirls. Then she fished a pen from her bag and peeked into the room—and found two men talking, one in the middle of getting dressed!

"Hello, sugar," said the handsome guy with his jeans around his ankles. "You need something?"

Ellie's gaze swept the tiny heart-dotted briefs covering his manly assets. Heat rushed from her chest to her neck faster than a prairie fire in August. "Uh, sorry. Wrong room," she squeaked, retreating into the hall.

Fanning her face with the notebook, she rested her back against the wall, the words "bad idea" ringing in her brain.

A moment later, the man stepped into the corridor. "Are you looking for someone special?"

She closed her eyes. "Ah, no. Not right now. I'll see you—I mean I'll catch you—ah—I'll come back later."

She made to leave, but he grabbed her shoulder, rooting her in place. "Take it easy, doll. No one's going to hurt you here."

Ellie gulped down her embarrassment, pasted on a smile, and turned. Her gaze wandered from his buff naked chest to the tight, well-worn jeans now covering his lower limbs. Quickly focusing on his face, she said, "I didn't think so. It's just that—"

"You aren't used to surprising cross-dressers when they're in the middle of—cross-dressing?" he asked, a grin etched on his *GQ* face.

"Uh, no—yes—uh—" Eye contact, Ellie. No fair looking at anything else. "I don't belong here. I should probably leave."

The man grasped her free hand and gave it a shake. "I'm Bill Avery, aka Eden Rose, and you don't have to leave unless you want to." He propped his well-muscled body against the wall. "And while you're thinking about it, tell me what you need."

"I'm a friend of Rob Chesney," she began.

"Our Bobbi Doll?" He raised a perfectly sculpted eyebrow. "You his girlfriend?"

"His girlfriend? Uh, no, I'm his dog walker."

"Good to know you're not spoken for." He continued

to grin. "Because if you're looking for a man with, say, *unusual* taste, I'm in the market for a new gal pal."

Gal pal? Heat warmed her cheeks again. "I'm already in a relationship."

Bill reached out and tugged one of her curls. "With a man?"

Mustering her courage, she slapped his hand away. "Yes, with a man. Now if you'll excuse me—"

"Hey, don't go off in a snit. People around here are flexible when it comes to sexual orientation." He shrugged. "If you're a friend of Rob's, I assume you understand his lifestyle. I've been looking for a woman who knows what a guy like me does for a living. It takes all kinds, you know."

Ellie swallowed. She did know, but not firsthand. At least, not until now. Bill seemed nice enough, when he wasn't being a tease. "I'm here because I want to help prove Rob is innocent of the crime he's been arrested for. I was hoping some of the girls—"

"Performers."

"Uh, the performers, might know something that would make the job easier."

"So you think he's innocent, do you? Hmm. Interesting."

"I have no reason to believe otherwise. Rob is a very nice man. He'd never do anything to hurt someone." When Bill arched that same perfect eyebrow a second time, she decided she'd had enough. "Look, I can see you're not the person I should be—"

"No, no. I'm sorry. It's just that I thought the police had already decided Rob was the one who did Carmella in. I didn't realize there were still questions."

The other man, who'd been inside the room, stepped out wearing a floor-length pink dressing gown and matching three-inch mules. "What's going on out here?"

"Uh, I'm Ellie Engleman." She held out her hand. "I'm a friend of one of the performers."

They shook as the man said, "Gary Wallace, but I'm better known as Sheleata Burrito. Just make sure you get the names right and we'll get along fine." He cut his eyes to Bill. "Is this guy bothering you?"

"Not a bit," Ellie said, feeling more relaxed. It was then she recognized the rather large Amazon with the last name of Burrito. "I remember you from opening night. You did that fabulous Dusty Springfield medley. It was great."

"Thanks. I try. This show is my chance to branch out in a more refined manner, if you know what I mean." Sheleata tossed her long black hair. "A girl has to do what a girl has to do."

"I'm just here to talk to some of you about Rob Chesney."

Sheleata narrowed her eyes. "Did I hear you say you were the one who takes care of Bitsy? Rob talks about you every once in a while. Almost had some of us convinced you were a saint."

"That's very sweet of him to say, but all I've ever done is listen when he needed to talk. I was here the night of the . . . incident, so I took Bitsy to my apartment. I'll be returning her to Rob later today."

The Amazon crossed her arms over her massive chest. Though she wasn't wearing a stitch of makeup, her actions were all girl. "That little baby is a cutie. I've been thinking about getting a dog, but not yet." She tied the dressing gown tighter. "So what do you want to know about Rob?"

"I have some questions about the—about Carmella, and I was hoping someone here might be able to help."

"Carmella, eh?" She glanced at Bill. "Have you filled her in on the charming Miss Sunday?"

"Not yet," said Bill. "Do you think we should?"

"Hey, Carmella was no pal of mine, girlfriend. Now that she's gone, why not?"

"What about Carmella?" Ellie asked, lowering her voice and taking a step closer. "If you know something that might point the cops in another direction—"

Sheleata waggled a finger and slipped into the dressing room. Bill motioned for Ellie to follow, which she did. Inside, the Amazon took a chair and crossed her legs, and Ellie prepared to listen.

"Go ahead, Eden, you start us off. Your info will be blah, compared to what I have to say," Sheleata stated.

Bill ran a hand through his hundred-dollar haircut. "Truth be told," he began, "not too many of us cared for Carmella. If you ask me, there are probably a dozen cast members who are glad to see her dead."

"See? Boring." Sheleata looked at Ellie. "He's just saying that because the bitch tried to steal one of his precious wigs." Her eyes cut to Bill. "Why don't you tell our friend what you thought of the girl?"

Bill scowled. "That's nobody's business but mine, and you know it. Carmella is—was—difficult with almost everyone." He nodded toward the room next door. "Lily and Pearl both had a bigger ax to grind."

"Lily? Pearl? They didn't care for Carmella either?"

"Absolutely not," Sheleata said. "But personally, I don't think it was someone from the show who did her in. I think it was someone Carmella was blackmailing."

"Carmella was into blackmail? Are you sure about that?"

Bill shifted in his seat. "Like most of us in this business, Carmella liked to blow her own horn. We go over the top because it's what people expect from the guys who live this lifestyle, but with Carmella, it was . . . different."

"That may be so, sugar, but I know more. Carmella used to brag about her conquests to whoever would listen. Said she'd been receiving 'friendship money'"—Sheleata used air quotes to set the words apart—"from a guy, and he was in line to become one of the city's VIPs. Said if he didn't come up with more cash, she was going to see to it that his time in the public eye was over."

"That was just wishful thinking," Bill insisted. Then he looked at Ellie. "You talk to Lily and Pearl if you want to hear somebody gripe about Carmella. Nita Zip, too."

Just then, another man walked in. "Hello, girls," the slender African-American said. Then he eyed Ellie. "And who are you, precious?"

"This is a friend of mine, and she was just leaving." Bill stood, drew Ellie to her feet, and guided her out the door and into the hall. "We'll get into this later, but not with Coco around. She was a good friend of Carmella's, and she's talked smack about your pal since before he was arrested."

Bill disappeared into the dressing area, leaving Ellie alone. Not practiced in running a real investigation, the way Sam did, she decided to write down the names Bill mentioned and whatever Sheleata and Bill had said about them. Then she heard a commotion in the main hallway and followed the noise, hoping to corral another performer or two into giving her insight. If she was lucky, she'd run into Nita Zip or one of those other people Bill had mentioned. She also had to find the two women Rob had told her were understudies.

She turned the corner and bumped into a pair of stagehands pushing a rack loaded with costumes. "Coming through," said one, while the other shoved her aside. Before she could right herself, a different guy, this one wearing a tool belt strapped over his baggy jeans, plowed past, muttering, "Damn queens," and, "That'll be the day."

Frazzled, she plopped into a chair, most likely the one she'd sat in the night of the murder, and checked her watch. She had just enough time for one quick interview if she planned to make her meeting with Anthony Rizzoli.

A cross-dresser wearing black leather pants and a matching bustier walked by and smiled. "Can I help you, doll?"

She stood and held out her hand. "I hope so. We've never met, but I was wondering—could I ask you a few questions?"

Sam stood in the doorway of a dressing room off the main hall, a few doors down from the crime scene, forcing his brain to focus on the matter at hand. But damn, it was difficult. He'd never watched a man put on makeup before, much less one who wore spike heels and a snug bodysuit in satin, lace, and close to a ton of glitter.

"Sweetheart, there are probably a couple dozen reasons why someone would want to kill Carmella," the black-haired she-male said, grinning. She then stroked on another coat of lipstick in a color that reminded Sam of a fire engine. "I, for one, wanted that girl's complexion. I mean, did you see her skin? It was carmelicious. Me, I never tan like that."

He resisted snorting. Before questioning Frieda deManeata—real name: Michael Woolsey—he'd interviewed a few other performers and received the same vibe from each of them. These drag queens were irreverent and entertaining and, as far as he could tell, truthful. He would never confess this to anyone, but he'd even lost the creepy feeling he'd had when he was here to watch the opening-night show.

"And the other reasons?" he asked, trying to keep a straight face.

"Well, this is between you and me, but"—Frieda waggled a finger to draw him near—"I heard she was arrested for prostitution a few times in the past. Can you imagine? I mean, no drag queen worth her thigh-highs would ever be that stupid."

Sam had already researched the victim's criminal history. He knew exactly how many arrests Carmella had, where they'd taken place, the charges, and the names of the other persons involved. Her last arrest, almost a year ago, had led to a trial, where she was given a slap on the wrist. Since then, there'd been no other police interaction, but he intended to speak to the men in her past over the next few days.

"Thanks." He closed his notebook and looked at his watch. "I take it the rest of the performers will be here soon?"

"They usually trickle in until about six and gab for a while, but they're putting on their war paint by seven." Frieda swung around in her seat and crossed her mile-long legs. "Have you talked to Angel Bebé yet?"

"He's—er—she's on my list. Why?"

"Because she and Carmella did not get along. And check out Nita Zip, too."

"I was told she was on the stage at the time of the murder," said Sam.

"Maybe so, but someone has to take Carmella's place as Bobbi's understudy, and Nita's been itching for the job."

"Did she tell you that in private?"

"Honey, very little is private around here."

Sam made another notation in his spiral. "I didn't realize they had understudies for the understudies."

"Not officially, but that doesn't stop a girl from dreaming." Frieda batted her inch-long eyelashes. "And if you're ever in the mood for information that's a little more personal, you know where to find me."

Relieved to be dismissed, Sam backed out of the room and closed the door. Then he shook his head. Until he'd met this crew of cross-dressers, dog lovers had topped his list of odd ducks and nut jobs. After grilling a couple of these faux women, he realized he owed Ellie an apology.

Frieda, as well as the show's director, had told him most of the performers wouldn't mind talking in front of the others, and suggested that he hang around while they got ready for the show, but Sam had no intention of watching exactly what was involved in cross-dressing. Instead, he opted to catch the performers as they filed in, but he also had to take a final look at the crime scene. It was possible he might find something he'd missed earlier; if he didn't, he had to give the room back to the participants.

After the backstage manager unlocked the dressing room door, Sam ducked under the yellow warning tape and perused the area. Flecks of blood still dotted the floor, even though the club had been given the okay to hire a cleanup crew for the worst of the mess. Forensics had to forgo the usual practice of preserving footprints because so many of the cast had tromped in and out when they heard the scream. Thanks to the traffic, the police had gotten little they could use in the way of shoe identification.

Scanning the room, he crouched down and spotted the hot pink dog carrier Chesney owned, still tucked where Vince had found it. The forensic team had returned and dusted it for prints, but just as he'd figured, they'd found only Chesney's. Taking it to Ellie seemed like a good idea, because she was babysitting the pooch that owned it, but he didn't want to give her a chance to quiz him.

In fact, he'd made a point of not contacting her since

she'd made that one phone call because he knew if they met, her string of questions would surely lead to a fight. He scanned the room, trying to think straight. Well, maybe not a fight, but certainly a heated discussion. And only because she considered Rob Chesney a friend.

He ran a hand over his jaw, thinking about the facts in the case. Chesney had opportunity because his number had been over for a while before the scream. They'd found him kneeling over the body with the weapon in hand. Since the shears were long and narrow, they'd held only partial prints, and most of those were smudged beyond recognition. Though he and Vince had yet to ferret out a motive, Sam was certain they'd find one eventually.

As the lead on this case, it was Vince's job to take care of the up-front stuff, coordinate with the DA, speak to the press, and answer to the top brass. That left Sam free to question witnesses and amass the data needed to prove Chesney had committed the crime. When he and Vince weren't side by side, they talked a couple of times a day, going over the clues and putting the pieces together. They'd worked out a rhythm that suited them, and they often rotated the lead on their assignments.

Except when Ellie was involved.

And that seemed to be happening more and more these days. He could forgive her the first murder. Finding a client dead could have happened to anyone. And she'd been a victim of circumstance in number two. He could even give her a buy on number three, but this fourth episode was too much. Was there something in her attitude that made her attract violent crimes like the dog crap she scooped attracted flies?

Worse, she was so used to snooping, she simply couldn't let things alone. In fact, he could practically feel her presence in his bones right now. He took a seat on one of the stools in the empty dressing room and began flipping through his spiral, hoping to put things in order, and then he heard a familiar voice in the hallway.

"We've never met, but I was wondering—could I ask you a few questions?"

At the sound of those words, Sam stood, jammed the notebook in his jacket pocket, and headed out the door.

Chapter 8

Sam closed his eyes and counted to ten.

What the hell was Ellie doing here?

He raised his gaze to the ceiling. Of course, she was here. A friend of hers, a fellow dog lover, was in trouble.

He straightened his tie, took a calming breath, and pulled out his badge. He thought he'd made himself clear the other morning, when she'd called to ask about Chesney's bail hearing. He should have taken the time to lecture her then on minding her own business, but it wouldn't have mattered. Ellie had never listened to him in the past. Why would she take his advice now?

Thinning his lips to enhance his I'm-in-charge expression, he strolled out of the dressing room, dodged several performers parading down the hall, and stopped at Ellie's side. Raising his shield to her face, he said, "NYPD. I need to see you in private."

Ellie jumped in place, but the cross-dresser standing with her had another idea. "Hey, wait a second, Mr. Man-with-a-Badge," said the queen in black leather. "She hasn't done anything wrong, so what's your problem?"

"My problem is none of your concern." He added a

snarl to let the she-male know he meant business. "The lady is coming with me."

"Sam—"

"It's Detective Ryder, Ms. Engleman. Now come along peacefully or I'll take you to HQ and arrest you for interfering with a police investigation." He clutched her elbow and led her into the scene of the crime. After slamming the door, he swung her around to face him.

"You have ten seconds to explain what you're doing here. And don't try lying, because that never works with you."

Ellie huffed out a breath and jerked her elbow from his grip. "Jeez, you don't have to get so bossy."

Sam slipped his badge back in his jacket pocket and folded his arms. "Unfortunately, I do." Fighting to keep his voice calm, he said, "Now start talking."

She ran her hand through her curls and heaved another sigh. "Okay, fine, but promise you won't get mad."

"I won't get mad."

"Yeah, sure."

"I won't get mad because I'm already beyond mad. I'm furious—wait, no. It's more than that. I'm incensed, irate, crazed with anger. How does that sound?"

She raised a corner of her mouth. "Like you belong in an insane asylum, if you want the truth."

He paced in front of her, using the time to regain his composure. When he looked up, Ellie said, "Is it okay if I sit for this interrogation?"

"Why not? You'd do it anyway, just to irritate me."

"That's not why I asked. This is supposed to be a crime scene, correct? Should I even be in this room?"

"You're asking me about proper police protocol? While you keep pushing your way into my homicide investigations? You're kidding, right?"

She fisted a hand on her hip and frowned. When he

didn't say anything, she pulled a chair out from under one of the tables and took a seat. "Okay, now what?"

"Now what?" He began to pace. "Let's see, where should I begin?" Ellie opened her mouth to speak and he held up a hand. "This is my party, so we'll play it my way, understand?"

She bit her lower lip and nodded.

"Why are you here talking to the performers about what happened the other night?"

"I'm here because I spoke to Rob, and he told me a couple of things that I thought needed looking into."

"And you couldn't have told me those things, so that I, in my official capacity as one of the officers in charge of the case, could see to it instead?"

She shrugged. "I thought if I got the answers myself, it might save you a step in your investigation."

Sam shook his head. "Please. Let's not go through this again. You have no right to be here in any capacity, and certainly not in the guise of helping me."

"Then I'm here to help Rob."

"Rob Chesney doesn't need help. As far as I can tell, he has a competent attorney, and I hear his sister is coming to town to hold his hand."

"But you believe he's guilty, and he's not."

"I believe he's guilty because the evidence points in that direction, which is why he was arrested, but the case is ongoing while we amass the data. Vince and I do the legwork, but it's the DA who decides the charges and presses for a trial."

She sat up straight in the chair. "So if I give you some new facts, you'd take them into consideration?"

"If it pertains to the investigation, yes."

"How about this one? Carmella Sunday was blackmailing someone—someone big in New York."

"And you know this because . . ."

"Because Sheleata told me so."

"Sheleata? Since when are you on a first-name basis with these . . . people?"

"Since I told them I was a friend of Rob's and he was innocent. I also found out there are a half dozen performers who are happy Carmella is dead. If that's the case, any one of them might have committed the crime."

"How about you give me their names, and I'll look into it?"

She moved to the edge of her chair. "Really, you will?"

He pulled out his notebook, just to prove he would. "Sure. Now talk."

"Lily and Pearl. I don't know their real names, but they hated Carmella. I'm not sure why, though I could probably find out for you if you wanted."

"Not necessary, because . . ." He flipped through the pages, and stopped when he found their names. "Both of them were onstage at the time of the killing. Next?"

"They were?"

"The director and two dozen witnesses say so, and I could probably corroborate that with a dozen more."

"Oh."

"Who else?"

"Nita Zip, but I don't know her real name."

Sam nodded. Ms. Zip was on his list. In fact, he'd planned on finding her until Ellie's voice had knocked him senseless a few minutes ago. "I have her down. In fact, I'd be talking to her right now if I hadn't found you snooping in the hall."

She huffed out a breath. "You make it sound as if I'm a pain in the ass who has nothing better to do with her time than step on your toes."

"And . . ."

"And I'm not. I'm the friend of a person I'm positive is innocent, and I want to make sure the police know it."

"Then I guess this all boils down to trust." Somewhere in the back of his mind, he'd known this day would come. "That's it, isn't it? You don't trust me to do my job. You think I'm incompetent."

"What? No!" Her shoulders drooped. "I know you're a good cop. It's just that—"

Sam raised both hands. If Ellie didn't trust him as a cop, she couldn't trust him as a man. And without trust, a relationship was nothing.

He stepped to the door and pushed it open. "This interview is over. Please leave the building. I have work to do."

Her eyes welled with tears, but he didn't let that stop him. "Now, Ms. Engleman."

She made a move in his direction, but he stood firm. "I said now."

Ellie swiped at the single tear trickling down her cheek. Hoisting her tote bag on her shoulder, she left the room.

Sam's gut clenched at her confused expression. What the hell else was he supposed to do? He'd already rescued her from three dangerous situations. One of these days she was going to be in a fix without him, and then what?

Ellie was the only woman he wanted in his life, but not at the cost of losing her to some nutcase killer. If they broke it off, maybe she'd take his words to heart and keep out of police business. It was the only way he could think to keep her safe.

Ellie had retrieved Rudy and Bitsy and just finished her second round of walks in the first two of her buildings. She still felt brain-battered by Sam's abrupt dismissal, and his statement continued to ring in her mind. She'd been prepared for him to argue with her about helping Rob, and maybe she could have chosen her words more carefully, but the big *kiss-off*? Did she deserve that kind of end to their relationship?

"Knock, knock. Anybody home up there?"

She gazed down at Rudy. "Did you say something?"

"Yeah, I said somethin'. I asked you a question."

"Oh. For a minute there I thought you'd switched from lawyer jokes to knock-knock jokes."

"Me? Never. But I am lookin' for a little info."

"Sorry—my mind was off on another planet." In fact, Sam's stinging remarks had been such a surprise that she'd rushed the walks she'd given so far. "What do you want to know?"

"I want to know how we're supposed to recognize this Rizzoli guy. Will he be wearin' a red carnation or maybe carryin' a great, big Dingo bone?"

She grinned at her boy, and her heart gave a painful squeeze. Men were a dime a dozen. If Sam decided to end their relationship over something as trivial as her being what he called a snoop, her heart would be broken, but she'd work her way through the pain. If she lost Rudy, on the other hand, she'd be so devastated she might never recover.

"I imagine he'll be alone, and he'll look like someone who has an appointment here in the building. If I see a good prospect, I'll just ask." She bent and lifted Bitsy into her arms. "As soon as we're done, we'll take this little girl to Rob and call it a day."

She was beat, mentally and physically. Meeting Sam at Guess Who had been a nightmare. After dealing with him and talking to over-the-top performers, she couldn't wait to get home, nuke a Lean Cuisine, and go to bed. Just then a young man wearing a leather bomber jacket, worn jeans, and scuffed boots came through the door and checked out the lobby. When their gazes locked, he headed in her direction with his hand outstretched.

"You Ellie Engleman?" he asked, pumping her arm.

"That's me, and I assume you're Anthony Rizzoli."

"You got it." He stepped back to eye Bitsy and Rudy. "These the dogs I'm gonna walk?"

Ellie didn't want to stare, but Mr. Rizzoli was one nice-looking kid, sort of a modern-day Fonzie from that old television series *Happy Days,* without the bouffant hair and chains. She thought of Joe Cantiglia and smiled. Some Italian men were definitely fine.

"This is Bitsy." She set the poohuahua down on the marble tile. "She lives in another building and I'll be taking her there after our meeting."

He scanned the foyer with a gleam in his dark brown eyes. "I never met anybody who lived in one of these swanky places. It doesn't look so hot to me."

She took note of the Cranston's newly installed front counter with a storage room behind it, which must have been constructed sometime today. The Cranston Arms had recently hired a new team of doormen who, she'd heard, were supposed to start work next week. Obviously, management would be making a few more changes to bring the place up to the standards of the other complexes on Fifth Avenue.

"Most of the buildings in this area have doormen, but the Cranston is undergoing renovation. From what I understand, they'll have a new crew in place soon. If you decide to take the job, you'll need to introduce yourself to them. We can do it together if you start working for me."

"A doorman? Is that one'a them guys who wears a uniform and tips his hat when he opens the door?" Anthony appeared to approve of this idea. "Sounds like an easy job to me."

Then maybe you should apply to their union. Ellie kept the remark to herself. There was no need to be snotty, unless this kid said something nasty about walking her pals. Then all bets were off.

"Actually, it's a very service-oriented position with lots of other duties as well. For now, let me introduce you to my companions." She couldn't wait to hear Rudy's opinion of the man. "The small dog is Bitsy. She's been staying with me for the past few days."

Anthony stared at the poohuahua as if she were a rabid rat. "That's a dog? Kinda small, ain't she?"

"I only walk small dogs." *Why didn't you crouch and give Bitsy a pat?* "Usually twenty pounds or smaller. My motto is 'little dogs—little poop,' but I do walk a few who weigh more. One lives in this building. You'll meet him in a couple of minutes."

"Ah . . . poop?"

"You'll see in a minute."

"Cut him loose, Triple E. He's a no-go in my book."

"How about we get started? Then you'll see what I mean."

"Uh—sure. Why not."

They entered the elevator and rode it to Freud's floor while Ellie talked about the job. When she used her key to enter the Gordon apartment, Anthony was impressed.

"Will I have keys, too, so I can come and go as I please?"

Ellie squatted to clip Freud to his lead. "The keys are used for planned walks only, and most of the time you won't go any farther than the doorway, where you'll hook up the dog. Then you'll lock the door like this." She demonstrated the action. "And bring Freud along to pick up the next pooch."

They took another elevator ride down a couple of

floors, where she repeated the steps. After she introduced him to Arlo, they continued their descent, picking up Rocco and Lily along the way. She was so busy telling him about treats and the time he had to spend, she forgot about Bitsy until they arrived at the Lowensteins'.

"This is the last pickup. Then it's off to the park." She knocked, then stuck the key in Sampson's door. When she opened the apartment, Mariette didn't appear, but Sampson was waiting with the leash in his mouth. After she attached the lead, she closed the door and locked it.

"Hold up a second, Ellie. We got a problem."

She gazed at Bitsy and her stomach dropped. The poor baby was trembling so hard she could barely stand. When the rest of the pack began circling the poohuahua as if protecting her, Ellie picked her up and held her close.

"What's wrong with the little one?" Anthony asked.

"I have no idea." She cradled Bitsy in her arms. "It's okay, sweetie," she said, leading the dogs to the elevator. Since it was not the time to discuss the poohuahua's problems with a stranger, she carried Bitsy out of the complex and across the avenue to the park.

Then she gave Bitsy's lead to Anthony. "You take her, and watch that you don't step on her while I show you the most important part of the job." She went over the steps he would have to follow after each dog did its business, explaining that a ticket for failure to clean up after a canine was the one thing she would not be responsible for during his employment.

Anthony did an acceptable job and copied Ellie's actions as she and her pack walked up the block and back again. Then, with her eye on Bitsy, she led them to the Cranston and showed him the last part of the job. About a month ago she'd compiled a sample report and taken it to a printer, where she had tablets made. Now, instead of writing a time-consuming note, all she had to do was fill in the canine's name and check off its performance. There was also a spot at the bottom for comments.

"After you make note of things on this list and set it on a hall table or kitchen counter, give the dog a biscuit, lock up, and go to the next apartment. When you're finished dropping off the pack, you're on your own until it's time to return for the second round of the day."

"Holy crappola," said Anthony when they rode the elevator down. "This is a lot harder job than I thought it would be."

"It's really fun once you get used to it, but if you don't think you can handle it . . ."

"I didn't say that. It's just that there's so much, ah . . ."

"Time involved?"

"Well, yeah."

They stood in the building's foyer, where Ellie set her tote bag on the new counter and pulled out paperwork. "You'll need to fill out these forms, and you have my phone number. If you want the job, call and let me know, and we'll meet here tomorrow morning. If I don't hear from you, I'll assume you decided against it."

Anthony Rizzoli took the papers and stuffed them in his jacket pocket. "Okay, sure. I'll call you."

When he turned and strutted out the door, Ellie gave her boy a grin. "Think we'll hear from him?"

"Not in this lifetime."

"I agree." She checked on Bitsy, who appeared somewhat calmer. "Okay, time to go to the Davenport and get this little girl home," she said, heading for the sidewalk. "She's not used to this much walking. I imagine it's tired her out, and that's why she's so upset."

Ellie had a lot more to worry about than one job applicant. There was Rob and his murder charge. And then there was Sam . . .

*   *   *

Kronk, wearing an almost-earnest expression, strode from behind the counter when she entered the Davenport foyer. "*Ell-ee*, my friend. I *haf* question for you."

She scanned the lobby, pleased that it was devoid of angry tenants demanding Rob's eviction. "Hello to you, too, Kronk. What do you need?"

"I need you to make nice for me."

"Excuse me?"

"To write letter to owners of build-*ink* and tell them I did right *think* when I ask tenants for their papers."

"You want me to write a letter—for you?" Duh. Wasn't that what the man just said?

"You tell them I did okay job, yes. I was polite and did not offense."

"Uh, sure," she said, intuiting what he wanted more than understanding his accented English. "Give me the company's address and who to send it to, and I'll write a letter." She headed for the elevator, afraid to hear the reason for the request. If Kronk was fighting for his job, he might actually encourage the management to toss Rob out. "I'll pick it up when I finish the walks."

The elevator door closed and she sighed. She didn't consider herself a friend of the Russian the way she was with Randall, but doing a simple task wasn't a problem. Someday, crazy Kronk might repay the favor.

After collecting the dogs, who seemed happy to see Bitsy, she led them across the street to do business and then back to the Davenport, relieved to find the door-man so engrossed in handling deliveries for the tenants that he couldn't bother with her. It was a little later than usual, but she'd had too many diversions to keep her on schedule today, and she still had to take Bitsy home and meet Rob's sister.

Walk time finished, she returned the dogs to their

apartments and aimed for Rob's floor, where she knocked on the door instead of using her key. While waiting, Rudy started to prance in place and Bitsy sniffed the bottom of the threshold, a clue that something was up.

"Bradley's here! He's here!" the poohuahua practically shouted, her joy clear.

When a deep *snurffle* seeped from under the door, she knocked again.

"Uh, Ellie," her boy intoned. *"Take it slow, will ya? This could turn ugly."*

"Ugly? Don't be silly. Bitsy's happy, and I know Rob wants her back with him." She heard a deep *woof*, then another *snurffle*. "See, Bradley's happy we're here, too."

"Maybe so, but—"

The door swung open and Ellie's knees went weak. Standing in front of her was ... a pony? Exhaling a gasp, she gave a feeble grin and focused on the woman standing next to one of the largest dogs she'd ever seen.

"Hi, I'm Kayla. You must be Ellie. Come on in."

When Bradley didn't move, the thin, attractive blonde shoved his back end. "Move it, love bug. Bitsy's home."

Love bug? Ellie waited, still unable to speak as the harlequin Great Dane stared her down.

Bitsy trotted in under the humongous canine's legs. *"Come on, Brad. These are my best friends. Back up a few."*

"Yeah, Bradley, back up," Ellie said to him, hoping to regain her composure. Maybe the sound of her voice echoing inside his head would shock the big pooch into obedience.

The Dane gazed at her with a look of shock in his eyes, but he didn't say a word. Nor did he budge from his guarding stance. Instead, he gave another growl, only this one was throaty and menacing.

"Ah, shut up, ya big moose, and get outta my way." Rudy tugged his leash out of Ellie's fingers and followed Bitsy under the behemoth and into the apartment, trotting after Kayla, who appeared oblivious to Ellie's predicament.

"Come on, Bradley. I have lots to tell you. We need to catch up," Bitsy called from down the hall.

Ellie crossed her arms and stood her ground. She had no intention of pushing a 125-pound dog around, even if she had him beat in the weight department. They were at a standoff until—

"Bradley, get your bony butt out here right now, and let the dog walker into the living room."

The Dane shook his foot-long head, took a step backward, gave a snort, and turned. Ellie waited a second, then walked in and shut the door. Bitsy wasn't kidding when she said Bradley was "ginormous," but Ellie'd had no idea she'd been talking about a Great Dane. There were heavier canines—Bull Mastiffs, for instance—and some Irish Wolfhounds might be taller, but for overall size, Great Danes won the prize.

She had the American Kennel Club listed in the favorites section of her computer. First thing after dinner, she would go to the site and check out the description of this breed. Maybe she'd learn something that would help her and Bradley get along.

When she arrived in the living room, the Dane was reclining next to his mistress on the sofa—make that on two-thirds of the sofa—and Bitsy was curled up between his paws, looking like a queen engulfed in a throne.

"Have a seat. Rob's getting ready to go to the club," Kayla said, scratching Bitsy's tiny head.

Ellie blinked when she saw Rudy perched next to the woman's feet. *The little stinker.* "If my boy is bothering you, just tell him to go away."

"Bothering me? Lord, no. He's a doll. Almost as sweet as my love bug."

Rudy licked Kayla's fingers and walked to Ellie's side. *"He's not so bad, Triple E. Just show him who's boss and you'll get along fine."*

"Did I hear a knock?" Rob asked as he stepped into the room. Dressed in a pair of chinos and a dark green sweater, he spotted Bitsy and went to the sofa, where she launched herself into his arms. "Welcome home, baby girl," he said, nuzzling her neck. "It's good to have you back where you belong."

Bitsy licked his chin, and Rob carried her to a pale yellow wing chair. When he sat, she snuggled against his chest. Raising his eyes, Rob gave Ellie a smile. "I don't know how I'll ever thank you for taking care of her."

Ellie took a seat in the matching chair. "There's no need for thanks, but I do want to tell you that Bitsy's been a bit . . . down. I took her to David Crane for a checkup, and he said she was fine physically, but neither of us is sure she's okay mentally."

"Mentally?" asked Kayla. She put a hand on Bradley's mammoth head. "Hear that, love bug? You'll have to make your cousin feel safe and happy while we're here."

"I see you two have met," Rob said, grinning. "Kayla is almost as empathetic with Bradley as you are with Rudy. You two should get along great." He furrowed his brow. "Any idea why she's upset?"

Ellie imagined the following conversation. *"Uh, yeah. Your pooch is suffering from post-traumatic stress disorder."*

"Really? And how do you know that?"

"Because she told me so."

Positive that wouldn't go over very well, she said, "When I figure it out, I'll let you know." Then she turned to his sister. "I know we haven't had a chance to talk, but I'm glad you're here, Kayla. Rob needs support until this is cleared up."

"As soon as the police find the real killer, my brother will be fine. He tells me you're going to lend the cops a hand with the investigation."

"Oh, boy." Rudy jumped into Ellie's lap. *"I knew this was gonna happen."*

She wrapped her fingers around his muzzle. "I think we'd better talk about that, but first—" She looked at Rob. "Kayla said you're going to the club, so I assume you plan to perform."

"You bet. I'm out on bail, and I intend to live my life as if I'm innocent—which I am. Kayla and I discussed it with my attorney and decided it would be good to show everyone, including the cops, that it's business as usual."

"What else did your attorney advise?"

"Not much. He said he had to wait until he got the DA's info before he does more."

Ellie sat up straighter in her chair, almost afraid to ask the next question. "So he's not hiring a private investigator to look into what happened?"

"He mentioned it, but I told him you were already on the job and he—"

Ellie held up a hand. "Rob, I'm not someone who can do that professionally. I don't have a license to detect, or whatever you call it. If I start snooping," *like I already have,* "the cops might throw me in jail for—for—" *What was it Sam had threatened her with?* "Interfering in an ongoing investigation, or obstruction, or—or—"

"That won't happen, because your boyfriend is one of the men in charge." Rob looked in Kayla's direction. "Sam's the one I told you about. The guy with the take-charge attitude."

"Rob, no. I mean, yes, that's Sam, and he is my boyfriend, but he doesn't want me meddling in this case."

"He told you that?"

"Pretty much."

"Oh."

"Maybe you could stay out of his way while you looked into things?" offered Kayla. "You know, sort of off the record. After all, Rob says you single-handedly solved a couple of murders already. The cops should feel lucky you're willing to help."

"I didn't realize Detective Demento had ordered you off the case, Triple E," Rudy yipped. *"What a putz."*

She closed her hand around his muzzle again. "I'm sorry, but I don't want to risk doing jail time." *And I don't want to lose Sam.*

"If it's money you want—" Rob began.

"A real friend wouldn't expect to be paid, little brother." Kayla rose from the sofa and so did Bradley. "Maybe it's time you left."

Ellie set her boy on the carpet and stood. "It's not that I don't want to help."

"That's okay. I understand." Rob stood, too. "Kayla's just acting protective. Always has, especially since Mom and Dad tossed me out of their lives like so much garbage."

"He's singin' a sad song, Triple E, but I don't buy it. I think he's playin' you."

"I'm sorry—really I am," Ellie said. "I'll be by tomorrow morning to get Bitsy at the usual time, if that's all right with the two of you."

"While you're at it, how about walking Bradley? I'm a night owl, and it might be nice for him to meet a couple of other dogs while he's here." Kayla's sharp blue eyes dared Ellie to say no. "I'll pay the going rate, of course, provided you truly are my brother's friend."

"Well, that's nice," Rudy griped. *"She really knows how to twist the knife."*

Ellie was speechless. The next thing she knew, she was standing in the outer hallway thinking about their conversation. How was she going to help Rob without getting in trouble with Sam?

And what was she supposed to do with Bradley?

Chapter 9

"Frieda deManeata? Sheleata Burrito? You have got to be kidding." Grinning, Viv scooped up a spoonful of Caramel Cone. "Could they be more in-your-face?"

"I think that's the point," said Ellie after swallowing the last bit of ice cream from her container. "Drag queens live to get attention, which will get them fans and exposure in show business. It's sort of like me passing out business cards to drum up clients, only it's all about persona with them."

"And their name is a business card?" Viv rolled her eyes. "Please, that's ridiculous."

"It's the only way I know how to explain it," said Ellie, running a hand through her hair. "I just wish Sam understood why I was at the club."

Vivian raised her eyebrows. "We both know why you do it. You enjoy searching for clues and helping your friends, and you love it when you're proved right about a killer."

"I do, but I don't want it to detract from my relationship with Sam. He means a lot to me."

"Stop dancing around the truth. Just come out and

say it. You're in love with him." Vivian's tone was almost accusing.

"I'd never deny it to you, but I'm waiting for Sam to say the words first. Until then, I'm keeping my feelings to myself." She rubbed her arms. Was it the ice cream that had brought on the chills, or was it discussing her feelings about Sam that sent her into the deep freeze? "Have you told Dr. Dave how much you like him yet?"

"No. I'm on hold with him, too." Viv frowned. "Why do men have to be such idiots?"

Ellie shrugged. "If women knew the answer to that question, there'd be a lot more happy unions in the world."

"If you ask me, men should be more like dogs. You know, loyal, kind, trusting."

"For Sam, that seems to be the magic word."

"Loyal?"

"Trusting. He says if I trusted him to do his job, I wouldn't interfere."

"Doesn't he know how you feel about your friends?"

"I've told him a hundred times, but he just doesn't get it." She heaved a sigh. "Actually, things have gotten a bit worse. Rob thinks all I have to do is snap my fingers and I'll magically prove he's innocent."

"How does he expect you to do that?"

"By finding the real killer, of course."

"What? He actually wants you to find a scissors-wielding murderer? You, the queen of nonviolence with 'Everybody is my friend' as her own personal mantra?"

"Guess so. Even his sister thinks I can do it."

"I forgot about her. What was her name again?"

"Kayla Janz. Apparently she's a writer."

"You're kidding? Kayla Janz?" Viv's complexion blossomed to a soft pink. "I'll be darned."

"You know her?"

"I read her," Viv answered. "Religiously."

"No kidding? What kind of books does she write? Romance?" Ellie hoped it was her favorite genre. She loved a happy ending, especially after being married to the dickhead for ten miserable years.

"Not exactly romance." Vivian grinned. "Guess again."

"Mystery? I don't read a lot of those, especially the gory ones." She hated blood and guts. She needed good vibes in her life, not bad.

"Try erotica."

"Erotica?"

"Naughty but nice. I love it."

"I don't think I've ever read one of those . . . and I'm not sure I want to." She didn't have to read about sex. She had Sam, and he was expert enough in that department for her. Still . . . "Do you have any of her books?"

"A couple dozen." Viv's green eyes darkened. "You want to borrow one?"

She might need to, if Sam dumped her. "Maybe. Can I take a rain check?"

"Of course." Viv stood. "You going to walk Rudy? 'Cause Twink and I will tag along if you like."

"Sure, but give me a minute to put on shoes and get my boy." Ellie went to the bedroom and found Rudy asleep on his pillow. Slipping on her flats, she said, "Last walk of the night, big man. You ready?"

Yawning, Rudy stretched out his front legs and wagged his butt in the air. *"If you insist."* He jumped to the floor. *"You and Viv talk about anything interesting, like the dopey detective's latest ultimatum?"*

"Sort of. I'm still not sure what I'm going to do about Rob and his problem. Maybe I should just leave everything up to Sam and the NYPD."

"You could, but what about Bitsy? She's got troubles

of another kind, and I think we should try to help her out."

Ellie would have liked to talk that over with Viv, too, but her best human pal would never understand how she'd been able to get to the crux of Bitsy's problem. "Okay, here's the deal. I'll continue to work on Bitsy instead of helping Rob. If Sam complains about my nosing around, that will be my answer. If I just happen to uncover clues about the killer while I'm helping Bitsy, so be it." They headed into the hall. "Think that will work?"

"Beats me, but give it a try. If the dopey dick doesn't approve, it's just like I been sayin'—he doesn't deserve you."

In the foyer, Ellie put on a jacket and hooked Rudy to his leash. They met Viv and Mr. T in front of their apartment and left for their stroll. She had a lot of ideas to mull over, especially the lying part. She hated dishonesty, and although what she was thinking about doing wasn't exactly dishonest, it was avoiding the truth.

She'd be okay if she didn't get caught, but if she did . . .

The next morning, Ellie heard the ringtone and fumbled for her phone, charging in the cradle on her bedside table. She couldn't imagine anyone phoning Paws in Motion at this ungodly hour, but it could be Anthony Rizzoli calling to accept the assistant's job. After she met him at the Cranston again, and signed him on, she would have to tell him the rules about phoning her before eight a.m.

"Ellie here," she said, suppressing a yawn.

"It's your mother, Ellen Elizabeth. Did I wake you?"

She groaned internally. Next time, she'd be smart and check caller ID in order to head off a sunrise ambush. The last thing she needed to start her day was a lecture from Georgette. Or a reprimand. Or a grilling. And any of the aforementioned might be the reason for the call.

"Yes, you woke me, but it's all right. My alarm would have gone off in another hour or so." She swung her legs over the side of the bed. Might as well take her medicine, or whatever it was her mom planned to dish out. "What's up?"

"We have yet to receive your RSVP."

RSVP? "Uh, clue me in, Mom. What reply are we talking about?"

"The one you should have sent back regarding Stanley's party on Saturday night, of course. Don't tell me you've forgotten."

Ellie imagined her fifty-five-year-old mother, dressed in a size four ice blue peignoir, sitting at her makeup table and frowning carefully in the mirror. Being a loyal user of Botox, there wasn't any other way she could frown.

Annoyed that she was placed in the middle of another lie, she knew the only way she could get out of this was if Georgette's radar was on the fritz. "Are you certain you sent me one? I don't remember receiving an invitation."

"But you did. I called two days after I gave them to the doorman, and you told me you had the envelope in your hand."

"Oh, *that* invitation. You're right. I got it. I guess I forgot to open it. Sorry."

"You *forgot* to open an invitation to one of the most prestigious legal events of the year, given by your mother and your stepfather?" After a long, reprimanding pause, Georgette continued. "Even so, I assume you'll attend."

"Me? Ah . . . I don't know."

"A few of your clients will be here, including one of the guests of honor and his wife. Norman Lowenstein and Mariette."

Ellie gave herself a mental head slap. As usual, her

mother was correct. Judge Lowenstein was one of three men being considered for some sort of prominent position in the federal judicial system. Apparently, a seat on this bench, or whatever it was called, carried the possibility of a future appointment to the highest court in the land.

"I do remember Stanley talking about it the last time I was over for dinner, but I don't think I'll be able to make it." What with taking care of Bitsy, placating Sam, and helping Rob, she doubted she'd have time for anything else over the next couple of weeks. "You'll have to give the judge my regrets."

"Tell him yourself, because he's sitting right here begging for the phone."

"What? Mom, no—"

"Ellie, my dear," said a familiar, jovial voice after a few whispers in the background. "Please say you'll attend." Judge Frye came through loud and clear, and surprisingly strong for a wheelchair-bound man of eighty-three. "I've told so many people about you and your fascinating business venture. There will be several opportunities to pick up new clients, so bring those adorable cards you usually carry."

Ellie couldn't help but smile. Her fifth stepfather was her absolute favorite, and she hoped with all her heart that his and her mother's marriage lasted until one of them went to their heavenly rest.

"I'm sort of busy, Judge. Do you really want me there?"

"You and your boy? Absolutely, and bring that upstanding young man you're seeing, too. It might do him good to rub elbows with a few of this city's more prominent law officials."

She doubted Sam would agree to go, even if he was talking to her by that point. "Okay, you twisted my arm.

I'm not sure about Sam, but Rudy and I will drop in for a little while."

"Good, good. You've made me a happy man. Now I'll give you back to my bride."

Ellie heard the *bride's* opinion in the muttered rant that took place in the background. Her mother demanded to know why the invitation extended to Rudy, and Stanley was stern in his reply. "Because this is *my* party, Georgette, and I want both Ellie and her dog to be here. That little fellow is quite entertaining, if you know what to look for."

"Are you still there, Ellen Elizabeth?" her mother asked after another minute of marital wrangling.

"Still here, Mom. It sounds like Stanley really wants us at that party."

"You, yes, but I'm not so sure about—"

"Georgette"—Judge Frye interrupted her from somewhere in the room—"that dog had better be here."

Grinning, Ellie shook her head. Stanley was one of the few people in the world who garnered her yorkiepoo's approval. In fact, even before Stanley and Georgette had tied the knot, the judge had announced that Rudy was allowed to attend any get-together he and her mother planned, or else.

"So you'll both be here?" Georgette asked, her tone strained but even.

"Is there a dress code?"

"Not a code, but it is formal. No pants for the ladies, unless they're Vera or Yves. A knee-length is fine, but it should be something designer."

Yeah, right. Like that'll happen. "I have one fancy dress, Mom, and no time to shop for another."

"Who is the designer?"

"I don't remember, but last time I wore it I went to

dinner and the theater with that creep of a lawyer you fixed me up with. It's that or slacks and a sweater."

Her mother made a choking sound, then said, "All right, last year's designer dress is better than nothing. See you Saturday at eight. And come early, if you like. Corinna misses you, and Stanley will be pleased that you're here keeping him occupied while the catering staff sets up."

After a polite good-bye, Ellie disconnected the call. What a charming way to start her day, arguing with her mother as if she were a teenager. Maybe instead of Sam, she'd ask Vivian to tag along. They could stand in a corner and play one of their favorite games: Face-lift Roulette. Viv was an expert at spotting most types of plastic surgery, and Ellie was slowly getting the hang of figuring out how many different procedures a woman had done and how long it might be before she'd want another.

But she would have to phrase her request to Vivian as if it was a done deal. Her best friend put spending time with Georgette just one step below a root canal. And she might have an evening planned with Dr. Dave. If that was the case, Ellie's one and only date would be a dog. Not that she'd mind, because sometimes, when Sam was immersed in a case, Rudy was much better company.

She swiveled on the bed and spied her boy stretching on his pillow. "Good morning."

"I take it that was the ex-terminator."

She couldn't help but grin whenever Rudy used Viv's favorite term to describe her four-times-divorced mother. "Yes, that was Georgette. You could probably hear her talking."

"As if she was in the room with us." He yawned. *"Why does she have to shout when she talks to you? She doesn't do it when we're at her place."*

"I think it has something to do with her role as a concerned parent. She wants to make sure I hear every word, so I can't deny what she said later." Ellie stood and peeked out her bedroom window, noting the sunshine and what appeared to be crisp, cool, springlike weather. "Looks like another nice day. I'll get dressed and we'll go out for a quickie."

"You cannot be serious," said Viv as she, Ellie, and the dogs walked to Viv's subway stop. "You actually think I'd believe you if you told me I promised to go with you to a party at your mother's?"

"It was worth a shot," said Ellie, annoyed that nothing slipped past her best friend's radar.

"And I'd give up a hot date with Dr. Dave to spend time with the ex-terminator?"

"A girl can dream, can't she?" teased Ellie. "I'd really appreciate your support."

"What about Sam?" They reached the stairs leading to the subway, and Viv rested an elbow on the upper railing before heading down. "He likes the judge."

"The judge, yes. Georgette, not so much."

"Did he say that or are you reading his brain waves?" Viv adjusted the strap of the Gucci Pelham handbag she'd bought on the Internet at a whopping 75 percent off. "Or is he still not talking to you?"

"We only argued yesterday, so I imagine it will take him a couple of days to cool off," said Ellie. "But I'll ask him if he calls. If he doesn't, you're my choice for a companion."

"Put a tux on Rudy and let him be your official escort," Viv said, grinning. "If I didn't have a date, and Mr. T was invited, that's what I'd do."

"Say what?" yipped the Jack Russell. *"The only way you'll get me in a tux is over my dead body, fool."*

Ellie's brain glided past T's comment and shifted into fourth gear. "How about this? I'll call Georgette and ask her if you *and* the vet can come. Dr. Dave might enjoy rubbing elbows with the elite, too."

Viv rolled her grass green eyes. "He already does. He was at Mariette Lowenstein's last night, checking on her Pug. It seems Sampson was having some sort of panic attack."

"Panic attack?" Sampson was one of the most easygoing dogs Ellie had ever cared for, when he wasn't obsessing about food. "That's ridiculous. He was perfectly fine when I walked him with my almost-assistant."

"What? Why didn't you tell me you had someone interview for the job when I was over last night?"

"I guess it slipped my mind. He met me at the Cranston and we went on a sample walk. He accepted the paperwork, but that was about it." She hoisted her tote bag over her shoulder. "I don't think he's a dog person."

"Then you shouldn't hire him." Viv glanced at her watch. "Yikes, I've got to leave or I'll be late. We can catch up later tonight." She took the stairs to the trains and disappeared.

"Viv's right. You'd be wrong to hire that Rizzoli character if he doesn't care for us canines," Rudy said. *"He doesn't deserve us."*

"Last thing we need is a human who don't get what we're all about," T agreed with a yip.

"Maybe so, but I've known people who weren't raised with dogs, so they weren't aware of the joy a good pet could bring. Anthony Rizzoli could be like that, but we don't really have to discuss it. He hasn't called."

The trio crossed Lexington and continued west to Fifth Avenue and the Beaumont. Ellie waved at Natter as they passed and went up to collect Lulu, Cheech and Chong, Bruiser, Ranger, and Satchmo. Minutes later, the pack left the lobby and headed to the park. Unfortunately, they practically collided with Eugene and his herd of eighty-pound pooches on the way.

"Jeez, Engleman," the other dog walker snapped. "How many times do I gotta tell you? Watch the fuck where you're goin'."

"Good morning to you, too, Eugene. Nice day, isn't it?" she asked, vowing to be polite to her obnoxious competitor. She glanced at his dogs and automatically took a head count. "Have a couple of your clients moved?"

"Moved? I wish. Some upstart stole 'em." He took a long drag on his cigarette. "Damn robber."

Stole? Robber? The terms catapulted Ellie back to the time she'd rescued Buddy and the other dogs who'd been taken from their owners, when she'd first started walking canines. "Are you saying they were kidnapped?"

After another drag on his cigarette, Eugene fell in step beside her and they crossed to the park, which, considering his normally unfriendly manner, was an oddity. "Businessnapped is more like it. Don't you read the papers?"

"I read when I can. What are you talking about?"

"The *Post* and a couple of other rags have been reporting an upswing in our profession. Seems this city is teeming with wannabe walkers, lookin' to steal our clients. Word finally got out about what a great deal this business is, once you build up a list."

Dog walking was a wonderful profession for a number of reasons. You made your own hours, the pay was off the books, and you experienced exercise and fresh air by the ton; it was a better job than working in a cubicle, waiting tables, or standing behind a counter all day. And dealing with canines was so much easier than dealing with people.

"I cleared over a hundred thou last year," Eugene continued. "How about you?"

"I did okay," she answered. No way would she share her personal information with Eugene.

Two of his dogs stopped to do their business and Ellie cringed at the size of the bag he needed to collect the waste. She was thankful all her pups together didn't weigh as much as one of his. But if she got any more clients in this building, she'd have to divide the walk into two groups.

"Just as long as I keep the dogs I have, I'm good, too, but I'll tell ya one thing." Eugene thrust out his jaw like a street fighter. "I ain't about to lose another one."

"I don't seem to have that problem," she told him. "I haven't lost a dog to a competitor yet."

"Well, lucky you." He ground the remainder of his cigarette under his ratty sneaker. "Don't worry. Your day will come." With that, he turned and marched his pack in the opposite direction.

"Good old Eugene," Rudy observed. *"About as pleasant as a case of pinworms."*

"You can say that again," Lulu yelped. The Havanese was Rudy's first love and one of Ellie's most outspoken dogs. *"He's always leaving cards with Nelda, hoping Flora will change walkers."*

Great. Just what she didn't want to hear. It figured her nemesis would do exactly what it was other walkers were doing to him. But her customers were loyal, and her rapport with her charges good. She doubted she'd lose a member of her crew to anyone.

When she brought the dogs back to the Beaumont, Natter waved her over. "I saw you talking with Eugene. Was he bothering you?"

"Eugene is harmless," Ellie told the doorman. "Most of the time he's just a complainer, but he was informative today." She waited while Natter tipped his hat to a tenant, retrieved a package from under the front counter, and passed it over. "He told me new people were trying to break into the dog-walking business and they'd already stolen a few of his clients."

"I probably have a dozen business cards from folks looking to hire on as dog walkers," Natter confessed. "I only pass the cards along if I know someone is unhappy with their current walker. Unfortunately, there are a few tenants in this building who don't care for Eugene's heavy hand."

Ellie had warned her competitor about losing clients because of his bad manners, but he'd ignored her. "Have you mentioned this to him?"

Natter shrugged. "I've tried, but he just waves off my advice, so I'm through talking to him. By the way, if you ever want to branch out into larger dogs, I'd be happy to recommend you to tenants."

"That's very nice of you, but don't bother. If I get one more of these little guys in the Beaumont, I'm going to have to break the walks into shifts or hire a helper, and I can't seem to find an assistant, no matter how hard I try."

"You want to take a look at the cards I have from the newbies? Maybe one of them would be willing to lend you a hand."

Now there was an idea she could work with. She'd talk it over with Vivian tonight and get her candid opinion. "Let me think on it for a couple of days," she told him. With that, she headed to the elevator and called over her shoulder, "I'll be back in a few minutes."

A short while later, the trio entered the Davenport and found Randall waiting. "I left before you arrived for your afternoon rounds yesterday, but I take it you've met Mr. Chesney's sister and Bradley."

"Oh, yeah," Ellie said. "And you'll never guess what."

"I already know what," the senior doorman said. "Bradley is now one of your clients."

She propped an elbow on the counter. "Did you give Ms. Janz that idea or did she think of it herself?"

"It wasn't me," he assured her. "But I know Mr. Chesney is thrilled with your service. I imagine it was all his idea."

"Rob has enough stress in his life right now, so I guess I have to give it a try," Ellie said. "If it doesn't work out, I'll think of something." She straightened her shoulders when a lightbulb snapped on in her mind. "You wouldn't happen to have one of Eugene's cards, would you?"

"Eugene? Don't tell me the two of you have become friends."

"Not exactly, but he did say he'd lost a couple of clients, and I know Kayla and Bradley don't plan on being here long. I thought I could give him a little help—just to let him know I don't totally disapprove of him."

"Bradley seemed like a perfectly fine fellow to me," said Randall. "Are you sure you want to foist Eugene upon him?"

"Unless I miss my guess, I'm not going to be able to handle the Great Dane with all the small pups in this building, but it will throw me off schedule if I have to take him out alone."

Randall searched a drawer, pulled out a business card, and passed it to her. "This is Eugene's contact information."

"Thanks." She stuck the card in her tote bag.

"I take it you've had no luck hiring an assistant."

"Nope. Why? Has someone asked about a job?"

"I haven't had anyone ask if a dog walker was seeking help, but I have been questioned by a few new people trying to drum up business. As far as I know, they have yet to find a client in this building."

When she'd first started walking dogs it had been difficult finding customers. Randall had been instrumental in growing her list; so had the judge and Professor Albright. Once she and Rudy caught the creep who'd kidnapped Buddy and those other champion canines, she'd picked up a half dozen of Bibi's clients and her business had taken off like the space shuttle.

"The doorman at the Beaumont told me the same thing. That's where I spoke with Eugene. This is a tough business to launch, but once you have a foothold, it's not so bad. I'll ask Rob and his sister about Eugene when I go up. See you in a few."

With that, she rode the elevator to Rob's floor, where she knocked on his door. Even though he and his sister had said they were night owls, she wasn't about to barge into a unit unless she was positive it wouldn't disturb the tenant. A moment later, the same *snurffle* she'd heard yesterday came from underneath the door. After giving another knock, she used her key.

"Ellie, Ellie, Ellie," said Bitsy, jumping like a pogo stick under the Great Dane's belly. *"See, Bradley, I told you they'd be here."*

Bradley stared, his brown doggie eyes rife with suspicion.

"Is Rob around? Or maybe Kayla?" Ellie asked, ignoring the pony-sized pooch. Eugene's dogs were big, but this hound would probably be the largest of any he walked. "I need to ask them something."

"They're still sleeping," Bitsy said. *"Is Bradley gonna come with us, 'cause I told him he could."*

Ellie did a quick calculation. If she took Bitsy and Bradley out alone, it would add about half an hour to her workload. She'd have to hotfoot it to her other buildings to get them done on time, but it was doable.

"I'm going to take the two of you out first, just to see how Bradley handles it. How does that sound?" She smiled at the Dane, whose head was even with her waist. "Bradley, you game?"

"He is. He is," Bitsy singsonged. *"Let's get going. I gotta pee bad."*

She brought Rudy and Mr. T into the foyer, where the Jack Russell gave a snarl when Bradley sniffed his butt. "Be nice, T," Ellie ordered. "He could swallow you in one bite."

"I'd like to see him try," T threatened.

"No biggie, Mr. T. He's really a cupcake," the poohua-hua said. Then she gazed up at Ellie. *"He's a nice dog, once you get used to him."*

Ellie ran her fingers over the Dane's sleek black-and-white head and snapped a leash to his collar, relieved that Bradley didn't growl or act aggressive. Then she led the four dogs to the elevator and they rode it down. On the street, she aimed for the park, where she encouraged the pair to be quick.

After Bradley did his business, he glanced at her with a doggie smirk, and she suppressed a groan. Cleaning up after a canine this size reinforced her company's motto: Little dogs—little poop.

"Yowza," Rudy yipped, eyeing the Dane's offering. *"He's got Sampson beat by a pound."*

"Way to go, big guy," Twink chimed in.

In response, Bradley lifted his leg and sprayed a river onto the stone fence bordering Central Park.

Ellie sighed. She was definitely going to encourage Kayla to use Eugene. When she returned to the Davenport and took the Dane and poohuahua home, Rob's apartment was still quiet as a tomb, so she squatted and had a talk with Bitsy.

"I meant to ask, how are you doing?"

"I'm better. I slept on Rob's bed last night, like usual, and I didn't have any bad dreams."

"Good for you. Have you remembered more about the . . . bad thing that happened at the club?"

"Not really, but I get the feeling it's right there, just out of reach. I know I'd remember if I had some help."

"Then I'll find a way to do that for you. Just give me a little time."

The poohuahua licked her hand. *"I know we can count on you, Ellie. You're the best."*

"Okay, then. I'll let you know what I come up with this afternoon." She locked the door and hurried to collect the rest of the pack. After she picked up Sweetie Pie, Jett, and Stinker, they went to find Buckley. Hazel answered when they knocked at the maltipoo's unit.

"Ellie, do you have a minute? I need to ask you a question," said the portly woman wearing one of her full-length floral-print dresses.

"Sure, but only a minute. I'm on a tight schedule today."

"It's about that man."

She knew exactly who Hazel was talking about, but she wouldn't give her the satisfaction of considering Rob some kind of maniac killer. "Sorry, but I'm not sure who you mean."

"You know. *That* cross-dresser accused of killing *that* other drag queen during the opening of *that* club." Hazel sneered. "So distasteful."

"What about Rob Chesney?" Ellie asked, gearing up to support her friend.

"I signed a petition asking management to terminate his lease. Have you heard anything about it?"

"No, but I'm sure you could phone them and find out." Then a second lightbulb clicked on in her brain, and she came up with an idea sure to lead the woman off the track and help Bitsy at the same time. "You've mentioned using a dog psychic for Buckley a couple of times. How good do you think she is?"

"Madame Orzo? Why, she's fabulous. I always get the feeling Buckley and I are connecting on a deeper level after they have their monthly session." She bent and scooped the maltipoo up in her arms. "Don't we, my Buckley-wuckly?"

"Disgusting," T snorted. *"Bite her, Buck."*

Instead, Buckley growled. *"She isn't worth the trouble, fellas. I'll pick my own battles."*

"Ah, well, then, I think I'd like to pay her a visit," said Ellie. "Would you happen to have her contact information handy?"

"Absolutely." Still cradling her boy, Hazel walked into the kitchen and returned with a card in hand. "Here you are. And please tell her I sent you."

Chapter 10

Ellie, Rudy, and Mr. T finished morning rounds and traveled a few blocks south, enjoying the warm sun and the cool but pleasant breeze. While the dogs sniffed everything they passed and lifted a leg on anything higher than a cigarette butt, she inhaled the fresh air and the scent of emerging greenery. Buds sprouted on the trees and bushes in the park, and crocuses and daffodils peeked up through the damp earth, greeting the world in patches along the walkway.

Tulips, which would appear in a few weeks, and daffodils, along with daisies, were her favorite flowers. She usually stopped at the fresh market next door to the nearest Joe to Go and bought a bunch to take home each Friday to brighten her weekend. Every once in a while, Sam remembered and bought them for her, but she doubted he'd be delivering bouquets anytime soon.

In celebration of the rosy weather, she stopped at Pop's lunch wagon. He'd returned to his regular spot this week, another sure sign that spring was on its way. After she and the old gent exchanged pleasantries, she took Rudy, Mr. T, the hot dogs, and her drink to a bench and sat down. It was an early lunch, but thanks to her mom, she'd been up since dawn and was now starving.

She took a bite of her wiener, savoring the spicy mustard and tart kraut piled on the bun. After washing the first mouthful down with a swig of Diet Coke, she grinned at the two dogs staring at her as if they were guards in front of Buckingham Palace.

"I guess you boys are waiting for a treat, huh?"

"Quit the chatter and toss us a bite, Triple E. T and I are hungry, too."

Tearing off two mini-chunks of the plain hot dog, she did as Rudy ordered. Since the boys would swallow anything she gave them in maybe two chews, size mattered. She had no idea how to perform the doggie Heimlich maneuver, and didn't want to try.

A moment later, they were eye-begging again, so she finished her wiener, gave them each a last piece, and sealed the remainder in a plastic bag. Rudy would get another bit, chopped into tiny pieces, in tonight's dinner. If Mr. T was good, she'd leave a section at Viv's when she dropped him off and suggest that she do the same for her boy.

After tucking the bag in her tote, Ellie searched for the business cards she'd collected from Randall and Hazel Blackburg. She didn't want to call Eugene and offer him the job of walking Bradley until she got the okay from Rob or Kayla, but she did want to contact Madame Orzo. Unable to come up with anything more she could do for Bitsy, she thought a dog psychic might help. She had to take advantage of every available option, even though grumpy Buckley griped that the woman was inept.

She dialed the number, ready to leave a message. She didn't plan on telling Madame Orzo the reason for the visit. If the woman was truly psychic, she'd be able to figure it out for herself at the appointment.

"*'ello. Theez eez* Madame Orzo. *'ow* may I *'elp* you?" asked a sweet-sounding voice on the other end of the line.

"Hi. This is Ellie Engleman, and I'd like to make an appointment for—my—er—a dog."

"But of course. What time would be convenient for you?"

Wow, thought Ellie, the woman was a fast worker. "Um . . . today? Sometime after six?"

"Af-*tair seex?* You make it at *say-ven,* yes?"

"Ah, yeah, sure. Can you give me your address?"

Madame Orzo recited an address in the Village, which Ellie dutifully wrote in her day planner. "Should I bring anything—besides the dog, that is?"

"Not unless you feel it *eez* important to the client."

"Oh, well, okay then. We'll see you at say—er—seven." She slipped the phone into her tote and leaned back on the bench, unsure of exactly what the psychic meant by her last statement. Should she bring the carrier Bitsy had been sequestered in at the time of the killing? A special toy? A picture of Rob?

If it was the carrier, she could pick it up at Rob's when she told him she wanted to keep Bitsy overnight. If he believed her, they were all set.

"Stop frowning. The ex-terminator wouldn't approve," said Rudy, nosing her knee.

"I've already given her my opinion on Botox, so I doubt she'd ever suggest that I use it."

"She knows how you feel about designer duds and diets, too, but has that ever stopped her? Noo-oo."

Her boy was right on that count. "I don't want to talk about Mother. I have to run an errand, so I'll give you and T two choices. You can go home and sleep for the rest of the afternoon, or you can come with me. What do you want to do?"

"Come with you where?" asked T.

"Club Guess Who. I plan to get a dog's-eye view of the scene of the crime."

"I thought Detective Doofus warned you to stay away from that place," said Rudy.

Ellie leaned forward and put her palms on her thighs. "He said I had to stay out of his investigation, but he didn't say I couldn't help Bitsy. I'm only going to scope out the room. Maybe if I put myself in her position under that table, I'll be able to figure out how to get her to remember what she saw."

"Yer really stretchin' things, Triple E. Somethin' tells me that flimsy excuse won't fly if the dippy dick catches you."

"Maybe not, but that will be my answer if he does, and unless he wants to call me a liar, I'll stick to it."

Rudy looked at T. *"What do you think we oughta do?"*

Mr. T shook from head to tail. *"That's an easy one. Home and sleep is my vote."*

"Ditto for me, but I do want to go on that appointment with you and Bits. I've never seen a dog psychic in action before. Could be fun."

When Ellie stood and headed for home, she caught a thirtyish, very attractive man, dressed in a Ralph Lauren tweed jacket and perfectly aged jeans, grinning at her. She nodded and smiled in return. This wouldn't be the first time someone had caught her talking to herself . . . or her four-legged pals.

"Hello," the guy said, moving in her direction. "I couldn't help but notice you earlier, leading a group of dogs into the park. Are you a professional walker?"

The inquisitive man had a great head of wavy brown hair, light blue eyes, and a killer set of teeth. He also reminded her a bit too much of Kevin McGowan, the creep of a lawyer who had used her to put the screws to a friend a couple of months back. "I am. Why? Do you need a walker?"

"Not exactly. It's just that— Oh, hell, I can't lie. I'm in a bit of a financial bind right now, and I'm looking to pick up a couple of bucks off the books. I'm willing to do just about anything, including dirty dog duty."

He appeared embarrassed to admit he was ready to undertake such a demeaning profession, and that didn't sit well with Ellie. She was proud of her work, not ashamed. "I assume you know the going rate, and the rules."

"Rules?"

"You need to be bonded and insured, so clients know they can trust you with keys to their apartments."

"Oh, right. A friend of mine mentioned that, but she also told me it was an easy gig, so I thought I'd give it a try. Unfortunately, I haven't had any luck finding a customer. You wouldn't need a helper, by any chance, or maybe know of someone who does."

"He's a pass, Triple E," Rudy advised from below. *"Let him talk some schmuck into lending him a hand— not us."*

There were times when Ellie doubted her boy's instincts, but this wasn't one of them. Two women she recognized, each leading a group of six canines, buzzed past just then and she tossed her head in their direction. "The tall girl is Roxy and the shorter one is Jane. Why don't you talk to them and see if they need help?"

"Sure. And thanks."

He took off after Roxy and Jane, and Ellie sighed. She hadn't heard from Anthony Rizzoli and no one else had called about the ad.

"Smart girl, gettin' rid of that bum," said Rudy.

"I wouldn't call him a bum, but he seemed a little off to me," she answered, going to the corner and crossing at the light. "What do you know that I don't?"

"I thought you could tell. He's a reporter."

"A reporter? Really? How do you know?"

"Trust me, I know," Rudy advised as they crossed Madison and headed for Park Avenue. *"He was feedin' you a line. Probably wanted to ask you about Rob and that murder."*

"What—how—why would he think I knew anything about that?"

"There's no tellin'. Kronk might have put him on to you in his quest for money, or maybe he staked out the Davenport and saw you walkin' Bitsy. Word spreads fast in this town. Far as I can tell, reporters are in the same category as lawyers."

She found it difficult to imagine a reporter hunting her up for a story because of a dog, but it was a possibility. Either way, she wasn't going to let it ruin her afternoon.

When they hit Third Avenue and hung a right, Rudy said, *"Hey, here's somethin' that might cheer you up."*

Ellie rolled her eyes. It had been a while, so she knew it was coming. "Let me guess. Another lame lawyer joke, right?"

"Just go with it, okay? It's pretty good. Why are lawyers buried twelve feet down instead of six feet under?"

"I haven't the faintest idea. Why?"

"Because, deep down, they're really nice guys."

Mr. T snickered. *"Good one, Rude."*

Suppressing a groan, she unlocked their building's outer door and guided the boys inside. At Viv's, she dropped off T, left a plastic Baggie holding a chunk of hot dog in the fridge, and wrote Viv a note about the Jack Russell's dinner.

"Where are you getting the new material?" Ellie asked as she and Rudy climbed the stairs.

"Around. And I'll be sure to pick up more at the judge's party. The place'll be crawlin' with those empty suits." He jumped at the door. *"Any chance I can have a Dingo bone while I'm takin' a rest? Pretty please?"*

"We'll see." Ellie unlocked her unit. After she unclipped Rudy's leash, she went to the cupboard, retrieved one of the mini-bones, and tossed it his way. She was a sucker for Rudy's demands, especially when he asked so politely. "Have a good nap, because you might need it. I have no idea how long it will take to finish with Madame Orzo."

Rudy trotted down the hall toward the bedroom. *"Just stay out of the dopey dick's way this afternoon. You got enough to worry about without him on your case."*

She locked the door and set out for the club. Rudy was right. She didn't need Sam on her case, but she did want him in her life. She just hoped he would understand that her main goal was to help Bitsy, not Rob.

When Ellie arrived at the nightclub, she checked the street out front and canvassed the alley before making her way to the rear entrance. She knew Sam's old Chevy by sight, and Vince's vehicle, too, and she could certainly spot a black-and-white. But if another member of the investigative team was on-site, she was screwed.

When she got to the rear door, she found it locked. At just past noon, it was a bit early for the performers to show, but she'd had the impression that this door was kept open during the day for deliverymen and workers, or in case of an emergency. And that was the reason she was here . . . sort of.

After rattling the knob, she knocked. Receiving no answer, she knocked again, this time harder. She was about to give it one more try when the door swung open.

"Yeah?"

She threw back her shoulders and looked up . . . way up. The giant who answered wore a scowl. "I have business in the building."

He stared at her through flinty gray eyes. "You're a woman, right? A real woman?"

Oh, boy, as Rudy would say. This might be a tough one. "I am. May I come inside?"

He propped his burly shoulder against the doorframe, blocking the entrance like a two-ton boulder. "Sorry, but I got orders. No one comes in unless they're part of the cast."

"I'm a friend of Rob—er—Bobbi Doll's. He—she asked me to pick up something from the dressing room."

"The stage manager should be here around three." He gave a too bad shrug. "Come back then."

When he moved to close the door, Ellie dipped her body into the entryway. "I promise this won't take long. Please?"

The man hoisted his low-slung belt and raised a bushy eyebrow. "I got orders from the stage manager. No one comes in this way unless they're on the payroll, and that don't sound like you." He poked her in the collarbone with a sausage-sized finger. "Now beat it."

"Ow! Hey, watch the hands." She rubbed the injured spot. This guy had to be a bouncer hired because of the murder. And she'd cover a ten-dollar bet that the big jerk had left a bruise, too. Just then, a hand touched her shoulder. Prepared to use a tactic she'd learned in her self-defense classes, she readied her elbow for a jab. But before she made the move, someone kissed her cheek.

"Hey, baby. I'm glad you're here. Hope I didn't keep you waiting."

Ellie grinned at Bill Avery—or was she supposed to call him Eden Rose at the club? "Hi. I hoped I would find you here."

"It's okay, Reuben," said Bill, eyeing the pushy bouncer. "She's with me."

Reuben stood like a mountain, giving Ellie another glare of suspicion. "I thought you said you were here picking up something for Bobbi Doll."

"I am, but—"

"She's also supposed to meet me, so be a nice boy and give us some room, okay?" Bill placed a palm on her lower back. "Go right in, honey bun. You're an invited guest."

The bouncer crossed his arms over his barrel chest and stepped back. Ellie passed him, breathing a sigh of relief. Thank God for Bill Avery. Mumbling a thank-you she walked straight ahead, until Bill again touched her shoulder.

"Hey, what's your hurry? I thought maybe we could talk."

Ellie turned. "I'm grateful for your help, but I don't have time to chat. I really do have to get something from Rob's makeup table."

"So stop in after that." He glanced back over his shoulder at the still-staring giant. "Wouldn't want to make ol' Reuben suspicious or anything."

"I'll try, but why is it so important we talk?" Unless . . . "Did you hear something that might help Rob?"

"Maybe. You can tell me if it's relevant after we have a little heart-to-heart." He nodded in the direction of his dressing room. "You know where to find me."

She decided to give Bill a business card when she went to his dressing room. That way, he could phone in whatever he had to report, and she wouldn't have to run the gauntlet to be allowed in the club again. After pressing herself against the wall to avoid a worker steering a costume rack down the narrow hall, she slipped into Rob's dressing room.

Hands on hips, she examined the space, relieved to

find it devoid of dead drag queens and police tape, and back to normal. Gone was the scent of blood. Instead, the smell of perfume, hair spray, and cosmetics permeated the air. She checked the entryway to be sure she was alone, then closed the door. Table by table, she switched on the bulbs surrounding the makeup mirrors, and did the same to the overhead fixtures.

She didn't have a great memory of the lighting in here on the night of the murder, but if the performers needed to come in and repair their makeup or change costumes, the room had probably been as bright as this. Next, she focused on the second chair to her left, which marked Bobbi Doll's table.

Ellie pulled out Rob's chair, crawled underneath the counter, and repositioned the chair. Closing her eyes, she crouched as she readied herself to be Bitsy. Over the past year, she'd done plenty of research on canines and learned that sight was the weakest of their senses, unless a dog belonged to a breed designated as sight hounds. That covered Borzois, Salukis, Greyhounds, Whippets, and a host of other beautiful dogs that depended on sight to chase and capture prey for their masters.

She also knew that contrary to popular belief, dogs were not color-blind. They didn't see in the entire spectrum the way people could, but they did recognize a range of colors in blue and yellow. They also saw four times better than humans at night. And although it was thought that canines weren't able to see the picture on a television screen, she knew of several dogs—Mr. T and Rudy, for instance—who loved to watch TV and could tell exactly what they were viewing.

Peering out from between the chair legs, she scanned the floor. Underneath the area directly across from her were a couple pairs of glitter-covered stilettos with open toes or slingbacks. One table housed a bag on wheels, the kind someone might take on an overnight trip. Under another was a Chanel bag, filled to the brim with what looked to be boas and scarves. If this was all Bitsy had to see to occupy herself during the show, she probably had been asleep during the performance, just as she'd said.

Ellie was ready to crawl out when the door opened and someone walked inside, but from this vantage point she had no idea who. Dressed in red spandex pants and wearing bright red slingbacks, the person heaved a sigh, headed for one of the tables across the way, and set a bag on the chair.

A moment later, another person entered, and Ellie remained still as a statue.

"Hey, sugar. You're here early. Come to welcome me to your headliner world?"

"Nita, baby, it's good to see you in here. I take it that means it's official?" The newcomer wore painted-on jeans and a pair of killer black heels with razor-sharp toes. She took a seat and crossed her legs. "You're Bobbi's new understudy?"

It was too late to crawl out from under now, unless she wanted to be labeled a fool. Worse, one of the cross-dressers might call the cops.

It was then she saw the spider.

Her heart raced. She hated spiders. And this one was a doozy. With a two-inch spread from leg to leg, it had big, googly eyes and a body the size of a dime. The fact that it was sitting calmly in the middle of a web on the underside of the table did nothing to quell her fear.

Closing her eyes, she concentrated on the people talking in the room. If she pretended she didn't see the mini-monster, nothing bad could happen . . . could it?

"It's about time I got my chance, don't you think?" queen number one said, easing into her chair.

"If you say so, sugar," said queen number two. "Any word on when you'll be takin' Bobbi's place?"

Ellie opened one eye and peeked at the spider. Had it inched closer since she'd first seen it?

"Shit, no, but once they go to trial I should be top bitch. I'm still amazed they let that diva back to perform. Killin' one of her own just ain't right."

Ellie sucked in a quiet breath. Between the spider and the drag queens, she didn't dare move.

"So you think Bobbi really did it? 'Cuz I don't."

"What you mean, ''Cuz I don't'?"

"What I mean is there was plenty of people who had it in for Carmella. As far as I know, Bobbi ain't never said a bad word to her or about her, though Carmella talked enough trash about Bobbi."

Ellie opened her eyes. This was better than she'd hoped for. Queen number one had to be Nita Zip, the cross-dresser who wanted Carmella's job. Too bad she didn't know the name of queen number two.

"And you think one of us did it?"

Nita gave a drawn-out chuckle. "Sugar, you don't know the half of it. Carmella, she was one stupid bitch. Bragged up one side and down the other 'bout her getting money from some big shot."

Queen number two's foot began to twitch. "And you think that's who did her in?"

"Coulda been, or it coulda been someone else. Carmella got herself arrested for bein' a skank a half dozen times over the past few years. Before we got Reuben, this place was as busy as Grand Central and just about as open. Anybody coulda walked in lookin' for Carmella, found her alone, done the deed, and slipped out before they was caught."

"So you're sayin' Bobbi was just—"

"In the wrong place at the right time is all. And there's somethin' else nobody knows."

Ellie held her breath. What! What?

There was a knock on the door. "You two decent?" asked another person.

"Honey, I'm always *un*-decent, if you get my drift," joked Nita. "What you need?"

"An opinion," said the voice in the doorway. "Got me some new titties and Pearl says they're too big. One of you want to come tell me what you think?"

Nita and queen number two stood and headed for the door. "Girlfriend," said two, "you couldn't keep me away."

The three cross-dressers left in a volley of girlish giggles. Ellie fell to the floor in a heap, looking for the spider. When she saw it was gone, she pushed out the chair and shot to a standing position. Then she did the typical stomp-and-brush dance she'd learned as a child when she thought a spider or other type of bug had landed on her.

At the door, she peeked into the hall and saw a bustle of activity. The number of people walking the corridor had tripled. Stagehands scurried past holding clipboards. A man in a suit pushed a couple of cross-dressers out of his way and received a shout of warning. Reuben and a trio of men were talking near the entry to the seating area, and another stagehand was pushing the ever-present wardrobe trolley to the back of the hall.

After situating the strap of her tote over her shoulder, she stepped into the corridor like she belonged there and aimed for the rear entrance. She'd put Bill Avery on the back burner for now. She'd heard enough to know she had a ton of stuff to go over, and she needed time to process it all.

Charging to the rear door, she checked her watch.

She had to pick up Rudy, make her final rounds of the day, and talk Rob into giving her Bitsy. She could call him and offer to keep the poohuahua so he'd be able to spend the weekend with his sister or she could wait here in case he showed up with Bitsy in her tote. She didn't have a lot of time to hang around, but a couple more minutes wouldn't hurt.

Opening the rear door onto the alley, she stepped aside to let a trio of performers in and saw more cast members coming her way from the street. Then she saw Rob—without the carrier.

When he noticed her, he broke out in a smile. "Ellie, hi. What are you doing here?"

"Um, waiting for you. I'm glad you're early."

"I have to talk with Nita. The producer chose her to replace Carmella, and, well, I don't want there to be any bad blood, if you catch my drift."

"So she's your new understudy?"

"Yep." His expression grew solemn. "When I first saw you, I thought that maybe you decided to work on my case."

"Ah, no, not exactly. I mean, I'm here for you, yes, but only because I have a question."

Jostled by another group of performers, Rob grabbed her elbow and pulled her aside. "I get it. There are too many ears in this place. You're here on the Q.T. just looking around and all that." He lowered his voice. "Okay by me, and I really appreciate it."

Ellie chewed her lower lip. "I haven't changed my mind about helping you. I just need to ask you something."

"Sure, sure, fine," he said, winking. "I understand what you're saying."

She raised her eyes skyward, ready to tell him he was an idiot, then changed her mind. The poor guy had been arrested for a murder he didn't commit. He'd grasp at any straw if he thought it threw a positive spin on his situation. "All I'm asking for is Bitsy. Can she spend the night?"

"You want my baby for a sleepover?"

"Just tonight. I miss her."

"I guess so. When you get to the apartment, tell Kayla I said it was okay." He swiped a finger alongside his nose, giving her the sign for "This is between you and me." "See you tomorrow. Just drop Bitsy off after noon."

She walked to the street and hailed a cab, telling herself she had not deceived her pal. Rob had read the situation wrong, and he hadn't heard a word she'd said when she corrected him. He'd come up with a story that made him feel secure, and that was all he wanted to believe.

Relieved when a taxi stopped, she slid inside and gave the driver her address. She had to pick up Rudy, make her afternoon runs, and collect Bitsy. Then she would have her first experience with a psychic.

Chapter 11

Sam scanned the details of the stabbing victim's bank records for the third time. He'd jumped through hoops to get hold of Art Pearson/Carmella Sunday's accounts this fast, but the news was good. The rumor he'd heard at the club, that Carmella had been into blackmail, looked to be true. The she-male had been depositing ten thousand dollars in cash, split into two accounts, every month for about two years, and he hadn't been paid that much at any of the venues he'd played before getting the job as Chesney's understudy.

That meant he might have had two suckers in his pocket, each paying five big ones a month, or he had only one, who had broken the money up to keep the IRS off his case. Either way, the info was a boost to their investigation.

If he believed the old adage—follow the money—all he had to do was connect the dots. Once Rob Chesney's bank released his transaction records showing monthly withdrawals for the same, they'd be a step closer to wrapping the case. When they figured out what secret Pearson had held over Chesney's head that warranted five or ten thousand a month, Chesney's conviction was a lock.

Of course, Chesney had already told them he had nothing to hide. His parents had disowned him in his first year of college, when he'd gone public with his goal of becoming a professional drag queen. His given name had been connected with Bobbi Doll for more than eight years, both on the Internet and around the circuit. He also insisted that he was straight, an unusual but not unheard-of preference in the world of cross-dressers. Sam had looked to confirm the fact with every person he'd questioned, and though many of the queens didn't know it for a fact, they believed Chesney was telling the truth.

He was so engrossed in studying the records he didn't think to check caller ID when his phone rang.

"Ryder."

"Sammy, it's me," his mother chimed. "Do you have a couple of minutes?"

He groaned internally. If he said no, Lydia would waste twice that long pestering him about why he didn't have the time to talk. Better to get the grilling over with ASAP. "Sure, Ma. What's up?"

"We haven't seen you or Ellie in a month. Is everything all right?"

He sucked up a second groan. Things between him and Ellie were definitely *not* all right, but that was none of his mother's business. "It's only been three weeks, Ma." Sam knew because he'd circled the date on his calendar. "And I'm up to my ears in work. I've got a high-profile case and a couple more hanging in the background—plus I'm due to testify in court this afternoon on another one."

"What about Sunday? Julie's going to be three months old, so we're celebrating."

"No can do. I have too much going on."

His mother waited a beat, as if forming her next question carefully. "What's Ellie been doing that she's so busy? I've told her she's welcome to drop in without you."

His mother had been trying to get Ellie alone for the past couple months, but using the celebration of one-quarter of a birth year as the excuse? That was so lame it didn't even deserve a comment.

"I can't answer for Ellie. You'll have to call her yourself," he said in a casual tone. If he showed any stress over the prospect, his mother would jump down his throat. "You want her number?"

"The number for Paws in Motion is tacked on the front of my refrigerator. I just didn't want to contact her without your permission."

My permission? Since when had his mother ever needed his permission to do anything? She was on a fishing expedition, but he refused to get hooked. "It's fine by me. Just don't be surprised if she's busy. Spring's almost here, so her business is picking up."

"I didn't think she walked dogs on Sunday."

"Not on a regular basis, but she's been babysitting a client's dog. She may have to—to house-sit." Sam inhaled a breath of relief at his logical excuse. "I'm not sure."

"She always brings that adorable dog of hers here to my house, so what's one more? Sherry and Susan love Rudy, and Tom does, too. It's important Julie gets used to dogs, so she won't be frightened when they finally adopt one."

He very much doubted that a three-month-old would be frightened of a dog, especially the kinds Ellie owned and walked. Rudy might be a pain in the ass with him, but he was always on his best behavior with Vince's daughter, Angela, who would soon turn one. And if Ellie was still caring for that hairy hamster of Chesney's, well, crap, that hound was too small to scare a mouse.

"I'm sure she'll agree to whatever you want, if you can catch her."

"Then I have your okay to phone her?"

Sam rested his elbows on the desk blotter. Ellie knew how to navigate around his mother, because she'd been doing the same fancy footwork with Georgette for years. They'd parted on a bitter note yesterday, but that didn't mean their relationship was over. It was simply on hold until she came to her senses, admitted he was right, and laid off pursuing killers. He trusted her to handle his mother the way she would her own: politely but without spilling secrets, especially things that were best kept between the two of them.

"Yeah, sure. Be my guest. Just don't be upset if she blows you off."

"Ellie doesn't have a mean bone in her body. I'd never take anything she said as an insult, and you shouldn't either. I see the way you look at her whenever she says something you don't approve of."

"Ma, I—"

"Have the two of you talked about moving in together yet?"

"What! Ma, no, I—"

"You should, you know. Sharing living space is the first step modern couples take before they marry, and you're not getting any younger. I'd like more grandchildren, but Susan and Tom want to wait a while, and Sherry can't seem to find the right man, so it's up to you to give me—"

"I gotta go," Sam said, reining in his temper. "We'll talk next week."

Snapping his phone closed, he swallowed a curse. If

he hadn't put an end to the conversation, he would have said a couple of things he'd regret. His mother had used the M word for the first time since she'd known he had a steady girl, and she was testing the waters for more info. She'd calm down eventually, and they'd be back on good terms in a day or so. Until then, he would keep his distance.

Meanwhile, the conversation was a wake-up call. He and Ellie had parted in anger, mostly because of him, and that wasn't good. But what the hell else was he supposed to do to keep her safe? Since they'd met, she'd been held prisoner in a basement, almost killed by an ex-con, and shot at and nearly poisoned by a nutcase woman.

There had to be some way to teach her the rules. They were so simple even the dumbest of people took them to heart. Just keep your nose clean and stay out of police matters. Period.

"Is that smoke I see coming out of your ears?" asked Vince, strolling into their shared office.

"I just hung up with Lydia."

"Uh-oh." His partner grinned. "Another badgering session?"

"Sort of. She means well, but—"

"She also needs to mind her own business. Mothers are like that—just can't seem to stop meddling in their kids' lives." Vince leaned back in his chair, swung his feet onto his desk, and crossed them at the ankles. "Have you talked to the lovely Ms. Engleman lately?"

Sam wanted to kick himself. Served him right for telling Vince about the way he and Ellie last parted. "No."

"Call her." Vince raised a brow. "Today."

"I'm due in court in an hour."

"Then do it on your way to court, or while you're waiting to testify."

"I'll think about it." Sam tossed the folder holding Pearson's bank records on his partner's desk. "This should cheer you up."

Vince's brown eyes roamed the pages, quickly getting the gist of the information. "You're right. Sponging ten thousand a month from some target is a good reason to get yourself killed. Considering the way the deposits fell, do you think he had one sucker or two?"

"That depends. Could be there was just one mark and Pearson was smart enough to split the money up so the IRS didn't get wise. But I'd say we definitely have our motive." Sam stood. "There's still a lot of digging to do."

"I take it you've already ordered Chesney's bank records?"

"They should be faxed here before five, but it could need follow-up, and like I said, I'm due in court. Think you can make a couple of calls to confirm the fax?"

Vince flipped open his cell. "I'm on it. You testify, then call me."

Sam headed out the door, stopping when his partner advised, "And phone Ellie."

He waved a hand and continued walking. He knew he should do what Vince suggested, but what the hell was he supposed to say?

After her information-packed visit to Rob's club, Ellie picked up Rudy and they finished three of their stops, ending at the Davenport around five thirty. When they walked into the building, Kronk waved her over, his expression just shy of cheerful.

"El-*ee,* my dar-*link* girl. You take care of my favor, yes?"

Oh, crap, no. She'd forgotten to write that letter to the building management like she'd promised. But the last thing she needed was an argument with the Russian bear. She kept on grinning as she came up with a response.

"Uh, I need the address. Once I have that, you'll be set."

The doorman fisted his ham-sized hands on his hips. "You write, yes?"

"Sure, I write," she answered, adding a "will" in her mind. "I just need something giving me the Davenport's headquarters."

"I thought I already gave address."

"If you did, I can't find it."

Kronk narrowed his eyes in thought, then reached under the counter and pulled out a business card. "This all I *haf*. You take and mail letter, yes?"

She dropped the card in her tote bag and headed for the elevator. "You got it."

"So much for hating to lie," Rudy scolded as the door closed.

"I didn't lie. I just omitted a key word."

"If you say so."

The yorkiepoo continued to berate her as they picked up Sweetie Pie, Jett, and Buckley. When the pack returned to the foyer, Buckley said, *"Hey, aren't we forgetting someone?"*

"Yeah, what about Bitsy and that gigundo pal of hers?" Sweetie Pie asked. *"Isn't he still visiting?"*

"I'm taking the two of them out after I bring you home," Ellie told them. "Bitsy and I have an appointment."

"Where you going?"

"You don't need to—"

"Can we come?"

"I don't think—"

"Hey, that's not fair."

Ellie heaved a sigh. She tried her best to treat each dog equally and not play favorites, but every once in a while, like now, it was impossible. "I'm taking her to someone who might be able to help her remember what happened the night of the murder. None of you has that problem, so you don't need to tag along."

"Who you goin' to see?" asked Jett.

Noting the temperature had dropped with the encroaching darkness, Ellie zipped her parka, pulled on her gloves, and stepped out onto Fifth Avenue. The wind gusted and she thought about her visions of an early spring. Even though there were clusters of crocuses and daffodils lining the edge of the park, the nippy air was a reminder that her second-favorite season was still four weeks away.

"Madame Orzo, if you must know," she said as they crossed the avenue. "Now hurry up and finish your business."

"You weren't kidding when you asked Hazel for her card? You're really takin' her there?" Buckley shouted over the rumble of rush-hour traffic. *"You gotta be kiddin' me."*

"No kidding. Bitsy needs help remembering, and I've run out of ideas. A dog psychic seems like the next logical step." After leading the pack to their favorite drop spot, she let them sniff for a few minutes before encouraging action.

Buckley hoisted a leg so high she thought he'd topple over. *"Don't be surprised if it don't work,"* he warned. *"The woman is all blab and no brains."*

"Believe me, I've heard everything you said about Madame Orzo, but I never did understand what it was that made you think so poorly of her. Care to clue me in?"

The maltipoo scratched his hind legs into the ground,

throwing up a shower of dirt, a sure sign he was per-
turbed. *"She said I was a grouch because Hazel treated
me like a baby instead of top dog. She also said I was
spoiled."* He gave the ground one more strike. *"Can you
believe that? Me? Spoiled."*

"Oh, no. Really?" Ellie bit back a grin. "How dare she
say such a terrible thing."

*"It's not funny. Just 'cause I'm the little guy doesn't
mean I'm not in charge."*

"You? In charge?" She shook her head, taking in the
seven-pound ball of fur with legs. "You're joking, right?"

Rudy sneezed. *"Go easy, Triple E. Buck is dead serious. After Twink, he's the badass in the group. I wouldn't
want to cross him."* He ended the statement with an eye
roll, as if to say "play along."

"Now, Buckley, think a minute. I spoil all the dogs I
walk, and their moms and dads do the same. It's only
natural for Hazel to baby you. She loves you."

"Yeah, yeah, yeah. Sing me another sad song," the
maltipoo said with a snort of derision.

"Okay, fine, whatever. Now move it along. We have to
give Bradley and Bitsy their walk and get to the Village
in an hour."

After the gang did as asked, Ellie and Rudy took them
home, passed out biscuits, and left progress reports. A
few minutes later, she and her boy were on the poohuahua's floor, listening to Bradley's snurffles from under
the door.

"We're here, so be quiet," she ordered Rudy. "I have
to talk to Kayla about Eugene, remember."

"You're gonna stretch the truth again, I take it."

"No. Well, sort of. We'll see."

She knocked, heard Kayla yell, "Come in," and used
her key. When she opened the door, Bitsy was again
jumping under Bradley like one of those windup dogs

the toy store sold to little kids. Ignoring the Great Dane's disapproving glare, she forged into the apartment with Bitsy on her heels.

"Hang on a second, you two, while I talk to Kayla."

"Kayla's in the big room, but I wouldn't bother her if I were you," the poohuahua told her. *"She's working."*

Ellie recalled what Viv had said about Kayla Janz being an author. Sure enough, when she turned the corner into the living room, the woman was sitting at a laptop, squinting at the screen in concentration. "Uh, Kayla. Can you spare a minute?"

Kayla's eyes never left the screen. "Uh-huh."

"It's about Bitsy. And Bradley."

"Uh-huh."

"I saw Rob at the club a little while ago, and he said I could take Bitsy home for the night. Is that okay with you?"

Kayla waved a hand. "Uh-huh."

Ellie frowned. At this rate, there was no point in talking to her about Eugene. She'd get the same deadpan answer, which really was no answer at all. "I'm taking them out now, but only Bradley will be back. I'll . . . um . . . see you in the morning?"

Another "uh-huh," accompanied by a second wave, was all Kayla had to say. Ellie turned and bumped into Bradley, who was standing close behind her. "Okay, big guy, let's get going."

When the Dane backed up a step and trotted to the hall, Ellie smiled. She specialized in walking mini-canines because she feared the larger ones might be too difficult to handle. She'd seen plenty of professional walkers stumbling across the avenue with eager charges rushing to get to the park. She'd even heard a frightening story about one girl who broke an ankle falling off a curb while she tried to control a pair of Mastiffs. At least Bradley did what he was told.

After clipping leads onto both dogs, she headed to the lobby with them and walked out the door. Once they crossed the street, Bradley wasted no time doing his business. Refusing to comment on his usual smirk, she ignored him, cleaned up his mess, and deposited everything in the trash.

When they returned to the Davenport, the lobby was clogged with tenants badgering Kronk en masse about something. Hoping to avoid attention, she hurried to the elevator. If the doorman was busy, he couldn't pester her about that letter to the management company or anything else.

"There they are," a man said above the noise of the crowd.

Ellie kept on truckin' when an inner voice told her she was part of the "they" the man was talking about.

"That enormous hound doesn't belong here, either," carped a woman. "I thought there was a rule about the size of dog a tenant was allowed to have in this building."

The elevator door closed and Ellie rested her backside against the wall. It didn't matter how much money some people had. Rude was rude. It sounded like the tenants were going to take their unhappiness with Rob's tenancy to a more personal level: his dogs.

"That group is nuttier than a jar of Skippy," Rudy pronounced.

"Yeah—some people," Bitsy added.

Studying the floor, Bradley stayed mum, which Ellie found sad. "It's okay, big guy," she said as they left the elevator. "Those people have no manners. Ignore them."

Knowing Kayla was busy, she unlocked the door and escorted Bradley inside. Then she removed the Great

Dane's leash and hung it on the wall hook. She left after giving the king-sized canine two biscuits and a grin. "See you in the morning. Be a good dog."

"Where you takin' me?" asked Bitsy when they returned to the elevator.

"It's a surprise."

"Oh, boy," snarked Rudy.

"Keep your thoughts to yourself," she warned him. "Unless you want me to drop you at home."

"What kind of surprise?" the poohuahua pleaded, a sliver of worry creeping into her tone.

"It's an experiment. I'm hoping it will help you remember everything that happened the last time you were at the club. You'd tell me if you recalled what you saw, correct?"

"Sure—and I haven't."

They passed the mob still harassing Kronk and arrived on Fifth Avenue, where Ellie hailed a cab. After giving the driver Madame Orzo's address, she pulled out her notepad and began compiling a list of questions for the psychic. Both dogs were quiet, and the ride passed without an exchange of words.

Madame Orzo lived on Grove Street, an area of neat and trendy brownstones a short walk from the entertainment and bustle of the Village. New York was one of the most expensive places to live in the United States, and the Upper East Side was at the top of the list when it came to rent and condo prices, but she'd heard this section of the city was comparable. Her neighborhood had the beauty and amenities of Central Park and Museum Mile, but the West Village had quaint shops, interesting architecture, Washington Square, and NYU.

After paying the cabdriver, she stepped onto the

pavement with the dogs. Gazing up at the five-story building with its neat brick construction, wide front porch, and concrete planters, Ellie was impressed. If Madame Orzo had an apartment in this building, the canine psychic business had to be booming.

The trio climbed the stairs and entered the front lobby. Checking the mailboxes, she saw that there were two units to a floor and Madame Orzo's apartment was located on the third. Preparing herself, she pressed the buzzer under the mailbox.

A moment later, a woman's voice said, *"Allo."*

"Madame Orzo? It's Ellie Engleman, your seven o'clock appointment. Can we come up?"

Instead of an answer, another buzzer sounded, and she pushed open the interior door. "You two ready?" she asked her companions.

"As we'll ever be," said Rudy.

They began their climb and Ellie noticed it was quiet. Very quiet. There was no noise from a television or sound system, not even an undercurrent of human voices. Odder still were the missing aromas of cooking food. The city was a melting pot of cultures, and in most of the smaller buildings it was rare not to smell Indian, Thai, Italian, or another type of ethnic cuisine wafting through the air.

"This place gives me the creeps," Rudy whispered.

"I don't think I want to do this," said Bitsy, stopping in the middle of the second flight of stairs.

"Don't be silly," Ellie told them, mostly for her own peace of mind. "You're both just used to bigger buildings with more tenants."

"Don't you mean live tenants?" Rudy muttered.

They reached the top of the stairs and Ellie looked to the right, where she saw a neatly lettered sign tacked to the cream-colored wall.

MADAME ORZO
ANIMAL PSYCHIC
PLEASE KNOCK BEFORE ENTERING

She raised her hand to follow the directions and Bitsy gave a whimper. "You okay, little girl?"

"Sort of."

"I thought Buck was lookin' for attention when he told me this place was a mausoleum," Rudy pronounced. *"Next time, I'll believe him."*

Ellie lowered her fist. "He said what?"

"He said this place reminded him of a crypt. You know, where they bury people. I thought he was being a pain, but now I see he was calling it true."

She dropped to her knees. "Well, now's a fine time to tell me. If I'd known—"

A rush of air fluttered the curls on her forehead. Looking over her shoulder, her gaze wandered upward from a pair of tiny black shoes, past a full-length black skirt shot with silver thread, over a long-sleeved black blouse, to a smiling, pleasant face.

"Uh, hi." Ellie stumbled to her feet.

"Allo," said the doll-like woman.

Towering over Madame Orzo, she imagined this was how Kronk felt, or the giant bouncer she'd met at Guess Who. If not for her funeral-appropriate clothing, the woman could pass for an upscale jewelry salesperson at Bergdorf's. With her closely cropped brown hair and bright hazel eyes, she appeared ready to tackle anything life threw at her.

"I'm Ellie. You must be Madame Orzo."

"Come *een,* come *een,*" the woman said, stepping back to give them room. "You are on time. That is good."

Ellie and the dogs entered and she noted that the interior of the apartment was painted in muted colors of umber, peach, and orange. Glancing down, she smiled at a pair of Italian Greyhounds gazing at her from around a doorjamb.

Madame Orzo waggled a hand as she made her way down the hall. "Come, come. We must begin."

Chapter 12

Once Ellie arrived in the living room, the elegant dogs took no notice of her, choosing instead to give a typical canine greeting to Rudy and Bitsy. When her boy didn't make a snarky comment after he sniffed and play-bowed with the new canines, she figured the Greyhounds had his stamp of approval.

So far, so good.

"Beautiful dogs," she said, hoping to get off on the right foot with the psychic. And she meant it. Italian Greyhounds were fine-boned, loyal companions with happy dispositions. Though she'd never had one as a client, she had always admired them.

"Thank you," Madame Orzo said, smiling. "*Mees-tee* and Spar-*kee* are my *cheel*-dren, so much more dependable than a man."

Ellie translated the psychic's odd pronunciation of the dogs' names to "Misty" and "Sparky." Madame Orzo's accent was a bit like Kronk's but seemed to include a touch of France, Spain, and Hungary for good measure. Asking the woman her country of origin might be construed as an insult, though. Even worse, the psychic's affected speech, as well as her talent, could be a sham.

"And this is my boy, Rudy. He's a pound puppy, but they thought he was a yorkiepoo, and he's worth more to me than any purebred," Ellie said. "I wouldn't call him my child, but he is my best friend."

"'*Ee eez* a very 'andsome fellow, no matter *'eez* breed." The psychic's brown eyes twinkled as they latched on to Bitsy. "And who *eez theez lee-til* girl?"

"This is Bitsy. I was told by her owner that she's a Poodle-Chihuahua mix, so I call her a poohuahua, but I doubt that's a combination anyone would recognize."

Madame Orzo's gaze returned to Rudy. After studying him for a moment, she left the room. Ellie thought maybe they'd done something to offend the woman, but before she could ask her boy about the possibility the psychic returned.

"'*Eer, eez* for you." She bent and offered Rudy a biscuit, which he quickly accepted. Standing, she said to Ellie, "Your boy was '*un-gree*. I '*ope* giving him treat was all right." Then she passed biscuits to her own dogs, who took the goodies to their beds in a corner of the room.

Ellie opened and closed her mouth as she gazed at Rudy. He'd already scarfed down the cookie and was curled on a corner of the rug. The least he could have done was warn her that Madame Orzo had read his mind.

"Of course not," she answered. "And he's not usually a beggar—" She hadn't seen him do a thing that would have been considered begging. "How did you know?"

Madame Orzo laughed. "I am good at reading their minds, no? *Eez* how I make my *leev-ink*." Focusing on Bitsy, who was standing next to Ellie, she squatted. "And you, *lee-til* one. I did not forget about you." She held out a smaller treat, luring the poohuahua near.

Bitsy sniffed daintily, then took the biscuit and began to chew. While she ate, the psychic lifted her up and stood. "She is troubled, yes?"

"Ah . . . yes," said Ellie, swallowing her surprise. Had she told Madame Orzo Bitsy was the dog that needed help? She glanced at Rudy, saw that he appeared to be sound asleep, and shrugged. "Are we—er—you going to start the session?"

The psychic nodded to a chair near Rudy. "We '*ave* already begun. Sit, please, and turn off cell phone, while *Beet*-zee and I continue in peace."

Ellie took a seat and did as asked with her phone, still unsure of what was happening. The woman was downright spooky, interacting with the dogs as if she could read their thoughts without any kind of voodoo or magical gestures. Then a lightbulb flashed in Ellie's brain and she swallowed her surprise. Madame Orzo's technique was close to what she did when she and her dogs spoke, except that this woman, instead of hiding her ability, advertised it for all to see. And Madame Orzo wasn't embarrassed or afraid of being ridiculed either.

Suck it up, Ellie told herself. She didn't do the exact same thing, and she never claimed to be psychic. And though she actually did hear dogs' voices in her head, she couldn't read their thoughts. Her charges simply chose to share them. She raised her gaze and watched Madame Orzo and Bitsy grow comfortable. If things kept going in a positive direction, the night might actually be a success.

Eyes closed, Madame Orzo cuddled the poohuahua in her arms. Bitsy appeared content, so Ellie relaxed. The last thing she wanted was to further traumatize the petite pooch.

"Ah, I see." Without opening her eyes, Madame Orzo spoke. "Let go of your fears and all will come to you, *lee-til* one."

Ellie tried to home in on Bitsy's thoughts, but nothing registered. "Do you know why we're here?" she asked the psychic.

"But of course. You already know that *Beet-zee*, she *'as* seen something *'or-ee-ble*. Even unspeakable. She cannot tell you about it because she has buried it deep in her mind."

Uh-oh. Ellie heaved a breath. The jig, as they said, was up. "Then you know what we—what I can do?"

Eyes closed, the psychic said, "You are blessed. I often *weesh* I could hear my *bay-beez* talk, the way you do, but it was not to be. It is enough I can read their thoughts, and do what I can to *'elp* other dogs." Bitsy squirmed and Madame Orzo frowned, gazing at Ellie. "You write what I say, in case you do not remember later."

Ellie reached into her tote bag and pulled out a pen and notepad. Time to stop talking and listen.

"I see what *Beet*-zee sees. That night, she was asleep, but she woke at the sound of angry voices. The voices grew louder, until one of the two humans standing in the room shoved the other. The next *theeng* she saw was a body dropping to the floor. And blood. So much blood."

Ellie choked back a gasp. "Can you tell what the people looked like?"

Keeping her eyes closed, the psychic pressed her lips on the top of Bitsy's head. After a second, she said, "No faces, only clothing from the legs down. The person who died wore a sparkling dress and shiny shoes. The other wore pants and shoes that were—" Madame Orzo stopped and looked at Ellie. "Shoes that belonged to a man."

So the killer was male? "Can you garner a little more in the way of details? Say, the color or size of the shoes?"

Madame Orzo furrowed her brow, then put her lips on Bitsy's head again. A minute passed before she said, "No color but dark and wide with flat soles."

"How about a scent?" Dogs' sense of smell was their keenest insight into what went on around them. She hadn't thought about it until now, but the poohuahua must have smelled something that made the killer stand out. "Does she remember if the man wore aftershave of some kind?"

Ellie wasn't sure, but it looked as if the psychic was deep in concentration. Then the woman shrugged and opened her eyes.

"The room was filled with odors. Cologne, makeup, *'air* spray . . . The scent of excitement engulfed the room. Bitsy has grown used to the smells, and didn't notice anything new. All that stands out is the scent of blood."

"That's it? She doesn't remember anything else?"

Madame Orzo pursed her lips. "I will *zee.*" A moment passed while the psychic concentrated. Then she shook her head. "No. *Eez* all."

Okay, Ellie told herself, no identifying smell for the killer. On the plus side, she now knew that the guilty party was a man. But that wasn't much to go on.

"Could you ask her—"

Madame Orzo frowned. "Sorry, but *eez* not a question-and-answer session. I can only put myself in her place and see what she saw. *Lee-til* girl is tired, as am I. She cannot *theenk* of more now—maybe later." She ran a hand down Bitsy's back. "I explain that if she recalls any-*theeng* else, she must talk direct-*lee* to you."

She set Bitsy on the carpet and the poohuahua gave a head-to-toe body shake, then scampered to Ellie and jumped in her lap. *"I did good, huh? I remembered the shoes and a little about the argument. You want I should tell you what they said?"*

"Now?" Ellie asked. Her gaze shot across the room. "Uh, sorry. It's just that—"

"You have a lot to discuss, I *theenk. Eez* fine." Madame Orzo stood. "We settle mon-*ee beez-ness* and you go, yes. I can do no more for you tonight."

Ellie pulled out her wallet. She'd never asked the psychic how much she charged, but whatever the amount, it was worth every penny. The poohuahua had recalled a couple of true clues. "I brought my checkbook," she told Madame Orzo.

"*Eez two* hundred doll-*airs*. You have driver's license, yes?"

She wrote the check out and flipped open her license.

"Tel-*ee*-phone number is the same?" the psychic asked, all business.

"Yes, ma'am." She dropped the wallet back in her tote, pulled out the leashes, and hooked up her dogs.

Madame Orzo walked them to the front door with the Greyhounds at her heels. "She *weel* be fine," the woman said, nodding at Bitsy.

"I hope so. And thanks again for your help."

Now on the sidewalk, Ellie zipped her parka with her right hand while she held the leashes with her left. The gusting wind seemed to seep through her quilted jacket and right into her bones. Glancing down, she watched Bitsy shiver as she tried to stay upright against the gale. Rob would be heartbroken, as would she, if she allowed something bad to happen to the poohuahua, like letting her get blown into the Hudson. If she'd been thinking, she would have dressed both her charges in winter coats before they left the apartment.

Raising her eyes to the heavens, Ellie viewed the thick cloud cover obliterating the stars and shading the moon. The weather had been so pleasant for the last couple of days, she'd forgotten it was still winter. She'd lived through many February and March blizzards in this town, even a few in April, and worried that might be the case by morning. Just because she hoped spring was right around the corner didn't mean Mother Nature planned to work within her timetable.

"Come on, baby girl. I'll keep you warm." Crouching, she collected Bitsy and tucked her inside the parka. "Rudy, you going to be okay?"

"If I had any nuts, they'd be frozen by now."

"Stay close. We're going where we'll have an easier time finding a cab."

The trio hurried to Sheridan Square, a more populated area. She wanted to question the dogs about their psychic experience, but the whistling wind, her chattering teeth, and the noise of the evening traffic made it impossible. She'd have to wait until they were in a taxi before they could talk, and maybe not even then if their driver turned out to be one of the chatty types and gave a running commentary on Manhattan's points of interest as he traveled the streets.

When a cab stopped, they piled inside and Ellie gave the man her address. Within seconds, he slapped on his earphones and began tapping his thumbs on the steering wheel, beating out his personal accompaniment to a rap tune blasting from his iPod. Between the blare of the music and the thumping of his thumbs, she could barely hear herself think, never mind talk to Bitsy or Rudy.

She breathed a sigh of relief when he took the most direct route to her street, sped around the corner, and slid to a stop in front of her building. Pulling a bill from her purse, she set it on his outstretched palm and left the cab.

Since the dogs had enjoyed a treat at Madame Orzo's and taken care of business in the Village, they were set for the night. But she needed a cup of tea and a warm bed, where she could hold a quiet conversation with Bitsy and get enough sleep to see her through tomorrow.

After charging up the stairs, Ellie unlocked her door, hung her jacket in the front hall closet, and headed to her bedroom with the pooches leading the way. The dogs jumped on the bed while she undressed, changed into a sleep shirt, and made a stop in the bathroom. She'd just finished brushing her teeth when the downstairs buzzer rang.

"Who in the world can that be?" she muttered, rushing for the door. She flipped on the intercom, but no one answered her. "Who's there?" The nonresponse got her thinking and she waited a few seconds. When she heard pounding footsteps on the stairs, she checked the peephole. Sure enough, she'd been correct.

Without waiting for a knock, she undid the locks and opened the door.

"Where have you been?" Sam asked, striding past her and into the hall.

Ellie had given him keys to her building and her condo about six months ago, with the understanding that he would use them only if he thought it absolutely necessary. And that had happened just once, when he knew she was in danger. What could be so important now? "Hello to you, too. What's up?"

"I called your cell a couple of times, but all I got was voice mail. I was worried about you."

He followed her as she walked past him and into the kitchen. "I've been visiting a friend." Which wasn't exactly a lie. She and Madame Orzo now shared a bond. It was possible they'd be friends in the future. "Turned my cell off so we wouldn't be disturbed, and I guess I forgot to turn it back on."

Ellie pulled the phone from her tote and checked the messages. Three from Sam, one from her mother, one from Rob, and one with a number she didn't recognize. She set the phone on the table and made a mental note to hook it to her charger. "I was going to make a cup of tea. You want to join me?"

"Yeah, sure," Sam said, taking his usual seat. "So, who were you spending time with? Vivian?"

She retrieved mugs from the cupboard, filled them with water, and put them in the microwave. Then she gathered tea bags and spoons and set them on the table. "Uh, no, not Viv."

Sam didn't speak, but she felt his stare on her back, drilling into her like a laser beam. When the microwave dinged, she removed the mugs and carried them to the table. "Careful, it's hot."

She dunked her tea bag, knowing full well he was still waiting for the details on how she'd spent the evening. After removing the bag, she placed it on a napkin and raised her eyes to find him gazing at her with a frown. "What?"

He made the same production with his tea bag before speaking. "Okay, don't tell me where you were. It's obviously none of my business, right?"

She blew out a breath. "It's not."

He slouched back in his chair. "Look, if this is about the other day, I apologize."

She sipped her drink, his words warming her more than the hot liquid. An admission of wrongdoing didn't come easy to Sam Ryder. "For ordering me around or for being nasty?"

He shrugged. "Both, I guess. But if you saw it from my point of view—"

"The might-makes-right point of view?"

"What? No." Leaning forward, he rested an elbow on the table. "I didn't mean for it to sound like I was bossing you around. I just—it makes me crazy when I see you getting involved in something that's none of your concern. Especially when it could be dangerous."

Ellie sat back and folded her arms. "Look, I know you're a good cop. Truth be told, I think you're stellar. But I'm an adult. I can take care of myself."

He raised a brow. "Like you did the last couple of times you got involved in murder?"

How could she argue with him when he was right? "Okay, I'll admit I've needed you to rescue me a time or two. Which should only prove how much I trust you. I know you're a professional, but Rob is a friend, and he pleaded with me to lend a hand in proving his innocence. I value my friends, so I try to help them whenever they ask."

He swallowed a jolt of tea. "I know you believe Chesney didn't kill that she-male, but right now the evidence says otherwise."

She-male? Ellie controlled the urge to laugh. "And you and Vince are doing everything in your power to support that evidence and gather more to make a case for the prosecution, correct?"

"We have to. It's our job."

"Well, I have a job, too, and that's helping Rob prove he didn't do it."

"It's not your 'job.'" He put air quotes around the word. "You aren't a law enforcement official, nor are you a private investigator. You're just a—"

"Friend?"

"Do you realize how many times you've used helping a friend as your excuse for running your own murder investigation?"

"I know, I know. But see it from my side. You weren't about to look for Buddy, and he was my responsibility, so you left that up to me, and finding the professor's killer was the only way I could make it happen. Gary asked for my help as a dying wish; how could I ignore a man's dying wish? Then Flora needed me. She's in her seventies, for Pete's sake. I didn't have the heart to turn her down.

"Now there's Rob. I already told him I couldn't help, but Bitsy isn't acting like her usual self, and I think it's connected to what she saw in the dressing room." She sniffed. "I'll do my best to stay out of your way while I help her, but I can't be certain I won't trip over your job while I do it."

He raised his eyes to the ceiling. "Again, with the 'helping a dog' thing." He stared at her. "Okay, if that's the best you can do, I guess I'll have to live with it. But how about making me a promise?"

"Only if I can honor it with a clear conscience."

"All I'm asking is this: If you get a good lead, something that can be used in court, whether it will help free Chesney or convict him, you'll tell me."

"If I promise, how far back would it have to extend?" she asked, feeling guilty before she even gave her word.

"How far back—" He groaned. "What did you do?"

"Not much, honest, but I guess I'd better share how I spent this afternoon."

Both of Sam's eyebrows bunched upward. "Something tells me it won't make me happy, but fill me in anyway."

She took a long swallow of tea while she thought. She didn't have to explain how she'd gotten the information, just confide what it was she'd heard. "I went to the club this afternoon to take a look at the room where Carmella was killed. It's back in use, and there's already a new understudy in place. Someone named Nita Zip."

"I know all about Ms. Zip. We've already documented that she was onstage at the time of the murder."

"You told me that, but I overheard a discussion Nita had with someone else and—"

"Who someone else?"

"I don't know. I couldn't see him—er—her from where I was hid—er—sitting." *Stop stumbling, Ellie.*

Just stick to the truth. "But I heard their conversation clearly."

Sam ran a hand through his rumpled hair, then pulled the ever-present spiral notebook from his inside jacket pocket. The NYPD had to be buying those pads by the case, the way every cop had one whenever she turned around.

He held up his pen. "Anything you tell me will be hearsay and not admissible in court, unless you're called to the stand during the trial. You understand?"

"Of course I do."

"Okay, shoot."

"This other person, the one I can't identify, told Nita she knew for a fact that Carmella was into blackmail. From the sound of it, it was only one guy, with a very public profile, and he'd been making the payments for a while."

Sam sat back in the chair. "I already know that."

"You do? How did you find out?"

"Legally, which is more than I can say for you."

"Ha-ha. Very funny."

"But true." He clicked the pen closed and returned it to his pocket. "Just keep what I'm about to say in confidence."

"You know I will."

"I already got a read on Ms. Sunday's bank records. From the look of it, she's been collecting payoff money for the past eighteen months or so."

A weight lifted from Ellie's shoulders. "That's great. When you find out Rob didn't make any regular withdrawals, you'll realize he isn't the killer."

"Not necessarily," Sam said. "It could mean he found a safer way to obtain and transfer the cash; a way that can't be traced back to him."

She drummed her fingers on the tabletop. "I still

don't believe the guy being blackmailed was Rob. He's told me a dozen times he's got nothing to hide, and he certainly isn't a public figure who has anything to lose."

"I'm supposed to have a conversation with the attorney handling Chesney's trust account. That guy might have a better handle on your pal's finances."

"I thought a lawyer had to honor attorney-client privilege and couldn't reveal stuff about someone he represented."

"Checking finances isn't the same thing. All I need is a court order and I can take a look at the bank records."

"Rob's attorney is Keller Williams. Is he any good?" She hoped so, and it would be nice if Sam agreed.

"He's an up-and-comer, though he's never defended a case I had a hand in. I heard your boy's trust attorney is the one who hooked them up."

"Mr. Williams got Rob out on bail, so he must know what he's doing."

"That remains to be seen." He pushed away from the table and stood. "It's late. Sorry I took up so much of your time." He collected the notebook and returned it to his jacket pocket. "I can see myself out."

This was not their usual way of ending an evening, and she didn't want Sam to leave without a proper good-bye. She was about to tell him so when they arrived at the door, but he surprised her by cupping her face in his hand.

"I don't like it when we fight, Ellie, but I like it even less when you get involved in things that are off-limits."

Relieved that he was still willing to talk, she smiled. "I'm well aware of that. I'm also grateful you look out for me, even if you don't approve of what I feel I have to do."

"So, we're back on track?"

She nodded. "We will be, just as soon as we say good-bye like we should."

A corner of his mouth lifted and he leaned close, brushing his lips across hers. She wrapped her arms around his neck and deepened the kiss, letting him know she forgave him. Telling him she was still his girl.

When he drew back, she sighed. "Stanley's giving a big party Saturday night, and he says you're invited, too."

He opened the door. "And your mother will be there?"

She grinned. "Unfortunately."

"What's the party for?"

"The judge is hosting a gathering for the three men who are up for some big-deal judicial appointment. One of my clients, Norman Lowenstein, is on the list, but according to Stanley all the men are equally qualified."

"Lowenstein? Why does that name sound familiar?"

"Maybe you had to testify before him? I walk the Lowensteins' chunky Pug, Sampson."

"The dog with the blue—"

"That's the one."

"Do I have to wear a monkey suit?"

"Only if you want to."

Sam's lips compressed into a thin line. "Can I think about it and let you know tomorrow?"

"Of course. Believe me, if I had anything else going on in my life, I wouldn't attend either, but I'm free. The best part is I can bring Rudy."

He gave her a cheeky grin. "Then let him be your escort."

"It's not the same thing. The judge asked me to bring him as a personal favor."

"So I'd be the third wheel to a pint-sized pound dog?"

"What? No. No!"

Sam laughed. "I'm only joking." He stepped into the hall and turned. "I'll call you." Pulling her near, he gave her a final knee-shaking good-night kiss and headed down the corridor. "That reminds me," he shouted over his shoulder. "You might want to check caller ID before you answer the phone for the next couple of days. My mother is on the prowl."

"What?"

He disappeared down the steps without answering and she huffed out a breath. Great. She'd managed to avoid a private conversation with Lydia Ryder for the past four months. At least Sam had given her a heads-up to keep the good luck going.

She walked into the kitchen, collected the tea fixings, and deposited them in the sink. Then she picked up her cell phone, ready to head for the bedroom.

"It's about time Detective Demento took a powder."

After jumping a foot, Ellie glared at her four-legged pal, standing in the kitchen doorway. "Stop sneaking up on me. I thought you were in bed."

"I was, but it's getting late." He trotted beside her as she paced down the hall. *"Bitsy's already sound asleep."*

"I was afraid of that." She tiptoed into the bedroom, plugged her cell into the charger, and pulled down the comforter. Rudy jumped on the bed and managed to curl up on his pillow without waking the poohuahua. Ellie slid under the covers, doused the bedside light, and reached out to snuggle her boy. "Did she say anything about Madame Orzo?"

"Some. Claims she's gonna think on what happened and tell you everything tomorrow."

Ellie stifled a yawn. "Do you think she'll actually recall anything more?"

"Maybe."

"What did you think of Madame Orzo and her psychic abilities?"

"Have to say, it was one of the weirdest things I've ever experienced. It wasn't like you and me, talking all nice and normal. It was more like she was inside my head walkin' around like she was shoppin' at the food store or somethin'."

"It was sort of spooky when she brought out those treats."

"Ya think?"

"Okay, fine. I'll let it rest for now. You and Bitsy can stay home tomorrow and I'll pick you up before the afternoon walks. Maybe you can help her remember more of what she knows."

"Don't worry. She'd never try to hide anything from you. She's trustin' you to save Bobbi-Rob."

"That's what worries me." Ellie scratched the underside of his chin, then rolled closer and kissed his nose. "Good night, big guy. I'll talk to you in the morning."

Chapter 13

The next morning, Ellie sat at the kitchen table, nursing a final cup of coffee with Bitsy in her lap. She'd showered, given the dogs a quick trip outside, and eaten a decent breakfast, but had yet to speak with the poohuahua about their visit to the psychic. Their session with Madame Orzo and the time she'd spent with Sam later had eased the load of worry she'd been carrying about Rob. It sounded like Sam would let her in on a few of the steps he planned to take in his investigation, and the poohuahua had remembered more about the murder. Both positive signs.

"I had a visitor last night, and by the time I came to bed you were asleep," she said to the pocket pooch. "I take it you had a good rest, no bad dreams or anything else caused by the incident at the club or Madame Orzo."

Bitsy gave a doggie grin. *"I slept real good. She got me to relax, and remember and . . . and everything."*

How much was *everything*? Ellie wondered. "I know, but I only heard what went on from her point of view." She held up a steno pad. "Now that we have a few minutes before I have to leave on rounds, how about you tell me more of what you remembered in your own words, so I can compare versions?"

Bitsy began by describing the performers' excitement in the dressing room the night of the killing, and how concerned they were about the show being a hit. After everyone left to put on the revue, she'd settled down for a nap. Her explanation slowed when she talked about being awakened by the sound of an argument.

"After the human voices got me up, I stared at the only thing I could see from underneath the table—their shoes. And believe me when I tell you if people looked at the world the same way we little guys do, life would be different. For one thing, they'd take better care of their shoes and their pants cuffs."

Since Ellie had shared Bitsy's experience of being stowed under Rob's table, she knew exactly what the poohuahua was saying. "Madame Orzo said you had shoes on your mind. Dark shoes with a thick sole. Is there more?"

"The shoes were definitely black or brown, and they were definitely man shoes. And they looked different, but I'm not sure how."

"Do you think you'd recognize them if you saw them again?"

"Maybe."

"And you don't remember smelling anything special about the killer? Something that would alert you, if you met them again?"

"That room is always full of smells. Most of the time it's girly and kinda sweet, but every once in a while it's pee-eeuw stinky. There's hair stuff, and spray stuff, and sometimes even food smells. One of the girls likes onions and horseradish on her roast beef sandwich. The stink's enough to make my eyes water."

"I'll just bet," said Ellie, coming to grips with the fact that although dogs' sense of smell is their strongest ally, it didn't sound as if it would help in this situation. "One more thing. What about the stranger's voice?"

Bitsy stood on her hind legs, rested her front paws on Ellie's chest, and stretched up until they were almost nose to nose. *"I think I heard that voice another time, but I can't be sure where."*

"Another time? You mean at the club?"

"Uh-uh. Somewhere else." The poohuahua dropped to a sit. *"I'm not sure, but I think so."*

"Then we should probably figure out where you've been since the murder took place." Ellie glanced at Rudy, who was lying at her feet. "Did you hear that, big guy? Chime in if you can help reconstruct the little girl's week."

Instead of answering, Rudy thumped his tail twice.

She didn't like the sound of that thump. "Are you feeling okay?"

He sneezed. *"Yack! Yack! Yack!"* The string of coughs made her frown. *"No, I'm not. I think I'm comin' down with somethin'. Prob'ly that freezin' wind last night."*

Talk about ratcheting up her guilt quotient. "What else? Sore throat? Headache? Chills?"

"A little achy. Yack! Like I slept on my bad side or jumped high and couldn't get my feet under me when I landed."

Ready to call Dr. Dave, Ellie said, "I knew I should have put coats on the two of you last night." She read the clock on the stove. "I've got to go." She set Bitsy on the floor and locked eyes with Rudy. "I'm going to leave both of you home this morning. You can stay here and sleep, and maybe the cough will go away." She walked to the pantry, opened a door, and began rifling through his treat basket. "I'm pretty certain I have some leftover doggie aspirin, from when Gary's brother slapped you around."

He stood and gave a full-body shake. *"No, no. I'm okay. A little exercise might do me some good, but maybe you should get my coat, just in case."*

Gazing out the kitchen window, Ellie saw frost still icing the pane. "It doesn't look any warmer than it did an hour ago, but all right, if you say so." She walked to the hall closet and slipped her jacket over her pale blue sweater, which covered a thermal undershirt. Then she reached up to the top shelf and brought down the red plaid coat he'd been given this past fall by canine design maven Lorilee Echternach. "There," she said, strapping the Velcro strips under his belly to keep the fit snug. "That should do it."

"What about Bits? She's gonna freeze out there."

"You up for a walk, too, Bitsy?"

"If I'm warm, sure."

She checked the shelf again and found a sweater jacket her boy never wore. "I don't have one of your coats, but this old sweater of Rudy's might fit." She slid the knit garment, more of a stocking with holes, over Bitsy's head. It was so huge, Ellie imagined two more of the poohuahua could fit inside. "Well, shoot, that won't work. Give me a minute to think."

When an idea hit, she raced to her kitchen and grabbed the scissors, then went to her guest bedroom closet with the dogs at her heels. Digging into a bag of used clothes she planned to take to a homeless shelter, she pulled out a faded black sweater and went to work with her shears. After a moment, she examined her masterpiece. "It's kind of ragged, but it should be okay until we get you home."

Ellie squatted and slipped the remodeled sweater sleeve over Bitsy's head and onto her legs. "What do you think?"

The poohuahua stretched, then wriggled. *"I guess it's all right. It seems warm."*

"Okay. We'll head out as soon as I put on my gloves."

Five minutes later they were on the street walking toward the Beaumont. The damp, chilly air and brisk wind still made her think of snow, and she hurried west, crossing Lexington, Park, and Madison at a marathon-walker pace. Finally at their first stop, the trio hurried inside.

"You three look toasty. All ready for that blizzard they're predicting?" asked Natter, the Beaumont's doorman.

"Blizzard?" was Ellie's response. "Darn, I knew I should have checked the Weather Channel before I left the house."

"You mean you haven't heard? We're supposed to get eight to ten inches by tomorrow morning. Biggest storm of the season. I just hope my shift is over before it gets here."

"Thanks for the heads-up," she said as they went to the elevator. The door closed and she leaned back against the wall. "We won't have a problem if it starts late this afternoon, but it's going to be trouble come tomorrow morning." Ellie heaved a sigh. "Good thing for us tomorrow is Saturday."

"You're right about that," Rudy yipped. *"Some of them humans with money would never walk their own canines. It's all they can do to give 'em treats and food."*

"Treats and food? Are you saying some of the dogs we walk are going hungry?"

"I hear things, off and on. Next time I get a hint, I'll report back what I heard."

"You do that. I want to know all the details. You understand?" The elevator stopped on the top floor and she knocked on Flora Steinman's door. "Remind me to put coats on Lulu and the rest of the gang if they want them," she said, ready to use her key.

Just then Nelda, Flora's faithful housekeeper, opened the door. "Good morning. Just give me a second to find the baby."

Ellie grinned. Many people on the Upper East Side treated their pets like children, especially the smaller dogs, but Nelda and Flora referred to the haughty Havanese as if she were a real baby. That was why Rudy's pronouncement about one of their dogs going hungry had upset her.

"Here she is," said the housekeeper, returning to the foyer from the direction of the bedrooms a moment later. "Ms. Flora already put on her new coat."

Her new coat? Blinking, Ellie studied the Havanese, who was dressed in her red-and-black-plaid outerwear. Then she looked at Rudy. "You are a stinker."

The yorkiepoo rubbed noses with his canine girl-friend. *"How the heck was I supposed to know what she'd be wearin'?"*

"You know because I told—" Lulu began.

"Ix-nay on the oat-kay," he muttered to Lulu.

Ellie grabbed the leash. Her boy was quite the actor, pretending to be sick so she'd dress him in a coat he knew was nearly identical to Lulu's. A coat that gave them the look of twins. "We'll be back in a little while," she told the housekeeper as they walked into the hall.

"I forgive you," she said when they entered the elevator, and rode it one floor down to Cheech and Chong's condo. "But all you had to do was ask. Thanks to that black lung act, I was worried you might need to see the vet."

"Can we talk about this another time?"

"Sure we can. Just remember you owe me one."

Forty-five minutes later, they arrived at the Davenport. The wind had calmed down, but the clouds still looked ready to dump a load of snow on the city. Stomping past Randall, who was chatting with a tenant, Ellie tossed him a wave and stepped into the elevator. It was then she remembered she wanted to ask Kayla if Eugene, who was used to handling larger canines, could take her place walking Bradley.

She pressed the button for Bitsy's floor and gazed at Rudy. "You and Ms. Pickypants looked very cute in your matching coats." She shook her head. "If you wanted to dress like Lulu, all you had to do was ask, you know."

He gave a doggie shrug. *"Uh, yeah. But I didn't want you laughin' at me for wanting to copy her."*

"Would I do that?" she asked, stepping out on the correct floor.

"Yes."

"Okay, you got me, but I would have understood."

"I knew, I knew. I knew what he was doin'," yipped Bitsy. *"Rudy's got a girlfriend. Rudy's got a girlfriend."*

When they arrived at Rob's apartment, she heard snurffling coming from underneath the door, a sure sign the Great Dane was waiting. No one answered her knock, so she opened the door and found Bradley staring at her as if she were a poison-laced Milk-Bone.

"Hey, big man. How's tricks?"

Glaring, the pony-sized pooch cocked his head.

"Is Kayla or Rob up?"

He nosed her arm, shoving her toward the leash hanging from a hook on the wall.

"No, huh? I don't suppose you have a coat?"

"Bradley's from Arizona. It's a hundred degrees down there, even in the winter," Bitsy answered for him.

She hooked up the Great Dane, locked the door, and gathered the rest of the Davenport pack, charging through the lobby and out onto Fifth Avenue in record time. Some of the dogs had asked for their coats and some hadn't, which was fine by her. The temperature had climbed a few degrees, so she doubted anyone would freeze.

Except for Bradley, all the dogs in this group held a special place in her heart. They were her first customers, had been with her when Buddy, a champion Bichon, went missing, and had known Gary, too. They keyed in on each other and her moods easily, and today was no different.

"Hey, Bitsy. How was the psychic?" asked Sweetie Pie, the ever-cheerful Westie.

"Yeah," grumped Buckley. *"Did she try to stomp around in your brain the way she does in mine?"*

Conversation escalated from there, with Rudy and the poohuahua rehashing their evening with Madame Orzo. After the canines did their business, she dropped them at home and wrote Kayla a note asking for her approval to contact Eugene about Bradley. If Rob's sister said yes, she would get the annoying man's promise that he'd take good care of his temporary client. She had never thought she'd see the day when she was friendly toward Eugene, but he'd been easy to get along with lately, and she got the feeling he actually accepted her as one of the area's legitimate professional walkers.

After seeing to the rest of her charges in the building, they moved on to Sara Studebaker's complex. When no one answered Ellie's knock, she figured her friend was at her new store, so she retrieved the rest of the dogs and finished the walks. Then the trio moved on to the Cranston Arms.

Their first stop was the Lowensteins', where she would pick up Sampson. Since Mariette had been home the last couple of times, Ellie knocked and waited before opening the door. A moment later, Norman Lowenstein greeted her with the pudgy Pug at his side.

"Ms. Engleman. Hello."

"Judge," she acknowledged. She knew men of his position expected a certain amount of respect for the job they did. She'd been careful with Stanley, too, until she got to know him. "I'm surprised to see you. Is today a holiday for the courts?"

"No, no. But I've cleared my calendar. Mariette's been under the weather, and I'm worried about her." He stuck his hands in the pockets of his cranberry-colored cashmere sweater. "I take it you'll be at the Fryes' tomorrow night?"

The Fryes? "At Georgette and Stanley's place? Yeah, Rudy and I will be there with bells on."

Judge Lowenstein raised a brow and focused on the yorkiepoo. "You do realize this is a formal affair in honor of the three judges being considered for the appellate court?"

"So Mother said, though it was Stanley's idea to invite Rudy. The judge has a rule: I'm not allowed to come to their apartment unless I bring my boy. Mother isn't an animal lover, so it was the only way he could guarantee that he and my dog could visit." *And who are you to say who I can and can't bring to my parents' party, even if it is in your honor?* "He'll be quiet. You'll hardly know he's there."

"Are you sure Judge Frye wasn't joking?"

"I'm gettin' a vibe here, Triple E. This guy don't like me, and he's nervous about somethin', too."

Ellie shushed him with a look. "I'm pretty sure he wasn't. He said—"

"Norman? Who's at the door?" called Mariette from somewhere in the apartment. Standing tall, the judge frowned, and it was then Ellie realized he was quite a bit shorter and thinner than his partner.

"I'm handling things, Mariette. There's no need for you to be involved."

Whoa, thought Ellie. He sure told her. "Can I do anything to help?" she asked as she hooked Sampson to his lead.

"Norm? Is everything all right?" Mariette's voice was high-pitched and warbling, not at all her usual commanding tone.

"Get control of yourself, Mariette. I'll join you for a cup of tea in a few seconds," the judge chastised, not an ounce of sympathy in his tone.

Ellie knew she was being dismissed, and not in a nice way either. "We'll be back in a half hour or so," she said, sidling out the door.

She led the dogs to the elevator, thinking about the Lowensteins. Mariette was usually a model of decorum. In fact, she was so adept at handling herself that the one time Ellie had seen the Lowensteins together, she thought Mariette was the alpha bitch in their relationship. Today, it sounded as if Mariette had experienced a mental lapse . . . almost as if she was in distress.

Ellie filed the experience away and led the group off the elevator and onto Freud's floor. She would see both the Lowensteins at the judge's party, and she might be better able to get a handle on Mariette's problem there.

She focused on this walk. Only one more unit and they were through for the morning.

Sam and Vince were in the office when their phones rang at the same time. After Sam answered his, he mouthed "medical examiner" to his partner and turned his chair around for privacy. Vince left the room a couple of seconds later and Sam centered his chair, then rested his elbows on the desk. "Sorry about the delay, Dr. Kingsgate. What do you have for us?"

"The autopsy and toxicology screenings on Mr. Pearson are finished. A lab tech is faxing the results as we speak."

"Maybe you could fill me in while I wait," said Sam.

"Our machines are always on overload for one reason or another."

"No problem. The toxicology screening came back clean and green. The victim was drug free, nothing in his system but the remains of an over-the-counter cold medication. Autopsy showed he was in good physical condition, just like Dr. Bridges thought. Death occurred as the result of a stab wound to the back of the neck between the third and fourth cervical vertebrae. The victim went into immediate spinal shock, disconnecting the brain from the body. He probably didn't feel a thing once he hit the floor."

"TOD?"

"Time of death approximately ten p.m. Smack in line with when you found the body."

"And the scissors Rob Chesney was holding?"

"Based on the width and depth of the wound, we believe the puncture was made by a weapon consistent with that type of object. We heard from forensics that they found tissue matching that of the deceased embedded between the blades. Gruesome, I know, but that's the whole of it."

"So we definitely have our weapon. Problem is, the fingerprints on the scissors were smeared. All we have is one clear partial belonging to Chesney. It makes sense, considering we caught him with the weapon." He leaned back in his chair. "Guess I'd better check the fax machine."

"You do that, and let me know if the reports don't show up. Dr. Bridges said to let us know if you need anything else."

He disconnected the call and drummed his fingers on the desk. The investigation was rounding out perfectly, just as he'd expected. Trouble was, he never cared much for an easy case, because something always happened to fuck it up. And knowing that Ellie was sniffing around didn't make it any better.

What in the hell had she been doing last night that caused her to turn off her phone? And why had she skated around the answer when he asked about it? The fact that she hadn't told him outright about her evening excursion could mean only one thing: She'd been snooping, and she didn't want to let him in on it.

Vince strolled in, tossed a handful of papers on Sam's desk, and added a manila folder. "This ought to make your day."

Sam examined the stacked pages, skimming the paperwork Dr. Kingsgate had promised. Then he opened the file and scanned the data on Rob Chesney's bank records. "Not exactly what we were hoping for," he said after a moment. "I take it you talked to the lawyer handling his trust account before you got these?"

"That's who called me when the ME phoned you. When I got to the fax machine, everything was waiting. It's all there in dingy black and white."

"The withdrawals from Chesney's trust account for his mortgage and credit card payments and his self-imposed monthly allowance are clear, but there's nothing that shows a regular withdrawal that comes close to the amount Pearson was raking in." He bounced the eraser end of a pencil on his blotter. "You're sure the trust attorney wasn't hiding anything?"

"Not so I could tell. He was open, sent me the paperwork as promised, told me if I needed to access the accounts on my own, he'd be happy to let me in. He just wanted to be careful, what with identity theft being so prevalent these days."

"You have to wonder, if there's no record of our guy making monthly withdrawals of ten big ones, where did Pearson get the dough?"

"You know the rule—follow the money. But it's going to be tough, seeing as all the victim's deposits were made in cash."

"And the attorney is certain Chesney had no other source of income?"

"Claims he made a couple of thousand a month from the clubs he worked as a drag queen, but it was nowhere near the amount we're looking for. He also said his client was a fanatic about living within his means. The only big money he spent was on specialty clothing, tax deductible because of his profession. Other than that, and a trip to Barneys a couple of times a year, Chesney never went through more than the usual living expenses. In fact, without counting the cash he needed for his bond, he'd never asked for any large amount." Vince rounded his desk. "That means we have to make a decision."

"After we talk it over with the assistant DA."

"Not we. You. Remember that trip Natalie and I are scheduled to take today? We're supposed to leave for south Jersey in the next"—he glanced at his watch—"twenty-seven minutes. Which means I'm outta here." Vince stood. "I hate to dump it on you, but this weekend has been planned since Christmas. It'll be the baby's first visit to Nat's grandparents' home, though Mr. and Mrs. Nunzio have been up here every month since Angela's been born. We have to leave now if we want to avoid that snowstorm they're predicting."

"I know how bad traffic on the Jersey Turnpike can be, even without the storm warning, so don't worry about it," Sam said. "Besides, you had to put off your last three-day break for the Northway case. I understand."

"Don't you have some big shindig set for tomorrow night? Something to do with Ellie's stepfather, the judge?"

Sam shrugged. "She got the invite, not me. I haven't decided if I'm going."

"What would keep you away?"

"Ellie didn't say, but I'm fairly certain the dress is formal, for one thing. Then there's the guest list. Lawyers, judges, city officials—no one I care to associate with."

"But you patched things up with Ellie, right?"

"Some. Trouble is, I'm not sure she got the message."

Vince cleared his desk and turned off his computer. "The message?"

"The same damn thing we've argued about since the day we met. Keeping her nose clean."

"I get the feeling that's a useless argument," said Vince, shaking his head. "Just learn to live with it. Your girl is stubborn and she loves to snoop. Those are traits I doubt she'll ever outgrow."

"I almost lost it a couple of months back, when I walked into her apartment and found that nut job threatening to shoot her if she didn't drink a poison-laced cup of tea." He ran his hands through his hair. "Carolanne didn't give a flying fuck about my job, complained, cheated, did everything she could to ruin our relationship. Ellie is the exact opposite . . . wants to know about my work, never gripes when I leave her for a case—" He heaved a sigh. "I just want to keep her safe."

"Why don't the two of you make a deal? She promises to tell you whenever she plans to do some scouting and agrees to report back on what she finds. Then she doesn't make another move without your okay. No going off half-cocked or putting herself in danger."

"We did that. I'm just not sure she'll keep her word."

"Trust me. She'll honor it," Vince said, heading for the door. "Ellie's as honest as they come. If you got her to promise, she'll do it. Just give her a chance."

Sam tossed his pencil on the blotter. "If I didn't care about her—"

"Sounds to me like this is more serious than you're willing to admit," said Vince. "Don't be stupid. Let her know how much she means to you, pal."

"Have a nice weekend, *pal*," Sam shouted to his partner's retreating back.

He ground his molars. Vince was right. He was serious about Ellie. She was funny, sweet, caring . . . all the things his ex had never been. She was also high class, though she worked hard to give a different impression. How could he keep up with a woman who made more money than he did and stood to inherit a bundle more? And money or no money, he would never be able to support her the way she supported him.

Maybe his mother was right. Maybe if he moved in with her, he'd be able to keep a better eye on her, get her to straighten up and fly right. Then he remembered her dog.

Lately, he and the miserable mutt had come to some sort of understanding. Rudy hadn't thrown him a single growl or snotty look for at least a month. Even slept in the guest room when he and Ellie shared her bed. If he didn't know better, he'd think the dog actually approved of his being around.

Sam spied the open folder and gazed at the financial information inside. He'd looked into Pearson's record and gotten the dates and other basic info on the guy's past arrests, but there were a couple of particulars he hadn't checked, because he hadn't thought they'd matter.

He replayed the scene at Guess Who in his mind. Chesney had looked shocked, kneeling in that pool of blood with the scissors in his hand, but the guy was a showman, so there was a chance he'd been acting. His story was plausible, just barely. What dope would walk into a crime scene and remove the murder weapon? Was Chesney such a humane idiot that he would truly do something that stupid? Did he really have no idea of the rules about contaminating a crime scene?

He snorted. Without a motive or the proof of a money exchange, there was a good chance the DA would drop the charges. Which meant he and Vince were back to square one. Who was paying Pearson and why?

Sam checked his watch, then made a call to the records department to start the investigation rolling in another direction. If the weather report was right, traveling tomorrow was going to be a nightmare. There was a tuxedo rental shop in his neighborhood and a damn good Chinese restaurant near Ellie. He could surprise her with dinner and stay the night, then retrieve his info in the morning. That would give him and his girl the day to get ready for the judge's party.

He might not be able to say the words yet, but tonight was the perfect time to show her how much he cared.

Chapter 14

"Wow. Bobbi-Rob really told his sister where to go when she pushed you about workin' on his case," said Rudy as he and Ellie left the Davenport. *"I got a feelin' she won't be pesterin' you about it anymore."*

"Good thing, too," Ellie agreed, heading toward the nearest Joe to Go. Rob and Kayla's discussion had been so single-minded, she hadn't even been able to ask the woman about Eugene walking Bradley. She was almost sorry she'd left Bitsy in the middle of the fight. "I'm glad he understands my position."

"Sure sounds like he does." He gazed up at the street sign. *"It's freezin'. Please tell me we're goin' someplace warm for lunch."*

"Joe's on Lexington. I want to hear what Sara said when he told her about my idea."

"Fine by me. We can huddle inside and get comfy. And didn't you say Joe's started serving sandwiches?"

"Yep. His turkey on whole wheat is great. You'll love it."

They arrived at the Joe to Go, where they found the owner standing behind the counter. Instead of taking orders or working the register, Joe had the same expression on his face that Bitsy's had earlier: lost in a day-dream. "Are you feeling okay?" she asked him when she got to the head of the line.

"Huh?" He blinked, then focused on her. "Uh, yeah. Why?"

"Because I thought maybe you were posing for one of Madame Tussauds' wax creations." She gave her order to the woman at the register and pulled out her wallet. "What's up?"

Head down, he hurried around the counter, grabbed her arm, and led her and Rudy to the only empty table in the room. "Wait here. Lunch is on me. I'll be right back with your food."

"Yowza. He's got it bad," Rudy said, circling before he plopped on the floor under the table.

She ducked her head. "Bad? Bad how? Do you think something happened to him after we left?"

"Remember those raging pheromones I told you Detective Doofus always sends out when he's near you? Well, Joe's sending out the same dopey signal."

"Raging what?" She sat up straight. Was Rudy saying what she thought he was saying?

"You talkin' to me?" asked the man at the next table.

"Uh, sorry, no. Just thinking out loud."

"Ri-i-ght." The guy drew the single word out to three syllables, stood, and carried his trash to a bin.

"Jeez! Some people," Rudy groused.

Before Ellie could comment, Joe arrived with her lunch. "You gonna order the same thing every time you come in here? Like the Caramel Bliss?"

She lifted half of the turkey on whole wheat, picked out a shred of meat, and fed it to her boy. "I like your version of the drink better than the one Starbucks makes, and this is a great sandwich, so I guess I will." She took a huge bite. Something was up with her friend and, thanks to Rudy, she had an idea what it was. After swallowing, she asked, "Did you get a chance to stop in the bakery next door?"

Joe blushed, something Ellie hadn't seen him do since college. "Uh, yeah."

"And?"

He squared his shoulders. "And nothing."

"But you met Sara and her girls."

He sat down across from her. "How's the sandwich?"

"You're avoiding my question." She took another bite.

"If this is how you act when you stick your nose where it doesn't belong, it's no wonder Ryder gets ticked."

Still chewing, she pulled off another clump of turkey and passed it to Rudy. After taking a sip of her coffee, she said, "How about you leave Sam out of this and answer my question. Did you meet Sara and her girls?"

He blew out a long breath. "Yes, I met Sara and her gir—er—dogs."

"And she liked my idea?"

"Yes, only . . ." He dropped his gaze to the tabletop.

"You're making me crazy," she countered. "Just tell me what happened between the two of you."

Joe's complexion washed from red to white in a nanosecond. Then he swallowed so hard Ellie thought he might toss his cookies right there in the shop.

"I think I'm in love." The words came out choppy but clear.

As usual, Rudy was right, though it was a stretch to believe Joe was "in love." "Considering you only met the woman yesterday, I think that's rather a strong statement, don't you?"

His face bled red again. "I can't help how I feel. It's just . . . there."

Joe had dated about a thousand girls in college,

each one dim-witted and, to a man's way of thinking, sexy as hell. He'd made slightly better choices recently, but the women Ellie had met still had that dumb-as-a-stick, "Don't hate me because I'm beautiful" attitude. She didn't begrudge Joe love, but jeez, Sara couldn't have been more opposite his usual type than beer was to champagne, and not the cheap kind either. Sara was more Cristal Rosé, one of the most expensive champagnes in the world.

"Are you sure you're talking about Sara Studebaker?"

"No. I mean Sara Schizophrenia," snapped Joe, slipping back into his usual teasing manner.

"How long did the two of you talk?"

"Ten, maybe twenty minutes." He glanced at the front counter and stood. "I gotta go."

"What in the world was that all about?" Ellie muttered aloud to her boy.

"He said he had to go," answered a school principal–type woman sitting at the table the grumpy man had just vacated. "Pay attention when people talk to you."

"Er—yes, ma'am." The woman had the perfect posture of a yoga instructor and the expression of a long-suffering saint. "Sorry."

"What are you sorry for? You didn't do anything wrong."

She tossed Rudy a look and smiled at the principal.

"And why is your dog inside? This is a restaurant. I believe there's a city ordinance that bars animals from entering places that serve food."

"Uh-oh. This I gotta hear."

"Rudy is a service dog," Ellie began, crossing mental fingers. "That means he can go wherever I go."

The woman stared at her as if she belonged in a petri dish. "Oh, really? And why might you be needing a service dog?"

"Tell her you hear voices, lots and lots of canine voices. That should shut her up."

"That question is a little too personal for me to answer."

"Yeah, it's for you to know and her to find out, right?"

"I can acknowledge your sentiment, but why isn't he wearing his vest?"

"Yeah, how come?"

Ellie closed her eyes. She had known this day would come; she should have been better prepared for it. "Ah . . . his vest is at home." Why hadn't she practiced the answer months ago? "I forgot to put it on him this morning."

"Then I assume you're carrying his card?"

"I told you this might happen, but did you listen? No-o-o."

She made a production out of looking at her watch. "Oh, gee, sorry, but I'm late for an appointment."

Standing, she hoisted her tote bag onto her shoulder, dumped her trash in the container, and hustled out the door with Rudy trotting along behind. She really did need to look into getting him certified as a service dog. She just had to take the time to do it.

Relieved to find herself in front of Sara's store, she went inside. The workmen were gone, the bakery cases were in place, shelves decorated two walls, and pictures of dogs hung on all the remaining free space. Sara had even posted an advertisement for Best Friends, Ellie's favorite animal charity, and the organization's magazines sat in a rack near the door.

"Hello! Anybody here?" she called, taking a seat at one of the four tables.

The sound of excited barking came from the back room. Seconds later, Pooh and Tigger danced in, their snow-white tails wagging. "Hey, ladies. Where's your mistress?"

Pooh and Tigger had never answered her, but they had a good rapport with Rudy, who rubbed noses with each Westie, then said, *"Sara's in the back. She'll be out in a couple."*

Ellie scratched Tigger, who was a bit friendlier than Pooh, between the ears. "Have you been a good helper today?"

Sara walked in smiling. "Ellie. I thought that might be you when the girls ran out. They're not much in the way of watchdogs, but they do know a friendly voice."

Sara wore a bright red apron over snug jeans and a black ribbed turtleneck. Her dark blond hair was pulled up in a ponytail, a dash of cherry-colored lipstick covered her generous mouth, and a little mascara enhanced her bright green eyes.

"You look great. Did anything happen today that you want to talk about?" asked Ellie.

"I'm pumped. The ovens are in, and they work like a charm. I called the city, and the inspectors should be here by the end of next week."

"So the business will be up and running soon?"

"My guess now is three weeks, but I'll need to build up stock before I open. There's a lot involved in making my treats, you know. I'm thinking of hiring someone to lend a hand."

"Good luck with that," Ellie told her. "I've been through three assistants in the past six months and interviewed a half dozen others. Joy was the best. I'm still hoping I can convince her to return."

"I just need someone to bag the cookies once they're out of the oven and have cooled, attach my tag, and stock the cases—and maybe sweep and straighten up."

"So you plan to open the shop and man the register, bake the goods, do inventory of the cases and shelves, and clean the kitchen, then close up for the day?"

Sara's eyes opened wide. "When you put it that way, I guess I'll need two assistants."

"You could stick a Help Wanted sign on the window."

"Great idea. It'll be up tomorrow." She rubbed her nose. "Have you had lunch?"

"I ate at Joe's," said Ellie, happy that Sara had given her an opportunity to pry. "He's my college buddy. I've known him for over ten years."

"Really. Funny he never mentioned you." Sara scratched Pooh's perked-up ears. "Pooh Bear seemed to like him on sight, which doesn't happen too often. She's a lot pickier than Tigger about the men she meets."

"Joe is a great guy. What did you think of him?"

Sara's lips thinned. "Ah . . . well . . ."

"I'm talking about a guy six feet tall, with a fabulous head of black hair, killer brown eyes, and a great sense of humor." Sara's bland expression made Ellie think maybe she had another man in mind. "That is who we're talking about, right?"

"The guy you're describing did come in, but all he did was stare at me, mumble something about running the coffee shop next door, and go on about me serving coffee here. He did pet Pooh, which I liked, but he was kind of weird."

"Hmm. Joe must have had something on his mind." *Like the hots for you.* "He's usually quick with a comeback or a clever line. And he's a talker."

"A talker? Uh-uh. Not this guy. Do you know what he meant when he mentioned something about serving coffee here?"

"Sort of. I think he's hoping the two of you can work out a deal. You give a coupon to each of the people who buy a dog treat here offering them a free cup of coffee at Joe's shop. He hopes they'll stop in, buy some of his people food, and become regulars. It's a giveaway for you and a business gimme for him."

Sara smiled at the explanation. "That's a good idea. And maybe he could give his customers a coupon for ten percent off anything they buy here as a trade-off."

"Now you're with the program." Ellie glanced at her watch and stood. "Oops, we've got to get moving. I want to finish my afternoon runs before the snow starts to fall."

"I'll walk you out." Sara pushed away from the table. "Will I see you on Monday?"

"We'll stop by if we can. And do me a favor?"

"Sure. Anything."

"Give Joe another chance. Drop in when his afternoon traffic slows and tell him your idea about the coupon exchange. He'll get better. Honest."

"I can do that," said Sara. She closed the door and waved through the glass, mouthing "Bye."

Ellie zipped her jacket and gazed at the still–dark gray clouds. "What do you think happened to Joe? Sara's description didn't sound at all like the man I know."

"I think Joe's a goner."

"I cannot believe he acted like a jerk." They headed across Lexington to Park. "Do you think she's telling the truth?"

"Why would she lie?" He gave a full-body shake. *"The weather report is right. It's gonna snow up a storm."*

"And you know this because . . ."

"Because I feel it in my bones. It's just somethin' I can tell. Animals are like that, you know."

"I do know." They crossed Madison and headed toward Fifth Avenue. "I was hoping to go to the club and talk to Bill Avery again. He wanted to tell me something the other day, but I never got around to having the discussion."

"You're gonna go out in a blizzard?"

A snowflake floated past Ellie's nose before she could answer. Then another . . . and another. Seconds later, the air was filled with big fat flakes, swirling like icy moths as they made their descent. "Okay, fine." They turned left on Fifth and headed for the Beaumont. "I guess I'll have to stop at the club tomorrow, after the roads are cleared."

"Good luck with that."

"It had better clear up enough that people can attend the judge's party. If Mother has to cancel, she'll have a conniption fit." They walked into their first stop and found Natter grinning. "What's so funny?" Ellie asked him as they aimed for the elevator.

"Not a thing. I just love a good snowfall, and I'm off duty in fifteen minutes."

She glanced out the door and eyed the swirling flakes, so thick she couldn't even see the traffic on the street. They raced into the elevator and rode it to their first stop. It was going to be a long couple of hours before they got home.

"I can't remember the last time I've been this tired," said Ellie as she and Rudy took the stairs into their building. The snow was falling full force now, and their afternoon walks had taken forever. Frozen and exhausted, she led Rudy up the steps to their condo. When they arrived on the second floor, the door to 2-B opened and Vivian stuck out her head.

"By the look of things, I guess you and the Rudster had a rough afternoon, huh?"

"You don't know the half of it. Lulu wouldn't walk, so Mrs. Steinman is ordering her booties. Sweetie Pie hates the snow so much she peed in the lobby of the Davenport, which killed Kronk's cheerful demeanor, and Arlo couldn't navigate the drifts, so I had to carry him, too. And don't even ask me about Sampson. That little lard-butt complained the whole walk about not feeling well, and when I brought him home his mom and dad were arguing about the judge's chances of getting that promotion."

Ellie stopped to take a breath. "That woman's blown hot and cold every day this week. I have no idea what kind of medication she's on, but I don't want any."

"I'm sorry to hear all that." Viv smiled. "Is there a chance you'd want to share dinner with Twink and me?"

"It depends on the menu." Ellie rested an arm on the banister. "What are you offering?"

"Italian. I stopped at Mama Bella's and picked up seafood Alfredo, garlic bread, and Caesar salad. There's more than enough for two, and it just needs a couple of minutes in the nuker."

Ellie raised an eyebrow. "Sounds like a special occasion."

"It is, sort of. Twink and I are celebrating."

"Celebrating what?"

"I'll tell you while we eat." Viv took a step farther into the hall. "We can do it here or at your place."

"It'll take me a while to get into something comfortable. You and Mr. T come to us. The door will be open. You know where to find the plates and stuff."

"Great. We'll see you in five."

She and her boy continued up another flight; then Ellie unlocked the door. All she wanted was a pair of sweats, a snuggly sweater, and a good dinner. Lucky for her, Viv had the last part under control.

Inside, she hung her parka in the closet and toed off her boots while Rudy raced down the hall. "Don't let me disturb you," she said when she entered the bedroom and saw her boy frantically rubbing himself on the spread.

He stopped to look at her. *"My fur's wet and I'm still freezin' my missing nuts off. I could use a good rubdown with a nice warm towel right about now."*

"Hang on while I change. There's a towel with your name on it sitting on the warming bar in the bathroom. Then we have to get ready for company."

Ellie peeled off her clothes, left on her black silk leggings, and slipped into her most comfortable fleece cover-up. Then she slid her feet into her bunny slippers. Fashion wasn't on the menu for the evening.

"I'll finish up in the bathroom and be right back," she said to Rudy.

Walking to the sink, she studied herself in the mirror and ran her fingers through her curls. She'd found a hair salon that was closer to home and still had room for Saturday appointments. Her initial visit was scheduled for tomorrow, and she hoped the name of the salon, Serendipity, would match her first time there, because it was serendipitous that she'd have a fresh cut for the party. If not, her mother would spend the entire night ragging her about her too long and unruly hair.

After removing what little remained of her makeup, she washed her face, dried off with the towel from the heated bar, and hung a new one in its place. Then she returned to the bedroom. "Here you go." She sat on the bed and Rudy scooted to join her. "Relax and let me do my thing."

After giving him a brisk rubdown, he rolled over so she could reach his belly.

"Ahh, that's more like it," he moaned, squirming on his back while she scratched. *"Yeah, yeah. That's the spot."*

When she heard the front door open, Ellie wrapped him in the towel and cuddled him in her arms. "I'm sorry you got frozen. Unless the weather report says it'll be warm, you'll wear a sweater from here on out." She nuzzled her nose in his neck. "I don't want you to get sick or anything."

"No worries there," he said, licking her cheek. *"Like I keep telling you, nothin' bad's gonna happen to us. We're together for the long haul."*

"I hope you mean that, because after Sam realizes what I've been doing you may be the only man in my life for quite a while."

He wriggled out of her arms and did a full-body shake. *"You still nervous about him finding out that you're helping Bobbi-Rob and Bitsy?"*

"He won't be mad about Bitsy, because he isn't going to understand the whole Madame Orzo thing. But he'll be furious if he figures out I'm still lending Rob a hand, even though I'm doing it as an aside." She stood and smoothed her sweater over her hips. "Ready to have dinner and spend some time with Mr. T?"

Rudy hopped off the bed and yawned. *"Try to make it an early night. I need my beauty sleep."* He skittered in front of her and rested his front paws on her knees. *"I just thought of something. Maybe you should take me to the groomer for tomorrow night, too. You never know who we might meet at the shindig. The last thing I need is Georgette complaining about my looks."*

Always amazed at the way she and her yorkiepoo tied into each other, she said, "I'm sure it's too late to get a grooming appointment, but don't worry. I'll give you a good brushing and trim you up a little. That should do the trick."

"Ah, not so fast with the scissors. I'm not sure I want you anywhere near me with the latest in murder weapons."

"Dinner's on the table," yelled Vivian before Ellie could answer. "Hurry it up."

"We'll discuss your concerns later. Now come on. Viv says she's celebrating. I can't wait to find out what's up."

They walked into the kitchen and she blinked. Candles burned on the table; her real dishes, not the paper plates she used when she and Viv shared a meal, sat on proper place mats; and wineglasses, not plastic cups, glistened.

"Wow, this looks great. Did you win the lottery?"

Viv brought white take-out containers to the table using potholders, a definite sign that the meal was hot and ready to eat. "Not the lottery, but it's good. I won't know for sure for about a month." She sat down and poured champagne in their glasses.

"Give me a second to make Rudy's dinner." Ellie aimed for the pantry and took out her boy's dry food and dish. "Does Mr. T want a nibble?"

"Darn straight I do," said the Jack Russell from his seat on Rudy's fluff mat.

"I already fed him, but I'm sure he'd eat something," Viv replied without hearing her dog's comment.

Ellie grabbed the can of Grammy's Pot Pie from the fridge, added two tablespoons of it to the dry food, and made an extra half portion of Rudy's gourmet dinner. She parceled out the meal and set their plates on the floor side by side. Twink and her boy were never aggressive about their food. They knew they'd get fed plenty of whatever they needed.

Once the dogs began to eat, she sat and shook out her cloth napkin. "Before we talk about your good fortune, I have to ask: Where's your current squeeze?"

"Dr. Dave's at some seminar on difficult canine-labor situations. Apparently there are some small breeds that have to be delivered by a vet. He wants to cover all the bases with the dogs he cares for."

"Have you already told him your big news?"

"I did, and he knows I'm celebrating with you. He's taking me to a fancy restaurant for dinner tomorrow night." Viv raised her champagne-filled glass. "Now here's to me."

"First tell me—what are we celebrating?"

"I got a promotion. A big promotion."

"Then congratulations are in order." They touched glasses and sipped the bubbly. "Now, dish. What's the job?"

Viv scooped a serving of the seafood Alfredo on her plate, then helped herself to the salad. "So you know I'm a securities research analyst?"

"Well, I know you do something with finances at Harrison Amero, but I've never quite understood what." Ellie served herself the Alfredo and salad. "It sounds confusing."

"It's not if you know what you're doing," Viv answered, chewing her pasta. After swallowing, she added, "Since H and A is a global bank, more than cash is involved. In my new position, I'll be a trader."

"Well, that certainly tells me a lot," said Ellie. She took another slug of champagne. "Let's get to something I can understand. How much was the raise?"

Viv grinned. "That's the good part. My base is two hundred thousand, but I could make more. It all depends on how well I carry out the role."

Ellie gulped down the mouthful of salad she was chewing. "Good grief, Viv. That's like a—a—twenty-five percent raise."

"You betcha it is. And I'm worth it."

They continued discussing Viv's plans, including a spa vacation to somewhere warm and a splurge at her latest favorite online site for shopping.

Ellie cleared the table and headed for the fridge

while her friend finished off the bottle of champagne. "Ready for some Caramel Cone, or are you stuffed?"

"I'm stuffed, but I'll take a couple of spoonfuls."

She retrieved their used cartons from the freezer and passed Viv hers. Sitting down, Ellie scooped up a spoonful of the creamy caramel-and-chocolate treat. "So, when exactly do you start this new position?"

"Bright and early Monday morning. I can't begin to tell you how grateful I am that you've been walking Mr. T for free all this time. Now that I got this huge raise, I can afford to pay you, so give me a number and I'll write you a check tonight."

Ellie opened and closed her mouth. "Vivian, we're friends. I'd bring T with Rudy even if I wasn't a professional walker. It's no problem taking him along and—"

"Yeah, yeah, I get it. You're my best friend, too, but I don't want to take advantage of you."

"Now you're being ridiculous. Taking advantage is what best friends do." Ellie got teary-eyed. "I don't have a sister, but if I could choose one, she'd be you." She sniffed and dabbed her nose with the napkin. "Now look what you've done."

"Hey, stop, okay." Vivian sniffed, too, then wiped away a tear. "I feel the same."

Ellie retrieved a couple of tissues from a box on the counter, passed one to Viv, and blew her own nose. "Speaking of sisters, have you heard anything more from Arlene?"

"Just this morning. She picked a wedding date for this July, and I'm invited to the house. It's supposed to be a huge deal, but I'm not sure I want to go."

"You're not sure you want to go to a huge deal in the Hamptons? Are you kidding? The way I understand it, that's the place to be in the summer. Mingling with stars, going to parties, sunning on the beach . . . I thought it was the dream of all the society wannabes of Manhattan."

"So I've heard, but—" Viv took a last spoon of ice cream, capped the carton, and snapped her fingers. "I know how I can repay you for walking Mr. T. Be my plus one at my sister's wedding."

Ellie gulped. "Me?"

"I know you've been there with Georgette."

"But what about Dr. Dave? Shouldn't he be your plus one?"

"Things got settled today. Dave is already scheduled to go to some big conference in San Diego. He wanted to take me along, but I'd already talked to Arlene so . . . Where did you go when you went with your mom?"

"I have no idea. It was years ago. And she hasn't been since she met Stanley. Now that they're married and he's in a wheelchair . . . Are you sure I'd be welcome?"

"According to my ditzy sister, every friend and family member she has will be there, and their dogs, too. I doubt she'll even know you're in the house."

"In her house?"

"Yes, hers. It's the one she and Myron lived in most of the time, and the only one she kept after he died. The summer cottage has five bedrooms and six bathrooms, a two-story guesthouse, and a fabulous view of the Atlantic."

Viv stopped to take a breath, then went on. "She said I can bring a plus one, and since I can't bring Dave, my plus one will be you. T and Rudy can come too. They'll have a ball."

"Viv, I—"

"If you don't want to stay with sis, she's putting the overflow up at Montauk Manor. It's a beautiful Tudor-style hotel with a fabulous spa on the premises. And they're dog-friendly, too." She put her hands together in prayer. "Please say you'll come with. It'll be my treat."

"But I don't have anyone to take over walking my charges."

"It's six months away. I'm sure you'll find an assistant by then." Viv returned her ice cream to the fridge, then began loading the dishwasher. "I'll call Arlene tomorrow and tell her we'll be there."

"I can't think that far ahead. Right now, the only thing on my mind is Mother's party."

Viv dried her hands on a dish towel. "I forgot about that big event. Did Detective Darling agree to be your escort?"

"I haven't the faintest idea. I asked him, but he never—" Ellie heaved a sigh. "Let's face it—I'm not on Sam Ryder's good list at the moment."

"So you think he'll blow you off?"

"Um, well—"

A loud knock interrupted her. "Who could that be?"

Chapter 15

Ellie opened the door and Sam breathed a sigh of relief. Seeing her made his trek through the blizzard worth every second of the slipping, sliding, and misery he'd endured for the past hour and a half.

"What in the world . . ." She stepped aside to let him in.

He held out a brown paper bag. "You mind taking this? I'm kind of strapped here."

When she did as he asked, he marched into the front hall and down to the kitchen, where he dropped his gym bag on the floor, hung a plastic garment bag on the refrigerator door, and set a six-pack of Bud Light on the table. Then he tugged off his snow-covered leather jacket and took it to the sink. After wiping it down with a handful of paper towels, he draped it across the back of a chair.

"Hello to you, too," said Vivian, who had propped herself against the counter to watch the show.

Surprised that he hadn't noticed her, he said, "Oh, hey, Viv. I didn't see you there. Sorry."

"Looks like you've been busy."

He spotted the Mama Bella sack on the counter

and bit back a curse. He was cold, wet, and thoroughly pissed. Once he'd found parking, he'd carried the tux, beer, food, and enough baggage to weigh down a camel at least four blocks in a near-blinding snowstorm. "I wanted to surprise Ellie with dinner, but I see you've already eaten." He sat and ran his fingers through his wet hair. "What I brought is probably cold by now anyway."

"That was so nice of you." Ellie laid a hand on his shoulder. "Why didn't you call?"

"Then it wouldn't have been a surprise." He entwined his frozen fingers with her warm ones. "The hard part was the snow. It made traveling hell. After I circled the block for an hour, I decided to use a parking garage on Lex, which will probably cost me a fortune. I had to walk through the storm lugging all this crap and—"

She nodded at the hanging bag. "What's in there?"

"A monkey suit. For tomorrow night."

"Oh, Sam." Ellie's eyes welled with tears. "Why didn't you tell me?"

Viv grinned. "Come on, T. Looks like we've just become a third wheel. I think it's time for a quick slosh outside, then bed." She walked to Ellie and gave her a hug. "I'm sure you two have things to discuss." Mr. T trotted to her side. "See you later?"

"Sunday maybe?" said Ellie, sniffing.

"In the afternoon," Sam added.

Vivian waggled a good-bye wave. "Have a great night."

Sam read Ellie's weepy expression and opened his arms. When she sat on his lap, he hugged her tight, too embarrassed to admit she felt good, damn good. So good, in fact, it was worth the trudge through the snow. "What are you crying about?"

"I'm— It's— I— That party is going to be sheer misery for me, so I can imagine how you'll feel. Why didn't you tell me you were willing to be my escort?"

He ran a palm down her damp cheek. "I just decided this afternoon, and since I wanted to surprise you with dinner . . . Well, I guess I thought to surprise you with that, too."

"You must be starving." She swiped a tear and stood. "I can nuke a plate for you. What did you bring, anyway?"

"Italian. But it looks like I wasn't the only one with that bright idea."

She took his carryout bag and six-pack to the counter. "Trust me, all Italian food is a bright idea." Digging in the sack, she opened the foil-wrapped package first. "Mmm. Garlic bread. Smells great." She pulled out a container. "Chicken piccata. Yum." Then she took out the last carton. "And penne. Very nice, Detective."

She took a plate from the cupboard, and Sam got a good look at her long legs, encased in some kind of stretchy black fabric. Checking her out from bottom to top, he enjoyed every generous curve, including the fact that she wasn't wearing a bra. No doubt about it, he was one lucky guy.

She put the food-filled plate in the microwave and set the timer. "It'll just take a minute. Vivian and I drank all the champagne, but I see you brought your own brand of high-class booze."

"Champagne? What was the occasion?"

"Viv got a big promotion. I'll tell you about it later. You ready for a drink?"

"If you don't mind."

"Of course not. And it's still cold, too."

He continued to watch her as she removed a Bud from the carton, then put the rest of the beer in the fridge. After opening the bottle, she brought it to the table and sat across from him.

"Did something happen today that I should know about?" Ellie asked. "Something professional?"

The microwave dinged and he raised a hand. "Stay put. I'll get it." He retrieved his dinner and found a knife and fork in the drawer, using the time to think of an answer to her question. She was probably asking about the Carmella Sunday case, but he had no right to tell her it was stalled, especially since he had yet to talk to the DA about the options.

He'd called and left a message while the rental shop tailor was hemming his suit pants, but the attorney had been in court. He had an idea where they should go from here, but until he heard from the records department . . .

Back at the table, he took a long pull on his beer, then dug into his dinner. "Sure you don't want some? It's pretty good."

"I'm fine. Thanks." She fiddled with a napkin. "Sam, what are you really doing here?"

Hoping he could get her to relax, he continued to eat. "Isn't that obvious? You said you needed an escort for tomorrow night, and the weather sucks. Since everyone was leaving the station before the storm screwed up the streets, I figured I might as well get that tux, find dinner, and keep you company for the night." He took another swig of beer. "No big deal."

"But you've been involved in this case—uh—several cases—for a couple of weeks now. I can't believe you'd suddenly put on the brakes because of a little snow."

"A *little* snow? Have you looked outside lately?"

She glanced at her frosted kitchen window. "Okay, I get the message, but still, why are you on downtime?"

"I'm not, really. I'm waiting to hear from the records department." As soon as he said the words, Sam knew he'd made a mistake. "Besides, my shift is over at midnight."

She rubbed her nose. "The records department?"

"And I'll be off duty in about three hours."

"Is the records department even open this late?"

"It's supposed to be, but who knows?" He leaned back in his chair, thinking of a way to veer off track. "Did I tell you Vince and Natalie were driving to south Jersey for the weekend?"

"Stop changing the subject and tell me exactly what's going on."

"Let's just say I've decided to take a break for the next twenty-four hours."

Ellie rolled her eyes. "That is such a crock of crap."

Instead of commenting, he tucked into the chicken. He wasn't looking forward to taking her to Georgette's over-the-top party, but it seemed important to her. If he couldn't reach the DA, and he had no idea when records would come up with his requested information, he might as well keep an eye on Ellie, make sure she didn't snoop and make her happy—hell, make them both happy—at the same time.

He swallowed the last of his food. "Why does the reason I'm here matter?"

She folded her arms, her face set in "wait for it" mode. Seconds passed while he drained the beer bottle and wiped his mouth with his napkin. Finally, he pushed away from the table and took his plate to the sink.

"By the way, did I say I was here for the night?"

"You know you're welcome to crash anytime."

He walked to her chair and took her hands, drawing her to a stand. "Yeah. So, now that I'm here, you got any idea how we can make the most of the evening?" He leaned forward and kissed the tip of her nose, trailing his fingers along her ribs until they cupped her breast. "I'm open to suggestions."

Ellie melted at his touch. It had been a while since they'd been intimate. She couldn't even remember the last time she'd had him all to herself for an entire night.

He ground his pelvis against her and she grinned. "Feels to me like you already have a few ideas of your own."

"Hey. I'm still here, and I need an out before you two go at it like humpin' hamsters."

Guilt-ridden, she pulled back. She hadn't thought about her boy once since Sam walked through the door. "I forgot. Rudy needs his nightly walk. Just let me get my boots and coat. It'll only take a couple of minutes."

"That's what you think." Rudy trotted to her side and put his paws on her calf. *"It might take me a while to pick the right spot and do big business. It could take so long that Detective Demento will get smart and go to his own home—where he belongs."*

Glancing down, Sam stepped back. "Want me to take him?"

Not sure that she'd heard right, Ellie thunked the heel of her hand against the side of her head. "Hang on—I'm having an out-of-body experience. I thought someone just said they were willing to take Rudy out all by themselves."

Sam shrugged. "I could, if he'd let me. Besides, you look all nice and warm, and I still have my shoes on. How bad can it be?"

"Pretty bad, if I have anything to say about it."

"Okay, but he might take a while," she warned.

"Not a problem. I'm tough." Sam took his jacket off the chair and put it on. "I'll do it."

Ellie went to the hall closet with both boys trailing

behind. After pulling Rudy's sweater off the top shelf, she squatted and slipped it over his head and front paws. Then she attached the leash to his collar. "You be good. It's freezing out, and I don't want either of you to get sick."

"A man's gotta do what a man's gotta do," Rudy said with a smug grin.

"Is he ready?" asked Sam, tugging on his gloves.

"I think so, but are you?" She poked around the closet until she found a long woolen scarf. After wrapping it around Sam's neck, she said, "There. That should help you keep warm. And I'm sure you'll only have to take him to the corner and back. Isn't that right, Rudy?"

"Maybe yes, maybe no. We'll find out."

She passed Sam the leash. "You sure you'll be all right?"

"It's one pint-sized pooch. How bad can it be?"

Ellie bit back a laugh. "Okay, be safe."

He opened the door, cupped her chin in his hand, and gave her a lingering kiss. "While I'm gone, why don't you get comfortable?"

Smiling, she closed the door, but left it unlocked. Sam still had the keys she'd given him a couple of months back, but this wasn't an emergency situation. She finished loading the dishwasher and turned it on, shut off the kitchen light, and picked up his gym bag. After clicking the hall overhead on, she took the bag to her bedroom, tucked it in a corner, and changed into one of the silk sleep shirts Sam had given her for Christmas. This one was teal blue—according to Sam, the same color as her eyes—with a row of easy-to-open buttons running down the front.

She brushed her teeth, turned on the night-light in the guest room, and pulled down the covers on the double bed. Rudy spent the night here whenever Sam stayed over, and she wanted him to be cozy. She even exchanged pillows, giving him the one he slept on from her bed so he'd be happy.

By the time she'd finished, Sam stood in the bedroom doorway, his shoes and jacket already off and his own shirt unbuttoned.

"Hey," he said, gazing at her through the dim light.

"Hey, yourself." She sat on the mattress and leaned back. "Time for sleep."

She felt the touch of his hands from across the room. "Give me a minute. I'll be right back."

"I bet he's in the bathroom, using that toothbrush you bought him, and doin' all that man stuff," came Rudy's voice from the side of the bed.

"What are you doing in here?"

"Me? Just reportin' my business. I did—"

Scrunching her nose, Ellie raised a hand. "Believe me, I don't want a blow-by-blow report."

"Okay, okay." He licked her fingers. *"Guess I'll see you in the morning."*

She ruffled his ears. "But not too early." Bending down, she kissed the top of his head. "Good night."

Rudy ambled out and Sam walked in, gazing at the dog as he passed. "I'm glad he knows his place."

"Ha!" she said, snuggling next to him when he settled on the mattress. "You're only in his spot right now because he's nice enough to allow you there."

Sam curled her in his arms. "That's what he thinks. This spot is mine, sweetheart."

On a normal night, that comment would have started a good fifteen minutes of teasing banter on the pluses of owning a dog. Tonight, all Ellie wanted was the man beside her. "Let's not discuss Rudy, or the records room, or even the snow. You're here for the first time in a couple of weeks and I'm looking forward to a night full of—"

He blocked the rest of the sentence with a long kiss that warmed her to her core. In seconds, he snaked one hand around her from underneath while he began undoing buttons with the other. Then he palmed a nipple and bit at her lower lip. "Shh. This is all we need."

A moment later, Ellie was so lost in sensation she couldn't even tell him he was right.

"Psst. Hey, you awake yet?"

The familiar voice rolled around Ellie's brain like dried peas in a can. Groaning, she opened one eye. "There is no need to shout," she whispered. "My hearing is fine."

Rudy inched his paws onto the mattress and licked her nose. *"Just checkin'. Detective Doofus is sleepin' like a rock, so I thought you might be, too."*

As if proving her boy's point, Sam took that moment to give a gentle snore.

"See what I mean? He sounds like the garbage truck when it roars up to the building at five in the morning."

"He does not." She yawned. "What do you want?"

"Now there's a genius question. What do I usually want when I get you up in the a.m.?"

He wanted his morning nibble and a trip outside, but she refused to play his baiting game. "What time is it?"

"Beats me." He gave a doggie shrug. *"But the sun's been up for a while. I think it stopped snowing, but I couldn't see out the window, so it's hard to tell."*

She opened both eyes and glanced at her bedside clock. Rudy had given her about an hour and a half of extra sleep time—not bad for a Saturday morning. "It's eight, so you did good. Can you hang on while I get dressed?"

"Sure. I'll wait in the kitchen, in case you and the dopey dick want to do the humpin' hamster thing again."

Ellie *tsk*ed. "Sometimes you are so gross."

Sam turned and wrapped an arm around her from behind. "Who are you talking to?" He moved close and spooned himself against her back, then kissed his way from her nape to her ear. "If it's me, and you're looking for an instant replay of last night, the answer is hell, yes."

"Oh, brother. See what I mean?" Rudy snorted as he trotted out of the bedroom.

Ellie waited until her boy left, then wriggled her bottom.

Sam gathered her in his arms. "You okay with this?"

"I'm always okay with this." She turned and he tucked a leg between her knees. "And that too," she said when his morning erection pressed against her pelvis.

He rolled over on top of her and she struggled to reach her nightstand drawer. "Condom time," she said, finding the box and ripping open a foil packet.

"You do the honors," said Sam as his mouth slid to her breast. "I'm busy."

She did as he asked, and he entered her in one sure thrust. Her fingers clutched his muscled arms and traveled down his back to hold him as he moved inside her. She nestled her nose in his shoulder as he rocked her to a fast and tender orgasm, then collapsed on top of her with a sigh of satisfaction.

"Good morning," he muttered, a smile in his voice.

She threaded her fingers through his thick blond hair. "Same to you."

"I suppose your dog has to go out?"

"You know he does."

He glanced at the frosted windowpane. "I'm happy to come along, provided we can find a place that's open for breakfast."

"The Bagel Bin is usually open no matter the weather. Lox and a schmeer would be perfect."

He stretched. "Do we have time for a quick shower first?"

"I have time, but only if there's no nonsense, like there was a few weeks ago."

"Has it been that long?" He kissed her ear. "I forget. What happened last time?"

"You know exactly what happened." She swung her legs over the side of the bed. Rudy could wait, but he'd been good so she didn't want it to be for long. "Now promise to keep your hands to yourself. Just soap and rinse, okay?"

"You take all the fun out of everything." Sam situated himself next to her, grinning. His face was creased from sleep, his hair stuck up at all angles, and his eyes sparkled from the great morning wake-up call. "I'll go in first and get the shower started."

Ellie watched him leave, admiring his sculpted backside, the breadth of his shoulders, his trim waist and taut butt. He was different from her ex in every way imaginable, a point for which she would be forever grateful. The D had shown little care for her feelings, while Sam never had a climax until she reached one first. And he always seemed in tune with what she needed to make the act special.

Thinking happy thoughts, she gathered fresh underthings, jeans, and a heavy red sweater, and came up with a plan. If Sam trekked to the Bagel Bin and picked up breakfast while she took Rudy around the block, that would save some time.

She could make her hair appointment, and he could check in with the station. After that, they'd be free.

Thirty minutes later, Ellie, Sam, and Rudy were out the door. "Wow, I don't believe it," she said, studying the building's front stoop. "Mr. Denopolis already cleared the porch and threw on salt. Someone from the tenants' association must have reamed him about the building's upkeep."

"Are you saying this doesn't happen with every snowfall?" Sam asked, holding her hand to guide her down the stairs.

"Hah! You're kidding, right?" She scanned the sidewalk, then took a look at Rudy, who was already lifting a leg on the side of the porch. "But I'm thinking salt might not be good for Rudy's paws. Maybe I should buy him boots."

"Cross that off your to-do list right now." Rudy gave a head-to-tail shake. *"And don't bring it up again, or you'll be sorry."*

"I think he'd look adorable in shiny red booties, don't you?" she continued, ignoring her boy's sassy comment.

They held hands as they walked to the corner. "Beats me, but knowing what a grump he is, I doubt he'll like it," said Sam.

"For once the clown is right."

"You remember Flora Steinman, don't you?"

"The older woman with that snooty little dog you handled at the Javits Center a few months back?"

"That's the one. Flora's housekeeper told me they were ordering a set for Lulu from a woman who specializes in designer doggie duds. And since Lulu's coat matches Rudy's, it might be nice if he had a set, too. Adorable, really."

"Well, why didn't you say so?"

"Sorry, but 'adorable' is not a word I'd used to describe your dog," said Sam, smiling.

"Me neither, but if I could dress like my doll baby—"

Stopping at the corner, they waited for a convoy of city trucks to pass. The neighborhood was a beehive of activity. Plows had come by and shoved the snow into piles of glistening white against the parked cars. People were now on the streets in force, clearing the sidewalks, tossing salt and chemical deicer, and shoveling their vehicles out from under the accumulated snow.

She loved the look and smell of a fresh snowfall, even if it would only last for a day before the fluffy stuff turned dingy with trash and dog urine. By Monday, the snow would be pushed into slushy mounds on the corners, covered in the accumulated filth of a huge city. She'd never actually played in the snow or made a snowman, but she imagined it would be nice to go somewhere like Vermont or upstate next winter, maybe for Christmas, so she and Sam could take their first joint vacation.

"I think snow is wonderful. It's like waking up to a magic kingdom, all clean and white and fresh."

Sam scrunched his forehead. "If you ask me, it's only good for one thing. A lot of these places are closed, so the robbery count goes down, as does the number of citizens who have physical altercations. But fender benders go on the rise, so it evens out."

"Do you always have to look at everything that takes place in this city in terms of how it might relate to a crime? That is so jaded."

"Somebody has to, and I decided ten years ago it would be me. My life is no picnic, babe, and you've been great at not letting it get you down. A lot better than Carol—" He raised his face to the cloudless sky and blew out a breath, then gazed into her eyes. "A lot better than most of the women I know."

"I can smell the schmaltz from here."

Ellie stepped aside to make room for people ready to cross the street. "Oh, Sam, that's so sweet. It could even be the nicest thing you've ever said to me."

Leaning forward, he kissed the tear she hadn't realized she'd shed. "You deserve someone who always says sweet things to you, Ellie. And I want that someone to be me."

The warmth of his words spread straight to her toes. She opened her mouth to tell him so, but he shook his head. "We can talk about it later. Right now, I just want to say one thing."

"Well, say it fast, because my paws are so cold they're stickin' to the cement."

Sam's sly grin told her the tender moment had passed. "Paying the parking garage a week's salary is worth it, compared to what I might have had to do if I'd parked on the street."

She slugged him in the shoulder. "You are such a romantic."

"You bet I am. Here's where we split up, correct?"

"Get movin', buster, before my tail freezes off."

Ellie was cold, too, but in a good way, and the morning had turned bright, even with Rudy's complaints. The sun was shining, the sky was a brilliant blue, and her world felt crisp and clean. "Correct. You go to the Bagel Bin to pick up breakfast while I finish the walk, go back to the apartment, and start the coffee."

"And I'll bring everything home, including enough bagels for tomorrow morning." He gave her a quick kiss good-bye and headed across the street.

Things couldn't be better. Sam had given her the best of all compliments. He'd compared her to Carolanne and she'd won. Since they rarely mentioned their ex-spouses, it was a big step. Now it was her turn to tell him how much happier she was with him than she'd been with the dickhead.

Thinking about what she would say, and when, she ignored Rudy's continued commentary, bought a newspaper with the spare change she found in her jacket pocket, and led her boy home.

In the apartment, Ellie hung up their snow gear, and Rudy followed her into the kitchen, where she mixed his morning nibble and set it on his mat. "Were you serious when you said you'd wear boots if Lulu wore them?"

He pulled his muzzle out of the bowl. *"If it'll get Lulu warm for my form, darn right I will."*

"I wouldn't go that far, but the two of you would look cute walking side by side wearing them. Maybe we should check with Miss Pickypants to see if she would mind, or just ask Flora to order two sets."

She filled the carafe with water and poured it in the coffeemaker, then measured the whole beans of her favorite dark roast into the grinder and let it spin. After she filled the basket and turned on the coffeemaker, she pulled her homemade caramel sauce and her latest local find—fat-free half-and-half—out of the fridge.

"The coffee will be ready in a couple of minutes. Do you want anything before I make a Caramel Bliss and start reading the paper?"

"A Dingo bone might be nice." Rudy sat at her feet. *"I believe I deserve it for lettin' you and Detective Doofus sleep in this morning."*

"I wish you wouldn't call him that. It's so insulting. But you were a good boy, so the rawhide chew is fine." She took the requested treat from the cupboard and tossed it in his direction. "There—now stay busy with that and let me catch up on the news."

A minute later, she poured steaming coffee into her favorite cup, added caramel sauce, the half-and-half, and a blue packet of sweetener. After taking her drink to the table, she opened the newspaper.

"What are you hopin' to find in that rag?" Rudy asked, sitting on the fluff mat with the bone between his paws.

She took a long swallow of coffee. "I'm hoping there'll be something miraculous about Rob and the murder, like how the real killer walked into one of the precincts and confessed."

"You do realize that's yesterday's paper you're reading."

She scanned the date printed on the header. "Well, shoot. And Sam probably would have told me if the real killer had confessed."

"Maybe yes, maybe no. It's hard tellin' with Detective Doo—er—Ryder."

"He would, especially since he knows I believe Rob is innocent." She took another sip of coffee. "He's been exemplary since he arrived last night." She glanced at the clock on her microwave. "Where do you think he is, by the way?"

Instead of answering, Rudy gnawed on his bone.

Ellie drummed her fingers on the tabletop. "It's been almost an hour since we left him at the corner."

"Maybe he got lost."

She took a swallow of her Caramel Bliss. "He couldn't be lost. The Bagel Bin is only two blocks up the street. You can practically see it from our front stoop."

"Stranger things have happened. He coulda got hit by a snowplow."

"That's a terrible thing to say."

"Okay, so maybe he shot himself in the foot."

"That's not funny. You can dream all you want, but the detective is in our life to stay."

Still, Rudy's silly comments got her thinking. When he stayed the night, Sam always hung his gun and body holster on the back of a kitchen chair, but he wore it whenever he went out, even if he was off duty. Though she hadn't seen him put it on before they left, it was gone, so she was certain he was wearing it now.

A siren sounded in the distance and her heart jumped. She took another gulp of coffee and the siren's wail grew louder. Standing, she again tugged her boots on and went into the front closet to get her coat, hat, and gloves.

Rudy followed her into the hall. *"Hey, where you goin'?"*

"That siren is driving me nuts, and I'm worried about Sam. I'm going to check outside."

"It's freezin' out there. Maybe the regular shop was closed, so he went lookin' for another one."

"Something's wrong. I can feel it." She jammed her knit hat over her curls and opened the door. "Stay here and be good. I'll be back as soon as I find him."

Chapter 16

Sam sauntered up the street, dodging the snow flying from shovels and, in one instance, a snowblower gone wild. As in most areas of the city, the people who were taking care of the sidewalks and stoops were a talkative bunch, calling out to complain about the lousy weather and to wish their neighbors well. Funny how something like a blizzard could bring out the best in folks.

He hated the snow, but Ellie seemed to love it, which meant he had to get used to it. Next thing, she'd want to take a walk in Central Park, where she'd probably whack him with a snowball. But it was a price he was willing to pay to keep her happy.

Stopping at the corner, he speed-dialed the records department, but all he got was a recording. At this rate, it would be a week before he received the info he needed on the judge who'd handed down a sentence in Carmella Sunday's final arrest. He was working on a hunch, but it was all he had until he brainstormed with Vince.

A block later, he arrived at the Bagel Bin, pleased to find it open for business. Out of habit, he took a look through the front window before he entered. It was then that he spotted the cashier, standing behind the register with his hands in the air.

Taking a step back, he again peered inside and got a better look at the man on the customer side of the counter—a lanky guy wearing a stocking cap and dark clothes, with his gun raised level with the clerk.

His heart shifted into overdrive. So much for blizzards bringing out the best in people. They could also bring out the worst. Breaking into a sweat, he speed-dialed and reported a Code 10, asking for backup. Then he prepared to do his job.

Raising his Glock, he stepped through the doorway, ducked to one knee, and pulled a table over for cover. The second he did, the clerk disappeared behind the counter.

"Police! Freeze!"

The gunman spun around and fired, but the shot went wild.

"Drop the gun!"

The kid stared him down, the weapon still in his hand.

Sam had no choice. He aimed low and fired, hitting the boy in his right leg. Screaming, the punk fell to the floor, and his gun skittered a few feet away.

It was then that every drop of air left Sam's body in a single rush of breath. He'd been in this situation before, but always with a fellow officer. On his own, and without backup, he had to follow proper procedure step by careful step.

Standing, he kept his gun trained on the downed shooter. His gut clenched when he saw the gunman was a boy of no more than seventeen. Hell, the kid should have been home digging his dad's car out of the snow, or shoveling walks to make a buck. Not doing this sort of thing.

Still clutching his lower leg, the boy moaned. Sam took a step closer and kicked the gun farther away. Sirens sounded in the distance and relief filled his senses.

The clerk rose from his hiding place, his eyes wide with panic. Sam gave a nod. "You okay?"

"Yeah. So you got him?"

"Take a look."

Inching over the counter, the shopkeeper stared at his assailant. "That's a lotta blood. Is he going to make it?"

The sirens grew louder, almost drowning out the clerk's voice, and Sam's blood pressure dropped a notch. "Best guess is yes."

"He's a kid. Where'd he get that gun?"

"We'll run a trace, but I doubt anything will turn up. Help's almost here. Hang tight until an officer comes in and takes your statement. Understand?"

"Yeah, yeah. Sure. Whatever you say."

The kid moaned again. "I need a doctor. I'm bleedin' here."

The sirens' screams blasted into the store; blue lights flashing from the street pulsed through the window. Sam set his lips in a grim line and stared at the boy.

"You have the right to remain silent. Anything you say can and will be used against you."

"Fuck off, buddy. I want a doc."

Three officers stepped into the shop, guns ready. Sam lowered his weapon and pulled out his shield. It was going to be a long morning.

Sam stared through the sea of blue crowding the Bagel Bin. The crime scene tech team had already found and bagged the bullet fired by the gunman, and Miles and Stanley, the detectives in charge, were taking the deli clerk's statement and talking to the two bakers who'd been working in the kitchen when the robbery began. Aside from waiting for his heart rate to return to normal, there wasn't a lot more he needed to do.

Just then, the patrolman covering the front door answered his radio and the voice of Frank Landon, the officer out front in charge of crowd control, came across loud and clear.

"There's a woman out here calls herself Engleman, Ellen Elizabeth. Says she needs to talk with Ryder ASAP. Claims she and him are in a personal relationship, and she won't leave until she sees him."

Sipkovitz turned and grinned, probably because he knew everyone in the store had heard the story. "You want to talk to a woman name's Engleman, Ellen Elizabeth? According to Landon, she says you two are—involved." He let the last word hang, along with the invisible finger quotes.

Sam stood and nodded, avoiding the snickers of the other officers. "Tell him to let her through." Then he held up a hand. There was blood on the floor and a spatter against the base of the counter. Ellie had seen a bloody crime scene before—just last week, in fact—but that didn't mean she needed to see this mess.

"Hang on. Tell him I'm coming out, and then let Stanley or Miles know I'll be back." Steeling himself for a scene, he heaved a breath. Meeting with his "bad penny" was going to be tougher than that appointment he'd have to keep with the department shrink because of the shooting.

He stepped outside and spotted Ellie. Except for a patch of pink on each cheek, her complexion was as white as the new-fallen snow. Chewing on a thumbnail, she stood staring at the door as if waiting for her executioner. The color in her eyes deepened when their gazes locked, and she gave him a thousand-watt smile.

He couldn't think what to do, so she made the decision for him. Throwing herself into his arms, she squeezed him so tight the air rushed from his lungs in one huge gasp.

"Hey, it's okay. I'm fine," he muttered, patting her back. Damn, but he was useless. Carolanne hadn't ever shown one minute of worry over him, even when he'd been nicked in a gang sting a few years back. Except for comforting his mother and sisters after his dad died, he'd never had to make a woman feel cared for. What the hell else was he supposed to say?

Ellie's shoulders shook, and he sighed. Her tears always threw him a curve, especially when she cried because she was relieved or happy. Why the hell couldn't women wear signs when they sobbed? Something like: HAPPY TEARS, NO NEED TO WORRY Or: MISERABLE. COMFORT ME, PLEASE.

"What can I do to make this better?" he asked, positive it was a dumb question.

"I—I'm—I—" She pulled back and rubbed her nose in her palm. After heaving a breath, she gazed up at him with a tremulous smile on her beautiful face. "You've already made it better, just by being here and not in the ambulance that pulled away a couple of minutes ago."

He led her out of the path of the crime technicians tromping out of the Bagel Bin, and again held her in his arms. "What are you doing here? I thought you were supposed to wait for me in the apartment."

"I was. I walked Rudy, made coffee, the whole nine yards. When I heard the sirens I knew—I just knew you were in trouble, so I threw on boots and a jacket and came straight here."

She sniffed and shivered, and he rested his chin on top of her head. "You want me to believe you heard the sirens and knew I was in a jam."

"It's true. You can ask—" She shook her head. "Just believe me, okay?"

"Sure, sure, fine." Anything to calm her down. "Did Landon tell you what happened?"

"Sort of. But someone in the crowd said that shots were fired, so I was a bit . . . distracted by the time I got to him."

"You thought I was hit?"

"I didn't know for sure, and Landon wouldn't say. When I saw the boy on the gurney, I almost collapsed. A thousand things ran through my mind. If you were the one shot, you'd have been taken out first, but you weren't, which meant you were okay or you were—you might have been—"

She started to cry all over again, and he cradled her against his chest. Landon grinned and he tossed the guy a "Women. Who the hell can understand them?" kind of look.

"I'm sorry I'm a mess." Drawing away, she pulled a crumpled tissue out of her coat pocket and blew her nose. "I guess I never really thought about what you did—what you sometimes have to do in the line of duty. This was all a little too real."

"You were there when that nut job drew a gun and fired last November." He tried for a teasing smile. "I was the hero then, if you'll remember."

"You were, but it was different. I knew old stone face was a loser. She had a gun, but it looked like a child's toy, and I knew you were behind a thick sofa and wouldn't get hurt. This was . . . different."

It sure was, but he had no intention of telling her so. "I'm fine. You're fine. Even that snot-nosed kid is fine. I got him in his right calf. Enough to stop him cold, but he'll live." She seemed calmer now, so he relaxed. "It was no big deal."

Her eyes flashed to that maddening green-blue color he never had a name for. "No big deal? You call a shoot-out in an armed robbery no big deal?"

"Okay, it was a big deal. Does that make you feel better?"

"Yes—no—I don't know." She bit her lower lip. "I guess it's a dumb thing to argue about now, huh?"

"I'd say so." He thought of something that might cheer her up. "Want to find a place that's serving breakfast?"

"Considering you made me wait for my bagel, that's a pretty good idea," she teased in return.

"Hang on a second. I've got to check out with the detectives in charge. Stay here and don't move."

Ellie nodded, still not sure if she was finished crying. Sam was probably bummed by a lot of things right now. He'd explained to her last November what would have happened if he'd actually had to shoot that crazy woman. For one thing, he would have lost his gun for the ballistics test, and then he would have had to visit a division psychiatrist for an evaluation.

But those two things took a backseat to today. Sam had shot a kid. Granted, he only wounded the boy, but he could have taken a life. Though he was full of brag-gadocio and snappy comments, she knew he would have been desolate if that had been the case.

He walked out the door and stopped to speak to Officer Landon, then brought the guy over for a proper introduction. "I believe you two have already met. Officer Frank Landon, this is Ellie Engleman, my better half."

Office Landon shook her hand and said something polite, but she didn't hear the words. Had Sam just called her his "better half"?

Impossible.

Before she could think, he tucked her hand in his

elbow and led her up the block. "Where are you taking me?" she asked when her brain cleared.

"Think that smart-ass college friend of yours, the one with the coffee shop, might be open?"

"Joe?" It was the first time he'd ever taken the initiative to stop at a Joe to Go. "Probably. He lives above the building. Worst case, he'll be manning the counter alone. I doubt he's received his morning pastry delivery, but I imagine he'll sell whatever was left from yesterday at a discount."

"Then we'll stop there. Don't you have a hair appointment or something later today?"

The comment hit her like a brick. She almost stopped and asked him if he'd been taken over by pod people. Last night, he'd walked Rudy without her. And he'd just introduced her to a fellow officer as his "better half." Now he was offering to escort her to a Joe to Go, when he was jealous of the relationship she and Joe shared.

And he remembered I had a hair appointment!

"I'm due there at one o'clock. I have time for a quick bite." They dodged people sweeping, shoveling, and tossing deicer as they traveled to the coffee shop. "What are you going to do while I'm gone?"

"Go to the station and talk to Miles and Stanley, see if they've identified that punk, make a date with the department shrink if I can. But I might not have any luck, thanks to the bad weather."

"Then you'll meet me back at the apartment?"

"Of course. I'm scheduled to escort you to that big party, remember?"

"We can stay home if you want." They hit Lexington, turned the corner, and stopped in front of Joe's place. "I'm only going because the judge insisted, though Mother acted as if she wants me there, too."

"Didn't you say the party was in honor of one of your clients? One of the two-legged kind?"

"I almost forgot about that. Norman Lowenstein, Sampson's dad, is one of the judges up for a position on the Second Circuit Court of Appeals."

Sam's eyes narrowed. "Then we'll go." He opened the door to the coffee shop. "I'd hate to miss my chance to see your unflappable mother flapping around a possible Supreme Court justice."

"Now that you mention it, it could be worth the fuss." She waved at Joe, standing behind the counter. "Now be nice or we won't get fed."

Chapter 17

"My, my, my. Aren't you just the prettiest thing. You look like a million bucks, and your little man does, too." Georgette's housekeeper opened the door wide so Ellie, Sam, and Rudy could enter the apartment. "Come in, come in." She gave Sam an appraising once-over, then said to Ellie, "Your big man is looking mighty fine, too."

Ellie wrapped the housekeeper in a bear hug. "We're happy to see you, too, Corinna. Excited about the big night?"

"Pshaw. Your mama and I, we done bigger parties than this one. It's all for the judge, of course. Mr. Stanley is the man of the evening, even though he says this shindig is in honor of those three muckety-muck judges." She took a step back and gave Sam a smile. "Welcome, Detective Ryder. It's a pleasure seein' you again. What have you been up to since Thanksgiving?"

"Keeping your girl out of trouble," he said, helping Ellie off with her coat. Then he slipped out of his trench coat and passed the items to a young man standing at attention next to Corinna. Bending low, Sam kissed the diminutive woman on the cheek she tipped up for what she considered a proper greeting. "It's nice to see you again, too."

"It's good to know someone's watchin' out for Ellie. Lord knows she keeps finding trouble wherever she goes." Corinna gave him a wink. "Are you ready for tonight?"

"I guess, but you should probably know this type of meet-and-greet isn't my strong suit. I may just hang out in the kitchen until everyone leaves. I can even lend a hand if you need me."

"I might take you up on that offer. Maybe you'd like to fill in as a bartender or pass the canapés? That could be useful, too."

Ellie smiled at the byplay between her mother's faithful housekeeper and Sam. From the moment they'd met this past November they seemed to share a bond, and it was nice to see that it still held strong.

Sam had been nothing but agreeable since he'd arrived home from the station late this afternoon. After taking his turn in the shower, he'd put on his tux without complaining and whistled his appreciation when she finished dressing. He even forgot to mention that the last time he'd seen her wearing the beaded navy blue sheath was the evening he'd caught her on a date with another man. Stanley had made a point of telling her that Kevin McGowan and his parents were not invited—one less reason for her to worry about tonight.

When Vivian came upstairs to give her official stamp of approval, she'd straightened Sam's tie, given Ellie a once-over, and pronounced them both ready for the red carpet. Viv's opinion had put her so at ease that she'd felt like taking a bet her picky mother wouldn't find a single thing to reprimand her for when they met.

"I have a better idea. How about bringing Sam to Mother?" Ellie teased. Sam was well aware that

Georgette was impossible to please. Best guess, he'd
rather direct traffic in Times Square on New Year's Eve
than be at her mother's beck and call. "I'm sure she'd
love a bit of attention from a handsome man."

"I'll pass on that suggestion," Sam said, rolling his
eyes. "But I wouldn't mind talking to the judge."

"That's a fine idea," Corinna agreed with a giggle.
"You'd be doing me a huge favor if you went to the library and found him. And bring Rudy with. Judge Stanley's talked about that dog all day. I believe he wants
your boy for a security blanket, while Ms. Georgette
needs a cool head to keep her calm." She handed Ellie
a bag graced with the name of one of the area's most
exclusive pet stores. "I already took a place mat and a
bowl of water to the library, and here's a little something
for your boy."

"It's about time someone gave me a thought," Rudy
yipped. *"Corinna always gets me the best stuff."*

The housekeeper held out her hand to clear the path
for a trio of men carrying chairs into the main living
area. "All right, young lady, it's your job to see to your
mother, 'cause I got more important things to do right
now."

"We're on it," Ellie said. "And thanks for getting
something special for Rudy." She watched the housekeeper head toward the kitchen, then turned to Sam.
"Do you remember the way to the judge's lair?"

He shrugged, nodding in the direction the set-up men
were traveling. "Back there somewhere?"

"Through the living room and into the rear hall, then
hang a left past the bathroom and guest bedroom. It's
the last door on the left."

"How about you provide a road map?" he joked.
They could put both their apartments into this pent-
house and still have room to spare.

"I'll only be a couple of minutes. I promise." She passed him Rudy's leash. "Take his coat off when you get to the library and drape it over a chair so it doesn't get lost. You won't have to do much else with Rudy, because the judge will take over."

"Thank you for that. And don't forget the treats."

Ellie bent and rubbed her yorkiepoo's ears. "You be good and keep Stanley occupied, okay?" She straightened and opened her evening bag. "Here are a few more goodies, plus what Corinna gave me. You'll be fine."

"If you say so," Sam answered.

She leaned forward and dropped a quick kiss on his frowning lips. "Cheer up, Officer Grumpy. I'll meet you there in a few minutes. Just let me see what Mother needs, okay?"

"Ten minutes and I come looking for you," he warned. Then he sauntered off with Rudy at his side.

Sam sat on the tan leather sofa in Judge Stanley Frye's library, feigning interest in a conversation the retired judicial legend was holding with Ellie's beast of a canine. If not for a debilitating stroke that had left him in a wheelchair several years back, the judge would probably still be on the bench handing out fair and concise decisions on all who appeared before him.

Sam found it hard to believe that Judge Frye and the many-times-divorced Georgette Engleman were a happy couple. Ellie's elitist and opinionated mother was a pain in the ass, while the judge was cheerful and approving of all who held intelligent and kind beliefs. That he loved Ellie like his own daughter made him number one on Sam's list of people he admired.

For the past few minutes the judge had interacted with the four-legged stinker Ellie referred to as "her boy." The little demon had played to the wheelchair-bound senior as if he were the deciding vote on an Animal Planet talent show.

The moment they'd arrived in the library, Rudy had vaulted onto Stanley's lap and licked his face as if they were long-lost brothers. Then he'd jumped down and begged for a treat. After receiving the reward, he gobbled it down and proceeded to roll over and play dead.

The entire act was a con, of course. All done for the big payoff: Corinna's marrow bone.

The judge gave Sam a grin as he watched Rudy gnaw at the bone. "Such a fine little fellow, don't you think?"

"Sure," Sam lied.

"And so entertaining. Do you know how many tricks are in his repertoire?"

Tricks? "Uh, no."

"He can sit up and beg, shake, roll over, play dead, and fetch certain toys by name alone. He also watches television. We've sat through several games of *Wheel of Fortune,* and he even knows when the contestants call an incorrect letter."

"You're kidding," Sam deadpanned.

"Not at all. One bark means yes, right letter, and two means no. And after every double bark, I can almost hear him say, 'Wrong choice, loser.'"

"Amazing," Sam said, keeping his opinion of Ellie's fuzzy troublemaker to himself.

"I think he understands exactly what a human says. He simply can't form the words to answer."

Sam recalled all the one-sided discussions he'd heard his girl hold with her dog. "Ellie would probably agree with you there."

"I'm sure she would." The judge stopped watching Rudy and gazed at Sam, his blue eyes flashing. "You are aware she holds full-blown conversations with him, are you not?"

"I've seen her in action, so, yes, I'm aware."

"And you approve of her doing so?"

"I approve of almost everything Ellie does."

"*Almost* everything?"

Tread carefully, bud, Sam warned himself. "I don't care if she talks to her dog, the television, or her toaster. What I do mind is her meddling in police business."

"Ah, I see. Are you afraid she'll prevent you from doing your job? Or maybe solve a case before you do?"

Sam prayed for patience. "I'm *afraid* she'll get caught in the cross fire, like she did a couple of months back, and I won't be there to save her."

"So you enjoy leading the charge to rescue a damsel in distress, eh, Detective? A modern-day Robin Hood to her Maid Marian."

"Uh, sorry, but I'm not sure what you mean."

The judge shook his balding head. "Come, now, I see the way you look at her. Does she know?"

Oh, crap. "I don't believe that's any of your business, sir," he said, trying to be respectful.

"Oh, but it is. I consider Ellie my daughter in every way possible except birth. I only want what's best for her, and that includes making certain she finds the right man." The judge raised a bushy white eyebrow. "She's in my will, and she'll inherit quite a bit when I'm gone."

Sam's blood began to boil, but he kept a tight grip on his temper. "Neither your money nor what she'll inherit from her mother has anything to do with my reason for lov—er—dating Ellie. She can take all the cash she gets and set it on fire, for all I care."

Stanley smiled. "I doubt she'll burn it, but I can see her donating it to some animal charity. I believe Best Friends is her primary concern, but the ASPCA could benefit as well."

"Fine by me." Rescued by the sound of the doorbell, he stood. "I think your guests are arriving."

"So you support her in everything she does?" Judge Frye asked, continuing the questioning.

Sam imagined how sharp the old guy must have been when he was district attorney for New York County. "Everything but her snooping."

"Snooping?"

"Like I said a minute ago, I draw the line at her sticking her nose where it doesn't belong." When the doorbell rang again, he breathed a sigh of relief. "I'm sure you're wanted out front. Is there anything I can do before we get there?"

"I believe I'll take it from here, young man." The judge patted his lap and Rudy jumped on board. Then he pushed a control on the wheelchair and headed for the door. "Come along, if you want, and join the festivities."

After brushing the invisible wrinkles from her dress, Ellie checked her thigh-highs for runs and inspected her three-inch navy Louboutin pumps. If she hadn't gone to that closeout at Saks, she never would have bought the pricey shoes, red soles or not. Positive that her clothing was in order, she ducked into the foyer powder room.

Not bad, she thought, glancing in the mirror. Lisa, her new hairstylist, had done a great job with her "look." Her hair gleamed like polished copper, while her makeup complemented her fair skin. No doubt about it, the woman was a miracle worker.

Convinced that there was no more she could do to make herself presentable, she headed through the dining room, took a left, and entered the master suite. After a soft rap on the door, she opened it and stuck her head into the room.

"Mother, it's me. Are you decent?"

"Come in, come in."

Georgette's voice sounded muffled, which meant she was in either the bathroom or the dressing area. Ellie stepped inside and walked to a closet as big as her bedroom.

"Mom? Corinna said you might need help."

Georgette turned and heaved a sigh. "I'm a mess. I don't know if I can get through this evening." She raised a full-length fuchsia gown with a lovely ruffled halter. "Here's my Valentino." Then she lifted her other hand. "And this is a Vera Wang." The pale pink slip of a dress had a plunging neckline and fell to the floor in a ripple of fabric.

The mere fact that her haute couture mother was asking her off-the-rack daughter for fashion advice only proved how nervous she was. "The Vera is sort of sedate, something you might wear to an opening at MoMA. I think the Valentino demands attention, but it won't hog the limelight."

Georgette nodded. "Just what I thought." She passed the ruffled gown to Ellie, returned the Vera to the hanging rack, and slipped off her dressing gown. "Now help me into this thing. I still have to touch up my face and hair."

Impressed by her mother's toned and trim size four figure, Ellie did as asked. Though she'd received the best of both her parents' gene pool offerings, Georgette, with her twice-yearly injections of Botox and Juvéderm, could have passed for Ellie's fashion-forward, always-in-style older sister.

She propped herself against an opposing wall and waited while her mother wielded a rapier-thin eyeliner brush, then a mascara wand. After touching up her nose and cheeks with a bit of pressed powder, Georgette covered her lips with a color that perfectly matched the Valentino gown.

"How do you do that?" Ellie asked.

Georgette held up a hand mirror and checked the back of her expertly coiffed head. She then gazed in the dressing table mirror and caught her daughter's eye. "Do what?"

"Find the exact lipstick or eye shadow needed to enhance what you're wearing?" To Ellie, pink was pink and purple was purple, while her mother could list a hundred variations in each color. "You even find clothes the same shade as your hair."

Georgette turned and gave her a once-over. "You have a good eye, too, when you choose to use it, though I doubt you'd find anything to match the color of your hair. Which looks very nice, by the way. Not your usual frizzy mop." She twirled her finger and Ellie moved in a circle. "And your hose and shoes do justice to that dress. Elie Saab?"

Ellie had found the dress on a closeout rack in a small boutique near Bergdorf's. Because the label had been removed, she had no clue to the designer, but her mother was probably right. "I'm not sure, but I'll say yes if anyone asks."

Georgette straightened her shoulders. "I now pronounce us ready to dazzle the soon-to-arrive guests."

Coming from her quick-to-judge mother, the words were practically a rave review. "Shall we find Stanley?"

Georgette pursed her lips. "I assume he's with your dog. You did bring him for the evening, as requested?"

Her mother pronounced "your dog" as if accusing Ellie of bringing the bubonic plague to her home. "Sam took Rudy to see the judge, and he's promised—er—I've told him to be good. I'll try to keep him in the library, unless Stanley wants him by his side."

"How nice. You've come with that adorable detective you brought to dinner on Thanksgiving."

"Sam is here, but he's not thrilled about it. He's in the middle of a serious investigation, so his mind is on his work, not mingling with the upper crust of Manhattan politics."

"Speaking of upper crust, did Corinna tell you the bad news? Because of this terrible snowstorm, Judge Sotomayor won't be attending."

"Oh, Mom, I'm so sorry. I know you were hoping she'd be here to lend an air of prominence to the night."

"Yes, well, the flights from D.C. were grounded. She did send a telegram of sorts. Stanley's going to read it to the attendees. It's a word of good luck to whoever is chosen for the judgeship."

"Who else is coming?"

Her mother's eye's brightened. "The mayor, for one. And a few of the city officials. I was hoping for the governor, but again, the weather didn't cooperate." She heaved a sigh. "Enough talk about the guests. I heard the doorbell, so I'm certain Stanley is waiting for me."

They linked arms and walked through the closet and bedroom and into the dining room. "Tell me, how are things going between you and Detective Ryder?"

"Going?"

"Yes, going. Is there any news about future plans?"

Ellie swallowed. "Future plans?"

"Ellen Elizabeth, stop playing dumb. You know what I mean. Are the two of you going to—"

Corinna saved the day by flying through the kitchen door as if her tail was on fire. "Lordy, Ms. Georgette. What's taken the two of you so long? I just heard that Judge Stanley's greetin' guests all by himself, with Rudy on his lap, no less."

Georgette gasped, then grabbed Ellie by the hand. "Come along, daughter, and take control of your dog."

Sam stood at the rear of the spacious foyer, eyeing the stream of guests walking through the door as if they'd all arrived on the same double-decker tour bus. He figured the downstairs doorman had his hands full, keeping the limos moving up Park Avenue while greeting and directing the A-list crowd.

Attendants took coats, and Judge Frye called each person who entered by name, then introduced him or her to Rudy. After exchanging a few pleasant words on the upcoming evening or their corresponding love of dogs, he instructed the guests to partake of the champagne and canapés that were offered by a group of waiters, who magically appeared from the dining room.

Corinna arrived two minutes later, with Ellie and her mother in tow. Georgette joined her husband at the door, and the housekeeper began supervising the troops, while Ellie walked to Sam's side.

"How did things go in the library?"

He took her hand. "Fine."

"That tells me a lot. Was Rudy a good boy?"

"How the heck should I know? He did a couple of tricks and ate the stuff the judge gave him. It made Stanley happy, so, yeah, I guess he was good."

She opened her baby blues wide. "Rudy did tricks? What kind of tricks?"

"Sat up and begged, laid down like he was dead. The judge loved it. Did you know that he and Rudy have watched *Wheel of Fortune* together? He claims your dog understands the letters called on the show."

"What? No."

"Yes."

Ellie focused on the judge and her dog, who were holding court at the front door. "Maybe I should remove him from Stanley's lap before Mother has a cow."

"From the way she's smiling, that might be a good idea." He nodded toward Georgette. "Those guests must think she's got a piece of glass up her butt."

Ellie *tsk*ed. "You are such a guy. I'll be back in a minute. Do you have Rudy's leash?"

Sam pulled the item from his pocket. "Just don't let your mother have it or Rudy could end up at a hanging."

When she grabbed the leash and took off in a rush, he shook his head. Even though Ellie was uptight about the evening, she looked beautiful and in control. She belonged with these upper-crust A-listers. Unlike him.

It had been damned disconcerting listening to the judge talk about leaving her money. Ellie already made more green walking dogs than he did protecting the citizens of this town. That she worked hard wasn't the issue, and neither was her salary. What burned his shorts was the cash she would receive when Judge Frye passed away. And her mother.

He was pretty sure she would give all of the judge's money to her favorite charity, which was Best Friends, just as she had the money she'd inherited from that homeless guy. But family money? That was a different matter. He'd be happy if she tossed it out the window or sent it to another of her animal rights groups, but what if she decided to keep it?

He watched the judge shake hands with Captain Carmody. Then he spotted Ellie, holding the little white dog they'd rescued when he and Ellie first met. Bobby? Billy? No . . . Buddy. The captain had brought Buddy to the party.

When Carmody waved him over, there was no escape. Pasting a smile on his face, he made his way across the foyer. The captain held out his meaty hand and Sam shook it.

"Captain."

"Detective Ryder. It's good to see you here."

"Detective Ryder," Mrs. Carmody said. The attractive woman grinned from ear to ear. "Do you recognize our baby? When Judge Frye called and insisted that we bring him, we just couldn't say no."

Unsure of how to comment or what to do, he gazed at Ellie, who had tears shining in her eyes. Oh, hell. Now what?

"Sam, look. It's Buddy. Isn't he adorable?" She nuzzled the dog's fuzzy white head. "I've missed him so much, and you've missed me, haven't you?"

Captain Carmody stepped aside and ushered the group out of the flow of guest traffic. "Stanley said you'd be surprised. You going to be okay?"

Ellie smiled. "I'm going to be just fine. But I think I'll take both boys into the library so they can get reacquainted. Corinna set up a water bowl and a cashmere throw they can share, and we have treats, too. Unless you want to keep him with you."

"No, no. You take him," Mrs. Carmody said. "He's wearing that distinctive Bichon smile, so I can tell he's happy to be in your arms. Mitchell and I will mingle with the others. I'm sure the guests of honor will be here soon."

"Detective. Ellie." The captain nodded. "We'll find you in a bit."

Sam turned to Ellie, who had put Buddy on the floor. All of a sudden the huge foyer felt as small as an elevator. "Let's get these guys to the library," he said, taking both leashes from her hand.

"Okay, sure." She sniffed back a tear. "I'd like to spend a little time alone with Buddy."

He guided the dogs through the crowd, where many of the guests commented on the Bichon and asked Ellie about its unique haircut and happy demeanor. It took a good ten minutes to get back to the library, where Sam breathed a sigh of relief.

"I think I'm going to sit here for a while and play with the boys, if that's okay with you," Ellie told him.

Sam's cell phone rang before he could answer her. He checked caller ID, held up a finger, and stepped to the desk. "Ryder."

"Detective, it's Battaglia. From the records room. I don't mean to bother you on your night off, but Stallings said you wanted this info ASAP, so I decided to call."

"Not a problem. Just give me a minute." He held the phone to his chest. "I've got to take this. Do you mind?"

"Not at all," said Ellie, giving each of the dogs a treat. "I've got plenty to do here."

"Do you think it's all right for me to borrow a pen and paper?" he asked her, scanning the desk.

"Go ahead. Stanley won't mind."

He opened a drawer, where he found a pencil and notepad. "Okay, shoot," he told Battaglia. A minute passed; then Sam said, "You're sure about this data. The dates and the trial's wrap-up are correct?"

"It's correct unless the info was recorded wrong, but I doubt that happened."

"Okay, thanks." He tore the slip of paper from the notepad and tucked it and his phone in his pocket. Then he walked to the sofa. "I have to talk to a couple of people out front. Do you mind staying here alone?"

Ellie gave him the okay and he aimed for the door. Scouring the crowd was the last thing he wanted to do, but he had to make contact with one of the guests. If he was willing to talk here, he'd ask a few questions, but eventually, the person would have to come to the precinct for a bigger sort-out session.

Tonight was no longer one of easy conversation and rubbing elbows with the city's bigwigs. Now tonight was business.

Chapter 18

Sam had been gone for about an hour when Ellie decided to leave the dogs and search for him. During the time she'd spent with Buddy and Rudy, she'd played with the Bichon and given lots of belly rubs. Rudy, on the other hand, didn't exactly play the way most dogs do, but he did accept his fair share of praise and attention. Right now, while sitting like a watchful Buddha, he continued asking his old pal a round of questions.

"So, Bud. What's it like, livin' with a cop?"

Buddy rolled to a stand and gave a head-to-tail shake. *"Captain Carmody is great. Different from the professor, but still a good human."*

"Then you don't think all cops are dopes?"

"I guess not. Besides, I spend most of my time with Mom. She takes me places, keeps me warm and safe, feeds me, lets me sleep in her bed the way you do with Ellie."

"And the big guy doesn't complain about you being on the mattress?"

"Sometimes I have to wait on the floor in my own bed, you know, for when Mom and Pop are doing the—er—they're—"

"We know what you mean," Ellie told him. She gave

Rudy the evil eye. "Enough with the personal questions. The Carmodys' life is not your concern."

"I'm just tryin' to find out how other canines handle living with a demented detective, or bein' tossed out of bed when their owners play humpin' hamster."

"That's it. I've heard all I want to for the moment." Corinna had dropped in twice to say that Georgette was looking for her. "I have to show my face at the party for a while. You have water and Mother's beautiful cashmere throw to keep you cozy. Do you need anything else?"

"Maybe another beefy bone?" Rudy suggested, his eyes sad and pleading.

She crossed her arms, vowing not to be swayed. "The answer to that is no. You've each had one already, plus the Pup-Peroni from home. I even sneaked out to the buffet table and gave you a nibble from my own plate. More food will just make you sick."

"You take the fun out of everything." The yorkiepoo dropped to a sit on the throw. *"C'mon, Buddy. I say we go on strike."*

Reaching down, she scratched Buddy's fluffy white ears. "I bet you don't feel that way, do you?" she asked the beautifully groomed Bichon.

"Who, me? Nope. I'll take seein' you any way I can. You haven't been to our house since Christmas. I miss the professor, and I still miss you."

"What a sweet thing to say." She gave Rudy a pointed look. "I wish all my dogs were so nice."

"He's just trolling for another treat," Rudy warned. *"He's not foolin' me."*

"Buddy knows Mrs. Carmody wouldn't approve of more snacks. He's much better at listening to his superiors than you are, my friend."

"Please tell me you're jokin' about that 'superior' thing. I thought you and me were partners."

"We are, but when there are decisions to be made about your welfare, then I'm in charge." She moved toward the door. "I'm going to do some scouting, but I don't want to cut you off from the world, so I'll leave the door ajar. Why don't you take a nap? Better still, sit tight and I'll see if I can get one of the attendants to take you for a quick walk."

She slipped out of the library and into the hall, where she ran into a group of women standing in line near the restroom.

"Ellie. I was wondering when you'd turn up," said Mariette Lowenstein. "The judge and I have been here for at least thirty minutes. Georgette said you were occupied, but she wouldn't say what you were doing."

"That's because I've been babysitting Rudy and another dog in Stanley's study. She doesn't approve of them being here, so I doubt she'd say anything to a guest."

"Too bad I didn't know Rudy was going to be here. Sampson hates staying home alone." Mariette moved up in line when a guest left the restroom. "He could have kept your boy company."

"Uh, well . . . I don't think Mother wanted anyone to bring a dog. The way I understand it, Stanley issued the invitations."

"Are you saying Georgette isn't a dog lover? That's hard to believe, knowing you're in the business and all."

A regal-looking woman wearing a full-length purple gown and a mass of diamonds turned before Ellie could comment. "Excuse me, but I couldn't help overhearing. So you're Georgette's daughter." She held out her hand. "I'm Nadine Spencer. Martin and I got an adorable little mini Schnauzer for Christmas from our daughter. We've been looking for a dog walker since the first of the year."

"Mother told you about my profession?" Ellie asked,

grateful she'd remembered to put on the three-diamond pendant that Sam had given her for Christmas. Most of the women in attendance were wearing enough gems to stock Tiffany's. "She said I walked dogs?"

"Not Georgette, but Judge Frye was happy to talk about you. Martin and I have been sharing walk duty with our housekeeper, but Ziggy is still learning the ins and outs of potty training. I'm sure you realize how difficult that is when one lives in a high-rise. We've interviewed a few walkers, but none of them seems as caring as we'd like. When Stanley told us about you, we thought maybe we could talk you into stopping by."

Ellie gave her schedule a mental once-over and decided there was no way she could add another dog. "I'm sorry. My client list is booked at the moment. Unless you live in one of the four buildings I already service, I don't think I can help." She opened her bag and took out a card. "Of course, there are times when someone moves away and a slot opens up, and I am looking for a helper. Give me a call so we can discuss where you live and we'll see."

Mrs. Spencer took the card with a rueful smile. "Fine, and thank you. Oops, looks like it's my turn." She ducked into the just-vacated bathroom, leaving Mariette and Ellie alone.

"Judge Frye is supposed to make an announcement in the next ten minutes or so, introducing Norm and the other nominees," said Mariette. "It wouldn't look good if I missed our big moment."

"Great. I'll wait and walk out with you. I want to see your husband's big moment, too." She leaned against the wall and heaved a sigh. Good thing Mariette hadn't found out about Rudy and Buddy being here before tonight. Georgette would have thrown a fit if her special event had ended up being a dog-sitting party. Luckily,

Stanley had used common sense and kept the invitation to only two canines.

Just then she heard the conversation level in the living room fall to a drone of voices. Mariette stepped out and Ellie said, "I think Judge Frye is about to do his thing. Let's go in."

Mariette turned in place, then stumbled. "My feet are killing me. Bunions, you see. I'm so nervous. What do you think?"

Mrs. Lowenstein had played down her rather masculine appearance with a softer hairstyle and a triple strand of dime-sized pearls. Her flattering full-length black sheath gave some shape to her broad frame and pooled elegantly at the floor.

"You look fine. Now smile and be ready to applaud."

When they entered the crowded living room, Mariette squeezed Ellie's hand. "I've been waiting for this moment for so long. I only hope our appointment goes through."

She swept off to find her husband, leaving Ellie a bit confused by her parting comments. *Our big moment? Our appointment?* Which of the Lowensteins was up for this judgeship, anyway?

She scanned the room and found Sam standing in a corner, watching Judge Lowenstein stalk off. Then he sidled to the other side of the room and began a discussion with a distinguished-looking gentleman. By the time Stanley called Judge Lowenstein's name a second time, Norm and Mariette were beside him.

Ellie frowned. What were Sam and Norm Lowenstein talking about? And why did the judge look angry enough to spit nails? And who was the second man Sam had cornered?

"Ladies and gentlemen," Stanley began, commanding her attention. "Georgette and I would like to welcome you to our gathering. We're here, of course, to celebrate the appointment of one of these three judges to a premier position in our nation's judicial system."

His blue eyes twinkled. "Now some of you might ask why we didn't wait to celebrate until after the official announcement, but I thought that all three men should be lauded, since it is a great honor to even be considered for such a prestigious post. Besides, the lousy weather gives us all the more reason to hold a party. Don't you agree?"

Suddenly Sam was at Ellie's side. "Taking a break from dog duty?" he asked, his expression grim.

"For a while," she answered in a hushed tone. "What have you been up to?"

His coffee-dark eyes inspected the room. "Me? Not much."

"I saw you talking to Judge Lowenstein. What was that all about?"

Before Sam answered, the group applauded, and Ellie felt obligated to listen to Stanley's introduction of each appointee. In the first two instances, when he announced Judge Arnold Simpson and Judge Henry Wilde, the wives took a backseat and let their husbands bask in the limelight. But when he named Norm Lowenstein, Mariette appeared center stage, right beside the judge, beaming as if she were the nominee.

"Well, that's interesting."

"Interesting how?" asked Sam.

"What? Oh." She didn't realize she'd spoken out loud. "Ah, just Mariette."

"Judge Lowenstein's wife?"

"Yes. She's acting— Never mind. It's not important."

Sam narrowed his eyes. "If you think so, then it is. Let me in on your thoughts."

"You never did say why you were talking to the judge," she said, sidestepping the question.

"What judge?" He surveyed the crowd. "There are only about a dozen in attendance tonight."

Ellie gave an eye roll. "You know exactly who I mean. One of the guests of honor. Norman Lowenstein. And that other man on the opposite side of the room. Who's he?"

"Funny how you're stewing over Mrs. Lowenstein, while I have issues with her husband, isn't it?"

"Issues? You have issues with Judge Lowenstein?"

He raised an eyebrow. "You're avoiding my question."

"And you're avoiding mine," she said, mimicking his annoyed expression.

Sam grabbed her elbow, led her into the library, and sat her on the sofa. "You've walked the Lowensteins' dog for what, a year now?"

"Just about. Why?"

"What kind of people are they?"

Ellie cocked her head, thinking. "I haven't spoken to them very often. Mariette is hardly ever home when I pick up her Pug. Seems she's a health nut, works out at a gym every day, does weight training, that sort of thing. And the judge is rarely there when I arrive."

He closed the door and sat next to her. "Have you ever seen them interact?"

"With each other?"

"Yes, with each other. Do they seem loving? Involved? Polite? Or are they more like roommates?"

Ellie blinked. What the heck was Sam getting at? The one time she'd seen the Lowensteins interact was last week, and it hadn't been a pleasant scene.

"I'm not sure. I've only—" Just then, she felt a paw on her knee, and she dropped her gaze. "Hey, little man. How are you?"

Buddy whimpered. *"I'm okay, but where did Rudy go?"*

She glanced around the library, then stared at Sam. "Do you see Rudy anywhere?"

Sam rested his elbows on his knees. "What does your dog have to do with the Lowensteins?"

"I just realized that I left two pups in this room, but only one is here now. I can't think of anything else until I find my dog."

"Oh, for—" Sam muttered a not-so-nice phrase under his breath. "Stay here. I'll scout the place."

The second he left, she reconnected with the Bichon. "How long has Rudy been gone? Did he say where he was going?"

"Uh-uh. He just said he wanted to find you, wedged his way through the door, and took off. But that was a while ago."

"Okay, you stand watch. I'll be back in a minute." She peered into the hall, made sure Sam was nowhere in sight, and headed into the crowd. She doubted Sam would do much in the way of hunting for her boy, but she could see him getting into another heated discussion with Judge Lowenstein. Maybe even Mariette.

Before she got a foot into the living room, her mother approached, a scowl gracing her face. "Do something about your dog."

"I'm trying to find him. Where is he?"

Georgette heaved a sigh. "He strolled into the middle of the three guests of honor right after Stanley introduced them. They were accepting congratulations from a group of well-wishers, including two reporters. The next thing I knew, he'd jumped onto Stanley's lap and become the center of attention."

Oy. "I'm sorry. Where is he now?"

"How should I know? The judges went to have their pictures taken near the fireplace. I tried to tell you having that dog here would be a disaster. If only you'd—"

Ellie left her mother sputtering and took off. Things were going to hell in a handbasket. Next thing, Rudy and Sam would get into it somehow. She could see the headlines now: LOCAL DETECTIVE AND CANINE BRAWL AT JUDICIAL FESTIVITIES.

Weaving through the guests, she made her way to the fireplace and its brightly blazing electric logs. Stanley and the three nominees were giving an interview, but there was no sign of Rudy.

She edged past the invitees sitting at small tables the caterers had brought in, and slipped by guests clustered in groups, holding drinks and chatting. When she arrived in the foyer she heard a shriek and stopped in her tracks.

The powder room door flew open and a woman raced out, her face the same color as her red dress. "There's a dog in the bathroom," she shouted to anyone who would listen. "A real, live dog."

Great.

Georgette took that moment to rush to the woman's side. "Mrs. Thachette, I'm so sorry. Let me get an attendant and have him removed." Her mother put an arm around the woman's quaking shoulders. Searching the foyer, she glared at a young man wearing a white jacket and a grin. "You. Go in and get that canine out of there."

Then Georgette focused on Ellie. "I swear, Ellen Elizabeth, if that animal isn't out of here . . ."

"Mother, it'll be fine. Why don't you take Mrs. Thacker—"

"That's Thachette," the woman said, correcting Ellie as her lips quivered. "And I'm highly allergic." She put a hand on her barely there chest and fingered a ruby necklace. "I've never been so frightened in my life."

"Take Mrs. Thachette to your private suite and help her get settled," she said to her mother, Then she opened the bathroom door and stared at Rudy.

What! What? I was just lookin' for you.

Ellie stepped inside and closed the door. "Where have you been?"

"Pickin' up a ton of lawyer jokes, and collectin' a lot of interesting facts. I tried to tell a couple of them legal beagles to XYZ, but they ignored me."

"XYZ?"

"Examine your zipper." He snickered. *"Most of those guys are incapable of lockin' up their privates."*

She shook her head. "You are the most—" Opening the door, she called the still-smiling attendant over. "Please follow me. I need a favor." Spinning around, she hoisted Rudy in her arms and headed for the library.

Sam's head was growing heavy. He'd watched Ellie pace for a good ten minutes, and had to admit it was as tiring, and about as boring, as watching a Ping-Pong match on ESPN. Worse still, when she paced she didn't walk in a straight line, but went in whatever direction struck her. His neck ached from following her erratic lines and looping turns.

"Will you stop?" he finally said, stepping in her way.

She raised her gaze to meet his. "I can't. Something tells me I've made a stupid mistake. That attendant told me he was familiar with dogs, but what did that mean?" Her eyes sparkled with unshed tears. "He's been gone for close to thirty minutes. What if he walked into traffic and got smacked by a cab? Or maybe one of the dogs slipped its leash and took off running. Rudy knew I was annoyed. What if he decided to go home on his own, and that attendant is chasing him down Sixty-sixth with no clue to where he's going?"

"Listen to what you're saying. There's no trick to walking a couple of dogs—"

"Oh, really." She gave him the look. "Remember who you're talking to, fella."

Sam groaned. "Okay, okay. What I meant was there's no trick to walking a pair of well-behaved dogs who know this area and are familiar with city streets. Is that better?"

She sniffed. "I guess so."

"And how would Rudy know you were annoyed with him? What did he do—tell you?"

"Yes. No." She ran her fingers through her curls. "But Mother's furious. The judge thinks she's blowing what happened to Mrs. Thachette out of proportion, and that's only making her madder. In the end, I'll be blamed for everything and anything that went wrong to-night, no matter what I say or do."

Sam gathered her in his arms. "So what went wrong? Rudy drew some attention away from the guests of honor and frightened some society woman in a powder room? Big deal. Who cares?"

She gulped out a laugh. "Okay, okay. When you put it that way, you're right. He didn't do any real damage, and most of the people here, except for Mrs. Thachette and a couple of other stuffed shirts, all like dogs."

"Now you've got the right attitude. Far as I can tell, your only real problem will be Georgette, and you're used to her complaining. You can handle her." He loos-ened his grip and looked her in the eye. "Am I making any sense?"

"You're making lots of sense," she told him. Stepping away, she went to the desk, opened a drawer, and pulled out a tissue. "I'm sorry. It's just that—"

There was a knock on the door; then the attendant brought the dogs inside with a flourish. "All done," he an-nounced. "The little guys really know their stuff. I took them around the block twice because they were so good."

"It's cold and they aren't wearing their coats," Ellie began. "And I thought I told you to make it—"

"Thanks so much," Sam interrupted, patting the kid on the back. "We'll take it from here." He passed the young man a twenty and led him out the door. Turning to Ellie, he grinned. "See. No harm, no foul. The dogs are fine." He bent and unsnapped their leashes, then put them on the desk. "You feeling any better?"

"A little."

When she squatted and pulled Rudy near, Sam figured it would be best if he let Ellie do her thing.

She linked an arm around Buddy's neck and gazed into his eyes. "You two had me worried. Was that kid nice to you?" She cocked her head. "Really?" Smiling, she dropped a kiss on his muzzle. "I'm glad you had a good time."

He shrugged. If there was any guarantee he'd get as much attention from her as these mutts did, he'd grow a tail and a second set of legs. Another knock on the door sounded and he went to answer it.

"Sam, my boy, mind if we come in?"

"Of course not, sir. It's your office." He opened the door wider to allow Stanley and the Carmodys inside.

"Ellie, thanks so much for taking care of our little man," said Mrs. Carmody. "I heard they just got back from a nice, long walk."

"Yes, ma'am," said Ellie. "Did you have a good time tonight?"

"More importantly, did you?" the woman asked her.

When they huddled and began to chat with Stanley, Captain Carmody nodded to Sam. "I saw you bending Judge Lowenstein's ear a bit earlier," he said in a low, even voice. "Then you held a conversation with Judge McDonald and the district attorney a couple of minutes after that. Is there anything you want to tell me, Detective?"

Sam looked him in the eye. "I have a theory cooking

in the drag queen case, Captain. I may need your assistance if things get difficult."

"I thought that was a done deal."

"It was until yesterday afternoon. Then the case veered off track. Detective Fugazzo and I had to go at it from another angle, and some interesting things started turning up. Things we didn't expect."

"Are you going out on a limb, or are these 'interesting' things solid?"

"I'll know better in the next forty-eight hours. I have to do a little more digging, which is why I needed to speak to Judge McDonald and the DA."

Captain Carmody nodded. "Let me know if there's anything I can do, but make certain your information is on the money. I'd hate to see you ruffling important feathers for nothing. It's always tough digging out from under if things don't pan out the way you expect."

"Yes, sir. I know that. I'll do my best."

"That's all I ask of you, Detective." He gazed at the two women, sitting on the sofa and chatting with Judge Frye. "I want to thank you again for putting that bug in my ear when you wrapped up the Albright case. I haven't seen my wife this happy in several years. Owning Buddy has done her—done us both—a world of good."

"There's no need for further thanks, Captain. I'm beginning to understand how some people feel about their pets."

Carmody rocked back on his heels, a grin splitting his Irish face in two. "I just bet you are. It's nice to see that you and Ms. Engleman are still together."

Sam didn't say a word. He couldn't.

"Well, it's time the Mrs. and I head for home." The captain walked to the desk, picked up Buddy's leash, and brought it to the sofa. After he hooked the lead, the

Bichon jumped into his arms and began licking his chin. "Judge Frye, always a pleasure."

The judge held out a hand and Mrs. Carmody clasped it in her own, stood, and said, "Ellie, Detective Ryder, it was nice seeing you again. Good night, Stanley, and thanks for inviting us. We'll just say our good-byes to your charming wife and be on our way."

"I'll follow you," said Judge Frye, guiding his wheelchair behind them. "I should be at the door with Georgette for the grand exodus."

Sam was beat. The night had proven to be an eye-opener, and he had a ton of crap to do before he assembled his paperwork and presented it to Judge McDonald. If his theory proved to be a dud, he'd have to walk on eggs and take a shitload of ribbing from Vince and his pals for the next couple of months.

"How about you and I join that mass retreat? My guess is your mother won't be able to make a single negative comment with so many important people around to hear her complain."

He snapped the leash on Rudy's collar and Ellie came to her feet. "You're probably right." Leaning toward him, she kissed his cheek. "Thanks for being so understanding." Then she grinned. "But don't think I forgot about that conversation you had with Norm Lowenstein. I'll just save the grilling for tomorrow."

Chapter 19

Sunlight streamed through the bedroom window. Ellie checked her nightstand clock, and saw that it was almost nine—late for Rudy, who usually needed to go out by eight even on weekend mornings. Well, the little stinker could just hold it a while longer if he thought giving her extra sleep time would get him back in her good graces.

She had yet to talk to him about his behavior at the party, mostly because Sam had stayed the night. It was tough having a serious discussion with your dog when someone else was in the apartment. Someone who didn't condone or even understand what you were doing.

After arriving home from the party, she'd been so beat all she could do was undress, wash off her makeup, and tumble into bed. Now, with a solid eight hours of rest under her belt, she was ready to face the world, and her boys. First, a nice bit of private time with Sam, and then she'd cook him a good breakfast and ask him about his conversation with Norm Lowenstein and that other man. And after he left, she'd have a sit-down with her yorkiepoo.

But her hope of spending time with Sam died when she turned over and found Rudy curled on the pillow.

"Don't rush getting up or anything," he said with a yawn. *"The dopey dick already took me out."*

"Excuse me?" she asked, not sure she'd heard correctly.

"He left a note. It's around here somewhere."

She rolled to the edge of the mattress, sat up, and took a deep breath. Rudy had to be telling the truth, because he'd never be this complacent if he were lying. But why was the dopey dick—er—Sam being so interactive with her dog? It was the third time in twenty-four hours that he'd given her help with Rudy's care.

The apartment was quiet—no sound of the shower, no kitchen racket, and no smell of brewing coffee. Standing, she faced Rudy, who was in full stretch mode, his front feet out and his bottom up.

"And where, exactly, might I find this note?"

"Search me. For all I know it could have accidentally got lost—or something."

"Or something?" Now at his side of the bed, she inspected the pillow, then dropped to her knees and searched the floor. "Aha!" She picked up a wrinkled piece of paper covered in teeth marks and smeared ink, and read it out loud.

"Ellie: Had a ton of work to do. I'll call you later. Sam."

She gave Rudy a look. "Something tells me this note was on the pillow when he left."

"Maybe so, but that's my territory." Jumping to the floor, he gave a full-body shake.

"We'll discuss this later."

After setting the note on her dresser, she pulled clean underwear from a drawer, went to the closet, where she found a navy sweater and jeans, and took everything to the bathroom. Twenty minutes later, showered and presentable, she was in the kitchen, starting a pot of coffee while Rudy watched her from his corner.

"You ready to talk yet?" he asked when she retrieved her homemade caramel sauce and whipping cream from the fridge. Nothing fat-free this morning. She needed the real stuff.

Thinking to teach him a lesson, she kept quiet. Maybe her boy would use the time to get his priorities straight, because Sam was in her—their—life for as long as things worked out. He had done his part lately, easing up on her involvement in Rob's murder charge, agreeing to take her places he really didn't want to go, and helping her with Rudy.

Her dog could complain, make nasty wisecracks, even eat Sam's notes. But it was time he stopped putting himself between her and the detective.

"It looks warmer outside. The snow's melting. I could be convinced to take a trip to the ex-terminator's, if you wanted to talk to her about last night."

Still ignoring him, she sat at the table and smiled. Sam had picked up a morning newspaper and—she inspected the bag sitting next to the paper—a sesame bagel with cream cheese, capers, tomato, and lox, just the way she liked it.

Ooo-kay. This was getting spooky. She usually had to repeat what she wanted a dozen times before he remembered. Either an alien being had taken up residence in his brain, or he was going to drop a bomb. She just couldn't wrap her mind around which it might be.

Rudy put his paws on her knee. _"Hey, I got a question for you."_

She raised an eyebrow.

"What do you throw to a drowning lawyer?"

Ellie groaned. "I'm not in the mood for one of your ghastly lawyer jibes."

"Come on, give it a try."

She shrugged. "A lead life preserver."

He gave a doggie grin. *"That's pretty good, but it's not even close."*

"Okay, give me the punch line."

"His partners."

She couldn't help but giggle. "Where do you hear all these terrible jokes?"

"Lotsa places. I heard a couple dozen last night, and some of them are good. Besides, you look like you need a little cheering up."

"Making me happy is simple. All you have to do is listen to what I say, do what you're told, and stay out of trouble."

He dropped to the floor and slid into his Buddha pose. *"I hate to say this, but you sound just like the doofus detective."*

"I what?" She blinked. "I do not."

"Oh, but you do. Listen to yourself. You're all bossy and 'do what I tell you.' Who does that sound like to you?"

Flustered, she opened and closed her mouth without saying anything. "I—er—well—" She stood up and went to the counter. She hated when Sam bossed her around, but they were equals. She had every right to expect things to be done her way if she was right.

Rudy was a dog.

"I might be a dog, but I thought we were partners."

Mouth agape, she stared at him. "What did you say?"

"You heard me. I thought we were partners. Leastways, that's what you said yesterday."

She stirred the caramel into her coffee and added a squirt of whipped cream. After carrying the cup to the table, she plopped into her chair and took a long sip. The sweet, hot liquid calmed her senses, woke her up, and gave her the chance to regroup.

"We are partners, but this can't be a fifty-fifty relationship because you need me more than I need you."

He again put his paws on her thigh. *"Yeah, I know. But there's nothin' I can do about that."*

"And it makes you sad."

"Not sad, but I do have to ask, if I wasn't here, what would you do?"

What would I do? Her throat began to clog and she opened her arms.

Rudy jumped into her lap and licked her face. *"That's just what I thought you'd say."*

Closing her eyes, Ellie squeezed him tight and sniffed back a tear. Rudy was her boy, the one thing she could count on in her life. Sam was here, but for how long? Viv was here, too, but she had Dr. Dave. Stanley loved her, treated her like a daughter, but he was eighty-three; there was no telling how much longer he'd be around to take her side.

And how could she forget her mother? The idea that Georgette would be there for her was a laugh. Her mother would disown her in a heartbeat if she thought her daughter was clouding her own social standing or embarrassing her.

Another sloppy lick brought her back to reality. She had Rudy, and he was all she needed.

Heaving a sigh, she nuzzled his fur. "I'm sorry for getting angry with you, but you have to see it from my point of view. Yes, we're partners, but other people don't understand where we're coming from, so we have to keep it a secret. Maybe you could look at it like an undercover relationship?"

"You mean a 007 kind of thing?"

"If that works for you."

"Then I need a code name." He pressed his muzzle against her chest. *"How about Agent Badass—or—wait. I got it. Agent BTS."*

"BTS? What the heck does that stand for?"

He gave a doggie smirk. *"Better than Sam, of course. Because I am."*

"Okay, if that will make you happy, Agent BTS it is." She ruffled his ears. "Now, tell me what you found out during last night's snoop session."

"For one thing, those lame lawyers, judges, and politicians blow a lot of hot air. They love talkin' about themselves, and the more limelight they can steal, the better."

"That's probably true, but I don't think it's going to help me with Rob's case."

"Then how about I tell you what Detective Demento and Judge Lowenstein were arguin' about?"

"You were in on that conversation? I didn't see you near them when I spotted them talking."

"That's because I was under the table next to 'em. They never knew I was there."

Ellie closed her eyes, trying to remember what she'd noticed when she saw Norm and Sam, but nothing clicked. "Okay, I believe you were there. Tell me what they said."

Rudy hopped off her lap and did the pensive Buddha thing again. *"Sam asked the judge if he would come to the station to answer a few questions about a case he presided over when Art Pearson was arrested. When Lowenstein said it wouldn't be convenient, Sam pushed, and ol' Norm said flat-out 'no.' Then Sam said he could get one of them court order things. That sent the judge into overdrive."*

"Why would Sam ask Judge Lowenstein about Art Pearson?"

"If I knew who this Pearson person was, I might be able to figure it out."

"Art Pearson is the real name of Carmella Sunday, the murdered drag queen."

"The one Bobbi-Rob was accused of killing?"

"One and the same. Does that help?"

"Not really, but that must be why Sam went to Judge McDonald."

"Is he the other man Sam was talking to? Did you overhear that conversation, too?"

"They don't call me Agent BTS for nothin'."

Ellie frowned. "This is getting complicated."

"There was a lot of gabbing goin' on and they were talkin' on the Q.T., so I didn't hear it all, but when Sam talked to McDonald, he said he was following the money. Then he said somethin' about a court case. I heard him mention Judge Lowenstein's name, and that was it."

She rested her chin in her palm. "I'm sure all of this is important, but I need to know a little more before I can figure out how. Sam's busy. He might not even answer his phone if I call. And I certainly can't ask him about something I'm not supposed to know, so there's not much I can do about it now."

Thinking hard, she took a bite of her bagel and another sip of coffee. Then she tore off a piece of smoked salmon and passed it to her boy. "Maybe you and I should go see Mother. If I can get a couple of minutes alone with Stanley, he might be able to shed some light on things."

Corinna opened the door wearing her usual welcoming smile. "How nice. It's two of my most favorite visitors. And twice in twenty-four hours. Come in and take a load off. I'll get Ms. George—"

"Corinna, wait a second." Ellie put her hand on the

housekeeper's arm and kept her voice low. "I need to speak to the judge first, and I want to do it without Mother waiting in the wings." She slipped off her jacket and passed it to Corinna. "Please tell me Stanley is free and he's alone."

The housekeeper opened the foyer closet and took out a hanger. "The judge is in the library, where you spent most of last night, and your mother is in the kitchen helping me set things right. The cleanup crew for the party left about thirty minutes ago, so she's taking inventory of the liquor." After hanging up Ellie's coat, she closed the closet door. "You wouldn't believe the amount of food and drink those bigwig politicians and lawyers can put away, and most of it eighty-proof."

"So maybe you could go back to the kitchen and take your time?" Ellie asked, crossing mental fingers. "Fix a bite of lunch for us, and don't tell Mother we're here until you're finished."

"If you don't mind leftovers, that won't be a problem. There's filet mignon and some of that lobster salad, and we even got a tray of shrimp skewers and a pile of spinach soufflé that should heat up good."

"That sounds wonderful. Thanks."

"Just don't ask me to bring your little man. Ms. Georgette is still steamed about what happened to Mrs. Thachette. Seems she's the wife of a city official, and your mother is sure she's gonna get X'd off of everybody's A-list if word gets out about Rudy. If she sees that he's here, she'll be outta that kitchen in a New York minute."

"I know she's upset about it, but—"

"It wasn't my fault."

"I don't want to get into it with her. Fifteen minutes is all I'll need. Maybe less. Please?"

Corinna headed toward the dining room. "I'll do my best."

Ellie took a look around as she made her way to the library. The house and everything in it looked perfect. The small dining tables and chairs were gone. Not a speck of dust floated on the air, and there wasn't a stick of furniture out of place. From the way Corinna described the alcohol and food consumption, Judge Frye must have spent a small fortune on the party. And even more to have things sparkling clean this early on a Sunday.

Turning into the rear hall, she stopped and dropped to one knee. "Please be quiet while I talk to Stanley," she told her boy. "I want to get this over with quickly, and I won't be able to if you keep sticking your two cents' worth into the conversation."

"How about you take the leash off so I can do some reconnoitering?"

She unhooked the lead and dropped it in her bag. "Okay, but stay out of the kitchen and away from Mother. And come back soon, because I know Judge Frye will want to see you."

"You got it."

Ellie grinned. Rudy skulked off as if he was on the prowl, which was silly because she doubted he'd find a piece of lint to report on. Feeling better about their morning, she entered the library and saw the judge reading the *Times*.

"That newspaper is so dry I'm surprised it doesn't crumble to dust when someone opens it," she said, walking to his desk. "I like a paper that has comics and an easier crossword puzzle."

"Ellie, my dear. To what do I owe the honor of seeing you again?" Judge Frye asked, smiling up at her.

"Good morning." She bent and kissed his bald head. "Have you recuperated from last night?"

"I'm fine, but Georgette is a bit frazzled. Mrs. Thachette was a royal pain in the you-know-what. The woman acted as if she'd been bitten by a rabid raccoon when she found Rudy in the powder room." He grinned. "Really, how could anyone look at that innocent little face and think badly of him?"

She suppressed an eye roll. "Speaking of innocent, thank you for allowing the Carmodys to bring Buddy. He's such a sweetie, and he was good company for Rudy."

"Think nothing of it," Stanley said. "If your mother would let me, I'd get a dog just like him. Georgette and Corinna always seem to let me have my way, but keeping a canine in this house is the one thing your mother won't allow."

After living with her dickhead of a husband, Ellie knew exactly how the old guy felt. Finding a dog was the first thing she'd done to celebrate her divorce, and it had made a world of difference in her life. If Georgette and Rudy got along better, it could help the judge's cause.

"Bichons are wonderful little dogs. Hypoallergenic, no-shed, and very happy. Mother loves you. Keep working on her. You might be able to wear her down."

"I'll try. Now, what can I do for you?"

"I need to ask you a few questions, some personality-specific and some legal, if you don't mind."

"Legal, eh?" Stanley nodded to one of the leather wing chairs. "Then sit and get comfortable. I'll do what I can to enlighten you."

She took a seat and tried to form a question that made sense. "Let's tackle the personal first. Can you tell me a bit about Judge Lowenstein? What he's like as a person, not a court official."

Stanley leaned back in his wheelchair. "I've known Norm for a long while. He's always been aboveboard, honest, a good judge. Of course, there were a few small transgressions, things he did that didn't sit well with the DA, but that's to be expected when—"

"Things? What sort of things?"

"Soft sentences every once in a while, things like that. No matter how hard a judge tries to abide by the rules, he can't help but let his personal feelings get in the way. When that happens, well, let's just say some felons get a bye."

"A bye?"

"No jail time at all. It happens to the best of us."

"Did Judge Lowenstein do that often?"

"Not to my knowledge, but I haven't been on the bench for a good ten years. I only hear the gossip, so I might not be the best person to ask."

"Any idea who would be?"

Stanley tapped his lower lip with the tips of his steepled fingers. "I'm afraid the legal profession is somewhat like the medical profession. No one wants to talk out of school about another of their kind."

Ellie stared at the ceiling. The judge wasn't telling her anything she didn't already know, unless . . . "Is there anyone who might be able to give me a more candid view of Judge Lowenstein? Someone more current with his activities on the bench?"

"Hmm. Well, perhaps Judge McDonald would be willing to speak with you. He and Norm have had words several times. Tell him I sent you, and I'm sure he'll tell you the real story. But I can't guarantee he'll even have the time."

Judge McDonald? She wanted to jump up and high-five the air. "Could you give me his phone number so I can call him?"

Stanley checked his date book, jotted the information on a sheet of paper, and passed it across the desk.

"If I'd known you wanted to talk to him, I could have set something up last night. Perhaps you met him or—"

She glanced at her watch. "To tell the truth, I met very few people at the party. I was in here with Rudy and Buddy. Then there was that other business, and— Can we move on to the legal part of my question?"

"All right. Ask what you will."

"How important is this position the three justices are up for?"

"Very. The judge who makes it to a circuit court of appeals has usually reached the pinnacle of his or her career. The next stop on the judicial train is the Supreme Court, and only a few have ever had the opportunity to serve there. Sonia Sotomayor came from this circuit, as did several past members of the Supreme Court. And they must have a pristine background to get that appointment."

"And would one of those small transgressions we talked about manage to knock them out of contention for the position?"

"That would depend." Stanley cocked his head. "Could you be more specific?"

"I would if I could, but—"

"There you are." Georgette's voice rang out from the doorway. She marched into the library with Corinna following behind and carrying Rudy in her arms. "Your little miscreant was in my kitchen, trying to snitch a bite of filet mignon. Honestly, Ellen Elizabeth, how could you bring him here after what he did last night?"

Ellie stood and Corinna passed Rudy to her. "I'm sorry, Mother. I thought he was in here—"

"Well, he wasn't." Georgette narrowed her eyes. "What were you and Stanley talking about? Nothing that would tire him out, I hope, because last night was very trying for him."

She walked to the desk, grabbed the handles of the judge's wheelchair, and began pushing him toward the door. "Now that you're here, you might as well join us for lunch." She stopped and turned. "And where is that animal's leash? Put it on him if you expect to be fed."

Corinna grinned at Ellie, then followed Georgette out.

Ellie sat on the sofa, pulled Rudy's lead from her bag, and snapped it to his collar. "Thanks a bunch, wise guy," she said, standing.

"Anytime." He trotted by her side. *"Anytime at all."*

Sam disconnected the call. Some Sundays sucked, and this was one of them.

It had been a rough couple of hours, trying to find the right district attorney to take up his cause, then jumping through hoops to catch Judge McDonald at home. Tougher still was convincing both of them he needed to officially investigate two years' worth of bank records of a highly respected judge and obtain a search warrant for his home.

But if the pieces fit the way he hoped, the Carmella Sunday murder would be wrapped by tomorrow afternoon.

After getting permission to search bank records, he'd pulled strings and, thanks to a pal who owed him a favor, Judge Lowenstein's information was on its way. If the money trail made sense, he'd drop in on the judge as soon as he got the search warrant, probably tomorrow morning. All he needed was a single piece of evidence, one small thing that would help tie everything together, and they were home free.

But it was going to be an uphill battle with the judge. He'd shown no interest in cooperating. Claimed he'd already been vetted by a background check from the U.S.

government. The judge asked what a flatfoot expected to find when he'd already been cleared by Uncle Sam.

Sam knew the federal government didn't spend a lot of time digging through personal finances in this type of investigation. Government inquiries were more interested in the professional background of the person they were checking on, and Lowenstein's bench performance had come out okay.

Of course, the big boys didn't know enough to tie things together the way he did. And if he was right . . .

He eyed his watch and frowned. He should call Ellie and give her a heads-up, not on the Pearson/Sunday case, but just to let her know he was sorry he'd left her without a good-bye. She'd looked so angelic this morning, sound asleep in the bed. Especially since she'd had such a crap-hat night.

Not that her spending time with her old four-legged pal had been a problem. She'd enjoyed playing with Buddy and her own pain-in-the-ass dog. And she seemed to enjoy people watching and evaluating the A-list attendees at the party. But her mother—well, that was a different story.

To put it plainly, Georgette Engleman Frye, or the exterminator, as Ellie and Viv liked to call her, had been a bitch. In fact, she was such a disagreeable woman she made his mom look like Mother Teresa. And that was tough to do, because Lydia Ryder was no slouch in the mothers-who-should-give-it-a-rest department.

There was no love lost between him and Ellie's dog either, but Georgette made out like everything the little mutt did was her daughter's fault, and he knew damn well it wasn't. Her pint-sized Cujo was wise to each and every person and situation around him.

Sam was just damned glad the little creep had finally accepted that he was going to be in Ellie's life from here on out. At least that was the way the pup acted, but who the hell knew. He wouldn't put it past Rudy to be plotting something nefarious, like crapping in his shoe or chewing up his shoulder holster—or worse.

One look at the pile of paperwork covering his desk and he knew he had to lay off obsessing over Ellie's mutt and get some work done while he waited for a call from the DA.

If things progressed the way he wanted them to, he'd have his hands full tomorrow. He decided to call Vince and clue him in about what was going on. If things didn't work out, he didn't want his partner coming home to an ugly surprise.

Chapter 20

Ellie woke before the sun rose on Monday, her mind on Sam, the Lowensteins, and Rudy's spy report. She'd left one message on Sam's phone last night, and she wasn't going to leave another. His note said he had a ton of work to do, and so did she. If Agent BTS was right, something was going on in the Carmella Sunday case, and she wanted in.

After taking Rudy for a first quick walk, she showered and supervised their morning routine. Then she put on a coat, hat, and gloves, ready to get an early start on the day. "Do you need your sweater?" she asked her boy before they went out the door.

"Nah. It was warm on run number one. I'll be okay."

Outside, they walked west on Sixty-sixth. The brilliant sun and blue sky brightened her outlook. The melting snow was washing away the salt and chemical deicers, and warmer temperatures and clean sidewalks meant she wouldn't need to stop and put coats and booties on every dog she walked.

With one less thing to worry about, she had time to work on all the questions flooding her brain. Questions with no answers, unless she found the solutions herself.

The who, what, when, where, and why of Carmella's murder were driving her crazy.

Instead of internalizing, she began to mutter. "Why would Sam want to talk with Judge Lowenstein in private?" They crossed Third Avenue. "What does Judge McDonald have to do with it?" They waited for the light to change at Lexington. "And why did Sam want to know about the Lowensteins' personal life? There's a connection. I just can't figure out what any of it has to do with Rob's case."

Before they crossed Madison, Rudy broke into her thoughts. *"I think you're barkin' up the wrong tree, Triple E. Let's take a look at what we do know instead of what we don't."*

Ellie smiled. "How come your brain is always one step ahead of mine?"

"I got more senses to work with than you. You can see and hear okay, but I got the nose. And right now I smell somethin' as rotten as a fish left out in the sun too long."

"Okay, we'll go at it from your point of view. What do we know?" They turned left on Fifth Avenue and aimed for the Beaumont. "One: Someone, either a performer or a stranger, entered Rob's dressing room on the opening night of the revue." She began ticking off fingers. "Two: Said person and Carmella Sunday had an argument, and a man grabbed a pair of shears from a dressing table and stabbed her dead. Three: Carmella was blackmailing someone, and that someone is probably the killer."

Rudy inspected a pile of yellow snow hiding his favorite fire hydrant and raised a leg. *"Keep countin' down."*

Walking into the Beaumont, she waved at Natter and aimed for the elevator. "That's all I've got. According to Stanley, Lowenstein is a good judge, but he's made a few enemies along the way. So what?"

*"All that has muscle, but you're forgetting one impor-
tant thing. We still got Bitsy, and she's our ace in the hole.
Why don't we use her?"*

They rode the elevator skyward, picked up Cheech
and Chong, Lulu, Bruiser, Satchmo, and Ranger, said a
pleasant good morning to each dog, and continued to
discuss the situation. "Yes, but do we bring her to the
Cranston and let the chips fall, or do we bring her to
Madame Orzo for another psychic experience?"

*"Forget Madame Orzo until you see how Bitsy's doing.
She might have had a breakthrough over the weekend
all on her own. She could have remembered something
about what the hit man wore, or figured out what Carmella and the killer were arguin' about."*

"Ooh, I love it when you talk like a detective," Lulu
broke in. *"It's so—so—*Dragnet, *or* Perry Mason. *Wait!
Make that* Quincy, *or—or—*Kojak.*"* She stopped walking
and danced around Rudy. *"I know, I know!* Columbo.*"*

Ellie raised an eyebrow and Lulu sniffed. *"I can't help
it if all Flora watches is those ancient TV detective shows."*

With that, Rudy skulked into his wolf-on-the-hunt
pose. *"I just wish I could figure a way to get INS over
here,"* he mumbled, giving the evil eye to the two Chi-
huahuas. *"Maybe I should make a citizen's arrest."*

"You're both being silly," said Ellie as they crossed
Fifth to the park. "Forget about Cheech and Chong and
those corny television detective series and get back on
track."

The canines did their business while Ellie stewed.
Rudy was right. Bitsy was the key. She'd been to the
Lowensteins' once or twice, and that was when she
had relapsed into her seriously upset routine. Ellie had
blamed it on nerves, but maybe she'd been wrong. Had
she made a mistake? Had she missed an important clue?

She led the crew back to the Beaumont. "I'm going to

change up the walks. We'll pass the Davenport, and do Pooh and Tigger's building next. Then we'll backtrack to the Davenport, walk the normal group, and take Bitsy on a trip to the Cranston."

"And once we're there, something will ring a bell in her tiny brain, and we can unravel this mess for good."

Relieved that she finally had a plan of action, she returned the pack to their apartments, then rode the elevator down while she continued to talk. "If Sam thinks he has a ton of work to do, he needs to live in my world," she said under her breath.

"Yeah," mumbled Rudy. *"We got a friend accused of murder, while Detective Dipstick is botherin' judges, and we got the answer to the murder right in the palm of our hand—er—paw."*

"All we have to do is put the pieces together," Ellie agreed.

"Say, Ellie?"

"Our problem is how to convince Sam we have an eyewitness to the crime."

"Hey, Triple E!"

They landed in the Beaumont lobby, and she finally paid attention to her boy. "What?"

"I know you want to work this out, but you gotta stop talking out loud. There were other humans in the elevator and you never even knew they were there."

She nodded to Natter as they headed out the door. "Are you saying I talk too much?"

"Not too much. But you're so used to gabbin' with us canines, you've started sayin' everything out loud. One of these days, the wrong thing is gonna slip out and you'll be in trouble."

"Fine. I'll try to contain myself. Just don't get mad if you're the last one to know my plans."

They passed the Davenport and entered Sara's building. When she got the dogs on the street, they were so busy nosing piles of slushy snow they didn't speak. Which was good, because she had enough on her mind without having to intervene in a canine squabble or answer silly questions.

"I bet we're gonna put ten extra miles on today, makin' all these trips back and forth. I'm dizzy just thinkin' about it," complained Rudy as they headed for the Davenport.

"Oh, hush. Once we're finished helping Rob, we'll be back on our regular schedule." They walked into the complex. "Good morning, Randall."

"You're here a bit early today," the older man said. He wore his standard uniform, complete with a bright red carnation. "Is something happening I should know about?"

"Nope, but I have to do the building in a single run today. It's everybody out and back, Bradley included."

"Ah, yes. The big dog. He reminds me of a pony I had as a child. All he needs is a saddle."

"Just don't try to ride him, or you'll end up losing a chunk of your arm."

The doorman grinned. "Right you are. See you in a few minutes."

They collected their regular charges, then stopped to pick up Bradley and Bitsy. When she heard a *snurffle* from under the door, Ellie put a finger to her lips and gazed at her pack. "This is important, guys. No fighting, and no smart comments. I want this run to go fast and clean, understand?"

The canines stared back, their faces solemn, their voices quiet. She decided each of them would get an extra biscuit when she took them home, as a thank-you for being so cooperative.

She knocked, then used her key when no one answered at Rob's. Opening the door, she found Bradley staring with his usual suspicious glare while Bitsy jumped under his belly. "So, Bits, how did the weekend go?" she asked as she clipped the poohuahua's lead on.

"Quiet. Rob did his shows and came straight home. He didn't even take me with him."

The pack entered the elevator and rode it down. "Did that give you time to think?"

Crossing the Davenport lobby, they arrived on Fifth Avenue. *"I thinked a lot, and I know somethin'."*

Now on the park side of the street, Ellie cocked her head and Rudy did the same. "Good for you. Can you share?"

"The argument the bad person was having with Carmella? It was about money."

She nodded to her boy when Bitsy did her squat and drop. *"Do you remember anything else?"* Rudy asked her. *"Like the sound of the voice? Was it familiar?"*

Bitsy shook from head to tail, and it was a regular doggie shake, a big relief to Ellie. "What if we asked you to come with us to another building? The building where I think you heard a similar voice? Would that be okay?"

"If it'll help Rob, I'll do it."

"That's the spirit. We'll drop the gang off, go to the Cranston and take that crew out, and when we're done, we'll stop at the Lowensteins'."

Frustrated, Sam huffed out a breath. He'd been on the phone all morning and he still didn't have his gun. According to regulations, he wouldn't get it back until he talked to the department shrink, but Dr. Garber was out for the next two days and booked solid for the rest of the week, so how in the hell was he supposed to do his job?

"Stop pacing," said Vince, tapping at his computer keyboard. "I'm on it."

"What's taking so long?" Sam asked, running a hand through his hair. "You talked to the judge and the DA two hours ago."

"Don't look at me, pal. The DA's running the show now. He'll let us know when the warrant's ready."

"Yeah, fine." Sam sat in his desk chair. "Our *probable cause* is shaky. I bet I blew it with McDonald when I approached him at that party."

Vince raised his eyes to the ceiling. "Just give it a rest. The DA agreed with the request, which means he thought it was fine. When we get the warrant, we'll leave. Who do you want to send to the judge's chambers? And how many officers do you want at the apartment?"

"Two should be enough for the courthouse. I can't believe he'd take anything from the murder there, but we have to cover the bases. Two more and a forensic team for the apartment. I didn't find a firearm permit for either the judge or his wife, so I don't think we'll have a problem. If I remember correctly, Ellie said Mrs. Lowenstein went to a health club every day and the judge left early for his office." Sam hunched over his desk and snapped open his cell phone. "I'm gonna make sure Lowenstein is where's he's supposed to be."

Ten minutes later, he disconnected the call. "Judge Lowenstein cleared his calendar for the day. His clerk told me he got the message late last night, which means he did it after I grilled him at the party."

"Hell. He could be home right now, getting rid of evidence." Vince stood and headed for the door. "Give me ten minutes. I'll get the officers and forensics on board, and rattle the DA's cage." He pointed a finger at Sam. "You sit there and chill. Get the search straight in your head."

Sam didn't know what they'd turn up, but time was running out. He'd jumped the gun grilling Lowenstein on Saturday night, but he'd been following protocol. Now that he had the court records and the bank info, it all fit like a custom-made glove. Lowenstein had presided over Carmella's last trial for prostitution, a trial the DA was positive would send the cross-dresser to jail. Instead, the guy had walked.

Three months later, the judge made his first withdrawal, and after that, like clockwork, he'd withdrawn five big ones from two different banks every month. The next day the same amount, give or take, had been added to Art Pearson's account.

The Pearson/Sunday stabbing had been a crime of passion, not premeditation—of that he was certain. If Chesney, a cast member, or one of the workers inside the club hadn't done the deed, the killer had to have come from outside. Since it was the freakin' middle of February, the perp was probably wearing a coat, maybe gloves. With all the blood at the scene, something he wore had to have a trace of the spatter.

So that was where he would start the search: closets first, in every room, including the bath. They'd collect all the judge's shoes, coats, scarves, anything that might have a trace of bodily fluid.

Sam drummed his fingers on the desk. He had thought the apartment would be empty, but that was a pipe dream. Since the judge wasn't in chambers, he could be home, so they'd concentrate on the apartment. If Lowenstein was there, they'd bring him in.

Vince stuck his head in the doorway. "Okay, pal, rise and shine." He waved a few sheets of paper in his hand. "We've got what we need."

Ellie, Rudy, and Bitsy arrived at the Cranston and walked across the polished black marble floor. The interior, with freshly hung burgundy wallpaper, appeared more spacious than she remembered, probably because the walls were devoid of artwork while the remodeling was going on. She imagined that once the decorating was finished, this building would look as upscale as the other complexes on the Upper East Side.

When they stood at the desk, the new doorman, an older fellow with a shock of white hair that resembled a cotton swab, looked up from the papers he'd been sorting and stared through shifty gray eyes. "Name?" he asked, tapping a pen on his clipboard.

"Ellie Engleman," she said, smiling. She held out her hand, hoping to get off on the right foot with—she read the name on his badge—Sherman Farkas. "I'm one of the building's dog walkers. It's nice to meet you, Mr. Farkas."

Ignoring the gesture, Sherman shot her a look of impatience. "You're down for Three-C, Keene; Four-A, Fielding; Nine-C, Dorfman; Ten-B, Heinz; and Eighteen-C, Gordon. I've been told by the Lowensteins in Twelve-G that your services are no longer needed. Please turn in your key."

"Say what?" yipped Rudy.

The Lowensteins are firing me?

Dropping her hand, Ellie stood there in shock. "I'm sorry. There must be some mistake. Neither of the Lowensteins called me to say I was off the job."

"Yeah, well, them's the breaks. Oh, and they asked me to give you this." He passed her a business-sized white envelope. "Key, please."

She fished the ring from her tote, found the correct key, and unclipped it. "Are you certain about this?" she asked him, still clutching the metal.

"Just doing my job, lady." He tapped his pencil on the desk and held out his other hand. "Key, please."

Well, crap. There was no use making a scene. The guy

was following orders, though he didn't have to look so happy while he did it. "Okay, here you are." She dropped the key in his open palm. "This is a surprise, so if you don't mind, I'd like to see what's in this envelope before I go up."

"Whatever." Farkas returned to the clipboard.

"Read it out loud," Rudy demanded. *"I got a right to know why we're bein' let go, too."*

Ellie dropped to one knee and slit open the envelope. "Okay, here goes," she whispered. 'Ms. Engleman. In regard to Sampson, please accept this check for one month's service as termination of our verbal dog-walking agreement. No further contact is necessary. Judge and Mrs. Norman Lowenstein.'"

"Well, that says a lot."

"Sort of odd, don't you think? Especially since Mariette and I had a nice conversation about Sampson at the party. Do you think the judge's discussion with Sam had something to do with this?"

"Are you kidding? It downright stinks. No need to tell you I'm smellin' dead fish again."

"I'm sorry, Ellie," Bitsy added. *"Rob and I would never do that to you."*

Standing, she led them to the elevator, pushed the call button, and stepped inside before she spoke. "Okay, let's think about this." She leaned against the wall. "Something is definitely up with the judge and Mariette. The other night she acted ecstatic when she saw me, and today we're through."

"Who do they think we are? Chopped liver? It's like sayin' so long, and don't let the door hit you in the butt on the way out."

"I can't believe it's Mariette's doing."

"Gotta be that snooty judge. I never did like him."

"Maybe so, but I'm still going to try to say good-bye

to Sampson properly. That's the least they should let us do." She missed the chubby Pug already. "If we're lucky, the judge is gone and Mariette's at the gym."

"So what are you gonna do? Knock on the door and see if Mr. Pudgy answers?"

"Don't be silly. I have a ring with extra keys, remember? And I'm fairly certain it's not legal for me to use them once I've been dismissed."

They gathered the pack and Ellie explained that they might have lost Sampson, which brought out a round of boo-hoos and snarky comments. She let the group complain while they walked, and she went over things in her mind.

Bitsy was here, and she'd brought the little dog quite a distance for this experiment. If she knocked on Twelve-G and no one answered, she could open the door, give Sampson a good-bye hug and be done with it. Then she'd have to think of another way to let Bitsy hear Mariette's and the judge's voices.

When they arrived back in the Cranston lobby, the charming Mr. Farkas was nowhere to be seen. She breathed a sigh of relief and aimed for the elevator, telling herself this was something she had to do. After dropping off the last dog, she pushed the button for the twelfth floor.

"So we're gonna take a stab at it, huh?"

Hands on her hips, she gave Rudy an eye roll.

"Sorry, that was a bad pun."

The elevator stopped and the door opened. "You two ready?" Neither dog answered, so she took off down the hall. Lucky for her, the apartment was at the far end, away from the others. If there was a scene, it might go unnoticed.

But when she reached the door, she heard a rumbling of voices. Either the television was on at full blast, or

Norm and Mariette were having one doozy of an argument. Rudy stuck his nose on the doorjamb and began snurffling. Raising her hand, she knocked and waited.

No answer.

"Are you getting anything?" she whispered, not sure what to do. When she knocked again, there was a scratching from the other side of the door.

"It's Sampson. He's upset and he wants us to come in."

Ellie cringed. Poor Sampson. When moms and dads argued, some dogs hid under the bed or cowered in a corner. A family altercation was as traumatic for a canine as it was for the humans doing the fighting.

A loud whimper sounded from behind the door, and she made up her mind. Using her spare key, she opened the door, and dropped to her knees to face a quivering Sampson.

"Ellie, Ellie, Ellie. I'm glad you're here. Big Momma and the judge are fightin' something fierce. I'm scared."

"Oh, you poor baby." She ran a hand over his head. Angry voices carried from the rear of the apartment. "What can I do for you?"

"Come in and make 'em stop. Please."

Standing, Ellie realized she'd gotten in trouble the second she unlocked the door. Could one more tiny transgression make it any worse? "Why don't you find your leash? We can take you for a walk. Maybe by the time we get back they'll be finished."

"It's on the kitchen table. Big Momma dropped it there after my morning quickie. I can't reach it."

"Go on in, Triple E. With all the racket them two are makin' I doubt they'll hear a thing."

It was then she spotted Bitsy, quaking in the doorway. This was ridiculous. She had three upset animals on her hands. She had to do something, even if it was something beyond the boundaries of the law.

Raising a finger to her lips, she signaled for silence, then tiptoed down the hall and made a left into the kitchen. Relief washed through her when she spotted the leash coiled on the table. Picking it up, she turned.

"What are you doing here?" Norm Lowenstein demanded, his angry brown eyes staring her down.

"Uh, Judge, sorry. I knocked, but I guess you didn't hear me."

"And why would you knock, Ms. Engleman? Didn't the doorman tell you your services were no longer needed?"

Ellie straightened her shoulders so she was eye to eye with the judge. "He did, but I wanted to say good-bye to Sampson."

"Say good-bye? To a dog?" He sneered. "I'd heard rumors about your animal antics, but didn't believe them, even after you and your hound caused that commotion at the party. You're probably the one who put your boyfriend up to sticking his nose into my business, too. Talk about having a couple of screws loose."

Mariette hobbled into the doorway. "Who are you talking—" She blinked, openmouthed. "Ellie. What are you doing here?"

"It doesn't matter, Mariette. I'm escorting her out." Norm took a step toward Ellie, and the three dogs scattered like leaves in the wind.

Mariette shrieked as they flew past her and up the hall.

"Get those mutts," the judge shouted, following his wife and the canine trio.

Ellie tried not to laugh, but good Lord, the situation was like something out of an old Keystone Kops movie. She took off after the humans, who were after the dogs, and they were heading who knew where. Sampson had led the charge, then Rudy, with Bitsy scampering behind. She could only imagine the two adults trying to corner three rambunctious canines.

She stopped just short of the room at the end of the hall. Judge Lowenstein was shouting, the dogs were yapping and snarling, and Mariette was dithering as she tried to sort out the mess. The situation quickly turned into a brawl. The pooches snapped and tugged at a black trash bag, while Mariette and her husband tried to wrestle it away.

Ellie figured she had two choices. She could wait until the dogs and the Lowensteins tired each other out, or she could walk inside and take control. Sampson and Rudy ripped the bag open and she decided to do her thing.

"Everybody! Step back and let me get the leashes!"

Ignoring her, the judge stood, swung a leg back, and kicked Sampson into a corner of the room. Mariette screamed and ran to her Pug. Bitsy whimpered and backed up.

And her boy, her hero, latched on to Norm's leg, snapped his muzzle over the calf, and hung on for dear life.

Norm started hopping on one foot, trying to shake Rudy off, but her little guy wasn't about to let go.

Steeling her spine, Ellie let out a "Hey! Leave my dog alone!" and pulled at the judge's arm.

The judge twirled in place and slapped Ellie hard across the face with an open hand. Dizzy, she staggered back and tried to regain her balance.

Norm grabbed a lamp off a table and raised it high, as if to smash it over Rudy's head.

She gasped and lunged, clutching his arm. The judge swung around, trying to shake Rudy off while attempting to whack her with the lamp.

Ellie grunted as she ducked. Staggering to her feet, she again lunged for the judge.

She heard some kind of noise behind her, but didn't care what it was. Rudy needed her.

"Police! Everybody freeze!" Sam shouted a second later.

Ellie wasn't sure how much time had passed. She'd positioned herself in a corner of the room so she could watch the proceedings and still stay out of the way. And while she cuddled Bitsy in her arms, Sampson and Rudy sat so close that their bottoms rested on her feet. Things had sorted out quickly, but she was still trying to get a handle on the story.

The Lowensteins were handcuffed and led away before Sam turned to her. "You okay?"

"Yes, but—"

"You mean you don't get it?"

"Ah, no. I mean yes." She heaved a sigh. "No, not really."

Sam grinned, obviously happy he was the one who could fill her in. "Mariette was the killer, not the judge."

Ellie blinked. "So that's what their argument was about. They kept screaming and accusing, but none of it made sense. He insisted she was stupid, and she insisted he'd ruined their lives. He meant the stabbing while she meant the affair, right?"

"Probably. She was sick and tired of the blackmail, especially after Pearson tripled the rate when he heard the judge was up for promotion. She could live with a bisexual husband, but she refused to be publically humiliated if news got out about her husband's affair."

"And the judge kept paying because he'd be disbarred if the truth was known."

"Seeing as his and Pearson's relationship started while he was hearing the case against Carmella, that's the way I see it. He and the wife were going to take the clothes and the pair of *his* shoes she'd worn to commit the crime to a trash dump somewhere in Jersey today. It sounds as if the dogs smelled the blood and decided to take a look for themselves."

Ellie gazed down at the Pug. "There's no one to look after Sampson. Would it be all right if I took him to my place?"

Sam shrugged. "I don't see why not. This isn't a crime scene, and we've removed the evidence. What do you plan to do with him?"

"Keep him for a while. Maybe you could find out if the Lowensteins have children? If not, I'll check with Pug rescue. They have a great group here in Manhattan."

He touched her cheek, the one that still stung from the judge's slap. "Good thing there were other cops around, or I would have 'accidentally' got in a punch for this."

"It's no biggie," said Ellie. She nestled her nose in his palm and smiled. "Do I have to go to the station and give a statement?"

He raised a shoulder. "I don't think that's necessary. By the time the suspects are booked and their lawyer arrives, it'll be all over. If we need your version of things, you can come down tomorrow."

Ellie breathed a sigh of relief. "Thanks for that. So . . . I guess you need to leave."

Sam backed up a step. "There's still a lot of work to be done, so yes. You going to be all right?"

She thought about her afternoon. "I'll walk Bitsy home. Then Rudy, Sampson, and I will catch a cab to my place. I still have a second round of walks, which means I'll worry about getting hold of Pug rescue tomorrow."

He leaned in and kissed her aching face. "You going to lock up here?"

Ellie nodded. "Yes, and then I'll stop at the doormen's station and give them the news."

"I'll put in a word, too. Take it easy, finish your runs, and get a good night's sleep. If I can, I'll let myself in and spend the night. There's something we need to discuss."

She waited until he walked down the hall and slammed the door. Fairly certain what the "discussion" was going to be about, she slid to her knees and caught Sampson's muzzle in her hand. "Hey, big boy. Are you okay?"

The Pug shuddered. *"I just want out of here. Are you really gonna take me to your house?"*

"Sure am." She kissed his nose. "You're a trouper. Things will be fine. You'll see."

She stood, collected the leashes, and headed for the door.

"Hey, what about me? Don't I at least get a thank-you?"

Stopping, she dropped to a squat in front of Rudy. "Sorry. I forgot to tell you how proud I am of you. And thanks for trying to protect Sampson and me. You saved my bacon again."

"Bacon? Did you say bacon?" whimpered Sampson.

"I love bacon," Bitsy yipped.

"Not for you, big butt," Rudy sniped. *"If I don't get any, neither do—"*

Ellie grinned. Bacon or no bacon, listening to her boy gripe told her that things were almost back to normal. A normal she loved.

Epilogue

Vivian poured Ellie a glass of white wine, set it on the kitchen table, and took a seat. "I still can't believe the story. The way things just 'happen' to you"—Viv used air quotes—"makes me think you should exchange the caramel you put in your coffee for Jack Daniel's. That might help get you through the day."

Ellie sipped her Pinot Grigio. It was after seven, and she was beat. "The wine is fine. Thanks. But if things continue the same as today, I'll need more than a shot of booze to keep me sane." She slumped over her kitchen table, while Rudy stood next to her with his paws on her thigh. "God, what a mess."

"But it's over, right? Rob's free?"

"As a bird. His attorney had called him by the time I arrived for the afternoon run. Kayla and Bradley are leaving tomorrow. She and her boy hated the snow. They can't wait to get back to Phoenix."

"And the Lowensteins have been arrested for murder."

"Involuntary manslaughter, actually. And only Mariette. That's the charge levied when a murder is committed in an act of passion. She didn't bring a weapon, just fell apart and used what she found to do the deed. The judge is an accomplice of some kind." She drank another gulp of wine. "The legalese makes my head ache. I need to go to bed."

"I understand." Vivian took a swallow of her Merlot, then stood and set the glass in the sink.

Ellie ruffled her boy's ears. "So where is our pudgy houseguest?"

"He's in the spare bedroom, asleep. He's pretty bummed about what happened."

"I know. I have to bring him to Pug rescue tomorrow. They said they'd foster him until the judge and Mariette are out on bail. Poor little guy."

"I still can't believe Mariette was the real killer," said Viv, reluctant to leave. "I bet that was a surprise."

"Ya think?" Ellie heaved a sigh. "Thank God Sam sorted it all out, because I was lost. Even after she told me she had bunion trouble, I didn't connect it with her wearing her husband's shoes."

"Imagine, being so vain she didn't want the surgery. And being willing to live with a man who has sex with other men."

"According to the judge, it was more like a couple of quick boinks in his chambers. And Mariette didn't mind staying with a gay husband, as long as they kept it a secret. But if word leaked out, she'd lose her socialite standing as the wife of a prominent judicial figure. Her husband would be disbarred—"

"Is that what they call disciplining a judge who has sex with the accused on a case he's trying?"

"It's more than that for Norm Lowenstein. Since he's what they call an Article Three judge, Congress has to impeach him. It's going to be a total humiliation for both of them."

"I still don't get exactly what happened on the night of the murder."

"Apparently Mariette had been simmering over the extra ransom request ever since Carmella made the demand. When Norm left for one of his gay hangouts, she decided to confront Carmella and tell her no dice. She dressed in slacks, a sweater, and a long black coat, and put on the pair of shoes she'd confiscated from the judge. Then she sneaked in the rear entrance of the club and waited for her target—"

"And Carmella just happened to be in her dressing room," said Viv. "Talk about an unlucky coincidence."

"For sure. They argued and Carmella refused to be swayed. When she turned around, Mariette spotted the scissors on one of the tables and *blam!* Carmella got it in the back of the neck."

"And this morning?"

"When the judge realized she still hadn't gotten rid of the clothes, he went ballistic, and I walked in on the fight."

The downstairs buzzer rang and Vivian raced to the intercom. "I'll get it."

Ellie heard the muttered conversation, then heavy steps on the stairs. Putting her elbows on the table, she rested her head in her hands and locked gazes with Rudy. "Do you think Sam believed me when I told him I used my key because I wanted to say good-bye to Sampson?"

"Beats me. But us bein' there helped the cops, so how can he be mad?"

Viv's voice echoed from the front hall, and Ellie recognized the second voice. "You might want to leave the kitchen. This could get ugly."

"No way am I gonna miss this." Rudy trotted to his fluff mat and parked his bottom. *"I'm here if you need me."*

Sam walked in and, cool as ice, hung his jacket on the

back of a chair, then removed his empty shoulder holster and draped it over the jacket. His face composed, he took a seat. "I got away early. Since Vince is number one, he told me to leave, he'd take care of the rest."

"Are the Lowensteins out on bail?"

"The judge is, but not Mrs. Lowenstein. Her charge is more serious, so it might take a while." Sam leaned back in his chair. "Thanks to Mariette's weight training, she was a strong woman. The scissors were handy, and she was able to hit the perfect spot on Pearson's neck."

Smart Sam. Who else would have thought to check back two years, and go for a judge's bank account info? Ellie held her breath, waiting for the promised *discussion*. She had a good idea what it would be about and needed all her strength to rebut the accusations.

"You look a little green. Stomach upset?" he asked her.

"Nope. I'm just waiting for the ax to fall."

He raised a brow.

"I figure you didn't give it this morning because you were in a hurry and I was upset. Now that things have cleared, you're here to give me the 'I told you not to mess in police business' lecture."

"Yeah, big man. Accusing Ellie when she was helping a friend . . . a canine friend."

Ellie tried not to smile. Rudy had an answer for everything.

Sam's lips curled at the corners. "You were messing in police business? When?"

She heard Rudy groan. "Ah, I don't know. Maybe by showing up right before the search warrant fiasco?"

"You were there, but Vince and Captain Carmody say you were legal. It's not your fault the door was open and the dogs were fighting over the bag holding the shoes, coat, and gloves of the killer."

"We weren't fighting. We were uncovering evidence."

Grinning, she glanced at Rudy. "I believe the dogs were helping find the evidence."

"Okay, that'll work." He stood, walked to her chair, and drew her to a stand. "Vince and the captain are on your side."

"I just have one question," Ellie began, still hoping to avoid the promised *discussion.* "What did Judge Mc-Donald have to do with all this?"

"Yeah, what?" Rudy yipped.

"Ah, well, I got the court records for Pearson's last three busts. The first two cases were heard by McDonald. Number three was Lowenstein's. McDonald warned Pearson that his third arrest would be jail time, but Lowenstein let him go. That frosted McDonald's ass, so I went to him for the search warrant."

"And he was happy to okay it?"

"Correct."

Ellie sank into the warmth of his chest. It sounded like maybe, just maybe, she was off the hook for this one.

"Now it's time for that talk I promised you."

Uh-oh. She raised her head, and he kissed the tip of her nose. "Okay."

"I've been thinking. We're pretty tight when you mind your own business—"

"Excuse me. I always mind my own business."

"Okay, we'll skip that. How about if I mention how nice it would be if we could share a bed—on a more regular basis."

"It would be nice, yes, but— Hey, are you saying all I'm good for is a steady roll in the hay?"

When his face flushed, her heart flipped over in her chest. What was he getting at?

"No. No!" Sam cleared his throat. "But I've been thinking. Since all I want is to keep you safe—"

"Which would be nice—if you didn't bully me."

"Okay, so maybe that happens, but I think I've found a solution to our—er—my problem. Don't take this the wrong way, but I decided you need a keeper, and I'm volunteering for the position."

"No, no! A thousand times no! I'm her keeper," Rudy ruffed. *"For now and for always. That's my job."*

Ellie opened her mouth, but no words came out.

"It's time we thought about a more permanent solution."

She was torn between running to her boy and telling him she needed two keepers or hugging Sam tight. Rudy would always be her number one, but having Detective Doofus near in a more personal way couldn't hurt.

Then Sam kissed her again, and every thought in her head disappeared. A minute later, he let her go and gazed into her eyes. "I think we should move in together."

"What? Nooooo!"

She took a breath, exhaled slowly. "Move in—as in *live*? Here?"

He grinned. "Uh, yeah. I thought that could work. Your place is bigger, there's more closet space, and—"

"Stay where you belong, you idiot. Out of our lives."

Ellie caught a glimpse of Rudy, now lying flat on the floor with his front paws over his eyes. "You want to live here, with Rudy and me?" She bit her lower lip, thinking. "And people would know?"

"Well, of course people would know." His gaze narrowed. "Do you have a problem with that?"

Thoughts of her mother, of Vivian, and the guys on the police force flashed through her mind. Biting her lower lip, she cocked her head and smiled at her boy.

Sam lifted her chin with a finger and she read the love in his eyes. "Ellie, hey, I'm up here."

She smiled and heaved a sigh. "Okay, sure. We're flexible. We can handle it. Right, Rudy?"

"Oh, brother."

Read on for a preview of Judi McCoy's
next Dogwalker Mystery,

Till Death Do Us Bark

Coming from Obsidian in August 2011

When Viv's sister mentioned her fiancé, Vivian set her empty wineglass on a passing waiter's tray and put her free hand on her hip. "I'd be happy to help, Arlene, but you're forgetting something. I have yet to meet the man. I thought you'd been hiding him somewhere for a big unveiling."

"Hiding him? Of course not. He's been with patients all afternoon. He gets so involved in caring for them, he sometimes forgets to come up for dinner. I sent Julio to get him at least twenty minutes ago." She huffed out a breath. "And where did Mickey go? If that man went to the cottage and corralled him into talking about business, I'm going to pitch a fit." She scanned the terrace. "And Dr. Bree? Where the hell is everyone?"

Ellie gazed over the crowd and saw why Arlene might have been concerned. The bull-doggish Mickey appeared to be missing, and it sounded as if he was a business acquaintance—not a real uncle. But who in the heck was Dr. Bree that Arlene thought she was so important?

Arlene stomped her foot. "This is crazy. It's our night to celebrate, and he's supposed to be here." She heaved another sigh. "And his so-called close friends, too."

"Maybe he got cold feet after he met some of your family," teased Viv. "Just remember, you can't blame me."

Arlene missed the humor in her baby sister's statement. "Something must have happened to him, but I can't imagine what." Spinning in a circle, she broke out in a full-fledged dither. "Julio! Julio! Oh, where is that man?"

Awwwk! Julio! Awwwk! Where is that man! Awwwk!

Mimicking Arlene's voice to a T, a large parrot who'd been tucked in a corner near Ellie burst into the fray by flapping his wings and wagging his head. Ellie had watched his beady eyes follow folks as they passed and kept to herself. Birds were not high on her list of animal favorites, and she hadn't wanted to rouse his curiosity, so she'd kept her fingers to herself and ignored him for most of the night.

The guests laughed, but Arlene began to wring her hands and pace. "I'm going to send a few of the catering staff out to look for the four of them. How can we have a prewedding celebration when the groom, the best man, Martin's only true friend, and the head of the hired help is missing?"

Awwwk! Missing. There's money missing, Marty, and I want my share. Awwwk! Or I'm gonna! Awwwk! Julio! Awwwk!

"Oh, hush, Myron," Arlene admonished. Flapping her arms much like the parrot, she tottered off on her stilettos talking to anyone in her path.

"I don't know how Arlene lives with that crazy bird imitating everything she says." Viv gave the parrot the evil eye.

"I was meaning to ask," Ellie began. "What's up with him?"

"Myron is an African Grey that Arlene rescued from

a pet store that was closing after the first Myron died. She said he kept her company while she grieved, but I don't understand how. All the idiot does is imitate whatever he overhears."

"Sounds kind of spooky, if you ask me," said Ellie. "Who's voice was that just now asking for his share?"

"Beats me, but the parrot's been living in the doctor's office while the interior of the house was being painted. She probably should have left him in there until this whole affair was over." Viv shook her head. "I'm starving. I hope the other guests arrive soon so we can eat. And Dr. Kent, too. I can't imagine where's he's been hiding."

Ellie had snacked on a dozen delicious canapés, so she was fine in the food department, but it did appear the other guests were getting restless. When she glanced across the terrace and no longer saw "hunky guy," she thought to take her friend's mind off eating by questioning her about the stranger.

"I've met just about everyone, but what's up with the tall, dark-haired man who was standing alone in the opposite corner a while ago? No one introduced us."

"I wish I knew, but I have no idea who he is either," said Viv. "I thought he might belong to Dr. Kent's family, since he's not a part of mine, but Arlene's already told us who's here from Dr. Kent's side."

"I'm sure we'll find out before the weekend is over." Ellie gave her wineglass to another waiter. "I'm going to check on Rudy for a minute. You want to come to the pen and see Mr. T?"

"Okay, sure. Lead the way."

They took the stairs down to the lawn and searched for Rosa's teenage daughter, Maria, who was supposed to be supervising the canines, but she was nowhere to be found. Ellie opened the gate, walked to her boy, and stooped to ruffle his ears. "Hey, how are things going?"

"*Boring, boring, boring,*" Rudy gruffed. "*That Yorkie is a pain in the behind, and so is some Jack-a-Bee named Greta. T and those Boston Terriers do not get along, so it's a good thing nutty Arlene brought them upstairs. It's been quiet since they left.*"

Ellie looked to her right, where Viv was giving Twink a belly rub. "He looks fine now."

"*So when can we come up and mingle?*"

"I'm not sure, but I'll find out. Right now, our hostess is in distress. Seems she can't find her fiancé."

"*I'd be in distress, too, if I had those pointy things she calls shoes on my paws. Arlene acts like she's had one too—*"

A round of shouts, not Arlene's or Myron's, broke out and Ellie stood. Glancing across the yard, she saw a man wearing a catering jacket running toward the house from the guest cottage.

"*El doctor, es muerto!* Help. *El es muerto!*"

Also Available from

Judi McCoy

Hounding the Pavement

A Dog Walker Mystery

**MEET ELLIE ENGLEMAN,
PSYCHIC DOG WALKER**

The newest dog-walker on Manhattan's
Upper East Side has a talent—she can hear
what her canine clients are thinking. So
when a dog's owner turns up dead, Ellie
must bone up on her sleuthing—and perk
up her ears to find a killer.

Available wherever books are sold or at
penguin.com

Also Available from

Judi McCoy

Heir of the Dog
A Dog Walker Mystery

Professional dog walker Ellie Engleman is more than just a pal to her pooches—she can also read their minds. When Ellie and her terrier mix Rudy find the corpse of a troubled-but-harmless park-dweller in Central Park, the dog walker becomes a prime suspect for murder.

When it turns out Rudy is the sole beneficiary of the victim's inheritance, Ellie, Rudy, and Detective Sam Ryder follow the trail of clues to a key to a safety deposit box that just might point to the motive and help them sniff out the real killer.

**Available wherever books are sold or at
penguin.com**

OM0019

Also Available from

Judi McCoy

Death in Show

Professional dog walker Ellie Engleman doesn't know much about the ins and outs of dog shows. But when one handler is killed, Ellie will learn that it's a dog-eat-dog world. Especially since the killer might now have it out for her. Now, she and her sometime boyfriend, Detective Sam Ryder, will have to dig up the truth faster than a speeding bulldog if they're going to stop this madhound.

Available wherever books are sold or at penguin.com

Sofie Kelly

Curiosity Thrilled the Cat
A Magical Cats Mystery

When librarian Kathleen Paulson moved to
Mayville Heights, Minnesota, she had no idea that
two strays would nuzzle their way into her life.
Owen is a tabby with a catnip addiction and
Hercules is a stocky tuxedo cat who shares
Kathleen's fondness for Barry Manilow. But beyond
all the fur and purrs, there's something more to
these felines.

When murder interrupts Mayville's Music Festival,
Kathleen finds herself the prime suspect. More
stunning is her realization that Owen and Hercules
are magical—and she's relying on their skills to solve
a purr-fect murder.

**Available wherever books are sold or at
penguin.com**